CITIES & COUNTRIES

1st Edition

About the Author:

Roman Payne was born in Seattle in 1977.

He left America in 1999 and currently lives in Paris.

For more information about the author, please visit:

www.romanpayne.com

Acknowledgments & Legal Statement:

This book is a work of fiction. Names, characters, places, and incidents either are products of the author's imagination or are used fictitiously. Any resemblance to actual events or locales or persons, living or dead, is entirely coincidental. This book is published by ModeRoom Press.

ISBN 978-0-6151-3787-2

© 2005, 2006 - Roman Payne / ModeRoom Press

Cover Design: Roman Payne

CITIES & COUNTRIES

by Roman Payne

Chapter I

Allow us our memories of that time we walked through the foreign city streets among strangers and madmen.

––––––––––

We walked along the canals past the opium dens, past the rathskellers and rows of doorways over which hung thick smoke heavy and motionless in the still air. And from the murky waters of the canals came the fumes and the gamey odors that mixed with the smoke, and also with the steam that rose up off the bricks of the streets when the rains began to fall.

As the rains grew strong, we walked along, our shoes clopping on the cobblestones like the hooves of horses. Beneath our step, puddles gleamed like black oil slicks. Our way was lit by the dull hazy whitish-yellow glow of fizzling gas lamps, burning in the darkening night, illuminating the streets through halos of steam.

When the storm commenced, we hurried down a narrow passageway empty of all people, save for a few shadowy figures taking cover under overhangs or in doorways. Rain poured in sheets off the rooftops, down the drainpipes, while rivulets of dirty water rushed down the gutters. And with the assault of the wind and the rain and the falling darkness, it soon became impossible to see. And it was then that I lost your hand and you were gone.

The storm came in swift and passed; and soon, all was calm again. The only sounds left were made by the residual waters dripping from the rooftops, and the flowing of neat little creaks down the cracks in the streets. I continued on through the narrow lanes, walking in the dark, looking for you, but you were gone; gone as if you awoke in your dreams or fluttered off into the eaves in mine.

It was then, while I was standing in a doorway, alone on an empty street, that I heard someone approaching. I looked down the lane and saw coming towards me the figure of a man. He emerged from the mist like a ship coming off the sea through the fog in the night. His form was tall and he wore a long black frockcoat and carried a leather satchel with what looked like to be the barrel of gun protruding from it. When he came close, I could see the lines in his face, his fair-colored hair dripping with rain. His strides were long and rhythmic, and he walked quickly as though in a hurry, coming nearer and nearer to the place where I stood; and it was then, as he walked by within an arms reach of me, that he looked into my eyes with a cursory sidelong glance.

To tell of the strangeness I saw in that singular gaze of his…

In the depth of those eyes, I read of a thousand histories; all the heroes of myths scattered through the centuries. Visions flooded my mind. Potent visions akin to madness: I saw the great allegorical wanderer. The gondolier guiding lost souls on dark eternal lapping waters. I saw the fabled traveler of the frozen steppe carrying the silk of time on a sledge driven by barbarous beasts. I saw the fiery sailor who sailed tumultuous seas, scorning the land until the ocean be tamed as smooth as a puddle of glass. I saw the lonely soldier who, in seeking life, sought Death for a game of chess, and played while laughing on the barren fields as his final breaths swam away. I saw the wandering balladeer who strummed and sang the Roman hymns with a blade and string on Afric's shore…such a look in the eyes of a human I had never seen before. And once I saw it, I sought to have it. For within his gaze, I believed was the secret to all greatness. Yet, as soon as his eyes met my own trembling eyes, after looking at me for only a moment, he turned away and resumed watching straight ahead as he continued on his way, quickly, hurriedly, down the narrow passageway. After he had gone, I stepped out from the doorway and watched his figure growing fainter and smaller in the steamy darkness of the winding lane. It was then I started after him. I began to follow him. I had to!

I kept pace through the numerous narrow lanes, drifting like a shade between doorways so as not to be seen. At one point he crossed a wooden bridge over a canal where the boats were roped-up and were rocking after the storm. I too then crossed the bridge and pursued him along the quais and down another series of streets lined with closed-up shops, seedy inns, and train depots. Then came the moment, while I was slinking along the walls of a building not so far behind him, that he suddenly turned around and stopped. He faced me and I froze still. His eyes moved upwards. What was he looking at? I ducked immediately behind some crates stacked near a doorway of a brick building and peered at him through the slats of wood. Although he was turned towards me, he wasn't looking at me. his head was tilted back, looking upwards at a train that was passing overhead with a *clack, clack, clack, clack* as it flew across the tracks of an aerial bridge. His eyes followed the last car until it was gone. Once out of sight, the sound of rumbling far in the distance, he reached into his satchel and took hold of the barrel of his gun or whatever was inside. He then looked my way. He stared at the plywood crates behind which I was hiding. My heart beat quickly. I prepared to act. Yet, before I did, he looked away. He turned around, and walked off as quickly as before. I continued on after him.

Our way led from the narrow lanes back to the quais, then back to narrow lanes. At times, I followed very close; other times, I discreetly allowed him to gain so much distance as to almost be out of sight, assuring myself that he could then neither see me nor hear my footsteps. A few times during the walk, he turned and looked at me, distinctly – as if he knew I were following him – though this might have just been my fanciful imagination.

It was after he turned down the boulevard leading out of the district of canals – the quarter of midnight dens and drinking rooms – that I almost overtook him in an elegant neighborhood, on a quiet street. Instead, I stopped and waited. Breathing heavily, I hid myself behind a pillar of a redbrick garden and allowed him to gain some distance. When he was again out of view, I continued on through the quiet street until it ended suddenly in a cul-de-sac, which then led into a small passageway, which in turn emptied out into a large square.

It was then I found myself standing in a large, silent and majestic square, planted with billowing trees and lined with tall palaces. In their windows gleamed the luster of chandeliers, casting creamy ivory light on draped curtains. In the center of the square, within gates of iron, within an ancient park, statues and slopes of grass were lit by a moon emerging from the clearings of the parting clouds thinly drifting in the mild night. As always following a heavy rain, the air was perfumed. Smells of blossoms came from the gardens, while sounds of nightingales came from the trees.

I stood there looking around the square, surveying the walls of the palaces. With eyes like searchlights, I looked around the gates of the garden. And then, to my delight, I saw the object of my pursuit. He was on the far-side of the square, approaching the entrance of a building; not one of the grand luster-windowed palaces, but one on the opposite side of the square facing them: a tall, narrow and average-looking building of white stone with a zinc slated roof, leaning slightly to one side from centuries of age.

When I saw his figure in the distance, I hastened through the square along the perimeter of the iron gate. I could see him turning the lock in the door as he clutched his satchel at his side. I almost leapt upon the place where he had been standing, but alas!, by the time I reached the doorway, he had already entered and had closed the door behind him.

I tried the latch on the door. It was locked. I tried to peer into the entryway, yet the glass was patterned, obscured, and it was of no use. I stooped and pressed my ear to the door and from within I could hear the sounds of his footsteps growing fainter and fainter, quieter and quieter, as he ascended the stairs and was gone.

———————

This man who had been followed through the dark streets on this night, his name was Alexander and he was a stranger in this southern city of numerous canals, in a country where the sultry subtropical winds blow and the air is mild in the winter. Where he had traveled from, snow still lay on the ground; but now he was far from all of that.

On this night, he traversed the numerous winding streets joining the various quarters of the city, navigating quickly through the intermittent storms, carrying his leather satchel which contained merely a bottle of wine he'd purchased from a subterranean cavern. He walked quickly, anxious to return to his room, suppressing the urge to linger along those canals which intrigued him so much. Only once did he stop on the way. It was when he had walked under a railway bridge and had heard a train coming, one of the grand-line trains; he turned to watch it pass overhead, and was struck with nostalgia. It reminded him of when he himself had passed through this place for the first time on such a train, while traveling from one country to another. For a few brief moments he had had a glimpse of this strange capital city from the deck of that train, and he'd decided then that he needed to return one day, some day, far in the distant future.

Now he was back. It was a different period of his life. And on this singular night, he was in the midst of it all as he hurried alone through the narrow streets that were alight with the glow of streetlamps. After he had stopped briefly to watch the train pass overhead, he took a moment to take hold of the bottle of wine in his satchel to make sure the cork was securely in place. As he was doing this, he was startled by a noise coming from some wooden crates stacked up by a nearby building. Just a clowder of cats, he assumed, looking at these crates; stray cats digging through trash. He shrugged it off and turned and continued on then at his hurried pace, paying attention to the street signs he passed so as not to get lost. Though he'd been in this city for a mere week, his orientation was good and he did not get lost. With ease he found his way through the mazes of passageways; and eventually he came to the large square where his room was, on the top floor of a white stone building overlooking opulent palaces and a grand Arcadian iron-gated garden.

After he entered the main door of the building and ascended the stairs to the fifth floor, he turned the key in the lock and went into the tiny furnished room that he rented. A noise could be heard out in the hall. Crickets, he thought. He closed the door behind him and turned the bolt two times to lock it. He then took off his frockcoat and turned his back to the window to hang it on the hook on the door. The moonlight came through the panes of glass and passed over his shoulder lighting upon the beads of rainwater on the fabric of the coat, while water dripped and gathered around the soles of his shoes on the wooden floor below.

His coat hung up, Alexander then threw his gloves and satchel on the bed and went over to stand by the mirror that was provided with the otherwise bare and spartan room, having besides only a single table and chair, a mattress on a steel frame, and a tiny lamp of tarnished silver. He stood at the mirror and wrung the rainwater out of his hair with his hand. He scratched the bristly whiskers on his broad square chin. There was a razor in the pocket of his coat and he thought to use it. Finally he decided against it, but his eyes remained fixed on this coat for a many moments. Then with a sudden gesture, he grabbed the coat and felt in the lining. He reached his hand in one of the inside pockets and pulled out an object. He held it up and turned it to catch the light of the moon. It was a medal of gold – a military decoration on a black, white and red striped ribbon – the type worn by officers awarded high-honors for bravery in battle. He looked at this medal with a peculiar eye, as though he were seeing it for the first time; though in fact he often looked at it in this way. After a moment, he returned the medal to his pocket, and turned his attention to his reflection in the mirror. He again rubbed the whiskers on his chin, and smiled at himself – not a carefree smile, but the type of thoughtful smile one makes at times when offering solidarity to oneself, privately in the mirror. When he smiled like this, faint wrinkles branched out from the corners of his blue eyes and ran like train tracks out to his temples.

Following this exercise, he walked over to the table and turned on the lamp which flickered and buzzed, sending faint light across the walls. He took off his damp shirt and draped it over the wooden chair. He then walked around the room several times looking for the satchel he had thrown somewhere or other. Hadn't he set it on the floor? No, it had been on the bed. When he found it, he picked it up, pulled the bottle of wine out, threw the satchel back on the bed and stood there quietly thinking for a moment. He thought seriously about several things, and then he stopped and just listened. Everything, the building included, was quiet.

Suddenly, he turned to the window with a startling thought. He saw the moon through the glass. It was three quarters full. Below it, lay the city. Suddenly, snatching up the bottle of wine, he ran over to the window, put his hand on the latch, turned it, and flung the shutters open…

"Oh, holy city, I don't even need to imagine you!" he called out to the night.

The wind flew in fresh and mild, carrying in its gusts, traces of the rancid air from the odorous canals of the city below. He looked at the silent square, then above at the silver quilts of clouds. Between the trees planted within the garden gates, he could see the numerous clusters of ancient buildings that extended as far as the horizon. Their dark orange and red tiled roofs were still wet from the recent storm and they sparkled luminously, glimmering in the starlight, in the moonlight. And between these clusters of stacked-up buildings, canals wound around enlaced, appearing like black snakes slithering quietly in the darkness; while little bridges spanned them here and there.

"And what a strange city you are."

And what strange city was it? It is of no use to know now, and not even Alexander's own thoughts were concerned with this city any longer. After having said this, his attention turned to the grand palace directly across the square. He looked at the tall windows with their elegant draped curtains illuminated by the ivory light of the chandeliers. It was beyond those windows, he mused, that noblemen lie with their brides and girls in beds of silk in high palace rooms. "I wonder how many…" he began. "No, Alexander, just look."

It was then while he was looking at the palace, that he caught something moving out of the corner of his eye . . . something among the bushes, beneath the gas lamps, in the square below. For a moment he thought he saw a person's figure scurrying along the iron gate of the garden.

"No matter!" he called loudly from the window, "Let us scurry together! But first . . . the wine!"

Grinning at the night, he took his wine bottle and pulled the cork out with his teeth and set it on the sill. He pressed the bottle to his lips and drew from it a long, slow drink of the cool sanguine wine. It tasted spicy and clean and it cured his thirst. It warmed his throat and the sensation passed into his arms and his body and his head, instantly softening his thoughts.

"Oh, good brother, wine." He took another drink. "My most charming wine." He drank again and his words ran on... "What a long path I have led myself on. And to think of all I have seen and known." The wine was passing through his body, changing his thoughts, softening his vision, making him feel increasingly thoughtful and romantic. He looked out lazily over the city and the stars glimmered brilliantly in his light glazy eyes. Above the rooftops, the moon sat softly on a glowing nest of clouds.

"So that was my life," he said to himself, "...and so this will be my life. How beautiful it all is." So like a dealer goes through a deck of cards, so Alexander shuffled through the recollections in his mind. As abundant as the stones which form the streets and structures of the greatest ancient city were the memories in his possession – as plentiful as the cloudlets which sail over the skies of the vastest country. And those who had been his friends, or his lovers, or those who had simply at one time met curiously his gaze were more numerous than all who dwell in any such city, and all who roam through any such country.

He gave a last look at the wisps of clouds coming in over the rooftops of the city.

"If those clouds knew my story," he wondered aloud, "would they hear of greediness?...of senseless wandering?" ... "If those rooftops heard my tale, would they hear of days squandered and hours lost? Or would this city drink my words like wine and sing of a life well lived?"

He looked down and reached into his pocket and took out a silver watch on a long chain. It was engraved with two initials – two letters roughly scratched into the silver, as if done so by hand with a nail. He opened the cover and looked at the time. Approaching midnight. The second-hand ticked. He mused on the date. "Yet, could it have only been two weeks ago that I was there?"

How far away it all seemed to be. Yet it had been almost exactly two weeks ago that he was standing there in the thawing snow, waving goodbye to the two of them – to that stranger with his simple and benevolent face; and to her – blessed woman – with her soft tired eyes, her hand that rested on the curve of her swollen belly.

He closed the watch and returned it to his pocket. Who were these two, is neither of any use to know now, and not even Alexander's own thoughts remained with them. As his eyes turned back to the city beyond the window, so his thoughts returned to this city, and to the other cities he had seen; and he thought of his long past. Visions came to his mind of faces he'd known, of places he'd traveled to, of conversations he'd had, and gently his whole life played back before him.

As he rested against the midnight windowsill, a mild wind blew on his bare chest, on his wounded shoulder and sinewy arms; and it blew through the trees in the square, rattling their leaves. And with this, his attention turned to them. He looked at these trees in the garden, towering above all, even the rooftops on the horizon. And he watched them swaying in the gentle wind, their silhouettes black against a sky lit by the silver moon cached in the patterned clouds, and it reminded him of something from long ago. And suddenly he was reminded of the very beginning, of the time and place where it all had started, and from which everything had stemmed. He could remember clearly the two of them, he and her, and how they had been; and he remembered that place, though long ago it was and so many things had come to pass since then. He had since dwelt in the basement and walked in the garden. He had bathed himself in the tenements and tin and the golden sunshine all in turn. He had seen the feasts and the massacres, the love and the loss, the rise and the glory; and he had become a man. But this was before all of this. This was when it had just been he and her, in that idyllic place. A boy and a girl, in a time which can be painted now in this pastoral scene, in the Great Northern Woods, upon the arrival of spring…

Chapter II

In a time of youth and ease...

Whilst the birdlets flew and lamblets grazed, through the treelets' maze, they went and gazed at the last light of the late white evening sun which came from beyond hillside yonder. Then evening fell, and between the tall black figures of cedar, swaying needles of pine, the moon appeared, as if by design; and though it was only a crescent, it illuminated their two bodies huddled together in the wood. It was late March, the equinox of spring.

Thus, with winter at their backs, and spring on their brows, they had then what only youth allows, and they both, two singular people, felt it together and knew what the other knew while neither of them spoke. Then, with their lives waiting back in the house, they bid farewell to the night, toasted their childhood gone away and walked arm in arm down the old summer path, which led to the winter home.

Back inside, besides the light of the moon coming through the cracked windowpanes illuminating dust on cedar walls, smoke from the hearth, embers dying in the fireplace, three old chairs silently sitting, two bowls of broth quietly cooling, and an old overcoat drenched and dripping; besides a heavy table filled with dishes, a plate of black bread and salt, uneaten crusts; three empty glasses, two with the dregs of tea, one with the froth of beer; besides these and other things there were they: two figures propped in the hallway. She like a wooden fish draped in a nightgown. And he like a firm stone dog holding up a candle. His wrist caught the dripping tallow. The walls caught the light so sallow and the copper knob on the hall door gleamed. And when the knob turned, out came the third.

The brother stood poised and the sister trembled, and her chin on his chest and his waist gave her a place for her hand, small and white and wet with cold sweat.

Shuddering, she stood; and still, he waited; and soon the door opened and the immense figure that was their father came out into the hall and cast a vast, dark shadow down the corridor. So grand was he. Black wiry beard and heavy fists, thick black brow and how he allowed himself to hover over their youthful bodies, which, though grown, seemed no taller than the toadstools sprouting through the cracks in the floor.

His blue eyes were heavy with sadness, swollen and old from the days and long nights spent awake by the bedside in the far off bedroom, in the holy part of the house, in the room where the brother and sister never once ventured.

"She will soon die."

It was certain in the voice of that rueful-speaking massive man. Head bowed low, he dropped loose hairs from worry. Each hair that fell, it landed with a sound like a broom sweeping across the floor. The father's giant fist shook with fright, and trembled with unholy sorrow, and the candle caught the shimmer of blood fresh on his wrist and hand.

Two children had he, and other reasons for joy, but no man felt more alone and more abandoned to the fiery ugliness of this world sometimes wicked than he then, their dear father. And hereby holy, on this evening he perched his lips to the neck of the world and waited to drink while the blood of their mother dripped to the wooden floor, and mice scurried in the walls.

Neither brother nor sister spoke. Her head dropped low, her body fastened to the former's arm. And he, leaving his father there, led her off down the hall and up the hollow stair, the rickety way to the garret. The father, now alone, took to the bedroom once again, and breathing solemn heavy sighs, he closed the door and closed his eyes.

Upstairs alone in the tiny attic room, furnished with a bed, a table, a basin and bath, the brother and sister sat facing each other on a mattress of feathers and wool. The brother reached under the bed frame and retrieved an old amber bottle filled with wine. Dislodging the cork with his teeth, he poured a glass. After lightening the red with basin water he added a gram of table sugar, which he stirred into the wine slowly, melancholically, with his rose-colored finger. A drop of wine ran down the side of the glass, dispelled, and fell, soaking the bed linen. His sister, seated cross-legged before him, rubbed her wet cheek on her thigh and a tear rolled down, soaking her nightgown. She coursed with her fingers her soft bare knees, which she pulled up against her chest. Her pretty face was swollen from crying and the curtain on the tiny window in the center of the far cedar wall blew with the March evening's wind, while a wisp of cloud passed by the moon. A rattling sound was heard. And then, far off, the sounds of wolves.

"I wonder if Mother is dead yet," she uttered softly to her brother.

"If not now, then soon enough." Alexis had the low and crackling voice of one deprived of sleep, "Take a glass of wine if you want."

"I don't want."

Each one took a breath. Alexis then turned away from his sister and drank from his glass. The diluted wine was acrid yet and made him wince. He added another grain of sugar, stirred and sipped and bowed his head, lifting it again when he was spoken to.

"Can I stay here with you tonight?" She leaned forward on his bed and embraced him, and he her; while the linen on the bed and his arms, and her gown, breezed and blocked the blowing March wind coming through the window, through the trees on forest-side yonder. The windowpane rattled again and his sister ended the embrace, stood, abandoned him and walked to the window. She leaned on its ledge and looked to what remained outside.

"I wish at least the moon were more than a sliver tonight. It is so dark. I wish the winds would stop." All trace of tears gone from her eyes, she spoke only with a voice of longing, "I wish those trees were taller, and broader, so as to keep us warm. Brother, it is especially cold tonight."

Alexis wiped the wine from his lips and joined his sister at the window. He looked out as far the night would permit - shadows of distant trees cast black cut-out shapes against a violet sky, "I wish I were beyond those trees. I wish I were on that sliver of a moon. It is so vast this forest, and we are so small within it."

Confused were her eyes, and strange were his words. She looked at him with misunderstanding and drew off to go lie in his bed. There, beneath a thin blanket, her body shivered. Her long golden-loom hair lay against the headboard. Eyes and lips swollen, she looked at her brother standing at the window who in turn looked out over the trees, and she asked him, "Will you be long, now?"

"No, I won't be long," he responded. Or perhaps he didn't respond. More likely it is that he just kept standing there silently, looking out the window.

Young Lise then blew out the lamp and all was dark. Her brother, after gazing a long time over those broad trees, whose needles and leaves rattled with the torrents of wind, drew the curtain closed and came to bed. He lay beside her. Her breathing was hard and her body was warm and she shivered as she slept - perhaps more from frightful dreams than from cold.

He remained awake, gazing at the slanted ceiling of the attic room, which could not be seen in the darkness - only imagined. He could hear his sister breathing, he could feel her breath on his skin. His father's, he could not and he wondered where he was - and where his mother was too.

These wonderings wandered for some time in the room which grew still and more still. Though also cold, not a shiver escaped him. Though also tired, not a dream overtook him. He lay awake and thought of many things, of those far and near, of then and now; and soon he found himself; and he wondered where his time had gone and wasn't sure if he had slept, though it was morning in a clear light room and a frigid misty northern wind blew with a howl through the trees coming in with the faint white sun through the open window in the attic, where he sat up and dressed, leaving his sister to sleep awhile longer.

Outside, a brook took water off into the forest, a silver film of clouds hung heavy in the sky, a dull drizzle drifted down, down to the soiled earth below. Blue smoke from far off fires floated up into the sky. And our young man, just a lad, laced his boots and looked from yonder's window ledge, again as far as he could see.

"The tree line seemed nearer last night, though the horizon seemed oh so incomparably far. The world is vast, yes. But as vast are the strides of a young man's legs, when his mind is clean and his eyes are wide and when he is bent on travel."

Alexis inhaled deeply smelling the scent of cedar wood burning, coming from over the forest in plumes of smoke from the recesses of trees where hunters were gathered by firesides cooking. The cold morning mist touched his bare chest and it pleased him. His body was firm and stood like a young Apollo carved in white marble, weight on one leg, hairless, supple and strong - the color of bone from a long winter's passed that saw no sun. Now, on this first morning of spring, the vernal sun - a little white disc beyond the mist - emerged a time or two, lighting the room with a new and unfamiliar golden light.

"How long have you been awake?" His sister stirred in his bed. The blankets rustled on her skin and fell to the floor, revealing her legs - bare feet, calves, until white, soft trembling knees, too like the marble of a young Artemis leaving her dreams of the hunt behind. And the morning fell on her face as she sat up and yawned.

"When did you wake up?"

Alexis turned to her. He told her many things and explained a great deal but in actuality he stood silent and said nothing.

"Did you sleep?" she began again.

Again he began not.

"Brother? Where do you think you will go? ...Now, I mean. Now that it is over."

"I don't know where I will go. But it will surely be far and I know I will be gone a long time." He looked away again, back to the misty tree line on far horizon's edge. His sister's eyes grew wide. She bit her lower-lip, stood, and covered herself with a blanket to approach him at the window.

"But it is just spring now and we always, in spring...."

"Lise," he interrupted, "last year was the last spring. Do you want me to be a man, or remain a boy?"

"Well, of course, a man. But I didn't say...." And she didn't say, but hesitated. After a moment, words fluttered out, "Anyway, I want yet to be a girl, and so I will stay. Or even if a woman ... but I will stay." And here her brother abandoned his sister's side; while her words, having nowhere else to go, floated up to the ceiling of the attic and seeped into the wood. As if alone, he walked over to the basin to wash his glass from the night before. Stopping to cast a glance in the mirror, he became lost in his gaze. Finally, a distant voice far-off came: "But you know I will stay here. Alexis, you know this."

"I know this, Lise. Come, let's go downstairs."

Alexis and Lise...

Whilst beyond the house the goatlets grazed, within its walls those two were raised, and fed all their years from a mother's hand ... a hand, which kept the stove water simmering and the oven coals a-smolder; so as to bake their little cakes, to please their little eyes; to cook their little breads - their bubbling little pies. And while as babes they climbed the walls, their mother swept up with a broom, and as they hid 'neath barrel lids, she tidied up their rooms. When on summer eves, the garden table was laid, the mother watched to the yard, where her young ones played. And on winters dim when the oven coals smoldered, she tended the soup while the short days folded - and nights came forth, and moons arose; the stars passed o'er, the lakelets froze. And the little growing children besides, they took their form and mother's eyes; and took their nightly tired rest, upon their mother's swollen breast.

But alas this poem had to end, as all sweet summers had before. Time ticked along, ticked along to the time they sat, on this singular misty morning, in an empty cold kitchen, which now only housed a week's worth of brandy and a day's worth of bread.

Dust in the corners, the broom went unused; cold morning air, the stove stayed unlit; all laughter gone, the children had grown; and now all alone but for the two of them, they sat at the table of wormwood planks, amid a spread of cups and plates. Alexis' sister, in a bit of a tremble, smoothed the wrinkles from her dress and looked to her brother, who in turn looked to the ground. He spied two beetles who chipped at a crumb. Two termites fought for a flake. Then, startled by the sounds of the birds in the rafters, he glanced up again and saw that his sister had left.

Standing at the sink, she wrung-out a rag. Her eyes searched the yard through the windowpanes for some flowers to put in a vase - a vase to place on the table. But no flowers were growing. It was still only March and the twigs of the trees were barren of leaves and empty of green blooms. With this realization, and others too, something akin to despair arose and a cold fever struck our young girl. She dropped the sopping rag on her bare foot and almost lost herself in a faint until Alexis helped her to the chair and sat her down. He remained with her until the dizziness passed, until her head grew heavy again. He remained with her longer, until she was calm, until she was quiet. And then she became upset.

"Why are you upset, Lise?"

"Why are you waiting, Alexis?"

One wonders if he knew. Standing, he nodded to her, left her to sit, and took his necessary march down the hallway – down the sallow lightless corridor, to the far end, to the door – while alone, she sat. Alone, she sighed and looked on ahead. Then, upon seeing Alexis returning from the hall through the corner of her eye, she again sighed and looked on ahead.

"He went to go bury Mother."

A sweep of silence. Then the rustles of needles and leaves on the rattling trees in the yard.

"But why do you look like that?"

She didn't look like anything. Her body was hollow. Her gaze was absent. Her hands shook. Her lips were a-tremble. She was thin as gauze and blank as bone. It was then that she left him. It was then that she stood and walked away; walked off to her room; the room where her bed was; the room which she hadn't entered for more than a week.

Chapter III

"Leaving Youth and Ease" - the sorrow and the sacrament...

Whilst the wolflets bayed, a grave was made; and then with the strokes of a silver spade, it was filled to make a mound. And for two cold days and three long nights, the father tended that holy plot; and stayed by where his wife was laid, in the grave within the ground. Then on the morning of the third day, as a mist swept over the land, he bade farewell to his wife, and offered up an offering. Upon the grave, he let fall a leaf. He laid down the bones of a lamb. Then, taking his gaze up from the mire, he cast his head back to the sky. All was calm and halcyon. From behind a blanket of copper clouds came the blue of azure fair. And in the golden light of the morning sun, he squinted his eyes into diamond slits, and brushed back his wiry beard, whereupon his lips became wet and his cheeks grew inflamed. Then, with a deep growl which resounded across the forests wide, he raised his fist and dropped his spade. His eyes burned with white fire. His mighty fist trembled with unholy fury. And this-upon, the heavens seethed and covered over with an iron sheet of rumbling, roaring thunder. Violent rains commenced pouring down in heavy sweeps, drenching and tearing apart the land. The rains beat upon his body. The winds tore at his flesh and shook his balance as he stood trembling by the grave. And only then did he let fall his fist. And all grew calm again.

Having learned from the heavens that he had lost, and realizing then he was truly lost, and his joy would live no more, he let tumble his gaze. He bowed his weary head. He sunk his broken brow; and treaded the wasted earth below, dragging his massive legs along. And on and on, he walked on and on, down the once happy path that now led to the house of sorrow.

Back inside, besides a low fire crackling sap, scalding logs; besides the singular flight of a dragonfly up above in the bend of the rafter's bow; besides the view of the lonesome yard from yonder's window ledge, which the sun at times came and lit - that sun that sometimes cached itself with the capricious beginnings of spring; besides these and other things, there was he: the immense figure that was their father, sitting gravely mourning in a silent chair by fireside. He waited for something or waited for nothing but here he remained alone: now smoking a pipe and gazing out of the window, now whittling a block of wood with a knife. His silence was deep, his sorrow profound, so great it appeared it would never leave.

It was then while the mother of Alexis wilted in the vernal ground, that her son appeared behind his father who was seated in a chair carving a block of wood.

"Father?"

And there was silence.

"Father?"

And then some.

"Father," Alexis spoke louder, "I am leaving for the city."

There was still no response from the grief-stricken man, and so his son called again...

"Father?"

"Yes Son, for which city?" He finally responded. His voice was empty. His gaze was elsewhere. He sat motionless – all but for his hands, which chipped at a block of wood. "Perhaps you're going to Krüfsterburg. It's not so far."

"No Father, not to Krüfsterburg. I'm going far. To the Great City. I am going to live. For good. I am leaving home, Father. I have grown and it is time."

"Well, I knew this day would come. I didn't know when it would be but I knew it would happen like this." The father's shavings of wood grew in an untidy pile around his mud-caked, unlaced leather boots. He reached down with his giant hand and sifted through the shavings. He pulled a large worm from the flakes of wood, and it squirmed in his grip until he threw it into the fire where it crackled and burned.

Alexis waited, watched on. He grew nervous and wanted then to take back his words, to tell his father it was nonsense, to tell him he would be staying. But it was not nonsense. He would not be staying. And so he stood silent and said nothing. Soon, his father broke the silence...

"Well my boy, be careful. It is a hard life out there. You'd be better off to stay."

"Better off to stay!" These words sizzled on the nerves of the lad. They kindled fire in his ornery glands; and so he grew bold and replied, "I am not your boy, Father. And I will not stay!"

"Very well, then. Don't stay." His father dropped his eyes low and resumed his task of chipping wood into the pile of flakes at his feet. And this pile it grew into a nest of splinters, shavings crawling with tender worms, while beetles hatched from their eggs in the fibers. And the sun and moon, they revolved in the sky casting changing shadows on the still and silent figure that was the father, who was now alone in this room, where he chipped and chipped and waited and thought.

Two days passed. And on the third, Alexis returned to where his father was sitting. The man in mourning was still occupied by his task. His head was bowed low. His son looked to him, and then looked to the nearby door which led to the room where his sister lived. Then he looked back at his father, "She hasn't left her room in days."

The father reached down and cupped in his hand some shavings of wood, and these he threw into the fire. "I know," he said, "your sister knows a great deal. But she will come out soon. She will be with us at the table tonight. It is an important night." He tried to smile at his son with a fatherly smile – a smile both warm and endearing. But his eyelids sagged, his cheeks sank, while his blue eyes glimmered, and this only made him look more sad; and so, knowingly, he let it go.

More hours passed and soon it was eve. Dusk fell on the house, and Lise came out to lay the table for the feast. She placed bowls and cloth and cups and rings. She lit a single candlestick. Then she returned silently to her room.

"She is dressing now," said the father who was now seated at the table. His face was lit red from the candle glow, while his son's radiated yellow fire. The flickers of flames, in their eyes they changed. The father's, they glimmered. The son's grew wide. While the rest of the amber candle glow fell on the top of the table below. "She is dressing now," he repeated, "She wants to look nice. Be kind to her tonight. Be gentle. It is important."

Soon the three were seated at the table of planks. It was there the three feasted in silence. Turnips were eaten, beets were enjoyed, as was a creamed cabbage stew. Once the bowls were drained to the dregs, the father gave his son a knowing look - a look whose meaning filled the room. When his daughter saw the expression on her father's face, she immediately understood, and got up from the table and gathered the dishes to go wash them at the sink.

Once the table had been cleared and was bare, but for a candle alight in its center; a candle which flickered and flung tallow into the grooves of the wood in the table as it burned, the father looked at his son with eyes that changed in the candlelight from lead to iron, from copper to bronze - and he picked his teeth with a splinter.

The father looked at his son, and he looked away. Then his eyes cast across the room at his daughter who stood washing the dishes in the sink, and he called out to her...

"Lizbeth!"

Lise turned her head quickly, trembling nervously from being called as such. And with her chin on her shoulder she looked at him and answered, "Yes, Father?", while continuing with shaking hands to dry the wet plates with a cloth.

"Lizbeth." His voice was slow, deep and steady. "Bring the black bread and a bottle of vodka. I will get the glasses. Vodka for your brother and for me. Sheep's milk for you."

Lise obeyed, set down the plates and the cloth, and left the sink. She brought the bottle of vodka, and a cup of sheep's milk for herself. There was black bread on the table.

"Two glasses, my son. The rim of yours is broken. Drink quickly so as not to cut your lips."

The father filled the glasses, and he and his son looked seriously at each other. There was nothing of laughter in either's eyes. Lise, wide-eyed and pale-faced, watched the procession as she hunched over in her chair, motionless, clutching her cup of sheep's milk. Alexis and his father sat across from one another, eye to firm eye, and silently they toasted glasses. The father's perfect glass clinked the glass of his son with its broken rim. And the two commenced to drink.

Alexis pressed his lips to the jagged rim of the glass for only a moment, and tried to drain it in one swift sip, so as not to cut himself. But he could not drink quickly. The liquor was too strong and he choked and pulled the glass away.

"Son," his father said with a powerful voice, looking firmly at the youth, "ignore the strong spirits. Ignore the broken rim. Drink to the bottom with your father. When we meet again, it will be a different kind of meeting. But now has to go exactly as it is going... to the bottom!" ... "Lizbeth," he turned to his daughter, "drink your sheep's milk and serve the bread."

Lise, who had hitherto stood frozen, unable to move, watching the two with an open mouth - her wide eyes reflecting the flickering candle flame, her teeth like little pearl rocks, wet from saliva, and glimmering in the candlelight - she now jolted. She trembled as though quite afraid. She then tried to drink her sheep's milk. She tried to serve the bread and salt. But the ceremony was coming to a climax, and she could only now stop and observe.

Alexis put once more the glass with its jagged edge to his lips. He kept it there, and he drank. With his eyes cast upwards, he looked at his father, and he drew the liquor into his mouth, while the broken rim of the glass cut his lip. And his lip, it bled. The dark ruby blood ran down the inside of glass, filling it, tingeing the once clear vodka.

Lise, who was a witness to this ceremony, grew completely pale and put her small fist into her mouth upon seeing her brother bleeding so profusely into his glass – bleeding, though continuing to drink, as if unaware that his lips, his chin, his neck, and his hands, and his glass were covered with dark red and sanguine blood. He pressed even harder the broken glass to his lips. He held it there, with a trembling hand and eyes fastened on his father's, as he drank and allowed the strong spirits to continue their course into his mouth and down his throat; while his blood it coursed and was drawn and continued dripping, filling the glass and dropping on the table and floor. Yet Alexis did not show pain. He did not show fear. He simply drank, and bled.

His sister, Lise, looked on all of this with a mixture of fear and respect, horror and admiration. She watched on at her father as he sipped his clear, clean vodka from his own glass slowly and steadily until it was empty. She watched on at her father, as he watched on at his son who continued to drink and to bleed. But soon she could take no more. As if caught by a sudden piercing pain, her pale face, the color of bone, flushed red and she began to cry. And her eyes flashed from her brother to her father, then back again to her brother; and she stood from the table and ran upstairs – stopping beforehand quickly to kiss her brother on the shoulder.

He took no notice, for he was drinking and bleeding and looking at his father. But she stopped to kiss his shoulder and her tears soaked into his shirt cloth. She turned and hid her eyes and ran up the stairs. And with her gone, Alexis continued on with the procession, silently sitting there, watching his father as he drank and bled.

As soon as every drop of blood-tinged vodka was drained from the glass, Alexis set it down on the table next to the clean empty glass of his father. His father looked on approvingly, and then said, "It is time, my son. You are a boy no longer. Go. Go and wander far, and speak nothing of us to those you meet. Now your mother is gone and your sister is changing. She will now become the woman of the house, and you will become a man of the world."

Chapter IV

"Alone in the world" – at last!...

The following morning at dawn, Alexis left the home of his father and sister in the Great Northern Woods and skipped off alone down the vernal sunlit path, carrying only his youth and a bundle. The silver coins, which his father had given him at last to help him get his start in the world chimed in his pockets as he ran along kicking rocks and taunting the sheeplets nipping at his heels. A traveling sack slung over his back was filled with his father's good shirts of sturdy cotton; and tied to the strap was a yellow silk handkerchief – gift from his sister – which flapped in the wind as he ran along. So full of eagerness was he, so full of youthful folly. He fled off into the direction of the eastern horizon where the spring sun was rising, and a great joy resounded within him; although time and again the image returned to his mind: that of his sister crying at the window with nothing of gladness in her swollen eyes, as she waved goodbye.

The sun pierced through the trees lining the path, illuminating the dust to create a soft matinal haze. This path took Alexis into the dense part of the woods where the canopies of trees allowed no light to enter. And in this darkness, the dampness and residues of winter lingered. Here, he passed stumps of rotting cedars covered in moss. He passed marshes covered in algae where cattails were growing and the early mosquitoes were hatching. He saw upon the trunks of the trees those brackish yellow shelf mushrooms, hideous creatures who survive even the coldest winter frosts. In the cracks of the rotting trunks sat sleeping toads. In the meat of the trees crawled fleshy worms, and dragonflies hovered all around.

Brittle tree limbs cracked and swayed above his uncovered head. One limb fell across his path. He laughed as he leapt over it. How puerile they are, these trees...how boyish compared with he who becomes more and more a man with each advancing step!

"With these woods," he called out in his peculiar ceremonious way, "I leave behind all vestiges of my boyhood. When I enter the first town, I shall bring with me only those characteristics which belong to the realm of man. ...Now, onward path!"

The trail continued winding, and Alexis continued on. As the day advanced, the woods changed and became less familiar. New kinds of plants grew and new fragrances came in abundance.

Along the way, Alexis found a bush where pink winterberries were growing. Hungry, he knelt down to eat some. But these were not pink winterberries! These were a new kind of berry, soft and fleshy, with a taste like warm sweet brine. A taste he had never known. He delighted in them.

He came to a tree upon which mirabelles were growing. But these were not mirabelles! They were a new kind of fruit, bigger than plums – juicy and milky, with waxy skins. They secreted a nectar that one may dream of finding in the breasts of sleeping Eve, resting in her far away garden. He drank from these fruits, he feasted on them, he fled!

Such fantasies filled Alexis' mind. If only he had really found fruit! A hunger began to pass through his body, but he disregarded it and continued on. So much there was still to discover. He could do without eating for the time being. He really had to hurry!

Soon the woods changed and the clearings between the trees became greater and the sun once again lit upon his path; and all that was cool, dark and damp, became warm, light and dry. Toads ceased to croak. Shelf mushrooms ceased to grow. And finally, that path through the woods ended altogether and Alexis found himself standing at an old blue-painted wooden fence, next to a long country road.

It was the road that was to take him far away from the Great Northern Woods. He hopped over the fence, stood at the side of the road, and listened.

Why no sound? He looked right, off into the southward direction. It was certainly a long road. To the south, it curved through brightly-lit pastures and wound around through rolling hills tinged gold by the sun; hills which led on to more hills, also rolling and also tinged by the sun; and finally at the horizon, it was crowned by a distant range of purple mountains.

"Beyond those mountains," Alexis pointed and declared, "or beyond other mountains, lies the Great City!" It was afternoon now, and he started off down the country road.

Traveling along, he looked about himself at his surroundings. Everything was new and unfamiliar. There were no more giant shadowy trees of needles and cones. Here instead, grew small, sunny broad-leafed plants abloom with flowers of peach and rose. Their petals, curved folds of skin laced with pollen; their stems quivered in the wind – a wind that blew warm and soft – and their green leaves glimmered in the sun like shards of jade. Now, with these sights, Alexis was struck by the sudden realization that he was finally, and for the very first time, out in the midst of the world. No going back! He laughed and skipped along and sang aloud, "Praise the earth! Praise the fields and flowers! And praise the city! Yes, praise the city! Onward Great City!"

It was getting late in the evening when Alexis arrived in a small quiet village off to the side of the long country road he had spent the afternoon walking down. He was relieved because he was hungry and tired and could profit from finding a bed.

He wandered through the narrow cobblestone streets of the village, passing rows of houses. These houses which were all identical to one another, with their shuttered windows and triangular slanted roofs jutting up to the sky, each with its own weathervane on top. The only structure in the town that was different was the church – it having a belfry, a more pronounced triangular roof, and no weathervane.

After passing the church, Alexis came to an inn. At least the painted sign said it was an inn. He stood outside a while considering if it was indeed an inn and whether or not he should go knock and ask about a bed.

At this same moment, inside the inn, a mother and her daughter were together alone in their brightly lit kitchen. The mother was a widow and was occupied with stuffing a fowl. The daughter was a girl in her teens with a name like Gretchen, and she was occupied with her sewing. These two women had no idea that a stranger was about to knock at their door. Although they ran an inn, very few visitors ever came, and almost none of these visitors were strangers who were traveling. Most visitors to the inn were local men who, for some reason or another, might want a place to stop and sleep a few hours off after spending an evening drinking in the tavern.

When a guest like this would arrive, he would be most amiable and greet the widow by her first name (as everyone in this village knew one another's first names), pay her the reasonable rates for the room and climb up to the bed upstairs to sleep. In the morning, the widow, or else her daughter Gretchen, would bring the lodger some biscuits which he'd probably refuse on account of a headache and a sour belly; then he'd jump with a startle realizing how late it was, run about the room a moment or two trying to pull his memory together. Perhaps he'd look for his hat. And finally he'd leave with a hurried goodbye and walk the two or three blocks home to his wife.

But on this late evening when Alexis came to the village, it was a holiday and the tavern was closed and the innkeeper and her daughter were expecting no knocks at the door – and especially no knocks from strangers. So when Alexis finally climbed the steps and gave a wrap at the door, they were most certainly surprised.

But who it could be?

The widow answered the door and Alexis introduced himself:

"I am Alexis, a traveler. I would like a room." Did they have one?

They certainly did.

And that was all it would cost? Perhaps he would stay two nights – see a bit of the town.

Alexis paid the widow a couple silver coins from his pocket. He entered the inn passing by the kitchen where the innkeeper's daughter was doing her needlework. She looked up as he passed and he saluted her politely, whereupon, she blushed the color of a baby mouse. He then went up the stairs to arrange the things in his bundle neatly beside the bed. He looked about the room. It was perfectly clean – not so much as a fly on the window – and smelled like vanilla soap. Moments later he returned downstairs with a washed face and inquired about something to eat. Of course he didn't even need to inquire, the widow was already preparing something for him to eat. The pleasure was all hers. She liked his bright blue eyes and found him dashing with his young smooth face; and besides, she loved to cook for her guests.

"And you haven't eaten today?"

No, he hadn't.

Well, she would have something on the table right away. "Gretchen, why don't you give me a hand ... no, just shoo! You're in the way!" Whereupon the child shrieked, "Mom!" and remained. Though she wasn't so much a child, she probably even had sixteen years already. Alexis looked at her curiously. She resembled her mother with her small upturned nose; though she was quite young, rather gangly too, perhaps even ugly, and had only small sprouts for breasts.

Alexis sat at the table and chewed on a doughy roll and looked at the two eager women while they clambered over dishes in the kitchen.

"I want to cook him my curdle-cake dish, Mom. Let me make it." Gretchen elbowed her way in, trying to take over. She put her little hips firmly before the stove.

"But I'm the one who taught you curdle-cakes!" her mother put in most offended, with a snap in her voice, shocked that her daughter should take the credit for such a delightful dish, "I'm the one who taught you curdle-cakes, and it's always too sweet when you make it...!"

"Mom!" Gretchen shrieked again, and became so flushed and embarrassed that she ran out of the room, and off to her bedroom in the back of the house. A few minutes later she slinked back into the kitchen and tried to say something quietly into Alexis' ear, but her voice only quivered and she again hid her face and ran out of the room. Foolish for a girl so young to try to compete with a mature woman like her mother!

"And would Alexis like anything else?"

No, he was full, thank you.

"Well, your quite welcome, we like to have a man around to feed." The widow smiled and sat with a cup of chocolate by the weary traveler. She complemented his shining skin.

He thanked her.

"And where are you from?" she asked.

"Far," Alexis answered proudly, putting his thumb to his chest, "I'm a traveling man and I've come a long way."

"But you have a local accent," she laughed, "You're from around here, I can tell."

"From around here!" ...Now it was Alexis' turn to feel ashamed. He was glad little Gretchen hadn't been in the room when the widow had said this. Alexis took this opportunity of uneasiness, having nothing to reply, to inquire about the best road to take to get to the Great City, as he really didn't know himself. The widow had never heard of anyone traveling to the Great City, nor even nearly half as far, but she knew of small city not so far to the west where he could get a train going south. That long country road, she told him, would be of no use to him. He could follow that for months and he'd only end up trapped in that endless range of purple mountains he'd seen on his way to their village. No, the best way to go was to take the little dirt road that wound west out of the village. He needed to take that until he arrived in the city she'd spoken of, then go to the station and certainly there he could find a train to take him anywhere he wanted. But he wouldn't be leaving first thing tomorrow, would he? No, he'd be staying at least another night, to rest and eat after that long day of traveling from his home in the woods.

That night Alexis sat on the bed upstairs and arranged his clothes and wiped clean his brown leather summer shoes, and looked out of the window at the first-quarter moon floating over the black shapes of the triangular rooftops of the village houses. The widow could be heard singing downstairs as she washed up the dishes.

"But you have a local accent!" he mocked at her words, *"You're from around here! ...* To hell with them both!

"...In the next town, Alexis," he reminded himself, "nothing of your boyhood will you bring with you. Only that which belongs to the realm of man. You are not to make any more mistakes, remember!"

Alexis lay on the firm bed in the village inn tracing with his finger the smiling green turtles carved into the headboard. He thought for a few moments about Gretchen, the innkeeper's daughter. No, she really wasn't pretty, but Alexis hadn't seen too many girls in his life other than his sister. Maybe she was to be the one after all... "Though Gretchen isn't even like a real girl. She is more like a clump of sand," he decided at last. "No, Alexis, there are other girls, better girls, crowding over yonder in the streets of the Great City!" And so his thoughts drifted from Gretchen to the Great City and sooner than later he drifted to sleep.

Alexis spent the next day at the inn going over his plans. The little innkeeper's daughter spent the next day following him around ready to offer him anything he wanted. Her eyes widened like moons when he came near. Each time he entered the kitchen, she would run to fix him a plate of something, always managing to make a clumsy mistake and spill something, whereupon she would flush red and tremble nervously until her jealous mother would come in, shoo her away and take charge.

The mother stuffed him with puddings and pies, and Alexis acted princely. Before dinner on the last night, Gretchen disappeared in her room for a while and when finally the food was served, she came to the table dressed in the most elaborate and overdone of Sunday dresses imaginable – complete with flounces, ribbons, lace, and a wide, tight-fitting crêpe choker which she wore around her thin little neck. Her face was powdered, her lips were glossed and she smelled heavy of floral soaps. Her mother watched on with a stilted look – pursed lips, her head tilted like a chicken – as her daughter made as if to glide into the kitchen with her head held high to seat herself royally at the table beside the young traveler who was already seated himself with a healthy appetite and a steaming plate of food, and who watched on at the girl entering the kitchen with eyes that didn't betray his astonishment; until finally her mother ended the scene when she set down the pan and spatula and blurted out, "Really, Gretchen! Orange bows with pink lace…you cannot wear orange and pink together!"

This-upon, little Gretchen turned so bright red – a color that clashed even more with the orange and pink of her dress – that there was nothing left for her to do but shriek, "Mom!" whereupon she gathered her ruffles in her trembling hands and ran out of the kitchen horribly ashamed and mortified. Then, her mother turned to Alexis and whispered, "She hasn't yet learned the secrets of being a woman!"

Gretchen stayed in her room and wept throughout the dinner and afterwards. Following the meal, Alexis went up to his own room to pack his bundle of socks and shirts. And only late in the evening did he return downstairs to tell the widow and her daughter that he would be leaving early the next morning.

When he entered the kitchen, the widow was making relish and her daughter was planting tulips for the windowsills. Gretchen was dressed normally now, and appeared to have recovered from the incident at dinner. She at first acted very nonchalant around Alexis, though she became visibly affected when he told the two women he would be traveling on the next day.

"But you're leaving in the morning?!"

Yes, he would be off. First thing in the morning.

Little Gretchen turned pale white. Her mother stood and blinked her eyes, looking surprised. It was then the widow made the mistake of suggesting Alexis would do well to stay and make this little village his home. "Why not stay here?"

To this, Alexis grew hot-faced and cheeky and said some rather insolent word: "Stay *here*?" She couldn't be serious! "...But yours is not even a proper town!" he told her, "It's just barely a village...a bandy little speck on the side of the road...a mere stop on the way...Pff! No, I won't stay here! I'm off for the Great City! A place where greatness awaits me!"

Oh, well. Youth forgives many things.

When Alexis finished with these words, the mother looked shocked and hurt and continued to blink her eyes; while mortified little Gretchen dropped a tulip pot on the kitchen floor, causing it to shatter. She then covered her mouth with her little hand and ran out of the room.

That night was calm as usual in the little village. In the morning, however, the spring winds came and sent all the weathervanes on the little roofs of the houses spinning; and this was the sound that stirred Alexis awake.

He sat up and rubbed the sleep from his eyes. He prepared his sack to leave – he'd decided that we wouldn't waste time eating at the inn, but instead would hurry along as early as possible – and as he was lacing his shoes, there came a knock at the door to his room. Actually, it wasn't so much a knock as a scratch, like the sound made by a hamster burrowing in sawdust. It was Gretchen, the one scratching at Alexis' door. Could she come in? Yes, she could. The door opened part way and she peeked her timid head through. "Alexis?" she tried unsuccessfully to look in his eyes. Finally she managed and asked, "So, you're leaving today?"

"Yes, today. Actually right this minute."

"Oh..." she began, standing at the door with her hands behind her back.

Oh, nothing. Alexis already had his shoes laced and his sack slung over his shoulder and was ready to get on the road.

It was then little Gretchen's cheeks flamed red and she ran into his room, went straight up to him and pulled her hands out from behind her back.

She had been holding something. "I made you these!" she said, plopping this something into Alexis' arms. He looked down. It was a pair of corduroy trousers. "I sewed them for you," her fragile voice flittered out, "...so you stay warm while you're traveling." After looking into his eyes for a mere moment, her nervousness seized her; and since Alexis made no reply, she gave up and ran out of the room.

Now alone in the room, he stood and looked at the trousers. "Hmph!" he shrugged. He took off his sack and stuffed them inside with his shirts. He then went downstairs and said goodbye to the girl's mother.

The widow was baking in the kitchen when Alexis entered. "You're leaving?" she turned to him, "Just like that?"

Yes, just like that.

It was sad, nevertheless, for the widow and her daughter. They had so much enjoyed Alexis' presence in their inn; and after all, they had been so kind to him, hadn't they? Why should it not be sad? Upon leaving, Alexis thanked Gretchen for the trousers – a gesture which thoroughly confused the mother and made the girl blush and fluster with some words about something or other so as to change the subject – then he turned to her mother, bowed a final time and promised to return to their village someday to stay again at their inn. This vow brightened the two women's faces beyond measure. The widow rubbed his shoulder and pointed again towards the road which would lead to the city where the train station was. Alexis smiled, waved, and walked down the steps and off through the streets of the village, alone and free once again.

His shoes clacked on the stones. The weathervanes spun on the triangular roofs of the houses. "Hell!" Alexis said aloud, "why did I say I would come back to this village someday and visit them? Why do I keep saying these boyish things? Be a man, Alexis! Tell them the truth! I will never return to this village. I am going on to the Great City. To live for good. This part of the world is finished for me. I'll never return. Do you hear? Now, onward!"

Alexis lectured himself with notions of the glory that awaited him; and with a joyful heart he walked the length of the village – some four or five blocks – and soon, the stone street turned into a tiny dirt road that headed west through morning-lit pastures. 'A new road,' he thought, 'this one even stranger.' He stopped there and took the corduroy trousers that Gretchen had made for him out of his sack. He looked at them for a moment. Then he scoffed and tossed them into the sticker bushes on the side of the road. "Pff!"

he said, "Country boy trousers. Not fitting for a man of the city!" and without giving them another thought he continued on.

Alexis walked down the road for the entire day without stopping. The weather stayed true to the capricious nature of spring. In the morning the sun shone and the wind blew. In the afternoon, rain fell and the dirt road became sodden with mud. In the evening there was some lightning. And in the night, it cleared up again and the sky was filled with bright constellations of stars.

"But this is no tiny road," Alexis said to himself after night had fallen. "I've been walking forever! That innkeeper sure made it seem like I'd come to a train station by noontime. Oh, no matter. At least she put some biscuits in my sack. I'll have something to eat when I wake up tomorrow."

Above the sky was dark and milky. The branches of an maple tree swayed over Alexis' head as he slept curled up with his sack on the grass at the top of the hill, off to the side of the long dirt road.

When he awoke the next morning at dawn, his teeth were chattering with cold, and he immediately stood and dug into his sack to find a dry shirt to change into. Luckily his father had handed him down quite a few – all of good sturdy cotton, all with his father's strong musky scent. He put on a clean shirt and continued down the road, hoping a farmer or someone would pass and give him a ride to this so-called city. But the day passed by and he saw no farmers nor anyone else, and there seemed to be nothing resembling a city or town on the horizon. In the evening, the rains started up again.

"Oh hell!" he cried, "The things a man has to put up with!" Soon his clothes were completely drenched, but his sack was a good one and its contents stayed dry.

As he walked down the silent road, the sky darkened, the rain kept on, and at one point it fell so hard he had to continue wiping the water from his face just to see the road in front of him.

Something then startled him. "That is odd!" He stopped and conversed with himself in a rather loud voice while touching his face, "That is very odd. I seem to have hair growing!"

It was true. The youthful Alexis, who'd never once needed to put a blade to the skin of his chin, suddenly had a light down of a beard growing. A light one, yes, but a beard, nonetheless.

"A beard?"

"Ha! Fancy that!"

This decoration of newly acquired manhood suited him just fine and he walked even quicker down the muddy winding road, excited to arrive in a place where there were people, so as to parade his plumes.

Alexis spent yet another night sleeping beneath a tree off to the side of the road. By morning, he had only one dry shirt left, he put it on and hoped the day's rain would be gentle. Luckily though, rain didn't fall on this day. The sky was clear, the sun shone and the air was unusually warm. He continued down the road, mostly clean and completely dry.

By afternoon, though, he was discouraged about the route the innkeeper had recommended. Surely she had never walked it! But just before sunset, all discouragement vanished. Alexis looked on ahead and saw a promising sight. What was green here, was grey up ahead. Here there were apples. There, there was asphalt. He walked on and the road changed from dirt to gravel to concrete. And there, in the distance at the end of the road, he saw what he'd never seen before: an cluster of smokestacks, chimney tops, and soot covered factories. He had arrived at last in the small city.

It was a grimy industrial town.

Chapter V

The appearance of a bearded traveler...

Alexis walked through the charred alleys and soot-covered streets of the small industrial town. By the time he had arrived, darkness was falling and he thought to hurry to find the train station.

"Station!" He called out when a stranger was passing by. The stranger hid his face and pointed to a structure not far off... "That's the station there."

Alexis hurried up to it, entered and found the ticket counter and asked for a ticket on the next train leaving that evening for the Great City.

"No trains tonight."

"No trains leave tonight?"

The ticket vendor confirmed it.

What could Alexis possibly do? No trains. No suggestions. Well, no matter. He could find cheap inn to stay at, at least. This town did have inns, didn't it? Surely it did. The vendor told him where he could find one and Alexis thanked him. "By the way," he asked, "what town are we in?"

"Municipality of Krüfsterburg."

"I'm in Krüfsterburg?"

Alexis was in Krüfsterburg.

He thanked the vendor again and told him he'd be seeing him the next day when he returned to buy his ticket. This bit of news didn't seem to impress upon the vendor too much. Alexis left the station, and walked through the dismal factory streets chewing the word Krüfsterburg over and over.

"Krüfsterburg... Krüfsterburg... Oufsterbergh... Burghestook!"

He knew nothing about this town, except that it was where his grandparents had come from. The people in the streets walked like shades with their heads turned away – as in the story he was told as a child about Candlemas and the hedgehog slaughterers. They weren't dressed like the woodsmen and hunters he was familiar with from the Great Northern Woods. These characters wore plain, drab clothes – green laboring suits, and such. Alexis thought it best to untie the bright yellow silk handkerchief from the strap on his sack and wear it properly in the breast pocket of his cotton shirt. Not that he needed to do this especially. Where he was wasn't the fashionable Great City. It was merely a smokestack town. But even so, he had decided to start acting like a man, hadn't he? Only a boy would tie a handkerchief to the strap of his sack.

Finally he arrived at the inn on Tritzel Street, where the vendor at the train station had directed him. It was a tall, two-storey house with no garden, no weathervane, and no neat little boxes of tulips on the windowsills. A painted wooden sign outside read AFFORDABLE INN. Alexis was glad it was affordable. He'd be needing to save as much money as possible for when he arrived in the Great City. He walked up the steps and knocked on the door.

"I'm Alexis, a traveler. Do you have a room?"

They had a room, indeed, and he was ushered inside by the innkeeper: a short, lean and snappy man named Viktor, who had blond thinning hair, and green eyes like a lizard.

The house was not nicely furnished and it smelled heavily of meat; but the room Alexis was given down the hall was mostly clean, and the bed had a thick down quilt.

"This is the room," said Viktor, "I'm turning in, but if you need anything...what was your name again? Alexis? Well, I'll be down the hall, Alexis, if you need anything. The room by the kitchen. Did you eat already? No? Well, there's some supper left over. I'll heat it up real quick. Come into the kitchen when you're ready ... Oh, and my daughters sleep upstairs. Don't pay any attention to them."

Daughters?

Yes, he had three daughters: Delilah, Delia, and Delina. That was their order from oldest to youngest.

Alexis paid Viktor for the room. It was a lot less affordable than the first inn he'd stayed at with the widow and her daughter, but that just meant that he'd have to find work immediately once he got to the Great City. Viktor went to the kitchen and Alexis stayed in his room and unpacked the bundle of dirty wet clothes. He'd have to find a way to wash them. He grabbed the bundle and went into the kitchen to ask Viktor about washing clothes.

"The neighbor does it," Viktor told him, "Just throw your bundle in the hall. They'll be cleaned in the morning," he added in a tired monotone, "It costs an extra three crowns. You can pay me tomorrow. I'll have some food ready in a minute. Then I'm off to sleep, I've been working on the damned roof all day."

Alexis thanked Viktor and left the kitchen to go wait in his room for the food to be ready. He was famished.

It was then, while passing the staircase in the dimly lit entryway, he spied what looked like to be a girl spying back down at him from the banister. He stopped and squinted to see her. Was it one of Viktor's daughters? She was striking, with raven-black hair and pale skin. Yet, a closer look revealed her to be not just one girl, but actually three girls; they were stacked up on top of each other like a three-piece Russian matrioshka doll. These three girls, all identical though their sizes varied, popped in and out of each other, all the while gazing at the stranger with their white wooden faces from the upstairs banister.

He snapped his gaze away from them and went off to his room to stir around a bit before returning to the kitchen to check on the food. He was given a kind of lukewarm potato dish served in a tin pan. He sat and ate it alone in the dark kitchen. Viktor slept with his door ajar, and the whole downstairs was dim and quiet. The three daughters had vanished.

The next morning, Alexis was woken up early by a knock at his door. The door opened and Viktor came in: "Here are your clothes. All clean!" He plopped them down on the wicker chair by the door.

"Already?" Alexis sat up and rubbed his eyes.

"Hep! She's fast, that neighbor of mine," Viktor clasped his hands. He was in quite the chipper mood. That sleep obviously did him good, "Just pay me three crowns when you can. When do you leave? Today?"

"Yes, today." Alexis was planning to leave that day.

"Well, hey," Viktor stalled, sifting through his thinning hair, apparently thinking something over. Alexis, meanwhile, inspected his shirts. They were clean and stiff and smelled like melons.

"You don't have much money, do you?" Viktor inquired.

Did Alexis have much money? What kind of question was that for Viktor to ask.

"I have enough," Alexis replied.

"Well, I just mean that… well, if you could use some more money, I'm going to be up working on the roof for the next couple days and I could sure use a hand, and I'll pay you for your work."

Alexis thought it over. 'Work on a roof in Krüfsterburg? What about the Great City?' Alexis was eager to get a move on to begin his new life. He didn't want to delay his glorious arrival. No, certainly he would not stay and help. Still, he'd be needing as much money as possible when he did finally get to the Great City. He wasn't sure if he had enough to see him through till he landed a job. Maybe he should. Sure, after all, he could do a little work, earn some extra money, then be on his way.

"So you'll do it?"

"No," Alexis replied.

"No?"

"Yes," he changed his mind.

"You're sure?"

"Sure I'm sure."

"Great! Meet me on the roof when you're ready."

Alexis got dressed and went out into the yard and climbed up the ladder to the roof. Viktor was already up there hammering away. He passed Alexis a hammer and nails and instructed him on shingle laying. Alexis got started driving nails. From this roof where the two worked, one could look out and see the factory skyline of Krüfsterburg.

"So, where are you from?" Viktor asked.

"From the Great Northern Woods."

"Oh yeah? And you're leaving! Sick of the woods? Where are you going?"

"To the Great City."

Viktor frowned. He looked Alexis up and down, but made no reply. Then he asked, "So who are you leaving behind in the Northern Woods?"

"My sister and father."

"Oh yeah? What are they like?"

Alexis almost answered but then he remembered the words 'speak nothing of us to those you meet' and said nothing.

The two hammered away until the sack of nails was empty. "Hey," Viktor asked, "run inside the house and get some penny nails, would you?"

Alexis climbed down off the roof and went into the inn. From the entryway where he stood, he saw Viktor's three daughters huddled in the dark hallway. They were all clumped together, the three of them, all with their white skin and black hair and devilish eyes, each one taller than the last – just like a matrioshka doll. They eyed Alexis strangely when he entered. He stood facing them. They neither flinched nor moved aside, they just observed him with their piercing eyes that followed his every movement.

Finally, he asked, "Do you know where your father keeps the penny nails?"

No answer. Well, did they know?

The three girls just looked at each other and giggled. A laugh, now quiet and girlish, now loud and wicked, escaped the lips of Delina, the youngest of sisters. She eyed Alexis with her black eyes and slowly glided into the kitchen where she pointed to a drawer where the nails were kept. Then she looked at him, and then at her sisters who remained in the hall, and laughed again.

Alexis helped himself to the nails, while the three girls stood in the hallway gossiping. Alexis passed them in the hall again on his way out to the yard. As he did so, he smiled; whereupon they stopped gossiping and looked at him with their six piercing eyes.

Silence.

"Nya-ha-ha!" they giggled.

Alexis turned and walked out. 'Ah, just like poor little Gretchen,' he thought, 'What can I do? These three girls are hopelessly in love with me!'

After he'd left the house, the girls continued on with their gossip:

"Did you see that hair on his face?" Delilah began.

"Repulsive!" said Delia

"Vile!" said Delina.

"And those eyes!" Whereupon their heads whipped around simultaneously as if caught off guard by something.

Outside, Alexis climbed the ladder to the roof and handed Viktor the nails.

"Yep, those are the right ones. You found them, uh?"

"Your daughters helped."

The two grabbed nails from the sack and began pounding.

"They are striking those three, your daughters…such black eyes, such black hair, and such pale skin!"

Viktor gave Alexis a bewildered look and said nothing. Alexis, worried that his words had been misunderstood, added, "…and pretty!"

"Hep!" said Viktor as he drove a nail into a shingle, "Of course they're pale. They never go outside. Me, I'm a blond man. My skin is tanned. But the sun hits me while I'm working. It's normal enough. Anyway, you wonder why I'm so blond and they're so dark-haired, well, you should've seen their mother. Like a crow!

"…Pretty, you say? Hep! You take a fancy to my daughters. Natural. All the young men who stay here do – old ones too. They're a competitive lot, those three girls. Take Delilah for instance, the oldest one. She thinks Delia is the most beautiful among them. Hates her for this. But Delia isn't the most beautiful, no. Not by a long shot! Delina's the most beautiful. That's for sure. But a girl can never judge the looks of another girl, Alexis. Just like a guy can't tell another guy from a rock on a fence – and that's the way it should be! Take you for instance… you could be a handsome lad, but I wouldn't know. For all I can tell, you could be snow! But still you could be a handsome lad. Though you need a shave and a haircut, you realize this?" Viktor slapped Alexis' shoulder, and continued talking to him, obviously taking great pleasure in the conversation, "Yeah, they're a couple of three girls! But when they're competitive like that, it just means they're up to tricks. I'd stay clear, Alexis, you hear? What would you want with women anyway? They a bunch of curvy little mousetraps, that's all. Devil take 'em!...

"Just like my three daughters. Sure they look sweet. One can even think they're precious and want to pet them. But just try! Give them a finger and they'll bite it off, chew it up and spit the nail in your face. Hep! That's for sure. Especially Delina, the youngest – she's a real fiery one. Devil take 'em, those women!"

The sounds of hammers pounded on through the morning. Alexis continued listening to Viktor's stories...

"I tell you, Alexis. I wish I'd had a son. He could help out with the repairs around the house and also go out and bring some money in from the outside. But I was unlucky. Just three daughters. Girls are an expense! Their entire purpose is to hatch scandals. The ones who do it openly are the more harmless ones. But they all do it. It's all they care about. Whether they're busy combing their hair to look pretty, or combing the locks of their toy horses, it's all the same... just plotting and hatching scandals!...

"But really boy, you don't need 'em. Say you get a woman and maybe she'll ask you to walk her to the park so you can eat little sandwiches. And maybe she'll let you stroke her little bare tummy while she's tanning in the sun. And sure, that tummy feels nice. But sooner or later it wants to eat again, and then she'll want to walk around and look at all the statues in the park. And you'll do this. And when she laughs at the ducks in the fountain, she'll expect you to laugh too. And she'll do this just to waste your time. And soon, stroking that warm bare tummy will feel less and less nice! Hey, you missed a shingle, lad! ...Do you really know how to lay a roof?!"

The two continued on hammering and nailing while the sun passed overhead, burning off the rest of the clouds. Viktor's head, which was barely protected by his thinning blond hair, began to sizzle in the noonday sun so that patches of skin on his crown turned red with sunburn; the sun being hot – unusually so, it being so early in spring.

Distracted, Alexis looked up from the roof of the inn and over the horizon – over the industrial skyline of the small city which appeared to chug up plumes of smoke like one giant machine.

"Viktor?"

"Yes?"

"Why do you live in this town?"

"Why? Hep…There's everything one needs here. Look down at those streets down there. Over there at Franzelsplat's market, he's selling sausages. And you can buy little fried pies from Mrs. Brundel's cart. And all those smokestacks you see over there are factories where they make useful things. Say you want to buy more penny nails…."

Alexis' mind began to wander.

"But wouldn't you ever want to live somewhere else, Viktor? Surely there is even more in a capital city. Wouldn't you want to, say for example, live in…" and here he almost mentioned the Great City, but stopped himself, "…to live in Marseille for example?" Alexis knew nothing about Marseille, except that his mother had owned an oil-painted canvas depicting this city. It had belonged to her grandfather. Now it hung in Lise's room. Alexis looked at it quite often when he was little. The painted skyline of Marseille looked quite impressive.

"Marseille!" Viktor started up, surprised at Alexis' words. "Marseille!" He wiped the sweat from his sunburnt head and stuck the hammer in his tool belt. "Who would ever want to live in Marseille?! I've been there, Alexis. Hep! I have been there, you believe me. It's in France! And I'll tell you something about the French. The French are bunch of picnic-eaters. All they're're picnic-eaters! Why, we here are working men. We get things done. We don't picnic. Now help me lay these shingles!"

Viktor knelt back down and resumed hammering. Alexis remained standing, thinking; while he looked out at the chugging factories on the grey sooty skyline of Krüfsterburg, he told himself… 'But I am not a roof-thatcher! I am not a shingle-shifter! What am I doing? I must go to the Great City where I will have influence!' … 'You see, Alexis,' continued Alexis, 'This is what sets you apart from the others. Whereas you seek greatness, they seek penny nails. And for this, you will find greatness and you will have influence!'

While Viktor drove nails into the roof, Alexis stood swinging idly his hammer at his side, looking out at the skyline, dreaming away… 'In the Great City, I bet I'll meet a famous actress and we'll fall in love. She'll be thin and glamorous and wear dark glasses and tight dresses, and we'll have to spend most of our time indoors, because when we're out in the street walking together people will talk about us and point. But that's fine. We'll stay home together drinking sweet wines and making love…" And he imagined himself living up high in a palace room with this beautiful actress, 'And our bedroom,' he decided, 'will have a view of the courtyard belonging to the Prime Minister.

And from there I will look down and laugh at all the washerwomen carrying linen to and fro across the courtyard; going into the palace laundry room, coming out...I will taunt the old grey-templed men wheeling service dollies across the yard, carrying trays of food and drink, taking them to serve the Minister's ministers.'

Alexis had a pretty picture in his head of these servants in their greasy aprons; he in his silk finery, laughing at the world from the window of his stone palace room, the sun falling on his face and a famous beauty waiting for him in the bedroom beneath fine satin sheets.

'And I will sit up there like a bird. Like a proud bird!...But first, I must get off of this roof!'

"Well, Alexis," Viktor suddenly said, interrupting his reverie, "looks like we're done. The rest I'll finish up tomorrow. Let's get off this roof and go inside a minute."

When he and Alexis entered the inn, Viktor's daughters were bunched together in the hallway. Viktor tossed his work-belt at them, "Scat, you three!" Whereupon they popped off, laughing wickedly, and disappeared between the walls.

Viktor and Alexis stood alone in the dimly-lit kitchen. Alexis wiped the sweat from his forehead. "Was it good work we did today?" he asked.

"Yes, good." Viktor's mind was set on something else. "Here's a little money for you." He dropped some coins into Alexis' hand. "You see, Alexis, a working man gets paid for his labor. No one makes anything by picnicking. Gotta work, you see?" ... "I'm giving you a little extra so you can go into town tomorrow and get a haircut and a shave." He handed Alexis a few more crowns and the latter thanked him, told him goodnight, and went off to his room to rest. The bed felt nice and the long hard day of work tugged on Alexis' eyelids and dragged him off away into a thick, heavy sleep.

The next morning brought dreary weather. Rain streaked down the windowpanes in the room at Viktor's inn where Alexis awoke and prepared to set off for town to see the barber. He decided he'd stay one more night at Viktor's inn and leave the following morning. Although he was sure he could benefit from having a friend like Viktor, Krüfsterburg was not his final destination and it was time to go. If there was one thing of which Alexis was certain, it was that great men knew when to terminate things, did so swiftly, and then moved on.

Walking on through the wet streets of Krüfsterburg, Alexis looked at the backdrop of steel grey clouds, against which white billows of industrial smoke puffed up from factory pipes. 'Viktor's a real kind of man,' he thought, observing the town, 'but too bad he's stuck in this mediocre place!'

Rubbing his little beard, Alexis walked along past the rows of warehouses. He passed Mrs. Brundel's cart where little pies were frying. He walked past Franzelsplat's market where leathery sausages were hanging in the windows. And soon he found a barber and had his hair cut, though he kept the beard.

By late-afternoon the sun had burnt through the thick clouds and by the time Alexis returned to the inn, it was evening and the sun was setting into the mist on the skyline. He saw that Viktor was up working on the roof, and he climbed the ladder to offer his help.

"Hi, Viktor!" he called, scratching the back of his neck which itched from the little cut hairs stuck in his collar. His pocket was weighed down heavily with money, and his hands were blistered from working the previous day. Viktor looked at him as he reached the top of the ladder. "Hiya, Alexis! I like your haircut! It looks more dignified shorter." But then Viktor frowned. He was upset that Alexis had kept the beard. "I don't know about that," he pointed, "Still looks like an animal is running across your face!"

The moon was caught between the chimney tops of Krüfsterburg. Another night had fallen and Alexis was in his room at the inn packing for his departure the following morning. A knock came at the door and Viktor entered. He was holding something in his hands.

"Well, tomorrow you're leaving, eh?"

Yes, Alexis would be leaving in the morning.

"So y'are! Well, I have a little gift for you. Since you're going to the big city, you might want to look a little more city-like. That haircut's a start. Still you should get a shave. You got some scruff there. They only wear scruff like that in the woods. Anyway, here you go…" And something wrapped in brown paper passed from Viktor's hands to Alexis', whereupon Viktor's face took on a bashful expression. He looked at the ground and scratched the flakes of sunburnt skin on the top of his head while Alexis threw him a questioning glance and sat on the bed to unwrap his gift. Viktor sat on the wicker chair by the door, while Alexis tore open the brown paper package…

Great Viktor! A new suit! Jacket and trousers of light-colored wool and a fine wristwatch, to boot! What had he done?! There could not have been a better present. Alexis thanked him several times.

"Oh, you're welcome, Alexis. It's for all your work on the roof yesterday...and besides...and well so you know..." and so on and so forth, Viktor stammered nervously. It was apparent that he who had but a flock of girls in his pasture was less than comfortable relating with camaraderie to other males.

"I have no use for a suit, so it was just in the way. It's well cut though, the tailor knew what he was doing. He was no layabout. And that watch is a good one."

Alexis fastened the watch on his wrist. It was a good one: heavy brass, an abalone dial, and a nice loud tick. Viktor watched Alexis put it on the way a father watches his child going off for the first day of school – a sorrowful farewell. That watch had obviously meant a lot to Viktor, but this moment with Alexis also seemed to mean a lot to him. He apparently decided he'd sacrifice it for the chance to have a son – even if just for a moment.

"But it's maybe it's too nice," Alexis told him.

"No, no, take it! You've earned it. Hard work pays off, remember. Too bad you're not staying. I could teach you how to lay a roof properly. It's as if you've never picked up a hammer in your life!"

With that, Viktor stood up quickly, said a hurried and clumsy goodnight, and left the room. Alexis then set his things down on the chair and went over to the window to let air into the room that was stuffy and overheated. After all was put in order, he went over to the mirror and spent many moments admiring his haircut and the progress of his beard. Following this exercise, he flopped down on the bed, leaned over and blew out the lamp. He stared up at the ceiling in the darkness and mused on his life in the way wanderers do from time to time when lying in unfamiliar beds. He thought about travel and he thought about the Great City. He fantasized about the world that awaited him. With the mild breeze that drifted through the window, came the smells of burning coal from the industrial town outside; and he enjoyed these smells and these thoughts and this breeze until he finally slipped and fell asleep.

The chimneys of Krüfsterburg coughed up the moon and it soared high in the night sky. Alexis stirred in his blankets, tangled in the wind; and when that wind caught the blankets it lifted him up like a kite. Uppity, oh! High in the air he soared, back and forth to the *tick-tock, tick-tock* of pendulum as he swung on a jeweled watchband. What a pleasurable dream! He was alone at first, but soon a girl came to join him. She came to swing on his band. Her blue cotton dress flittered in the wind, the side of her thigh touching his, as she laughed; and gusts of wind breezed through her fair locks of hair.

No longer on high, Alexis found himself sitting below in a warm color-saturated field of clover. Sunshine dripped off the blades of grass. And there, seated directly across from Alexis, was another girl. Was it the same girl? No, it was another. This one wore a golden dress, and hers was of yellow hair. She sat and hummed a sweet little song while spreading jam on glazed bread. When Alexis asked for a piece of the glazed bread, she looked up and smiled at him. She pointed over to the edge of the field and asked him, "Why are the trees all perforated? Do you know? It's as if one could just tear them right out! ... Ha-ha-ha!" She pointed and laughed.

Alexis didn't know why the trees were like that. He drew close to listen to her while she spoke. She then admitted to him that she wanted to go climb those trees – to hang on their limbs. Yet, Alexis wanted her to stay with him on the grass, to stay with him in the clover and spread her golden jam, but she didn't want that. She wanted the trees.

Oh, pretty girl and the warmth of the sun! Alexis dreamed and dreamed away while his legs spun and spooled the sheets in the bed at Viktor's inn. And it was while he dreamt that a little solitary brown mosquito flew in the window and settled on his foot. He jerked in his sleep and the mosquito took flight again and landed on his lip. With her slender beak, she punctured the tender skin on his lip and began to feed from him, taking blood from the same place where he had cut himself recently while performing the vodka ceremony with his father, drinking from the glass with the broken rim.

The mosquito nourished herself on his blood with her sharp proboscis probing his veins, and with this, his dreams rearranged and suddenly changed. He no longer dreamt of idyllic things, like prances with girls in clover groves. Every brightness dimmed, all colors faded, day turned to night, his dreams darkened...

Upon a moonless night, he was alone in the forest, wandering the darkened trails. Upward, downward, he roamed the hillsides – a powerful hunter, carrying an ax that gleamed of blood.

Onward! The flight of a cloud of bats.

Onward! The march of a band of coyotes.

And then with a crack, he lost his axe and was overcome by fear. Something came approaching. Was it shade or beast? He hid himself behind a growth of ferns near the trail and watched the path. He went unseen and carefully observed a lonesome hunter who came sauntering by. This hunter carried a rifle and a string of rabbits.

The night passed over, and the satisfied mosquito, withdrew her nourished beak from Alexis' lip and left his mouth, flying back out of the window and off in the night.

Alexis' body stirred in the bed at Viktor's inn. His finger tore at the lump on his mouth – while his mind brought forth the frightening vision of the vodka ceremony of past: seated with his father at the table of planks, he drank from the glass that cut his lip. His lip, it bled. The candle flame crackled. The forest night sky trembled. And his father's voice boomed: "Speak nothing of us to those you meet!"

Cold and clammy air seeped in through the open window early the next morning to wake Alexis before it was even properly light outside. He immediately sat up and sifted through the residues of his dreams, trying to salvage what he could and piece it all into some kind of meaning. But he could not remember more than a few fragments here and there. He felt then his lip had swollen up again from where it had been cut and he gnashed it with his teeth to ease the itching. He wasn't sue why his lip was again inflamed, the swelling had almost completely disappeared. His brain was still foggy with sleep. He scratched his itchy lip, then he scratched the hair on his chin. A pounding sound was coming from far up on the roof. "Pounding? Ah!" Then he remembered he'd be traveling on that day, going abroad. This was the day he was to take the train to the famous Great City. "A train," he told himself, "I can take a train now!" Krüfsterburg had a train station. No more walking all day down muddy country roads or sleeping at night in cold wet pastures. Now he could travel properly. He was a country bumpkin no longer. Now he was a man of the world. And so, with more than just a little excitement, he got out of bed and began to pack his things.

"Admirable!" he exclaimed, while inspecting himself in the mirror with his new suit of clothes. He slipped on the watch and combed back his hair. He posed for himself. "A real dandy!" If the world was ready for him, it didn't know it yet. So, with his father's shirts packed away in the sack slung over his shoulder, Alexis went out into the hall to go find Viktor to say goodbye. In the dark entryway he met his three daughters. Awake already? They were clumped together as usual, whispering to each other.

Alexis waved to them, "Farewell!"

They didn't respond.

Hadn't they heard he was leaving this very day for the Great City? Apparently they hadn't. He was sure those girls had never met anyone who'd ever traveled to the Great City before. – certainly no young man adventuring on his own, at least. He beamed his eyes confidently at them and with his thumb he flicked the hem of his yellow handkerchief that folded over his jacket pocket.

The girls simply ignored him.

Viktor then appeared from the kitchen and the three daughters slid off and disappeared somewhere between the walls, not to return again. "Ah, so you're off!" Viktor fumbled. He shook Alexis' hand and walked with him to the door. "That suit fits you well. You're looking grand! You sure you don't want to stay around here awhile. I could teach you a few things. It'd be nice to have another guy around to teach things to. No, you say? Oh well!" Viktor let his hand fall off Alexis' shoulder as the latter made his way out the front door and started off down the steps towards the street. Viktor called to him from the doorway, "So when do you come back this way?!"

"Come back this way?!" Is that what he asked? Alexis was astonished. "But Viktor," he called back to him, "I'm not coming back this way. I told you, I'm going to live in the Great City!"

"To live, are you? Hep! That place will eat you alive!" He rubbed his sunburnt forehead and smiled. Alexis took a few steps back towards the inn to better hear Viktor. "I thought you were just going for a visit – to stretch your legs a bit. You don't know anyone there, Alexis. And you don't have much money. I'll bet you be back up this way in a couple weeks. You mark my words!"

Ah! Was Viktor really saying this? These words burned in the furnace of youthful ambition smoldering in Alexis' breast. How dare he! "But, Viktor," he shouted back with insolence, "what are you saying? why would I come back? And especially *here*? to *this* town?"

These words left a scalded mark of injury on Viktor's forehead. "Well, I didn't mean necessarily you should come back to *this* town. I mean, I know you have no desire to stay in *this* town!" … "I'm sorry I suggested it!" Then, after a moment, "You know what I think? You'd be best off going back north to your father and sister. I'm sure they miss you."

"Go north?!" Alexis spat in frustration, "I'm not going north, Viktor. I'm going south! To the Great City. Ach! Goodbye Viktor! Adieu!" And all was final. With an annoyed wave, Alexis turned and started off down the street not to look back again.

Back on the stoop, Viktor stood and yelled after him, "Hey wait a minute!" Alexis, however, didn't turn around. "Okay then, Alexis," he shouted after him, putting his cupped hand to his mouth to strengthen his voice, "take your nice watch and your new clothes and go out into the world and learn what poverty is!"

Chapter VI

Onward Great City!

And so that morning, Alexis headed for the train station, walking in the misling rain through the grey and dismal streets of Krüfsterburg. Outside factories lining the streets, workers shuffled in methodically in double-file lines, tin lunchboxes in hand, for another day's work at the assembly line. Oh, pitiful creatures. Their clothes were drab and their faces were grey and each looked the same as the next.

"I just can't fathom this," Alexis stared in bewilderment at these lines of workers, "The world is theirs as much as it is mine. Yet they march into these sooty factories as if there is nowhere else to go." ... "Why, if they have but one jaunt on the surface of the earth, why do they spend their time slaving away in these mediocre mounds of bricks toting smokestacks? Why not live in the highest towers this world provides? Why not live in the greatest city this world owns. Don't they realize that the train that will take them there is only a few blocks away?

"Alexis," he reassured himself, "when you are in the Great City, you will meet no one like these workers. You will meet people who know the world is theirs; and who, for this, fight for their place atop the pillar, above all things, where the view looks out on everything that is beautiful and profound." ...

"Yes, beauty and profundity! I will meet extraordinary people, strange people…rich men driven by chauffeurs, eccentrics and geniuses, people of noble birth; I will meet sensual and experienced women…." And so in this fashion Alexis' thoughts ran about while his feet turned this- and that-a-way, to take him on past all the factories, shops and warehouses of that little industrial city.

"Fancy Viktor thinking I'd ever come back here! One day he'll understand, when news of my fame spreads far and wide. He'll read about me in the papers and think, 'Of course Alexis would never come back here! That clever young man knew what he was doing all along. The Great City gave him fame, while all Krüfsterburg could've offered him was penny nails!..'" … "penny nails!…

"Aye!" Alexis blurted suddenly as he tripped over a weed growing through a crack in the sidewalk. Then, after regaining himself, he looked around, "What is this here?" He looked up and saw a tailor shop. It was closed but Alexis stopped to have a look at the window display. In the vitrine, wooden mannequins were propped up wearing men's suits. He glanced them up and down, and spit mockingly… "You tree stumps look pretty sorry in your cheap suits!"

While Alexis was talking to these mannequins, two workers passed him on the sidewalk and began to stare. Alexis turned and stared back at these workmen but they quickly turned their heads away to hide them in the Krüfsterburgian fashion and walked on. Alexis returned his attention to the mannequins…

"If only you guys had eyes to see me!" he called out to their square wooden heads, "This is what a real suit looks like!" Then, seeing his own figure elegantly displayed in the reflection of the window vitrine, he was filled with pride, and walked away singing aloud:

"A father decides…" … "No!" … "A mother decides the day of your birth…The doctor, the day of your death…The tailor decides the joys in your life…and the beauty of your wife!

"Hey! What a great little rhyme I just made up!" And Alexis was quite happy with his little rhyme, and he repeated it over and over, singing it all the way until he reached the train station and went up to the ticket counter… "Ticket man! A ticket to the Great City on the next train, please. One-way." Did the ticket vendor not remember Alexis? Apparently, he did not. Must be the new suit.

The ticket vendor looked at his timetable: "Train to the Great City … Yes, one train leaving today. Leaves at ten o'clock. That'll be sixty crowns, please. Okay, how much do you have there? Yes, that will do. No, you take this back. Yes, that's it. Here's your ticket. Departs from platform one. Pleasant voyage!"

Alexis went and stood at platform one and waited for train to arrive. The drizzling rain slid down in streams, dripping from the glass roof onto the tracks. The rain enhanced the smells of the moist sod packed in between the railroad ties.

"To hell with them!" he suddenly said aloud, "That damned widow thinking I'd stay and live in her little pie-cup village. And then Viktor thinking I'd stay here in this grease-wrench town…I can't believe those two!" He scuffed his shoes on the platform a few times.

"Well, not to hell with Viktor. He was a nice man. And after all, Alexis, it was thanks to him that you have these handsome clothes and this expensive watch…and also this money in your pocket. This way you don't have to spend anymore of the money your father gave you – at least not right away. You can save it till you get to the Great City…

"Yes, Viktor more than paid for my train ticket. Now I won't be in such a hurry to find a job. Now I think I'll even buy myself a nice meal when I arrive. Yes, not to hell with Viktor."

It seemed everything was clear in his mind; and deciding that the train might be arriving soon he thought it was a good time to say goodbye to his country:

"Farewell, my Fatherland. You raised me well. I may never see you again." He bent down and touched the wet concrete platform with his fingertips. 'It may be a long time before I return, after all.' … "But, why would I return?" he demanded, unsatisfied with his previous thoughts. "What an absurd idea! You are a traveler, Alexis! Yes, I am a traveler…a voyager…a wayfarer…an adventurer…anything, but not a tourist. Only tourists go places and then return. Men of the world don't do that. That would be like growing up and then growing down again. Like learning and then unlearning. That's not progress. That's a mental swing-set! Life shouldn't go back and forth like that. Life shouldn't go in circles. Life should move forward! Onward!…

"Why would I return to where I started?" he asked himself as he stood on the platform turning circles on the ball of his foot. Of all the possible reasons… "Return so that I can rot away in my old familiar home, with nothing but my memories of those days when I once had energy for life? Then I can dream about what my life would have been like had I continued on, going forward, going farther, going deeper into the world... It's absurd!...

"I wonder how many men live not in the world, but instead only in their dreams of what the world could be like for them if they had the will and courage to meet the world and venture out into it. I'm sure most men are like that – dreaming about what it would be like to live the life of someone like...myself, for example. But of course all this is natural. There can't be too many great men. Most have to be average. I will be great, however. Why? Because I act. I move forward. Look, I left home, I'm on my way to the capital of greatness. I'm not sitting around dreaming about it. Great men don't dream, they act! One must be alert to the world. Sit there dreaming and the world just passes you by. And I'm sure it doesn't care if it passes you by. No, it doesn't give a damn. You're the one to lose. No one else is even interested in helping you. And anyway, I can't even fathom not having that ambition that overleaps itself to the other...huh?!" Alexis' reverie was then most suddenly interrupted by someone tapping urgently on his shoulder... "Young man!" this somebody shouted.

The somebody was a train attendant and he was tapping Alexis' shoulder to try to get his attention to help him "Young man!" he explained, "Your train is leaving without you. You'd better hurry!"

And sure enough, while Alexis had been busy daydreaming away, his train had arrived and all the passengers had boarded; and now the doors were closing and the train was beginning to chug off without him.

But that was the only train of the day! In a rush of panic, Alexis clutched his sack and ran down the platform... "There's nothing wrong with dreaming," he called to the rhythm of his shoes slapping on the wet concrete of the platform, "it just means that doing so is going to eventually cause you to have to rush and take a great leap if you ever want to go anywhere!" ... and it was with that great leap that Alexis passed from the platform across the gap and into the train car, through the doors which the attendants were busily closing; and the train then left the terminal and chugged off in the southward direction, away from the little industrial city of Krüfsterburg, off towards places new and unknown.

Aboard, Alexis found his assigned seat and sat by the window to look out at the changing scenery. 'A train,' he thought, 'what a strange thing to ride!' He sat on the hard bench and looked around the compartment at the other passengers. 'All these people are going to the Great City?' he wondered, 'Certainly they cannot be. Not *these* people!' His upper lip curled with disdain as he looked around the train car at the yokels sitting on the benches. A few appeared to be laborers – with their drab clothes of heavy material smeared with black grease; but most were simple country folk – many with bits of hay stuck on their clothes or in their hair. The train car smelled like tractor grease and animal beds. No, but Alexis was not worried. He knew these weren't to be his new compatriots. These people, he was sure, couldn't possibly be bound for a place like the Great City. The city would eat them alive!

After an hour or so the train slowed in a station and stopped. Alexis looked out the window to ascertain which place it was they were in. A sign was posted: NUSQUAMISH. Horrid little town, it was a rusty old settlement ensconced in fields of barley; and it was here in Nusquamish that the yokels and laborers – every one of them – got up and deboarded.

"All poor souls go to Nusquamish!" he laughed.

Now he was left alone in the train.

In the next town, the train filled up again. Here, a new flock of passengers boarded and took their seats around Alexis. He studied them. A most bizarre type of passenger: they were all women, all identical in appearance – without exception – wrinkled old ladies with covered heads and bright blue gowns. They shuffled in the train compartment like old birds hopping across stones on a pond. Once they were seated and the train began to move, they all simultaneously leaned forward in what looked like to be a sort of prayer. What sort of people were these, Alexis wondered. He tried to draw a clue from the embroidered words stitched into the fabric on the backs of their gowns. The words read: COUSINS OF THE CLOTH.

"Nuns!" he guessed. "Or socialists?" He wasn't sure. So many strange new things. Traveling was sure going to turn tricks with his mind. He rode along with these Cousins for hours before finally tapping one of them, "Excuse me?" he asked. The old woman's gown felt slippery like satin. She gave a startle and turned to face Alexis who was looking at her most expectantly. He asked her then if it was not the train to the Great City they were traveling on. The woman removed her head covering which let little tufts of white hair tumble down over her face. She pinched her thumb and forefinger together and drew it across her lips as if to signal that she couldn't, or shouldn't, speak. She then put her head covering back on and turned away from Alexis to resume praying.

"Well, whatever that means...I ask a question and get no response! Doesn't this lady know who I am?!" With this defeat, Alexis ceased to be curious about these old mute Cousins and sat there whistling a snatch of his own invention while tapping his foot on the bench. He then gave his thoughts to the place where he was traveling to. Could it really be that he was on his way to the famous Great City? That there was nothing to separate him now from his new life of greatness? Just some distance. But the train was taking care of that. He looked out of the window, and listened to the *clack, clack, clack* turn to the *drip, drop, drip* of the rain as the train slowed to a stop at another unfamiliar station. It was then, for some reason, that a stinging knot began to grow in Alexis stomach. It grew more painful until it made a piercing stab that made him gasp. From there it turned into a dull ache. "What is the cause of this?" The pain had come with Alexis' realization that he was now going out into the world and could never turn back. He tried to reassure himself... "This is a knot you must live with, my friend, keep courage, you are no longer a boy. Your life belongs to the world now. Where you are going you have no father to help you. But you need that no longer. Come what may, your life belongs to the world now. And remember, wherever you go, the world is on your side." And with that, the nervous sickness passed and settled into a dull acceptance of things and Alexis leaned back on the bench in quiet introspective thought about the meaning of the past, the conquest of the present and the mystery of the future.

After the train started up again, Alexis rested with his forehead pressed against the window watching out at the damp pastures of the changing landscape. He traveled along and he watched them turn unto fields of flowers. He watched clusters of red brick houses turn unto colonies of grey granite homes, turn unto windmills and granaries, peasant dwellings with their crude stone animal barns. Hours passed, the train chugged on, and the little crumbly wet farmhouses of the north disappeared altogether making way for the villages of creamy white stone houses of the south, with their black rooftops, walls the color of quartz that formed halos around cathedrals with spires and columns a-plenty; and with these sights Alexis knew he was passing through new and strange regions, and this pleased him very much.

It was while the train was moving along nicely, and Alexis was riding along not fearing at all that anything could separate him from his destination, that a strange noise began to resonate in the train car and it worried him. Could it be the wheels? Alexis didn't have much experience with trains. None at all. He listened carefully. A low-pitched droning sound passed through the train— a vibrating hum that grew louder and louder...Ah! Then Alexis realized it wasn't the train at all, it was just the silly Cousins. Part of their prayer.

"So they can talk after all!" Kneeling on the benches, the Cousins of the Cloth pursed their wrinkly mouths and pressed them into their cupped hands, and began chanting, repeating these phrases over and over:

Pray for the comfortable voyage unhindered of the sun and moon across the Heavens...

Pray for the safe passage of the puer aeternus, as he rides his reckless chariot...

"Well, fancy that!" Alexis exclaimed, "How withering souls love to pray! Pray for this and pray for that!" Why, Alexis, who was firmly on the ground and bound for the land of earthly delights had no use for such words; he had understood their prayer, but he didn't care if the sun's voyage was comfortable or not; nor did he care if the moon was hindered as it tumbled across the heavens, just so long as the train kept on and didn't break down. Still, he did like the sound of the Cousins' low-pitched droning voices; and so he hoped they'd continue singing their hymn. *"...Pray for the safe passage of those four feral steeds and our poor puer aeternus, flung upon a reckless chariot enflamed!"* ...And so on and so forth, the train flew southward across the spring-lit countryside and was gone.

Chapter VII

"Rooftops, Rathskellers, Tenements and Tin" – arrival in the Great City...

By the time Alexis' train crossed over the international border, the Cousins of the Cloth had long since departed. The new travelers were mostly businessmen, smartly dressed with dark-colored suits; upright sorts with black, glossy shoes that looked like puddles of oil on their feet. They carried calfskin briefcases with gold latches and most had little pointy beards – dark and nicely groomed – and black eyes like pinpoints with spectacles. These men spoke to their traveling companions in beautiful flowery language, with perfectly formed sentences and clear, distinguished pronunciation of words. Alexis knew by this – as by the fact that he had already passed many days of traveling, many nights of sleeping curled up on train bench – that he was nearing the cosmopolitan Great City. And nearing the Great City he was, and indeed these were the passengers whom he was among when he finally arrived at his destination on the brink of evening after what seemed like an eternity of travel. But finally he was there – in the Great City. At last, he had arrived!

His first view of the capital didn't come from the train window. Not that it was too dark to see out of the train, it was only dusk when he arrived; but the train had descended into an underground tunnel before entering the urban landscape and traveled underground for quite sometime before it slowed and came to a stop at North Terminal Station. Then came the clang of luggage racks, the stir of businessmen taking their briefcases; Alexis took his own sack, slung it over his shoulder and stood in line to exit. The train doors opened then and a buzz of people began fluttering here and flittering there. A commotion of voices, a bustle of figures running down the platform either shouting at porters or calling to friends they are there to meet, or hailing drivers and ticket agents; all the while vendors formed a gallery of shifting hands and brick-a-brack; and somehow or another, our confused and dismayed Alexis made it through the busy underground terminal to the moving stairs that carried people hurriedly upwards and downwards from one level to the next; and it was in this method that he ascended to the street level and went out to greet the formidable Great City.

Through electric doors he passed, and entered into the midst of the metropolis. There he witnessed a commotion of men and machines like he'd never seen nor could have imagined. Metal towers, streets and tracks, concrete overpasses intersected at all angles. Tram cars raced down boulevards, cables popping and showering sparks against their steel bodies. Immense buildings of concrete and stone shot up into the darkness. Grates on the street poured steam and the lights and the clamor of underground trains beneath grid-planks flickered. Gas lamps lined up like giant soldiers along bustling sidewalks where shadowy-faced pedestrians hustled along, weaving through honking horns, climbing through one another. A mob of furry hats, long coats and foreign voices all flew past, carrying garments and luggage, bags of food, purses and briefcases; all darting quickly past the lone traveler, stranger and foreigner, Alexis – who stood on the sidewalk with his drooping bundle, gaping in awe at all he saw.

Minutes passed.

"All right, my friend, why not find a hotel?" It'd be a good idea. He picked up his jaw and gathered his head and straightened his suit, fixed his yellow handkerchief, and wandered off through the dusky streets to find a place to sleep.

The lights of shop signs flickered along the avenue where he walked along, past bashed-in doorways and steaming vents. Streets stemmed from crossing streets; aerial bridges and avenues extended as far as one could see. In these, his first impressions, the city appeared incomprehensibly vast and alive. It undulated like the belly of a gypsy, like the tail of a fish. A city inconceivably immense, profoundly beautiful and simultaneously mortally disappointing. Feeble and omnipotent. Glorious and deranged. Like a broken swinging chandelier, casting blistering lights and dismal shadows. Gaping and gasping, Alexis wandered the streets with his head cocked back and eyes flung this- and that-away. He thought once of his old home, those Great Northern Woods that had spawned him. He wondered if those woods would terrify the Great City, should the two ever come face to face. He imagined one would be flared like a beast while the other kicked and squirmed. On certain streets a lonesome howl poured through the corridors of buildings and all felt desolate. One looked at these towers, rising up so high, and one wasn't sure if there was any sky above at all. This thought led Alexis to wonder if the sky really only existed solely to fill the empty spaces in places outside the Great City, where there were no immense buildings. This latter thought further led him to question whether the Great City was actually even built on top of the earth, or if the earth had been built beneath the Great City. And it was in this fashion of speculation, he walked on and on.

"Ô, holy city, I don't even need to imagine you!" What a pleasurable moment to behold. Farther up ahead, he saw some flickering lights he thought might belong to hotels and turned to walk towards them. The passage led to a crooked and dank row where people lingered on the sidewalks peddling things – a street where gamey-looking, sallow-eyed creatures scuttled by; while dark-faced men hunched over rickety tables, selling knives, rings and watches. Cripples leaned on sticks. Small gaunt women with scarves stretched over their chicken skulls lay curled up in doorways with sheepish hands outstretched to receive coins – for some, a few coppers sat in their dry palms. Tongues rattling strange words came from all directions. All foreign, all wild, and all obscene in their merciless movements. This was the Great City, capital of everything, far and wide; and now Alexis was really and truly out in the midst of the world and no one was even interested in helping him now.

The Ninth District, where his path returned to again and again, was a labyrinth of low-lying streets where pigeons pecked at garbage and twilled refuse pouring out of torn sacks, and train horns sounded low and wrathfully. On one street, he passed a man playing an accordion with a ferret perched on his shoulder. By his feet, sat a floppy hat containing some petty coins and a damp cigar. Alexis kept on this route and passed another man who shouted out to him. What could he want? Alexis turned to look at him. He was a small, emaciated specimen wearing soiled clothes and some kind of round little hat that looked like a loaf of black bread squashed on his head. He had hollow cheeks and little thin dry mustache and bloodshot eyes. He held out his hand to Alexis and asked in a wry nasal voice: *"Vous aimez la poésie? Un sandwich…c'est pas grand-chose. Je vous échange un poème pour un sandwich!"*

Understanding nothing of this, Alexis didn't respond but passed by, though he kept his head turned around to look back at this strange individual.

Minutes later, he passed another similar figure – though this one was hatless, much taller, and had blond hair and no moustache. His skin was scaly and there were contusions on his face. He wore the dusty green pants of an infantryman and black boots with the leather cut off in front, revealing scabbed and dirty toes. With an outstretched hand he called out: *"Mögen Sie Philosophie! Ich habe philosophische Ideen! Brot ist nicht so bedeutend. Ich tausche Ideen gegen Brot!"*

Again, not understanding, Alexis passed by without paying the courtesy of a response. 'What could they want, these people?' he wondered. He kept on walking forward, looking back with wide eyes, all the while gripping his bundle nervously close to his side.

Farther up ahead, he saw another man, also in rags. This one had black oily hair, long and wavy, and olive skin – short sleeves and greasy elbows. His face was horribly pockmarked and his front teeth protruded grotesquely between his large fleshy lips. With an outstretched hand, he bellowed: *"Ti piacciono le canzoni d'amore? Cosa vuoi che sia un gelato! Dammi un gelato e ti canto una canzone bellissima!"*

Alexis found a small hotel.

The flimsy knob rattled and the door clinked as he entered the sallow-lit lobby. Inside, it smelled like urine, but only faintly, and mixed with the smells of rose-oil and spices. Behind the partition, someone could be heard playing a whiny, out of tune stringed-instrument. Alexis apprehensively approached the counter.

Behind the counter, people were gathered. Alexis stood and looked at them. It was a family. They were seated on little crates eating a meal of some kind of saucy rice. Their mouths stayed drooped over their bowls, but they flipped their eyes up to Alexis when he approached. One child, gaunt and scantily dressed, had a bit of drool and a dab of chutney on his chin. Alexis looked past them at a curtain stretched behind the counter where an old woman was wrapping wet cloth over a hot iron. Steam poured off the iron, carrying with it, the odours of labour and foreign sweat. Next to her, on a little table, a baby in diapers squirmed on its back and howled.

The man of the hotel eventually stood up from his crate, left his family at their meal, and approached the counter to ask Alexis what he wanted. A room was what he wanted. Could it be done? And what was the price? The man's pinpoint eyes darted back and forth when the subject of money came up. Alexis studied him. He was a short, with a narrow head and jaundiced skin. He spoke in a strange accent, garbling his speech with the rice in his teeth. The room would cost a couple sovereigns.

And how much was a sovereign worth?

"That's all? I see...."

And where could Alexis change money?

There was no problem. The hotelkeeper was willing to help him convert his currencies. Alexis wasn't sure about this transaction and thought a moment to wander on, to change money elsewhere and find another hotel that was perhaps a bit different, perhaps one that smelled nicer. But no. The important thing was to keep things simple. The hotel seemed cheap enough, from the looks of things. Alexis could bare through anything for one night and he'd have plenty of time the next day to find better lodgings. And so it was settled. He dug in his sack and handed over his entire fortune to the hotelkeeper. He gave him the rest of the crowns he had been paid by Viktor, plus the remaining silver coins his father had given him. He would not be needing that kind of currency any longer. He had no plans of ever going back to his home country. It was settled. And so the jaundiced hotelkeeper wrote Alexis out a receipt for one night's stay and changed the rest of his money, dropping a handful of new sovereigns into Alexis' outstretched hand. They were beautiful coins, these sovereigns: heavy and nickel-coloured with gold serrated rims and strange engravings on either side – pictures of bridges and aqueducts and faces of men with curled lips and battle hats. Alexis studied one of these Great City coins while the hotelkeeper went to get the key from his wife.

The key hung from a string tied around a clunky broken tin doorknob. Alexis put it in the pocket of his suit jacket, where it made an unsightly bulge; and he walked up the thin-carpeted stairs to put his things away in the room that was his own until noon the next day.

He turned the key and entered. In a room lit by a single lamp casting faint light on stale papered walls, the guest walked in, dropped his bundle on the stained carpet and paced a moment. "Could it be?" he wondered.

He went over the bed, made up tightly, and felt the blankets. Stiff and dry, coarse and scratchy blankets – a few burn-holes from cigarettes. Pulling them back revealed yellowed sheets upon which, about halfway-up, waist-level to where one sleeps, there were bloodstains. Just a few drops, not more than a couple teaspoons full, but blood nonetheless, and of a sickly brown color, the way dried blood appears in fabric over time. Papered walls and a blood-stained bed…a holy virginal to Saint Vincent de Paul.

Alexis pulled the bristly blankets back up to cover the sheets and went over to the window, and with some effort, managed the shutters open.

"Could it be?" he mused aloud in a voice of awe, while looking out that first stubborn window at the small dark crevice of a Great City courtyard where pigeon nets were stretched and tied to drain pipes. "…Yet, could it be that I am really in the Great City after all? Could it be that my life has really taken me where it has? Just how I suspected it would?" … "Oh, now you see, Alexis!…a man's destiny is no less brilliant than the grandiosity of his willful decisions. And just as I was there and thought to be here, so now I am here…and think to be over…." He balanced his hands on the filthy windowsill of his hotel room and listened to the foreign pigeons mating, cooing foreign coos in the gutter ledges, "…And just as I am here now, thinking of the greatness I will have then, later on…oh, how it will be soon later on, and it will be then that I will have that greatness! That glory!" He strained to lean out the window and listened. The pigeons in the gutter ledges continued their cooing, mating and cooing,

"But why that sound?

"…Anyway, Alexis," Alexis continued, "and furthermore…" this, that, and so on, he lingered on his life of greatness to come. Lingered and lingered, but not for too long, as he was more than ready to abandon that windowsill and the hotel altogether, to jaunt about the new great capital he was now a part of. He, feeling now a distinguished member, picked up his bundle from the floor of the dim and not so clean room allotted him for the night – a room whose walls did none the good to hold out the smells of sweat, spices, flowers and urine – and this bundle, he hid in the small closet allotted to the room; and off he went with the key bulging in his pocket, out of the hotel, and burst like an opening springtime bud into the bustling city streets – off to explore.

He wandered in circles, not quite sure where to go. He watched for landmarks near the hotel so as to be able to find it once again. It was a dingy neighborhood around where he was staying. He looked and noticed there was a smudge of hotel on the shoulder of his nice light-colored suit. "Oh well!" With a carefree smile, he brushed it off and went on his way, walking with the strides of a gentleman. He was fully aware of his plume of silk handkerchief and his stubbly beard – the pride of a peacock – aware of his handsomeness in all its resplendent glory. So, now with his new position in this new society, where was he to go? What now? He had arrived in the Great City. Was there nothing left to do but live! "Okay, Alexis, go find a place to do the living!"

He looked around and found an older gentleman who was well-dressed and knowledgeable-looking. Alexis ran up alongside him and called to him...

"Stranger!"

The stranger stopped.

"Where should a man go in this city?"

The gentleman swung his cane and looked Alexis up and down. *"Jeune homme,"* he addressed him, "You would be fortunate to remain in the first district."

"The first district?"

"You're in the ninth now. It is not so far to the first. Just a few blocks down there, southward direction." The man tossed his eyes towards a narrow street past the intersection and pointed.

"Oh, but another question?" Alexis had the desire to detain this gentleman further, to ask him for more tips about how to get along in the Great City, as the man seemed to have fairly good knowledge of the place and was well presentable and quite distinguished-looking and probably very important in society; yet the latter made it all too clear that his time could not be spared, that he was in a definite hurry and would not pay honor to anymore questions – although he had seemed happy enough to help at first; and it should be noted that all the while he had been swinging his cane and pointing his suggestions that Alexis stay in the first district, he had been continuing on at a quick pace – his legs moving back and forth like a pair of scissors busy at work cutting fabric – and Alexis had to walk quite fast to keep up with him just to hear the conclusion of his forthright directions. So before Alexis even realized the man was gone, he was gone; and Alexis was alone and turned around this- and that-away, with his nose pointed luckily towards the street that would lead to the first district of the city, where things might be a little nicer.

"Why didn't he inquire about my accent," Alexis wondered, "Couldn't he tell I am was a foreigner here? How could it not be perfectly interesting to be accosted by a traveling foreigner with an accent?" This Alexis couldn't understand. He attributed it all to the gentleman's being in a tremendous hurry. "Perhaps his wife is in labor on the other side of town and he has to attend to her." That was the best reason that could be thought of for the man's behaviour. "No matter!" Alone and happy, head bobbing about in delight, and with fascination of the strangely constructed urban architecture setting the stage for this frantic play, Alexis walked on along down the street.

It was after being almost run over by two tramcars and a half-dozen people on bicycles, he came to a charming brick pedestrian street where things seemed nice, clean and vibrant. He peered into some café windows and was struck by the décor of the eating establishments. Some of the cafés had sheets of glass for walls and glowed with beams of coloured lights. People sat on white boxes as they ate. In the street, the air was mildly warm and many tables were set outside at which lovely couples sat drinking digestifs with their coffee beneath the warm bubbling flames of café braziers.

Alexis passed groups of people all dressed to go out. Glossy-lipped girls pranced along in gaggles, clutching little swinging handbags. They walked like birds in high heels, making clopping sounds like shoed ponies. Alexis smiled about this. He closed his eyes and imagined the street was filled with teams of horses trotting along – *clop, clop, clippety, clop!* He opened his eyes again to be reminded that there were no horses in the street. No horses at all! It was a herd of pretty girls out for a night in the Great City.

When the girls passed by, Alexis spun in the trails of their perfume. And what perfume! He reproached himself then… "How silly I was to think little Gretchen could have been for me! These girls here are a whole other species. How they look! And, oh how they dress! They smell beautiful from clear across the street!"

It brought Alexis a euphoria of the most painful sort to see these cosmopolitan city girls; and this painful euphoria made him swerve like a dizzy bee as he walked through the brick lane. A few streets farther down, he was alone again and came to a little urban park where he began to weave across the lawn. The pigeons saw him coming and scattered. His steps startled a squirrel and it ran up a tree. "But that was no squirrel!" he said, alarmed. It was a rat. "Can rats climb trees?" He looked into the branches of these trees planted in the park and asked them aloud if rats were able to climb them. Apparently city rats were. He squinted to see into the darkening night. Beyond the trees, there was a park gazebo. There were also some bushes and a few garbage cans. It was then, while surveying the park, that he heard chirping sounds coming from the same tree the rat had climbed up. He put one hand in his jacket pocket. The other, he waved about while talking to himself in this manner: "Though I don't know this country at all, I can safely say, based on my knowledge of the nature of beasts, that there could exist no bird of any kind that chirps in the evening whose natural habitat is a place such as we have here, with a mild temperate climate…especially not this early in spring."

Alexis thought then maybe it was the rat that was chirping and not a bird after all. He strained his ears to listen. "Bah, chirping rats…fancy that!" He took his hand out of his jacket pocket and stood akimbo. "What?" Now he could swear the rat was chirping words. A chirping rat can't chirp words…! Yes, they were words, after all! something about a 'little yellow handkerchief.'

"Strange! I also have a little yellow handkerchief," he said aloud.

He was about to leave the park and wander on through more city streets when he saw the source of the chirping. Those sounds had been coming not from the trees at all, but rather from a group of people sitting in the gazebo. There were two young men, and with them was a girl. They were laughing and talking the evening away, sharing a bottle of wine. They looked a handsome group from afar. As Alexis passed by, his shoes stepping soundless on the soft grass, the people in gazebo stopped talking and observed him. He fastened his eyes on them and walked sort-of sideways, baring his teeth at them in a friendly way as one ought to do in the city. The girl laughed and turned to say something to one of the young men. Alexis thought to hurry on his way and leave the park. It was then the man turned his ear from the girl and called out to Alexis. "Hey, you!"

"Me?" Alexis asked.

"Yes! Come over here a second!"

Alexis bit his lip. "What could they want?" He walked over to the gazebo to inquire. The fairer of the two young men handed the bottle of wine to his friend seated beside him. He then smiled at Alexis and pointed at his jacket pocket. "That's a nice handkerchief that you have, where did you acquire it? It's very novel."

So it had been these three in the gazebo who were chirping about the handkerchief. Alexis didn't tell him it was a gift from his sister. Neither did he tell them that he thought they were tree-climbing rats at first, though he wanted to. The fair-haired one invited Alexis to sit a minute with them and share their wine. Alexis accepted and this fair one then introduced himself. He was a young officer named Dominique. He had a smooth voice and a handsome face. There was a salesman's air about him, he was the kind of man one immediately takes a liking to. His eyes were strong and steady and he had an admirable ability to grin. The girl's name was Sidonie, and she dangled on Dominique's arm like a charm with wide eyes and a peal of laughter. She was fashionably dressed, wearing a robe of rhinestones and a jingle of jacks. She was also brash and spoke in a high-pitched, scratchy voice. Her waist was small and she had wide, flat hips. She looked rather pretty in a soft, leporine sort of way. The third person in their party was another young officer who went by the name of Federico. He greeted the newcomer with aloofness and didn't stand up to shake Alexis' hand like his friend had, but rather remained seated. This Federico was of swarthy complexion, had shifty eyes, and seemed exceptionally tall, but was otherwise unremarkable.

Sidonie and Dominique made room for Alexis on the bench in the gazebo and Dominique passed him the bottle. "It's a nice wine, this one," he insisted. "It's from the estate of Federico's father."

Federico's father had a wine estate?

"What was your name again?" Sidonie chimed in.

"Alexis," Dominique reminded her. He then turned back Alexis, "have another sip. Really taste this wine. Feel it on your tongue."

"It's quite good...Ah, yes. Indeed it is good!" Alexis said with a swallow, feeling the gentleness of the wine swirling in his head.

"So where are you from?" Dominique asked.

Alexis told him.

The three finished the bottle of wine and Sidonie tugged on Dominique's arm. "Come on, Dommie, let's go to The Rook. I'm getting bored here!"

"Listen, Alexis," Dominique said, "were going to go to a club. It'd be a pleasure if you would join us, that is if you desire...I'll pay you a glass."

"Ah yes,. I'd be glad to. I mean, if you wish that I come with you. But you don't have to offer me a drink...."

"Oh, don't worry about it, money's not so much of an issue."

"Did you hear that? We're leaving. Get up, Federico!" Sidonie took the tall officer by the hand and pulled him up to his feet. He sluggishly stood and followed the others out of the gazebo.

"You have an amusing accent," Dominique said to Alexis when the two were alone, walking past the shops and restaurants on the street. Sidonie was trailing several paces behind with Federico. "I mean that in a good way. And your dialect is interesting, too."

"How is it interesting?"

"Oh, just like I say words like 'pleasure' and 'desire,' and do you want to 'join us'...while you use words like 'glad' and 'wish' and that you'll 'come with' us...it's strange...it's different. I like it!" He continued: "...and here one says, I'll 'pay you a glass'; but you say, 'offer a drink.'"

"Huh," Alexis responded, and that was all. He liked it that he had an accent. He thought it was Dominique who had the accent, but maybe he was wrong. Or they both had accents, was probably the case. Anyway the wine was whirling gently in his brain while the two walked along and Alexis had not much to say but was altogether glad he met these new people. Federico and Sidonie lingered behind. Dominique walked with Alexis and told him stories of his success with money and women.

"You see this gallery?" Dominique pointed through the windows of an elegant art dealer. Inside, large canvases splattered with primary colors could be seen hanging on the walls. "The cheapest painting here sells for five-hundred sovereign. It's one of the greatest galleries in the city. And you know, Alexis, it was just last week I slept with the gallery owner's daughter." Dominique was beaming as he spoke. "What a sweet young flower she was!"

Alexis smiled and told himself in excitement, 'Yes, Alexis, this is the beginning of that greatness you foresaw. These are the people you are to meet. Real people...Ah! The beginning of life in the Great City...and it's only my first night here...unbelievable!' Alexis made several exclamations one after the other. His great hope and joy was mingling with the red wine he'd drunk and he was becoming increasingly thoughtful and romantic. 'I look into these people's faces here, and see that for all of us present, there is great meaning!'

Sidonie and Federico had caught up with them, but then lagged behind again. "Did you know I'm also a publisher?" Dominique asked Alexis. But no, Alexis had not known that. "You see, Alexis," he continued, "We're sort of princes in this city, Federico and I. We know all the important people. You could say this city belongs to us."

This information made Alexis smile with delight. Surely, the wine in his head made it all the more profound, yet still lucky for Alexis to be meeting the princely owners of the Great City. And already! Oh, surely Dominique was exaggerating – they didn't *own* the city – but still, Alexis could feel that great winds were blowing. 'It might take less effort than I thought to conquer the world!' Alexis thought to himself, while looking up at the high-up windows in the buildings they passed

"Hey Alexis!" Dominique suddenly exclaimed, "you'd be fortunate to watch your step. Someone didn't clean up after their dog."

'Fortunate,' Alexis thought, stepping aside, 'they always use this expression in the Great City... *You'd be fortunate to...* ...or so it seems. Why not say, *best if you watch your step*, uh? Strange dialect indeed!'

After a bit of walking they arrived at a rathskeller with a red velvet rope outside and a line of people waiting to get in. "This is The Rook" Dominique said, "It's a nice place. ...Well, you would call it a rathskeller. We call it a club." The four passed in front of the line of people waiting to get in, descended the stairs and entered a plush, dimly-lit room where music was playing and elegantly-dressed people were talking and drinking cocktails.

Dominique and Federico walked up and leaned on the slick surface of the bar to shake hands with the bartender. Dominique introduced Alexis to the bartender and they also shook hands. At the same time, Sidonie went to the backroom and installed herself on the cushions. She wanted to sniff some of the ether she had with her, and so she sought her favorite place to do it. She had called over to Dominique from the cushions, but he remained at the bar with Federico and Alexis. So there alone, she reposed herself in the nest of satin pillows, and touched up her lips with a stick of red. She then looked around herself discreetly and took a little metal flacon from her bag and poured some of the fluid inside on a small white cloth. Quickly, she pressed the cloth to her nose and breathed the chemical fumes. Leaning back, she inhaled deeper and deeper. At the bar, Dominique ordered a drink for himself and one for Alexis. Federico ordered his own.

"Alexis," Dominique asked, "have you ever tried Seraphome?"

"Seraphome?"

"Yes, it has a strange name, doesn't it? But it's a nice liqueur. No doubt, the finest. And this city is the only place in the world where one can get it. I insist you try it. It's a little pricy, but well worth it."

"Okay," Alexis agreed, "with pleasure!"

The bartender caught the signal and took from the shelf a bottle kept inside a burgundy velvet bag cinched with a golden cord. From this bag he took out a voluptuous corked chalice filled with a deep red succulent liqueur. He arranged two glasses, wet the rims, and poured the Seraphome into each, returning the chalice to its velvet bag afterwards. The drinks were placed on the bar.

Dominique and Alexis clinked glasses. Federico, who took for himself some port wine instead, toasted with Dominique; and finally succumbed to toast with Alexis, after the latter insisted.

A deep red light swooped through the bar. "Heavenly, isn't it?" Dominique turned his glass in his hand to admire the viscosity of the sanguine liqueur. Alexis took another swallow. It had a bitter taste which he liked immensely. "It's made essentially from pomegranates and wormwood," Dominique informed him.

Next to the glasses of Seraphome, the bartender set a couple complimentary cups of mint-water. Mint-water was the house specialty: crushed spearmint, gaseous water, and a splash of gin, garnished with a pickle. Alexis drank the mint water down quickly and enjoyed it, though he preferred the Seraphome.

Federico said something to Dominique which Alexis didn't overhear. He was busy sipping Seraphome. Dominique then nudged Alexis, "Hey, your glass is looking thirsty! You're drinking faster than all of us. Have a little more." The bartender overheard this and put another glass of mint-water in front of Alexis. He added an extra pour of gin.

Alexis took a swallow and Federico called over to him, "Hey, you seem a bit shaky! Why are you shaking, guy?"

Alexis turned to face the two men.

"Gla, gla!" he said.

"What?" Federico asked.

"Gla, gla!" cried Alexis.

"Well, you're getting a bit tipsy over there!" Federico turned to Dominique... "We give this guy some wine and a couple cocktails and he gets all tipsy on us!" Federico turned back to Alexis, "You are a little bit drunk!" He then made a wry smirk at Dominique, "*Gla, gla,* goes the drunk!"

Federico faded to the background. Dominique came closer, "How are doing?" he asked Alexis, putting his hand on his shoulder.

"Alright. I'm feeling a bit...Aye-aye-aye!"

The room spun and then stopped at a dead halt, slipping once and then stopping to view, counter-crooked, Federico walking at an angle in his tall, upright manner away towards the backroom. Alexis watched the tea lights on the bar fizzle. A moment later Federico reappeared with Sidonie on his arm. The two approached Dominique:

"I was waiting on the cushions for you, Dommie!"

"Well, Sidonie, I was talking to our friend, Alexis."

"My God, Dommie!" she shrieked, "Sometimes you treat me as if I'm not even a woman!"

She gathered herself then and started for the exit, "Fine!" she put in at last, "I'm leaving with Federico. Enjoy your night. Ciao-ciao!"

At the bar, Dominique and Alexis were alone again to talk. The latter fumbled to refrain from slipping off his satin stool. Dominique, returned his full attention to him. "So tell me, Alexis, what are you doing in the city?

"Oh, I'm here for thrills," he thought to answer, "see the world, look around a bit" But what did he really answer?

"Good, good, Alexis. Look around. See all you can. We'll have to stay in touch. I may have some opportunities for you."

Opportunities?

"Who, then, and why for...Oh, yogs!" Alexis was getting increasingly dizzy from drink and speech was difficult. The pickle in his cocktail glass seemed to grow infinitely large. The ice cubes clanked together noisily, making a crashing cacophony of horrid jingling, sounds like waves exploding on a beach and factory hammers slamming. No more sips, Alexis. He started to worry that he would certainly faint if he did not find his bed. He abruptly stood.

"Opportunities? But, Dominique, I don't know how I'll find you." He thought he said something to that effect and he probably did as Dominique then took out a leaf of paper and a shiny steel pen and wrote his address on it.

"I'm in the best part of town, my friend. The Ministerial District. It's the seventh district. Do you know what kinds of things sparkle there?" But Alexis didn't know what kinds of things sparkle there and wasn't able to care as he was then quite drunk and thinking just made him squirm.

"Here, write your address down." Dominique handed the pen to Alexis.

Alexis took the pen and tried to explain that he didn't have an address at the moment. He stood there digging the pen into the palm of his hand while eyeing some lights that were coming in through the corner of his eye. He tried to speak a couple of times. Dominique reassuringly said, "It's okay, keep the pen."

"I can have the pen? No, I can't take your pen." This is what Alexis thought he said while simultaneously dropping the pen into his pocket where it fell to the bottom and clinked against his doorknob. Here the room turned a demi-tour for him and he then left quickly, unable, or forgetting, to say goodbye.

Up on the street, Alexis wandered, weaving here and wafting there, until somehow or other, he found himself walking alongside a wench.

This wench stepped like a stork, her face was heavily covered in orange rouge. She joined Alexis for a few blocks.

"It's Monday night and everything's dead!" the wench was complaining. "How can everything be dead on a Monday night!"

Alexis kept on with the wench while holding his head to keep it going in the direction of his feet. The wench continued on with her story... "You know, I was in drinking in this bar. This man wanted to have me in the bathroom. He wanted to take me somewhere too. He had loads of money. I could've had whatever I wanted, you know...whatever I wanted! Why is everything closed? They're sweeping the streets. It's Monday night and it's dead! I don't understand it. Hey, you don't have a pill by any chance?"

No, Alexis didn't have any pills and his way somehow diverged when his ankles got caught on some wire mesh lining the street and the wench went on her way. He stopped then and leaned against the bricks of the nearby building and let his head fall into the palm of his hand, with sinking, clouding vision. Meanwhile, in countries far away, the banks of the Moldau River swelled to the tune of violins and seven swallows flew in unison over the city of Jerusalem.

Alexis woke up what must have just been two or three minutes later on a street bench. Still dizzy, but mildly so, and some energy restored, he stood with the sickness gone from his throat. Much relieved, he walked on straighter now. "Whew! That was close, I almost lost myself! Now to find my bed." He thought he recognized some of the buildings that he passed as being those he had seen upon leaving the hotel.

He came to a bum on the street a few blocks farther up. The bum called out to him, "How about a little coin?" his murky hand was outstretched. Alexis turned around and took a step towards him, and asked, "How about a big coin?" He reached in his suit jacket pocket and searched around. He felt the steel pen and the doorknob. He pulled out a largess, extending it out to the bum; but before the bum could take it, the coin dropped from his hand into a puddle in the sidewalk gutter.

"Ah, it fell in the mud," cried the bum.

"Well, can'tchya pick it out?" Alexis responded with impatience. The dizziness was beginning to return.

"Ah, but you're talking to me like I'm a bum," replied the bum, "I ain't a bum... I'm just a travelin' man down on my luck."

"Down on your luck?" inquired Alexis.

"Yes, down on my luck, you see? Tryin' to find a soup kitchen to sleep in." And after a moment... "what are you, some kind'v aristocrat? You'z dressed fancily! You're a good lookin' guy. The girls, they like you, I bet. Are you famous?" All the while the travelin' man was asking this, he was trying to get his heavy dirty hand into Alexis' to shake it, but Alexis kept on jerking his hand closer into his body as he started back off on his way, squinting on up ahead to see if he recognized a hotel. "You are famous," the travelin' man continued, "This big muddy coin means nothing to you, does it? Can I've another?"

"No, I'm not so famous," Alexis said, stepping away, "I'm a traveling man too!" He stuck his thumb in his chest and fanned his fingers out towards the travelin' man down on his luck... "I'm a traveling man up on my luck. I'm a gambler!" Alexis told him. "But soon I'll be down on my luck and I'll come to find you to ask for that coin back. Where will I find you? Will you give it back to me?"

With this, the travelin' man backed off. Alexis dropped his smile and let his hands fall in despair. "I'm looking for my cat, actually. I have to bring it in, and...you haven't seen a tabby around have you?...no, but I must go." He didn't feel like talking any longer.

With a floppy wave of his hand and a bob of his head, he departed company and continued off on down the street.

Alexis wandered in tired drunkenness for quite a while but couldn't find his hotel for the life of him. The key on the tin doorknob bulged grotesquely out of his jacket pocket, his shoes flopped along as he walked. He looked and looked, but could find it. Eventually, to his fortune, his tiredness overtook the drunkenness and he was no longer dizzy, simply foggy-headed. Soon he realized he'd made a full-circle. "I was just here!" he exclaimed when he found himself standing beside a red velvet rope that blocked off an entrance leading down to a rathskeller. A thick-necked doorman with a stern serious face, ever so tall, in a black suit, stood on the other side of the rope, guarding the entrance. Alexis thought to enter and see if Dominique was still inside. 'He'll lead me home,' Alexis thought. 'At least he'll lead me somewhere where I can sleep.'

Exhaustion gave him the feeling he'd do best to simply drift and fall down the steps to the rathskeller, but instead he waited by the rope of the entrance for the doorman to invite him in. A nicely dressed couple approached from behind. Alexis stepped aside. The doorman dutifully nodded to the couple, pulled back the rope, and allowed them to enter. Alexis decided it was his turn. He took a step forward towards the rope, and stopped. He looked at the doorman who didn't return the glance. Just then, a single man approached. The doorman looked at the single man, nodded to him and unlatched the rope to let him go through. He wished him a good evening, after which the man descended the stairs into the rathskeller.

Alexis then got full control of himself and stepped up to the rope. He smiled at the doorman. The doorman made no response but simply looked back as though expecting to hear a question. Alexis recognized this and asked one…

"May I enter?"

"No, sir," the doorman responded.

"No, sir?"

"No, you may not enter, sir."

"Christ! Why not?"

The doorman was unflinching.

"Why mayn't I?"

"Because you cannot enter!" was the response. The doorman stepped forward as if to suggest that Alexis would be best off backing into the street and away from the club. He stepped beyond the barrier, latched the red rope behind him, and stared firmly down at Alexis.

Alexis didn't care for this doorman. "But why can't I enter? Is Dominique here?"

"Who?"

"Dominique. Is he here?"

"I don't know who that is. Regardless, you cannot enter tonight."

"Is it a private club, this place?"

No, sir. It is not private." The doorman sniffed his nose, huffed up his chest and his eyes bounced back and forth to the periphery of his jurisdiction. Alexis sneezed. Just then, a single individual, dressed similar to Alexis, and resembling slightly Alexis, no older, no younger, approached the entrance to the rathskeller.

"Good evening," the doorman greeted the individual, while at the same time, he pushed Alexis out of the way to unhinge the red velvet rope, to allow this individual to enter.

Alexis stepped up again to the doorman… "Well then, do I need an invitation?"

"I'm afraid even with an invitation you could not enter."

"But is it the way I am dressed?"

"No." And after some pause, "You are dressed fine."

"Then is it my face?" Alexis grew angry. "You don't like my face? Is that it?!"

"No, it is not your face."

"Then you think I am drunk!"

"No, sir. You do not seem drunk."

"Is this The Crook, man?!" Alexis demanded, "or The Rook?…well, is it?!"

"No, sir, it is not."

"Well, then, what is it? Why can I not enter?! Tell me!"

Here the doorman again unleashed the red velvet rope and stepped beyond it towards Alexis, locking it again on the brass pole once he had passed to the other side; he gave Alexis a shove…"You simply cannot enter." Then another… "You are not going to get in by asking questions. So, go on, get out of here!" And with whirling muscular arms, the doorman threw Alexis out into the street, whereupon the latter toppled, tripped, almost fell; and then, realizing his chances were lost, he turned and walked on away from that club through more and more city streets.

Luckily, as if by design, Alexis stumbled upon his hotel after another hour or more of hopeless and tiresome searching.

"Ah, my hotel!" he exclaimed with a sudden resurgence of energy, "Luckily it was by design, and not by fluke!" He wiped his eyes and scratched the bump on his lip and entered the building. He passed the lobby quickly without looking at the woman who was in the shadows ironing rags. He ascending the sallow-lit stairs, weary from drunkenness and the late hour; he pulled the flimsy doorknob from his pocket and stuck the key in the lock. The old door opened with a snag on the rug. Alexis went in the dingy room and fell asleep on the twin bed with his clothes on, not bothering to pull the blankets down or dig around for a pillow. Outside the window, the sun was about to rise. A light rain started and then stopped and the winds died down and stopped too, and not a cloud remained in the Great City sky. It looked as though the day was going to be pleasant and warm.

Alexis awoke with fresh-eyed exhilaration at around eleven o'clock. He washed and shook out his suit, went downstairs and returned the key and the clunky knob to the hotelkeeper – he would not be staying another night. Then, with his traveling sack slung over his back, he stepped out into the city for his first daylight experience about town.

The sun was abound, and the air, mild. The tops of the buildings looked as though cut out of ivory. Alexis began to traverse the city. In search of an apartment and a job, he walked amidst dreams of glorious opportunities.

'Where can I find a meal? Something besides cabbage and turnips. This city's bound to have everything. What is all this trash in the street? Where is that clean neighborhood I found last night? Maybe he would know...'

"Stranger!" He called out to a passer-by. The stranger stopped. "Is this the first district? ... No, it is still the ninth? ... Okay, thank you!" He wandered on. "How the women look at me as I pass. It is the beard, no doubt!" ... "Yes, Alexis," he told himself, "don't underestimate the power of your handsomeness. It seems to make even fearful eyes wander!" ... "Good, good!" ...and things only got better. After walking all morning, he found the first district where he recognized a statue he had seen the night before. It marked the beginning of a pedestrian street paved with red bricks. He walked down this redbrick street watching the people with their shopping bags – strolling along with their big city lives.

"How is it these people live here?" He stopped for a moment by a street meter to ask himself, "I mean, these people actually are fortunate enough to live here?! They buy their food here, they meet their friends here...

"...Of all the crevices on this earth...I mean, they could be living in little weathervane villages, or no-name factory towns, but no...they live in the Great City! ...Ah, soon I will be able to say the same for myself...Wait! I already do live here! Ha, fancy that!

"...Just think of it, Alexis," he continued on with his prideful soliloquy while strolling along, "yesterday morning you were asleep curled up on a hard wooden bench on a train. Already last night you were drinking with the princely owners of the Great City. Today, you have some money in your pocket and your mind set on greatness. You see how fortune multiplies exponentially? Oh, soon you will have your high palace room, your famous mistress, your cosmopolitan worldly greatness and fame. The bounty of a sultan, the bread of a king...ah, but wait! That is the glorious future. There will be time enough for that. Let me just taste the present a moment. Yes, look here...

Alexis came to an outdoor marketplace.

There he was in the midst of a marketplace amid a clamor of vendors and buyers, costermongers, people of all sorts wheeling carts and the like. Stands were set up for various goods to be sold. Alexis, having never before seen anything like it, realized he had truly arrived in the land of earthly delights.

"So, this," looking around himself, "is the Great City. A place where all can be had!" He walked the aisles beneath the umbrellas. "One sovereign, two sovereign!" voices rang out. When he came to a salt stand, he stopped. There, hundreds of types of salt were offered: salt petals, rose salts, bulging bags of alkaline salts, salt bismuth, flowers of salt, cream of the sea salt, too!

He came to a mushroom stand. Here, all the world's mushrooms were for sale – all, save for the yellow shelf mushrooms of the Great Northern Woods – and they lay like fetid limbs ready to be bought and bagged: oyster mushrooms, fleshy peach chanterelles, kneecap mushrooms, crocus mushrooms, chartreuse finger-lily mushrooms, clam-cap mushrooms, button mushrooms of every shade of beige, pretty-door mushrooms, lid mushrooms, and more!...

Olive stands sold olives, grape stands sold grapes, oil stands sold oil. Oils of tournesol, coriander, and linseed; oils of Persian pepper-pods, oils of Sheba...!

Dead rabbits lay in a stall with cocked heads and metal pins jabbed into their ruffled bellies toting signs with the price written on them – one sovereign apiece!

Alexis wandered up and down passed the stands, looking at the foods and wares, eyeing the vendors and shoppers – these vendors with their calloused peasant hands. And the shoppers: some fashionable, lean and tall with glistening lips and eyes, others who were hunched over canes with grey flabby faces, clutching bulging shopping bags brimming over with foodstuffs. Young yellow-haired women held the hands of daughters in lily white dresses. They carried baskets of golden flowers. Tall, dark-haired, olive-skinned men with lean arms and smiles, handed these little girls more and more flowers; and how their young mothers thanked them! Alexis thought that although these marketplace people well-covered their flesh in a stitch to defend from the chilly spring winds, one could easily think they were marketplace shoppers in Eden in the time before the expulsion, before the innocents were exiled. Nude and alive, theirs was a land of plenty where fruits of every hue were abound and laced with forbidden treats.

"Peaches! Nectarines!" a vendor announced. Alexis swung his sack as he walked along. He sang a little verse he made up on the spot…

All earthly delights the world can conceive,

the bones of Adam and the breasts of Eve…

Some cash in my pocket, an arm in my sleeve,

the bones of Adam and the breasts of Eve….

It was while he was busily singing aloud, wafting away the smells of carcasses, dead fouls and fish; while his eyes were busy surveying a stand of marbled jellies and candied fruits a-glimmer with waxy skins, that the earth beneath his feet began to tremble.

Tremble, tremble! People screamed. Tremble, tremble!

Everyone was a scurry. The flower girls dove beneath the marketplace stands. Women took their babes from their baskets and cupped them to their breasts. Merchants flung themselves over their goods.

"Thief!" someone yelled.

"Earthquake!" yelled another.

Yet the feeling passed right away.

Alexis regained himself, as did the others around him in the marketplace. He had never felt an earthquake before. Strange sensation indeed! With his mind full of thoughts and impressions, he languidly left the area, left the crowds, and turned down a narrow lane which led onto a wide boulevard.

It was boulevard filled with bright sun and lined with tall oak trees. Alexis walked along the wide sidewalk thinking about the earthquake. The passers-by he crossed seemed to be going about their business as if nothing bizarre had just happened. 'Who knows, perhaps earthquakes are common in this city.' The matter ceased to interest him. He walked along admiring the gold-tiled conical roofs of the stone buildings that lined one side of the boulevard. On the other side, there was an immense gated park. It was the Imperial Gardens.

Stopping by the gates of the Imperial Gardens, Alexis was struck by the sight of a group of young people standing in a circle, talking. Five in all, they were all fashionably dressed, about the same age as Alexis. When he noticed these people, a pleasurable cold tingle went through his body. He had been struck by one of the members of the group in particular. It was a girl and she was standing with her front facing Alexis. 'What a girl!' he thought. He looked at her and could not turn his gaze away. He was frozen still and watched on, while she and the others in her group continued talking, gesturing their hands casually; as around them, children and parents flooded in and out of the gardens passing through the open gates.

Of the young men in the group, there were three. Two had blond hair and carried smart leather satchels. Among them, there was a second young lady, though Alexis noticed neither her nor the other three men at first. He was struck solely by the face of this girl whose front was turned towards him. She had light-colored hair, neither brown nor blonde, and full and sensual lips. She was rather on the short side of tall and was dressed in a fashionable black and grey checkered wool coat. After standing transfixed for many moments, Alexis quickly turned away and tried to walk on. He went a few feet and then stopped in front of a magazine stand. But where was it he was headed to anyway? If he could only peruse these magazines. 'Hmm, glossy covers…' He tried to, pretended to at least, but that face! Where had he seen her? He had only been in the Great City for one day, and she was so beautiful; had he seen her, he would have certainly remembered exactly when and where. Yet no doubt there were gaps in his memory from the night before. He had been quite drunk. Ah, he knew! He had talked to her at The Rook! No. Or outside, maybe? Had she exchanged words with him while he was trying unsuccessfully to enter that second club later on? Oh, he would have remembered that! But that face, he knew that face.

And so, Alexis drifted like linen drying in the wind around the perimeter of the magazine stand near the gates of the Imperial Gardens. He thought hard about that girl in the checkered coat and returned around and around again to the side where her group was to take another look at her. Maybe she was famous actress. "That's where I've seen her…on one of those giant advertisements posted up along the boulevards. I must've seen her face on one of those posters."

It was then, when he decided to leave the gardens and pay her no more mind, to go along his way, to wherever it was he was going, that he noticed from afar the group was splitting up. The second girl kissed the cheeks of two of the smartly-dressed young men and walked off holding hands with the third. The remaining two men walked off north-east together, in the direction of the Commercial District. While the first girl, Alexis' girl in the grey and black checks, walked on her own, unaccompanied, down a narrow street that led in the direction of the river. Alexis decided then to follow her. But why follow her? He had no choice. He had to!

He first let her go a little ways, walking down narrow roads past the art galleries and bread shops, past apartment houses – he followed some distance behind. As she walked, she turned once and again and looked back towards Alexis. Had she noticed he was following her? Or was it just his fanciful imagination?

She had put on dark glasses after leaving her friends to go off on her own, and they glamorously eclipsed half of her face. The sun had come from behind the clouds then, and perhaps it was too bright for her. Regardless, she had put on dark glasses and now it was hard to tell whether or not she was looking at him when she looked back. But he knew it. It was him she was looking at. Yes, she knew she was being followed! Maybe not, though. After all, she didn't quicken her pace. She kept on walking idly along the narrow street that led on towards the river. Idly, yet still in the fashion of one who has someplace to be. 'If only she would go into one of these apartment houses,' he thought to himself, 'then I will know where she lives and can return now and again and hope for a future accidental meeting.' … 'Oh, if only I could remember where I have met her.' He kept on after the girl, and in that last block before the river bank, she looked over her shoulder twice more. 'Still, she can't think I am following her. There are other people walking along the street, other people strolling between us.' Still, he fancied that she too had noticed him back by the Imperial Gardens and now noticed him again. It would be unusual for him to be so near to her now, now that she was quite far from the gardens. She had, after all, been walking for more than a quarter hour with Alexis walking right behind. 'Well, don't you think if she had met me before, she would stop to speak to me? Or at least wave hello?...that is, if she's seen me.' ... 'I must think of where I've met her, so I know that I've met her; so it will not be absurd that I am following her. But it is not absurd that I am following her. I am following her because I *want* to follow her. And *if* I want to follow her?!'

Then at the banks of the river, the girl in the checkered coat stopped to examine some postcards being sold at a stand. Alexis continued on towards her. How beautiful she looked standing there flipping through the cards! Alexis approached the quai where the postcards were, yet before he came to where she was standing, he turned sharply to the right and began to walk off in the other direction.

'Oh Christ, Alexis! Why? Why do you walk off?! This is the girl you must meet. It is her...you simply must! So why, Alexis, do you walk off like a puerile little boy? Damn you sometimes!' Yet, like a boy or whatever, he was still walking away. And off he went along the banks of the river in the eastward direction.

But he did not stray from her for long. After a minute he turned; and with renewed courage, he started back towards that postcard stand. Oh, how sweet those cards must smell! 'Perhaps, she had only stopped to browse those postcards so that he may catch up with her. That's what he began to think. She wanted him to accost her. Certainly it was so! He looked around the postcard stand, But what? She was gone!

She was not gone, though. Yes, she had left the postcard stand; but she had not drifted far. She was merely walking along the banks of the river towards the next bridge. His theory now was that she certainly had not cared a bit about those cards, but was lingering to give Alexis a chance to catch her up; and having done that, she decided he was interested in meeting her because he'd walked off, so she left to continue on her way. Perhaps she had not done this. Perhaps she wanted to look at those cards, after all.

So now, as the pretty girl in the checkered coat was walking her way along the banks of the river, Alexis was following her from farther behind. 'This time I mustn't let her go!'

When she came to the next bridge spanning the river, she began to walk across it. Alexis hid behind a stone pillar. It was a statue of a saint and a lion. There he waited. She, all the while, was continuing across and when Alexis peered from behind the pillar, he saw that again she looked over her shoulder at him. Yet this time when she looked back it was not as before, as if she had seen him and were staring through her dark glasses directly into his pupils. No, this time when she looked back, it was more in cursory way, as if searching; as if wanting to see something she couldn't find. Yet, he was far enough at a distance to be safe from sight, so once again she turned and resumed looking forward, keeping on her way and her usual idly hurried pace.

Once across the bridge, on the south-side of the river, she passed beneath an stone archway and turned down the outdoor corridor belonging to the National Museum. Alexis trailed her for a minute or so. Here on the museum lane that was paved with round stones, there were no other passers-by and it would become obvious very soon, he knew, that she was being followed. Alexis knew he had to stop. He knew that accosting her on this day would be impossible. His only chance would be if she were to enter into an apartment house. This way, he would know where she lived. He could happen upon her another time. But there weren't any apartment houses. Just a long empty stone corridor belonging to the National Museum and there wasn't another soul around, just the young lady in the checkered coat with her little shoes that clicked on the stone floor as she walked along. Alexis listened to the sweet little sound of her feet on the stones. How prettily her shoes clicked as she walked! 'Oh, I cannot turn down that corridor. My shoes too will click and she will turn to see me and the whole scene will become ridiculous.' And so it was here, without thinking about it, without giving it any conscious thought, that he turned away. He turned and walked off back away from the National Museum. He turned away once and for all and let the mysterious checkered girl disappear back into the fabric of the Great City. Alexis walked away from the National Museum, away from the archway, back towards the river, back towards the bridge, back across the bridge; back, back and away from her and away from his life as it would have been, had he managed to stop this girl and speak to her. "Oh maybe nothing would have been different. Surely it would have changed nothing. But certainly it would have. Oh what a life! What a strange business this life is with all the things that can happen!" Alexis was not distraught. He walked along the river bank by himself in quiet introspection, no longer following anyone, no longer near anyone worth following, and when he passed the postcard stand he didn't even stop to look.

Along the banks of the river, he walked for sometime, passing tourists where they stood at the railings, gaping at the marvelous architecture of the city. He passed musicians, policemen, tramcar lines. He walked by the river and when he came to a bridge, he crossed it, went to the end, stopped and looked around. He then decrossed it. Then he came to another and he crossed that one too, stopped and looked around, he then decrossed it. For sometime he weaved in this way back and forth across the bridges, tarrying awhile on each riverbank before walking on again.

He soon came to Our Lady's Bridge – a magnificent suspension bridge that spanned the river at its widest point; it saw a constant thoroughfare of people traversing on the wide walkways, parallel to these were several rows of tracks across which tramcars zipped along every minute of the day, making loud pops with their sparks of electricity on the cables.

It was here on Our Lady's Bridge that Alexis found some new acquaintances. They were two girls. They looked like twins with their bright golden hair and full apricot lips. Both were thin, both rather tall and both very pretty. As they came walking arm-in-arm across the bridge – the sun falling down, lighting up their bright heads of hair – Alexis stopped in front of them and stared. He stood before them, eyes wide open, the tails of his suit flapped in the wind that whipped across the bridge. Why he had stopped to stare at these girls, he wasn't sure. Perhaps it was because they were staring at him first. Regardless of the reason, he stood now here before the apricot-colored girls and the three just looked at each other and stared.

'They look like decorations, these girls,' Alexis thought to himself. They were standing there on the bridge jumping up and down ever so slightly like two little jingling bells. As they looked at Alexis, they jingled and giggled. Alexis responded with wide eyes and a mouth open.

Then came chiming those two jingling golden-haired bells simultaneously… "Who are you, boy?"

"I'm Alexis."

"Oh."

Hereupon the girls stopped jumping up and down, although they continued to ring. They took Alexis' arm, one on each, each on either side, and began to walk with him across Our Lady's Bridge.

"I'm Katya," one said.

"I'm Katarina," said the other.

"We're from Roussinia." They chimed together.

Roussinia? Where's that? These tall golden-haired bells were charming indeed. Without any ado, they led Alexis away from the bridge, away from the river and off through the colorful streets of the first district of town. After the three passed the Imperial Gardens, they came to the eighth district. Here was the quieter and more upscale neighborhood called the West-End, with the city's nicest and most fashionable restaurants and shops.

"Come on Alexis, let's stroll!" And why not? These girls from Roussinia felt very nice on his arms. Being with them made his lips tingle. What were their names again?

"Katarina!"

"And you?"

"Katya!"

Thus, Katarina, Katya and Alexis walked down the tree-lined boulevard of the luxurious Chancellery Prospect, where gentlemen sat on terraces in the crisp spring sun with well-dressed ladies in broad spring hats, eating salads with sweet oils and drinking sparkling wines. The weather was cool and breezy, but still bright, and the sun burned nicely.

Alexis asked the girl on his left arm some trifling questions. Was this one Katya or the other one? He couldn't remember. The one on his right arm all the while kept jingling along letting her head sway a little to the right to glance at the fabulous luxury items being sold in the windows of the fashionable shops on the prospect.

The three strolled happily along.

After fourteen tolls of the church bells nearby, the girls insisted they were hungry.

"Look at all these cafés with terraces!" Alexis suggested they stop and eat at one. It's okay. He would pay.

"Why don't we take this table? It's in the full sun. Here, you girls sit with the sun on your faces."

The waiter came over and brought menus.

"Oh, I love this dish!" said one of the girls. "And this one is absolutely divine! And we'll need a bottle of sparkling water...."

And so the three sat and ate chilled summer squash soup with grilled bread and espelette. It was a very nice light meal and the girls ate with great appetites.

The waiter came over with the check.

"No, I'll pay! It was a very good soup indeed!" Alexis beamed. "What a good day it turned out to be!"

After lunch, the three continued fluttering down Chancellery Prospect so the girls could eye the noble delights glittering in the windows of the luxury shops. They danced happily on his arms and Alexis was too busy enjoying their fresh faces and warm and slender arms to look around to see if the passers-by were looking on at him with envy and admiration, fancying him a lord with these two beauties on his arm. But certainly they were. He didn't need to look.

While strolling along the prospect, they came to a fancy perfumery where Katya found some smelling-lotions she liked. "Oh my dear, Alexis, I really do adore smelling-lotions!" And so she bought some with his money, and oh, they were dear! Alexis could stay in that dingy hotel from the night before for a full month with the money he spent on a couple tiny bottles of lotion. But Katya certainly adored her smelling-lotions. Why should she not have them?

The cool wind picked up later on, and the sun headed off behind some buildings, casting shade on Chancellery Prospect. This made it, though not unpleasant, less idyllic than before. The three walked along and looked at a few more window vitrines. Katya had received her present but Katarina hadn't and she wanted one too. And so, Alexis bought her some trifle to keep her fingers pretty that she seemed to not be able to continue living without. It cost more than the chilled summer squash soup, but it meant so much to her. She thanked Alexis tenderly with a kiss on the cheek. Oh, how his cheek could taste the honey sweetness in that kiss!

Lastly, Alexis came upon a window display where handsome men's furnishings were sold. He looked at the shiny shoes in the window and he thought of his own shoes and looked down at his feet. "I wonder how long I'll have these shoes," he wondered. They were good leather but a little scuffed and worn out. "I may have to replace them someday soon," He stared with great longing at a brilliant pair of dark dress shoes propped in that window display on Chancellery Prospect. 'Oh, but for the price of those shoes,' he sighed, 'one could probably buy an entire inn in Krüfsterburg.' Before he could fall too much in love, the girls dragged him away from the window display. Katarina was chattering away about something or other while Katya had her nose in her lotions.

Soon, the strolling hour was coming to an end. With the sun fully behind the conical-roofed buildings on the prospect, the three walked along together a little farther. Then, by evening, the two girls fluttered off like a pair of nightingales.

'Oh, well,' Alexis thought, 'It was pleasant while it lasted.' He still felt a lord, though his ladies were no longer on his arm. He stopped a moment to think beneath a street lamp that flickered as it got ready to light up for the night, and dusk came in dully and smoothly, darkening all that was around.

Alexis continued wandering for a bit. The twilight was impatient and darkness fell quickly on this new and strange foreign city. And with it the darkness, came the worries of finding a place to lay his head. Hunger began to gnaw at him. That chilled soup from noontime wasn't worth its weight. Alexis' belly felt hollow. He dug in his pockets and his sack and gathered his remaining money and counted it. It was certainly dwindling, no doubt about that!

"First I have to get out of this neighborhood," he told himself, "here everything is unbelievably expensive." Alexis headed to the east through the city, and as he did so, the scenery degraded. After he passed the Imperial Gardens, he went through the first district and entered the second by way of some scattered streets that looked more or less as dingy as the place where he had stayed the last night.

Along a boulevard of the Commercial District, where trams zipped through the darkness and passers-by walked in and out of the shadows, Alexis found a tavern that looked like a cheap enough place to get a meal. "I must keep my stomach's expectations low till I find a job," he told himself, as he went inside.

The barmaid was a blue-lipped girl, ghostly pale and sickly thin, and was bent over changing a keg. Alexis asked her if he could see the food card. "Something more than bread,' he asked.

Alexis was handed the card and looked around the room. Some elderly patrons sat on barstools, flopped over cups of wines. Middle-aged couples in working-class garb were seated at far off round wooden tables where they were eating. Alexis stood at the bar, unsure. He felt eyes on him. With great unease, he held the food card and scanned it. What was the cheapest thing on the menu? He leaned over the bar and called to the barmaid, "Miss?...What is this dish...this, 'Rice-of-the-Sea?'"

The barmaid didn't answer him at first. He asked a few more times and eventually she stood from the keg, turned around, and said in a dry, unhappy voice, "It's just green string plants."

"Are they hot or cold?"

"Hot."

"They're hot? Okay, I'll have those, please…and some bread!"

The dish cost only a couple of thalers.

After ordering the string plants, the barmaid took the card and walked off towards the kitchen. Alexis settled on a barstool. Then he noticed the person who had been staring at him the whole time. He turned and looked to see a man seated on a barstool next to him. This man had unabashedly turned himself sideways in his stool to study Alexis, so Alexis turned to face the man and study him back.

It was a man was about fifty, quite fat. A heavy-breathing, stertorous specimen with a lazy eye and a birthmark atop his bald head. He sat there nursing himself with whiskey while dipping his hand into a hot greasy plate of potatoes and cheese. With this he nourished himself between sips of his drink. "Do excuse me," said the birthmarked man to Alexis in a high-flown voice, "You don't mind if I strike up a friendly conversation with you?"

"Not at all," Alexis replied, impressed with the man's neatly constructed phrases. Despite his slovenly face, Alexis found some charm in this man's mannerisms and his stately voice; and besides, Alexis would have welcomed any conversation in this new and strange city where he knew practically no one. He needed all the friends he could find.

The man kept turned on his stool so close to Alexis that his plump knees bumped Alexis' leg. Alexis side-stepped away and remained facing forward as he rested his elbows on the bar. He sifted through the lose coins in his pocket, and counted up enough to pay his meal.

Moments passed.

Alexis expected the birthmarked man to begin with his friendly conversation, but none came. The man remained silent. Alexis turned again to look at him. The man had finished his glass of whiskey and now sat moving his lips silently as though he were speaking, but he articulated nothing. Little wet breaths of air puffed out between his flabby lips. Alexis waited and waited. He looked him up and down. The port wine birthmark on the top of his head, he noticed, was shaped like a snail. Alexis also took note that it was the man's left eye which was wandering away from his face. And his clothes? Well, now there's something. Alexis got a good look at the man's coat. Though the underclothing appeared worn and dingy, his coat was magnificent – thick purple velvety greatcoat like a Dionysian robe that a king would wear, Its folds of fabric were tucked into the man's belly rolls, and this made the man look extremely puffed up; both because of the amount of fabric on the coat, as with the fact that the man was himself extremely large, and was stuffed into a little armed barstool. Alexis noticed the buttons were torn off of the coat, and he wondered why. Pieces of purplish thread hung frayed from where buttons should be sewn on.

"How about that earthquake today?" came suddenly from the birthmarked man, "We've never had one before in the Great City. Well at least not since I've been here, and I've been here fifty-three years. I was born at Our Lady's Hospital just down the street and one must wonder when suddenly there's an earthquake when there hasn't ever been one before. Things are coming unglued!" He dipped his fingers into his plate of cheese and potatoes and brought his dripping mess up to his mouth and rubbed a little of the grease on his puffy lips. "Keeps them soft!" he exclaimed with a smack of his mouth.

Just then, the barmaid came over with a steaming plate of stringy green plants. She set the plate in front of Alexis. The birthmarked man eyed this newly arrived plate with focused attention. Turning his eyebrows downward, he made a little wet choking sound, "Urp!" and then he burped out matter-of-factly, "Rice-of-the-Sea!"

Alexis turned away from the man and let him dissolve into the background. No more conversation for the moment. He now wished to devote himself entirely to his food. The odor of algae poured off his plate and began feeding himself. What happened to the bread? No matter. Alexis hoped for undisturbed peace until his stomach was filled.

"You look like a noble young fellow," the birthmarked man started up again, "You have an elegant neck. I can always tell how noble a person is by the elegance of his neck. I'm going to pay you a glass."

"Oh no!" Alexis turned to him with some string plants hanging out of his teeth, "Thank you but no. I have to keep my head clear. I still have to work tonight."

"Oh, you work nights? Not me. I used to when I was your age. It's a tough life."

"No, I don't work nights. Neither days. But that's got to change. I have to find a place. A place to work and a place to sleep. It's already very late...." And here Alexis made an effort to present honest eyes and a charming smile to this stranger – though he kept his mouth closed to hide the food in his teeth. He knew that the world gives good credit to handsome people with honest eyes and nice smiles; and knowing this – though the man with the lazy eye was probably just a drunkard and could offer no assistance – Alexis thought there could be a chance that he knew of a job for Alexis or a place he could sleep. And from one of either, Alexis could have benefited greatly.

"Mm, you're looking for a place to sleep?" asked the drunkard. He scooped up some more potatoes, sipped a little more whiskey, leaned forward and looked as though he was going to stumble out of his stool – though his puffed up coat kept him harnessed – and continued saying, "But I am not a drunkard, in case you're thinking that. I'm an official."

Alexis nodded and smiled.

"So you're looking for a place to sleep?" the official repeated himself.

"Yes indeed," Alexis responded.

"Have one little whiskey with me and we'll talk. I have an idea for you."

An idea? ... 'He has an idea for me!' ... "Okay," Alexis agreed. He knocked the bar with knuckles, and turned to face the official with brightened hopes. Finally things were coming together. The official ordered the whiskeys. While the barmaid was pouring them, Alexis' mind wandered. 'Now who is this official? Must be someone important if he has sleeping places to dole out like that. The secretary of the Prime Minister no doubt. He must know actresses. This tavern is the place where he eats before going to his private box at the cabaret. With a puffy velvet coat like that one must have... '

"...Two rooms on Garibaldi," the official interrupted, "I have two rooms there. My sister occupies one, but she pays me nothing; and besides that, she's a nuisance. I've been meaning to send her packing. She's probably there tonight. Oh, certainly she is!

"...Listen, go there with me. Now's a good time. With you there I can send her away more easily. It will be a good way to pressure her. Then you can stay with me for a bit...till you get your feet on the ground, so to speak."

"But you're going to kick your sister out?" Alexis was appalled.

"Oh, she has it coming. She takes up too much space – the entire room I provide for her plus half of my own room. Her clothes are everywhere. Now is that fair? She needs…well, she needs to learn. She has no respect. And she's messy too, a regular mess heap!...

"…So come with me and I'll send her away. Why should she have warmth and shelter when there are people who are cleaner and more respectful?" And here, the official drew his pudgy little finger in a circle in the air as if he were winding a clock, "…well, like yourself, respectable people who have nowhere to go… Answer me that!"

"Yet, she's your sister!" Alexis tone reflected not a little disgust for the conversation.

"Ech! We're speaking frankly, you and I, we drank whiskey together, didn't we? And you know blood is thinner than whiskey!"

Alexis stared at the remaining half dram of viscous golden liquor in his glass. He thought the better of repeating the night before, and so let the remainders of the glass remain; while he resumed eating his plate of green vegetables as well as the butter and bread the barmaid had finally brought over. He looked out the window of the tavern. Darkness had fallen. It was night already and another spring rain had begun. Alexis was full of food and didn't look forward to walking in search of lodgings and work on this night.

Alexis' gaze drifted over to the corner of the tavern where a family was eating together. A child in the highchair had a napkin stuffed in his shirt and was eating yams. Its mother had bobbed hair, and the father wore a plaid shirt awkwardly tucked into his trousers. Alexis read suffering on this father's face. The eldest son was seated with his back to the window, through which shone the light of a streetlamp outside. The son appeared taller than the other members of his family. His mother looked at him with a sorrowful face; and in reply to his words which were inaudible she said, "I know, Son. We'll go home soon. As soon as they say it's okay." The son bowed his head and continued to eat. The plaid shirted father then said, "Come on, Son, drink with your father. Drink with your father." And he lifted his glass.

Alexis gave a start when he heard these words. He blanched and turned away. He then looked back at lazy-eyed official beside him and said with urgency in his voice, "Shall we go now? I'd like to see this place of yours."

The barmaid brought the bill and Alexis paid his meal. The official paid his own, plus the whiskeys, and turned the change tray over to show that they'd paid, and the two left the tavern.

Outside, a cold rain fell diagonally down on the evening city, passing in front of the streetlamps where it made halos and a mist of bronze light. The official stepped out to the curb – a tuft of wet garbage was stuck to his shoe – Alexis followed behind him. The official pulled his greatcoat in close to his immense bulging body making movements as if to button it – as if he'd forgotten the buttons were torn off. Finally, he let the coat drop and it flopped and hung like a plush velvet carpet flung over him. The two walked up the street alongside the racing tramcars.

"Garibaldi is past the reservoir. We'll go this way." The two turned down a narrow side street. "And right here." They went down a passage. "And left here," the official led him out into a wide boulevard. "I'm stopping in here a minute." Alexis looked up. The two had arrived at some kind of missionary center. "I have to go in and get an address from someone. Wait here. Do you have something to write with?" … "Yes? Good." Alexis felt in his pocket and found the steel pen that Dominique had given him the night before at The Rook. He handed the pen to his friend.

"I'll be right back," the official said, cinching his coat. Alexis nodded in acknowledgment and stared up at the rain that came sinking down in a weighty mist, moistening his forehead and clothes. The official started off up the steps into the missionary center, stopping once near the door to scrape the garbage off his shoe and glance back at Alexis who awaited him in the driveway by the curb.

Alexis waited for a long time.

Tramcars passed by, clacking on the narrow rails. Streaks of light from their lit-up windows fluttered through the misty rain that coated the street in black wetness, shiny as a mirror.

Alexis kept waiting. Still no sign of the official.

After a while, the door to the missionary center opened and someone came out. Alexis peered through the darkness to see if it was the official, but it wasn't. It was a little man jingling a ring of keys. He wore grey felt pants and a red scarf in his shirt, and looked rather like a plucked weasel with his thin neck and a small squished head. His head reminded Alexis of an earlobe the way it was flat and bulbous. Upon this head, sat a droshky driver's hat.

"Heya, guy!" the plucked weasel yelled to Alexis, "Ya can't stay out here! We're closed for the night. I'm shutting the gate. Got'sta move!"

"The street too is closed?"

"Come on, move past the gate!"

"Yeah, but listen," Alexis asked the weasel, "have you see the official who came in a while ago to get an address?" Alexis asked.

"There aren't any officials comin' in here."

"Yes, there was…just a little while ago!"

"Nope. No officials, but you need to officially move!"

Alexis was confused.

"Maybe a man with a lazy eye, then?" he asked, "No? Well, how about someone with a birthmark on his head? No? Not that either? Perhaps someone who was a bit drunk? No? Drunk people don't come here? Okay. Maybe you can show me where the backdoor is, I want to find my friend. You have no backdoor? Okay, I'm leaving. But, you're sure, no backdoor? … Oh, why do I care!"

Thus, Alexis was shooed out of the driveway of the missionary center. The weasel padlocked a chain around the gate and Alexis found himself standing in an empty alley. Baffled by what had just happened, he walked away scuffing his feet on the wet pavement. "Oh, well," he exclaimed, "A steel pen lost!"

He came out of the alley and entered onto another boulevard and continued along staring at the ground, now scuffing his shoes in a forward direction, now spinning circles on the cement. "Was all this for a damned steel pen!" he demanded, "It wasn't so much of a pen. I would have given it to him. Christ!...all just a set-up. A dram of whiskey gained, a steel pen lost. And now where am I?" Alexis looked up. "Hey, what is this strange-looking building?"

Chapter VIII

"The House of Sevres"

"What a curious sight!" Alexis exclaimed, looking up and around him. He'd been turning circles on the boulevard in lament for the loss of his pen and the loss of his new friend. Meanwhile, the night's sky was dripping wet and the rain was dampening his shoulders. When he finally looked up, he saw there before him a large and strangely constructed ornamental building built of some sort of stucco. On each storey of the building, there were balconies enclosed with wooden bars. They looked like bird cages and jutted out over the street. The roof was made of copper and sloped up like a playground slide. It was corroded with peeling green patinae. On top of the roof, triangular sheets of metal stuck up like the ridges of a king's crown. Out front there was a little patch of yard with a headless plaster statue next to a large post with a sign nailed into it. The sign read: THE HOUSE OF SEVRES.

"The House of Sevres," he muttered while looking at the sign from the street. "Fancy that! I'll just have a look..." He took a few steps closer and stopped. He then resumed and crossed over the little patch of yard and walked right up to the building. The windows on the ground floor were alight with a warm lamp glow. He could hear someone was inside playing a violin. All had a rather inviting feel to it. Alexis looked back again at the sign and repeated the name to himself: "The House of Sevres... A beautiful word, no?...'Sevres'! Was not Sevres the king of Arcadia? Yes, obviously. Don't you remember, Alexis? It was in that fable you were read when you were young. It was that King Sevres who fought the barbarian invaders when they tried to conquer Arcadia. They wanted to create a new Eden, but King Sevres fought them off. Then, having preserved the peace in his land, the King had enormous walls built around the perimeter, gave generous portions of gold to the workers, allowed the non-workers to spend as much time as they pleased frolicking in the warm streams in the gardens while eating the sweet sugary fruits of the Arcadian trees, and afforded himself the time to pursue his favorite activities, thus devoting himself entirely to his harem. Yes, that was the great King Sevres!"

Curious to see what went on in this House of Sevres, Alexis walked around to the side to peek in some of the windows. All the windows, however, were fogged up on the inside and he could see nothing. The violin playing had ceased and now all he could hear were the sounds of tramcars passing down the boulevards. He waited until all the trams went by and then he again pressed his ear to the window. This time, he could hear someone was inside playing on a rather tinny piano. With his cheek, he felt the windowpane was warm and he was sure there was quite a bit of heat inside. He was starting to feel a chill. The night was advancing and the temperature was dropping rapidly. It was starting to feel like wintertime. Alexis puffed out a few breaths and watched it to see if his breath was visible. It was too dark to tell. He walked back around to the front of the building and headed up the steps. There was a light overhead on the porch. He stood beneath the light and watched the gnats flying around it. "Goodnight, gnats!" he said to them. There was then a crashing noise. The front door of the building suddenly opened and man came out onto the porch. He was smiling softly and didn't seem to notice Alexis standing there. He made a kind of warble sound like a bird and floated gracefully by, off down the steps, through the yard, and out into the boulevard. Alexis eyed him. The door he had come out of was still swinging. Once the man was well enough away. Alexis grabbed the swinging door and went inside.

Upon entering the House of Sevres, Alexis felt a rush of heat flush his face. He looked around to see himself standing in a sort of lobby furnished with brown carpeting and wooden benches. There was a counter at the far end. Some chairs were off to the side. The sound of the tinny piano was continually heard from a room behind one of the walls. The place smelled musky and fragrant, like an unusual type of incense. Beyond the counter, Alexis could see there was a kitchen where a tall, lanky black-skinned man was busy washing dishes. Alexis surveyed the lobby with a careful eye. His gaze then fell on a woman whom he hadn't noticed before, but who was standing at the counter watching him, and had been since the first moment he had entered.

This woman was called Madame Chaussepied – first name, Mathilde. She was middle-aged, quite fat and wore a yellow blouse. Her lips were painted dark pink. When Alexis' eyes met hers, she gave him a look that was by no means welcoming. As Alexis didn't know what kind of establishment this was, or whether or not he should even be there without an invitation, he was cautious; and, as this woman continued staring at him with icy expectation, he decided the most proper thing to do would be to outright ask for a job. Yet, before he could open his mouth, the fat woman addressed him:

"Sit there and wait!"

Alexis turned to look at where she was pointing. She was pointing at an empty wooden bench in the corner. Beside it was a potted geranium. After Alexis had seated himself, she inquired of him, "Are you mad, or are you here for pleasure?"

"Am I what?" he stammered, "here for pleasure?...I...I'm afraid I don't understand."

"I said," the fat woman raised her voice, "are you mad, or are you here for pleasure? One or the other?" She was growing more and more impatient. From the far wall came the tick-tock of a cuckoo clock.

"Well it's one or the other!" she barked, bending her plump elbows to rest her hands on her wide hips.

Alexis didn't answer.

"Oh! You just sit there and wait, you!"

So Alexis sat there and waited, and while he waited, he played with his watch band. 'Nice watch,' he thought to himself, 'I hope she gives me a job.' The fat woman ambled behind the counter and yelled down a corridor that ran back by the kitchen, "Delphine! ...Damn you, Delphine! Can't you usher people in? My legs are tired...I need to sit!"

"Madame," the black-skinned dishwasher came to inform her, "Miss Delphine is asleep."

"What?! Sleeping again? Well, wake her up!"

"Madame," the dishwasher replied, "she won't wake up, Madame."

"Oh bleh! Doesn't anyone see my legs are tired?" The fat woman walked back around the corner into the lobby and approached Alexis. "What do you want, boy?"

Alexis was stirred out of a trance. She stood impatiently. Alexis noticed she had a peculiar smell – like old dried flowers.

"Well?!"

"Oh…" He sat up, straightening his back. He arranged the collar of his shirt and fixed the yellow handkerchief in his pocket. "I'm looking for work."

"What kind of work?"

"Oh most anything…but not washing dishes or sweeping." That was not Alexis' kind of work.

"Not washing dishes or sweeping? You boy, you come in here and ask for a job and tell me you won't do this or that?!"

Pause.

"Well, you're lucky Delphine's asleep and I'm fed up, I need to sit down. Can you count money, boy?"

"Oh, I can count money!" he replied. Honestly though he didn't understand one bit about these sovereigns and thalers that are used in the Great City.

"You can count money, you say!…oh, you'd better not try anything funny. I'll keep my eye on you, watch out!"

"But I don't do things funny."

"What's your name, boy?"

"Alexis."

"Strange name. You're a foreigner. How many tens in a hundred?"

"Ten," he replied.

"Ten. Good. You can have a job. But you can't spend all day sleeping, and you have to shave that hair off your face." She then turned her body around and the bare white skin on her nape bulged from between her shirt straps like the poultry flesh of a chicken tied up in string. "Marick!" she shouted at the dishwasher. "Marick, come here!"

"Yes, Madame." The black-skinned dishwasher ran to her beckoning.

"Marick, what do you shave with?"

"A razor, Madame."

"Well, go fetch your razor. This boy needs a shave. He looks like some kind of squiggly rodent." She turned to Alexis, "It's like pubic hair you've got on your face."

The dishwasher disappeared a moment. Then he returned. "My razor, Madame. He glanced quickly at Alexis and then gave the razor to Madame Chaussepied.

"It's filthy!" she blurted out, "Marick, you shave with this?!" She handed it to Alexis. "Here, boy. Take this razor and go shave. There's a sink down the hall in the bathroom. Come back afterwards. You still want a job, don't you?"

"Yes, Madame," Alexis replied, "as long as I don't have to wash dishes or sweep."

"Oh!" she growled, "I'll keep my eye on you. Don't be foul!"

Alexis walked down the stoopy little hall to the bathroom where an old shriveled woman was selling soap from a plywood box slung over her shoulders with leather straps. Alexis bought a handful of froth and shaved himself in the mirror with Marick's razor.

Madame Chaussepied was waiting for him in he lobby when he returned from the bathroom with a clean-shaven face, smooth and shiny. "There, you look like a damned prince now!" she said in her hoarse voice, "Good that you got that pubic hair off your chin. Now I'll show you how to count money and use the cashbox. But once I show you, you'd better not ask me again because I don't like to be bothered. I like to sit 'cause my legs get tired. I like to sit and read my women's magazines, so don't bother me, you understand!...

"...And don't try anything either, you...what is your name? Alexis? Don't try anything, Alexis, 'cause I'll be watching you. And you so much as pocket a sou and I'll slap you to the woods!...

"...Marick!" she turned and yelled back into the kitchen, "Tell Delphine when she wakes up that she's got some dirty work to do! Ach, the wastrel!...

"...Okay Alexis, whenever Hippolyte comes down, you give him the money he asks for and do anything he says. Then you lock the box up and smile at people when they come in. It's not your job to greet people. Just smile at them. If anyone tries to attack you or makes a screaming ruckus, you ring the bell. This bell here. *Ding, ding!* See? You work day and night. We're open all night, you hear? Hippolyte will tell you when and where you can sleep."

Alexis listened to the instructions, nodded and obeyed. Still having no idea what kind of place this House of Sevres was or what purpose it served, he took the keys to the cashbox and took his station; and for the hours that followed, he patiently waited for people to enter so he could smile at them, he waited for Hippolyte to come down the stairs so he could give him money or whatever was asked for. Meanwhile Madame Chaussepied sat in the back and read her women's magazines.

In the late night, everything was quiet. Alexis was hunched over the cashbox drinking coffee to keep awake. Boredom and weariness began to overtake him. He jabbed his fingers into his eyelids to keep them from shutting. And it was then while he was more or less standing, more or less awake, that a girl popped up from out of nowhere – popped up right beside him. Alexis was startled into alertness. He turned to the girl.

The girl was Delphine. She was a soft and pale creature about the same age as Alexis. The skin on her face looked like a puddle of cream and her eyes were large and bright – bright as though she'd been asleep her whole life. She asked Alexis calmly, without concern, who he was. He explained that he had just been given a job. "Oh," she responded in a slow, sleepy voice. Her face then began to drift away. He summoned her attention and asked her what kind of place this House of Sevres was. She then became more loquacious and explained to him what the House of Sevres was. The ground floor where they were, she told him, served as the kitchen – the kitchen and the lobby. There was also a room in back with some tables and a little piano. Upstairs on the first floor, it was explained, there were numerous satin-upholstered rooms that served for the pleasures of opium. The floor above that, the second floor, had no satin upholstery. It was all wood and housed insane patients.

"Opium and madmen?" Alexis asked.

Delphine explained that before the House of Sevres was just an opium den. But since they had that extra floor that wasn't being used, the government sent some surplus mental cases to be housed; and in return for taking them in, the government paid Mathilde some extra subsidies and tax-breaks.

'I see,' Alexis told himself, making sense of it all, 'an opium den and a madhouse…that's why the Madame asked me when I first entered if I were mad or was here for pleasure.'

"So, where did you come from…?" Delphine was in the middle of asking when she was interrupted by a shuffling sound coming from the back room, followed by the scuffle of footsteps. She gave a start.

"Oh," she said in her listless voice, turning back to him. "I have to go back upstairs now. It was nice to meet you, Alexis." Alexis watched the way her black little nostrils dilated as she spoke, and the way her words came out through her soft lips like a whisper. She then turned and was gone – disappeared in much the same way as she had first appeared.

Night went on.

At three in the morning, while Alexis was flung over his cashbox trying to fight off sleep, Madame Chaussepied could be heard from behind the partition turning pages in her magazine. The downstairs was otherwise empty and quiet. It was then this Hippolyte character came walking down the stairs and approached Alexis.

"Eyes open!" he snapped, scratching his nail on the counter by where Alexis' arms were resting. "You hear me, guy…eyes open!" He stood tapping his arms with impatience. Alexis gave a jolt. "I need fifty sovereign and two bones." Alexis gave another jolt. "Fifty sovereigns and two bones!" With that, Hippolyte flipped his hand open and cocked his head to the side while awaiting his orders to be carried out. "Quick-like!" he snapped again. Alexis fumbled with the cashbox. He opened the lid and counted out ten five-sovereign coins and handed them to Hippolyte. "…And two bones," the latter demanded, but Alexis didn't know what a bone was. "What d'you mean, you don't know what a bone is?" … "Mathilde!" he yelled back to Madame Chaussepied behind the partition, "who did you hire here? Guy doesn't know what a bone is!"

"Ach!" she yelled back, "Don't bother me! I'm reading my women's magazines. Just show him what a bone is!"

"A bone," Hippolyte turned to Alexis and began explaining in a condescending voice, "is a pipe for the opium smokers upstairs. When they break a pipe, we sell them a new one. It's five sovereign and we throw in a half-gram of opium. We call that a 'bone'…a pipe and a half-gram of opium."

"But how should I have known what that is, 'a bone?'" Alexis asked in defense.

"You watch your place here, guy," Hippolyte snapped sharply, "…Uh huh! You don't know where you're standing. You slip and I'll shove you off packing faster than you can cinch your belt!"

"Ooh!" Alexis growled under is breath. 'The way he talks to me, I ought to….Doesn't he know who I am?!' Alexis prepared to fire himself up. He then sulked his shoulders, 'Oh, what's the use? Up, down, balance, no, balance, yes…how am I ever going to get to my minister's palace like this? It's as if they think I'm their pup!' All the while thinking this, he was busy weighing-up a piece of black tar opium on the brass scales next to the cashbox in order to give Hippolyte the 'bones' he had demanded. 'This Hippolyte is absolutely intolerable. I've got to have a strategy. All great men had to pull a stunt of some kind to first get to those high palace places. No one just came and gave them keys. That's not how the world works. No one just comes and gives you keys. You have to steal them!'

Alexis had finished weighing the opium and it was a few minutes after Hippolyte took it and left with his money, his bones and clipboard to go back upstairs, that Delphine came down again. She was crying.

"Why are you crying?"

She explained to Alexis that she had been upstairs in one of the rooms minding her own business. She was sitting on the cushions, smoking her opium and wanted to sleep, but a man wouldn't let her. He was putting his hands all over her and wouldn't let her sleep.

"Well, don't go back upstairs," Alexis advised her. "If you want to sleep, sleep down here somewhere."

"I *have* to go back upstairs," she replied. While she spoke, tears ran in streaks down her soft cheeks. "If I want to keep my job, I have to stay upstairs."

"Well, have the man thrown out, then," said Alexis, "I'll throw him out myself!"

"Oh no!" she replied with a voice of sudden worry, "and not you…you can't especially!…and anyway, he's a regular customer. If he wants to put his hands on me, I have to let him. …Oh, I have to let him!" Her crying increased and she was now choking on her tears.

It was just then that someone started coming down the stairs. Delphine wiped her eyes and stopped crying. The two stood silently side-by-side while the person approached. "Is it him?" Alexis whispered to Delphine. She looked at Alexis, shook her head and rubbed her nose and turned back to look at the man who was approaching.

He was a tall and gangly thin type, with an immense shiny forehead crowned with tufts of orange hair. He had pursed lips and giant round eyes framed by an excessive number of layers of eyelids. He approached Delphine and Alexis and cleared his throat. "Eh, hem!" He then addressed Alexis specifically... "Who are you?"

But before waiting for an answer he continued speaking in a lofty voice... "So you should know, I am the Superintendent of this building and I must inspect the building and its employees. You..." he leaned towards Alexis balancing on the balls of his feet in the obvious attempt to intimidate, "Can I see your papers?" He said this in a thin nasally voice and while he spoke, his chin swung back and forth like a pendulum.

"Papers?" Alexis fumbled.

"Let me look at your fingernails, make sure they're clean."

Alexis stretched out his hands to show the Superintendent.

The Superintendent pushed his hands away, "No, first let me see your papers. I will be taking them down to the foreign embassy to ensure that you are not a..." His voice faded out and seeped into the walls as Delphine pressed Alexis' shoulder and whispered into his ear, "Don't worry, Alexis, he's not a Superintendent. He's just one of the insane patients. I'll have to take him back upstairs." Her face turned and quiet words drifted out. "Come on, Rodney, I'm taking you back to your room," She turned around once more and whispered, "Bye for now, Alexis."

Alexis studied Delphine as she walked up the stairs holding the slender, imbecilic hand of Rodney. He watched her taught rump, her hips that swayed languidly back and forth in their feminine fashion as she climbed the steps; the tired dusty soles of her thin sandals revealing themselves each time a foot left a stair to take another step. He watched her until she was gone. 'What a woman!' he thought, 'A whole other species!' There was something gamey and bizarre about this Delphine that Alexis enjoyed immensely. She was not a child like those innkeepers' daughters he had met. Neither was she glossy and stainless like the two golden bells from Roussinia. There was nothing fashionable about her to hold her in the ranks of the Great City female populace, as he had seen in Sidonie, the girlfriend of Dominique. This Delphine was a raw creature of earthly femininity – like a mother dog birthing wet pups in the woods; or perhaps, more accurately, like a working-woman of the Lower East-End of the Great City…yet, whatever it was, it was wild and tempting, it was delicate and nourishing – her soft voice, the round forms of her body, the way it moved and swelled, the smell it carried, all of this remained in his mind and he thought of her, repeating her name over and again until sleep overtook him, seized him with force, and pinned him down mercilessly against the cashbox.

Rat-a-tat-tat!

The sound grew louder.

rat-a-tat-tat!!…rat-a-tat-tat!!

"Oh, Delphine…where are you? Please tell me. The lamps are eating the candles. Can't you see it? Delphine! Where are you? Tired-eyed Delphine, I can't find you! The eels are swimming in frozen puddles. It's all a mess and we're here with…" All of this and Alexis felt the sensation of cold metal pressed against his cheek. A stream of saliva ran down his lip. These sounds slowly dampened and he lifted himself up, both easily and with difficulty, as if he were a crane lifting a heavy lead weight. Upon rising, he saw the image of someone coming slowly into focus. Was it man or beast? Neither, it was Hippolyte! He was standing in front of Alexis tapping a pencil on the counter next to the cashbox: *"Rat-a-tat-tat!…rat-a-tat-tat!* …Wake up!"

"Oh da…" Alexis began, rubbing his eyes in confusion.

"Don't worry, guy," snickered Hippolyte, hovering over him, one arm akimbo, his free hand fluttering a pencil in speedy annoyance, "I stopped your clock two hours ago, so you're not in any danger of being paid for the time you've been asleep. Anyhow, gather yourself. It's the slow time of the day so you're off. Clock back in at nine tonight for a double and report to me immediately."

'I'm off work?' Alexis thought, 'But if I'm off work, why did he wake me up?!'

"Oh, and," Hippolyte continued, "before you leave…someone vomited on the floor in salon number seven upstairs. If you could clean it up…."

'Ooh!' Alexis began to fume, 'No sweeping or washing dishes…and no vomit, either!' He breathed deeply to avoid losing his temper, "All right," he said, biting his teeth, "Salon number seven. Vomit. back at nine. Report to you. Understood." And with that, Alexis was left alone standing by his cashbox. Hippolyte had gone off to scold a stray lunatic.

"Christ!" Alexis cursed to himself, "what's a man gotta do to feed himself in this world?!" He looked around himself and tapped the cashbox lid. "Am I the only one on this earth who must jump through such odious hoops to attain greatness? Christ, indeed!" And thus he stood for a long while, wrapping his knuckles on that cashbox with bitterness.

'Very well,' he told himself after he'd regained composure, 'Just this once, I'm going to play this Hippolyte's game. Tomorrow, however, mark my words – oh, who am I talking like? – no but tomorrow, Alexis, listen to me... Come tomorrow, you are an enemy of anyone or anything that stands in your way of greatness. Is that clear? You will be a servant to no one. Do you hear me, Alexis? If you are a great man, act the part...after this, I serve no one!' And with that he walked off to find a mop bucket to take with him upstairs to clean up the mess.

The opium den at the House of Sevres consisted of the entire first floor at the top of one flight of carpeted stairs. It being early in the day, there were few customers in the den; and most who were there lay motionless on the satin cushions or on the floor beneath the great concaved bay windows through which a cold sunshine came from outside. The hall smelled sweet and musty – body sweat mingled with spicy burning resins. Alexis carried the mop bucket past the rooms, while looking about with one eye raised curiously at the strange types of men he saw sprawled out here and there. "Salon number three...salon number four," he counted the rooms bitterly to himself as he marched down the hallway reading the numbered plaques above the doorways. "I've got a good mind to break that Hippolyte's teeth!"

It was then while passing salon number six, that Alexis' torment reached the limit. What he saw infuriated him and he could not pass it off with a puff of steam. Stopped frozen, he looked across the room at the figures occupying the far cushions beneath the bay windows. There lay Delphine, asleep in a dream. Her sandal had fallen from her bare bruised foot and her toes were digging into the satin between the pillows. There she lay flung about the cushions, haphazardly, her hip jutted upwards, her belly twisted inward, one of her breasts was pushed into the cushions and her chin was turned in towards it. From her mouth, a long draw of sleep-ridden breathing fluttered out. Then, came a cackling sound from someone beside her, followed by a hoarse phlegmy cough. Next to her, a man was sprawled out. He was unkempt, with black teeth and yellow skin and a sharply sloping forehead. He had narrow, half-closed orange eyes, and reclined pressing a long brass pipe to his mouth, drawing sips of smoke through the gapes between his cracked lips and stained teeth – and while he smoked, he cackled. When Alexis met this man's demonic gaze, the man's lids folded over and fluttered like the wings of a moth. He seemed as though about to drop and fall off the earth. Another sip of smoke, he puffed again and the stem of the pipe slipped off his dry mouth. He fumbled with it in his scrunched-up little right hand, while with his left, he fumbled with the drooping breast of the sleeping Delphine. Alexis watched it all. This man sprawled out pinching greedily her breast; then letting go, he slipped his hand away and moved it up underneath her torn and wrinkled dress where he clung to her, clung to the sloping flesh of her waist; and as he moved his hand down between the thighs, her hips grabbed his fingers like a vice.

With a quivering mop handle and a splash of fiery blood in the flesh of the face, Alexis stood in the doorway and trembled with unholy fury. Clenching his fist in an anvil block, he tossed his mop aside and leapt across the room. He came down upon the little man and seized his wrists and pinned his hands against the window. "Arg-glug!" the man gurgled out in a half-conscious exclamation of shock. The pipe slipped out of his spout-shaped mouth and fell upon the pillows on the floor, where it smouldered in the satin, burning the old dirty fabric. Alexis shook this little man while he pressed his hands fiercely against the foggy windowpanes. Nothing doing…the man was gone. He didn't react. All that was left of his yellow heap of flesh were flaps of quivering lips stained black with pockmarked opium, and those sallow waxy eyelids that fluttered, heaving bright orange irises farther backwards into his skull. A shiver ran through Alexis. He let go of his opponent's wrist and the man collapsed in a dead sleep upon the body of Delphine, who herself remained rising and falling in the arms of her own Morpheus, soundly breathing silent.

Alexis was both defeated and triumphant. He looked down on his opponent who lay like a dusty carpet on Delphine, desiring only to crush his heel into the man's little skull. "Shall I permit this woman such a withered blanket?" he spat on the yellow man's back while a fever mounted in his brain. Such sudden passion, so strange a feeling, Alexis remained there not a moment longer. It was evident there was only one thing he could do. One thing must be done! And with this realization, he turned and ran quickly out of the room, kicking aside the bucket of spilled soapy water in the doorway. He passed the salons of sleeping customers, ran down the stairs and over to his cashbox.

When he reached the cashbox, he knelt down before it. He looked left and right. No one else was around, except that he could hear Marick washing dishes in the back kitchen.

Crouched in fury, Alexis felt back in the crawlspace beneath the counter on which the cashbox was nailed down, and from that crawlspace he got a hold of his traveling sack. He had stashed it there the night before when he first came to work at the House of Sevres. He got hold of the sack, pulled it out, stood up and slung it over his shoulder. From the back kitchen, came the sounds of Marick splashing in the sink. He was whistling a snatch of a tune. Madame Chaussepied also could be heard somewhere not too far off turning the pages of a magazine. Last glance at the House of Sevres. With firm intentions, Alexis ran through the lobby and out the front door and headed off in the damp and grey, cold drizzling overcast gloom.

He crossed the East Canal and went up Garibaldi, counting paces. He turned right from there and headed into the Upper East-End. The wind was frigid on his face but he walked quickly and thus perspired and felt warm. He felt sweat on his shoulders. Why couldn't he find what he was looking for? He searched the same blocks for over an hour, tracking and backtracking the same narrow streets of the dismal East End of the city. Like a crow, he pinned dark eyes to each doorway; like a hound, he memorized his trail. He was not to be lost again this time. Now his path was clearly laid out for him.

Eventually, he saw a sign over the doorway on a decrepit building and found what he was looking for.

It was a pawnbroker's shop. Alexis walked up the steps and opened the door. The handle jingled a string of bells hanging from the knob. The central heat burned with gaseous odours in the tiny cluttered shop. Behind the counter with a glass case, stood a tall lanky man with mousy-brown hair. In his case, knives and neckties, rings and revolvers, were on display to be sold.

"What can I do for you?" the pawnbroker asked.

Alexis was out of breath. He stood over the case and heaved to catch his air. The sudden heat of the shop flushed him. He eyed a revolver in the case. "I need to get some money for these clothes," he told the pawnbroker, "I have a watch too."

The pawnbroker turned his head to the side and surveyed Alexis in the customary pawnbroker fashion to see what his story was and whether or not he should be dealt with. "Let's see what you've got."

Alexis took off his watch and set it on the glass case.

The pawnbroker inspected it. "Ten sovereign."

He had hoped for more. He took off his suit jacket.

"You'll need that," the pawnbroker said. "This is unusual cold weather were having…especially for this time of year. I've never seen it so cold after February. You'd be a fool to walk around without a jacket."

"It's alright," Alexis said, "I live close by. I have another at home. I must swing it, I need more than ten sovereign."

"Well, I'll give you thirteen altogether – for the watch and the jacket."

"And these too." Alexis opened his traveling sack and dumped his father's cotton shirts on top of the counter. The pawnbroker reached his hand out for them. "Wait!" Alexis exclaimed loudly, reaching into the pile of shirts. He pulled out the best one, a cream-colored one. He decided to change into that one and get rid of the one he was wearing. If he was going to keep only one shirt, it should be his best one. His forehead was itching from the warmth of the pawnshop. With fumbled and feverish movements, Alexis took off the faded blue shirt he was wearing and put on cream-colored one, taking care to transfer the yellow silk handkerchief his sister had given him into the pocket of the shirt he'd changed into. He couldn't part with the handkerchief!

"How much for all this?"

The pawnbroker inspected the shirts.

"Fifteen sovereign altogether," he said.

'That's not going to get me very far,' Alexis thought. He looked around, thinking. He tapped his fingers on the glass. He eyed the revolvers in the case – shiny metal. A fever boiled in his forehead. Blood swished and swirled… "Wait!" he cried out. He pushed his now-empty traveling sack across the counter into the hands of the pawnbroker. "And this too!"

"Hmm, an old sack." The pawnbroker inspected the stitching in the oilcloth, "It's seen better days. Seventeen altogether."

"Seventeen," Alexis repeated. The pawnbroker began to turn the sack inside out. Alexis suddenly remembered something was still inside. "Wait!" he exclaimed. He grabbed the sack from the pawnbroker and reached his hand in it. Stuffed in the bottom was a blue piece of folded-up paper. He took the paper out and stuck it in the pocket of his trousers. "I'll need this!"

"Fine, Fine," the pawnbroker said, "is that all?"

"Seventeen, you say? Can't you do nineteen for all this? That's a good watch, abalone dial. And the jacket must be worth more than three."

"I gave you ten alone for the watch. Seventeen is where I'm stopping."

"Wait a minute!" Alexis bent down with fury and unlaced his brown leather summer shoes. Beneath them, he had on a pair of dark green socks which he'd been wearing for some time. They were slightly damp from the puddles he'd walked through on the way to the pawnshop and the toes were crimped. He slapped the brown leather shoes on the counter. "And these too!"

"You really wanna part with the shoes?" the pawnbroker asked, "You're gonna to freeze your feet off. I've never seen such a quick turn in the weather. Only yesterday it was warm outside, but now, well it might even snow it's so unseasonably cold, you wouldn't even…"

"Yes, the shoes, too!" Alexis cut him off, mid-sentence.

The pawnbroker took a breath.

"I'll tell you what," he said, "normally for shoes in this condition I'd pay no more than two sovereign. But I'm gonna to give you three. That makes twenty sovereign for all."

"Twenty…twenty…twenty…twenty…" Alexis repeated looking left then right, then left then right, trying to pin down thoughts which were flying by him like hornets. His eyes darted around the pawnshop while he tapped with his fingers on the case.

"Just a second!" Alexis had a thought. He reached down and grabbed his feet and pulled off the damp dark-colored socks he'd been wearing. He slapped them next to the shoes on the counter.

"Old socks?" asked the pawnbroker, "you wanna freeze your feet off?"

"Socks aren't much good if you don't have shoes!"

"You gotta point," said the pawnbroker, "A half thaler for the socks." Alexis nodded and the pawnbroker threw the socks back into a bin behind him and turned back around and asked, "Is that all you wanna pawn?"

Alexis, who was busily grinding his teeth, now jumped a step back and with bulging eyes he clasped his hand protectively over the yellow silk handkerchief in the pocket of his cream-colored shirt. He had thought he saw the pawnbroker eyeing the handkerchief when he asked if that was all he wanted to pawn. Not the handkerchief! There was no way Alexis was going to part with the handkerchief!

"I take it that will be all," said the pawnbroker, settling things up. It was not difficult to observe that besides the sacred handkerchief which Alexis held clasped in desperation, the single cotton shirt from his father and the pair of trousers that originally went with the suit Viktor gave him, he had not a stitch left on him.

"That will be all then?" the pawnbroker asked again.

Alexis said nothing, but just stood there looking impatiently at the pawnbroker with bloodshot eyes as he waited for his money. The pawnbroker counted out a stack of coins on the counter. Alexis watched him with hungry avarice. Saliva glimmered on his lower lip. He kept at it, tapping the case, shifting his weight from his left bare foot to his right, the wet hems of his trousers brushed on the tops of his clammy bare feet.

"It's all here: twenty sovereign and a half thaler." The pawnbroker dropped the last coin on the stack. Alexis scooped up the money and turned to run out of the pawnshop.

"Wait a minute!" the pawnbroker yelled after him.

Alexis stopped as he was grabbing at the door. He turned around shivering, and looked with bulging red eyes at the pawnbroker. "What?!" he demanded with impatience.

"You forgot your ticket! You'll need this to claim your items."

Alexis ran back to the counter, grabbed the claim ticket, shoved it carelessly in any old pocket of his trousers, not caring one way or the other, and ran out of the pawnshop.

Outside, night had dropped from out of nowhere, and the wind was whipping through the dirty streets of the East End. A light hail was falling. Pebbles of ice hit the ground with a sound like gravel sliding on concrete. Alexis pinched the knees of his wet trousers and picked them up so the sopping wet hems wouldn't get caught under the soles of his bare feet as he walked; and like a drenched spider he traversed the back alleys and streets along the East Canal, stepping quickly to keep his feet from freezing on the cold concrete as he made his way through the neighborhood.

"Never liked that sack anyway," he mumbled to himself as he walked along. Ridges of bumps of cold grew on his bare skin. He rubbed his arms to keep warm. "Last shirt, last pair of pants…but a pocket full of money." He continuously grabbed for the wet cloth of his trousers to make sure the coins that were weighing them down were still there. "Twenty, twenty…twenty sovereign and a half thaler. Half tavern and a twenty salver." A light came from a little boat trolling on the East Canal. Alexis crossed the bridge and spat in the water below. He was almost there.

When he arrived back at the House of Sevres, customers were coming and going in a cloud of smoke. Oblivious to the cold and the oppressive hail that fell, the men who were leaving drifted like cotton beneath the porch light, going off into the shadows of the building's environs where they disappeared forever. Those entering marched in the front door sheltering their heads with their greasy dark coats the way bats hide beneath black scaly wings. In they went and the House of Sevres swallowed them up.

Alexis, mounted the steps hurriedly and pushed a wavering and dizzy customer aside to enter. In the lobby, a puddle grew around his feet as he stood surveying the environment. The sound of a broken violin being played came from a back room far off. The air was warm and smelled of burning opium. The new arrivals didn't wait to be greeted, but simply took to the carpeted stairs to go up to the den on the first floor. There seemed to be nobody working the cashbox. Neither Hippolyte nor Madame Chaussepied were anywhere in sight, though the latter, no doubt, was sitting behind the partition with her magazines.

Just then, Marick came out from the back kitchen carrying a bin stacked with dishes. He glanced at Alexis who stood like a trembling fortress with sopping clothes and bare feet, but didn't seem to make heads or tails of anything. He merely bared the yellow-tinged whites of his eyes at Alexis and then looked away. Alexis seemed to be deciding what to do. His thoughts belonged not even to himself. He reached down and wrung out the wet fabric of his trousers, and water ran in streaks down his calves.

"Alexis!" someone suddenly called out in a suppressed whisper. It was Delphine. She had popped up from out of nowhere and was now standing by the cashbox. She looked almost blankly at Alexis while her fingers slid lazily over the metal surface of the cashbox. Her other hand was playing with the fabric of the pocket in her apron. A hint of a smile passed over her face, but Alexis couldn't tell exactly what it meant. He stared firmly at her, while his muscles tensed up. He combed the water out of his hair, and with the other he felt the heavy bulge of metal coins in the pockets of his trousers. "Delphine!" he called out to her boldly, "Come with me!"

And off they went.

The two left the House of Sevres together and walked in the night along the banks of the East Canal. Hail was falling now in less abundance and soon it stopped altogether, and the clouds drifted away from the center of the sky allowing the moon to emerge to light their way. Delphine did not ask questions, she simply held Alexis' hand and walked sleepily along beside him. Numbness had eased the sting of cold on Alexis' bare feet. The torn wet frays of his trouser cuffs clung to his heels. The untied straps of Delphine's apron dragged behind her as she walked. Their way continued, and as it did, Alexis' earlier delirium and blind urgency vanished and gave way to an awareness of a happiness and a sense of the meaning of this heroic moment came over him. He walked erect like a soldier and led her, as he were the shepherd, off in the southward direction. They crossed slippery wooden bridges over the canal. He held her hand on through the neighborhood of rathskellers and midnight drinking rooms. Over the doorways of dilapidated opium dens hung cloudlets of smoke. From between the clusters of buildings, the banks of the river in the south could be seen. Across its shores twinkled the lights of the train terminals of the East Station. Alexis strides were great and his fortune chimed in his pockets as he walked.

Every now and again, Delphine would stop for a moment beneath one of the fizzling gas streetlamps on one of the side streets or along the East Canal; and she'd look up at him with her sleepy sheepish eyes the shape of slender moons. And the moonlight as well as the light of the lamps reflected in those glazed and glistening, sad eyes that looked up at him so trustingly. And she would squeeze his hand, or she wouldn't. Sometimes she let hers go limp. But always she continued walking beside him – silent, trusting, solemn, and distant.

The air warmed up enough so that no more hail came, but when it finally started to rain again, the weather showed no mercy and it showered heavily. The couple turned down a narrow passageway and took cover under an overhang. They stood close together. Delphine looked out with her wide eyes at the dirty water pouring off the rooftops, flowing in rivulets down the gutters. She looked out across the river that now stood majestically before them. Alexis too looked out. He then looked at Delphine. He felt power and greatness, greatness and numbness, numbness combined with the fresh-eyed tingles that accompany the realization of a dream. He looked at her face and she hung her head low. He looked back at the river.

"That the road to greatness should wear such an unexpected mask," he said aloud. With this, her head dropped even lower. The pinging of the rain sounded all around them. Beneath that overhang, she stood silently with an air of obedience; while he reached into the pockets of his wet trousers and took out his entire sum of money – the large precious silver- and gold-colored coins with serrated edges – amounting to twenty sovereign. He fumbled with the thin half thaler coin and it fell from his hand and rolled down a gutter. He held those twenty sovereigns in his palm and reached out to Delphine and dropped them into the pocket of her apron. She looked up when he did this, but it didn't seem as though she realized what he'd done. Certainly she felt the weight in her pocket. She looked out at the glimpse of skyline beyond the passageway with childish eyes, as though she were startled by a strange noise. Then, with a sweep of silence, the rain stopped completely. A gust of wind blew with a howl through the passageway. Once it passed, all was still and the only sounds left were made by the residual water dripping down the drainpipes and the trickling of neat little creaks down the cracks in the streets. Alexis searched for Delphine's hand and led her off away from the overhang; and the two continued hand-in-hand through the old streets of the city. Their feet stepped sifting through garbage – wet newspapers, pigeon bones…all but broken glass. He who had no shoes, and she whose soles were thin, felt the wetness and gritty textures of the cobblestones upon their arches and toes no longer clopping like horses hoofs, but with footsteps dampened and silent.

As they neared a large square, Delphine stopped yet again and looked up at Alexis with her soft pearl-like face and moonlike eyes. He looked back at her and read in her gaze, now affection, now disgust; now submission, now distrust; and not knowing how to react, he bent towards her here. He leaned to her giving none of this any thought. Now so close that he could feel heat coming from her skin, with the edge of his finger, he stroked her cheek; and this-upon, the two fell together. Two breathless mouths collapsed in a kiss.

Sometimes as a boy, Alexis kept mirabelle plums in a net in the icy stream by his house to keep them fresh. And so at times when he would awaken with hunger in the morning, he would rush outside to eat one before washing his teeth. The fresh cold sweet taste of the plums would combine with the foul taste of morning in his mouth; and eating the fruit would produce a pleasantly disgusting clammy sensation. This was like Delphine's kiss. The first he'd had. Yet Delphine was a woman, not a plum, and so it was altogether different.

After they kissed, they held each other for a moment. When they ended the embrace, they continued walking together through the narrow streets of the dark neighborhood. Silently. Each seemingly cradling each own's thoughts. No longer holding hands. He had lost her hand. After a while, Alexis looked up and realized Delphine was gone.

"She's gone? … But where has she gone? … What happened?!" He asked himself these and other questions as he wandered looking for her here and there in the narrow lanes and dark streets surrounding the square, but nothing doing – she was gone, sure enough. Gone as if she awoke in her dreams or fluttered off into the eaves in his. Alexis raised his arms and then let them fall in despair. He looked around the dark passageway, and then suddenly he heard the sound of footsteps as someone approached. He turned his head around and saw a figure emerging from the mist. But it was not Delphine. It was a man carrying a leather satchel concealing a wine bottle. He wore a long black frockcoat. Alexis backed into a doorway and let him pass.

The cold rain resumed falling. A streetlamp flickered and burned out. A confused and distraught Alexis stood alone and shivered in the middle of the empty passageway. He wrung the water out his clothes that were in complete shambles. He stuffed his wet yellow handkerchief deep in his shirt pocket so it would not get lost. Something was stuck in his foot. He thought it might be broken glass, but there was no glass. It was merely a pebble. He picked it out of the waterlogged skin and then silently and gloomily, he walked off back in the direction from which he had come – back when he had been with Delphine.

It was late when he finally returned to the House of Sevres. He didn't know why he returned or what he wanted. Perhaps he just needed to sleep. A long dreamless sleep to help him forget. He walked up the porch not paying attention to the people coming or going. His body drooped as he dragged it along in its new meekness and tired worn clothes.

When he entered, a gust of heat fell on his skin – not pleasantly; he had been numb through his pores – now that numbness turned to hot prickling itchiness.

'Is that Hippolyte?' No, it was Madame Chaussepied; she was standing alone at the counter by the cashbox. "Has Delphine come back?" he asked, barely raising his eyes to the one he was addressing. He didn't expect a positive answer and so his tone was lifeless and there was little hope in his voice and posture. He hung there in the room for a moment. Suddenly, as though he had fallen asleep and was startled awake, he jerked. "Uh?" He looked around the lobby with his bloodshot eyes. There was no one besides Madame Chaussepied in the room, though Marick could be heard as usual in the back kitchen, splashing in the sink and whistling a discordant tune.

"Well imagine *you* coming back here!" Madame Chaussepied snapped at Alexis. She caustically slapped her rolled-up magazine on the cashbox and began chirping in an overloud voice, "No, Delphine isn't here…if it's any of your business!"

Maybe she didn't abandon him in the street after all. Suddenly a new hope crept into Alexis. 'She isn't here? ... Oh!' Maybe she wandered off by accident and got lost. Maybe she had been stolen! Maybe she hadn't abandoned him after all. Maybe she fell while the two were walking and knocked herself unconscious. She fell asleep in the gutter, is more likely. After all, she was so tired! Alexis chewed on his lip with his incisors. The kiss with Delphine had aggravated the lump where he had cut himself – 'oh, it seems so long ago!' It itched horribly in the sweltering heat of the room.

Alexis' surveyed the lobby of the House of Sevres. How wet and weary he was. If only he could dry himself in the restroom; buy a handful of froth from the soap vendor to clean himself. He looked towards the corridor leading off to the restroom. There, far of on the floor, lay a single sandal. It had a broken strap and a thin, worn-out sole and was dripping wet. A puddle of water gathered around it on the wooden floor.

"Oh," Alexis turned back to Madame Chaussepied and asked abjectly, "She's here, isn't she?"

Madame Chaussepied tapped her plump elbow with her fingers.

"She's here, but she doesn't want to see you."

"I see."

Alexis let his head drop completely and remain bowed so his neck looked like that of a bedraggled animal sipping murky water from a trough; whereupon, he began walking slowly towards the corridor, towards where the slipper lay in the puddle of rainwater. He probably just wanted to clean himself up in the restroom. Oh, he had not even the money now to buy soap froth...!

"Marick!" Madame Chaussepied suddenly yelled with great alarm into the kitchen. Alexis stopped dead in his tracks.

"Yes, Madame?" Marick appeared obediently from behind the partition. Madame Chaussepied didn't give him further orders, but rather – as if satisfied with her sudden reinforcement – turned back around to readdress Alexis.

"I said," she repeated in a wrathful voice, "she doesn't want to see you."

That's fine. Alexis did not need anything. Never mind about the soap, about the sandal, or about whoever might be down that corridor. There was no more reason for anything and he made no effort to move. He simply remained there in the lobby standing in inertia. Madame Chaussepied, meanwhile keeping her eyes on him, huffed and shook her head. She reached in her apron and took her ring of keys out. She put a key in the cashbox, opened the lid and pulled out a thick brown envelope. She shut the cashbox, locked it, and then walked around the counter and handed the envelope to Alexis.

"Here."

"What is this?"

"It's from her." She shoved the envelope into his hands. "Now go and find your way. No more working the cashbox. You're done here. I already paid you yesterday for the hours you worked already."

Alexis looked up at her.

"So go on!" she waved her hand. "Find your way!"

Alexis turned around and left. Wearily, with sagging eyes, he left the House of Sevres, and walked out into the darkness, off into the cold, drizzling streets.

"Well they skinned their dog...a few more bones to add to the pile...some kind of other...may as well be broken glass...in some city, birds are flying over..." Alexis wandered muttering disjointed phrases while drops of cold fever beaded up on his forehead. He no longer pinched his trousers at the knees to hold the hems from catching under the soles of his feet as he walked, and now the fabric was well torn and mud-caked and stuck to his heels. He walked up along the East Canal while wringing water out of his hair. It dripped into his eyes and made them sting. In one hand, he clutched the wet envelope Madame Chaussepied had given him. After few blocks he stopped. "What the hell am I doing?"

Stopped beneath a streetlamp, he stood in the gutter with his bare feet submerged in the rivulet of water running into the sewer grate. A constant dull drizzle drifted down. A mist rose over the rundown rooftops of the Upper East-End. He tore open the envelope and sifted through the contents. It contained twenty one-sovereign coins. Or he thought it did. He counted them. There were only eighteen. It also contained a note. Some water had seeped through the envelope and the creamy paper was damp. He had to peel it apart gently to keep it from tearing. The ink had run. He leaned against the coal black lamppost, which smeared his sopping light-colored shirt with dark grease.

He began to read the note.

"What a disaster!" It was quite obvious that Delphine hadn't written very many. The handwriting was like chicken-scratch. There were no capital letters, almost all the words were misspelled and there was no punctuation. The general idea of the message, if logically ordered, would have followed something like this: "Good Alexis…sneak away…sneak far, far away…you are better than this place…I would say the same whether I loved you or loved you not… you cannot save me, so save yourself…" and then something about the money.

Alexis folded up the soggy note and tucked it back inside the wet brown envelope which still contained the eighteen sovereign coins. He then left his lamppost and started off back in the direction he had come from – back towards the House of Sevres.

"It's throwing nothing away, Alexis," he mumbled on his way, "It's a spin of the wheel. Chancing nothing for all…or else all for something, anyway it will be done…and if 'twere done when 'tis done, let that be the be-all and the end-all…here."

When he returned this next time to the House of Sevres, he seemed to be more aware of his surroundings. He now noticed the people going in and out of the building. They drifted beneath the porch light with placid movements, lint-like in their drunken sleepy states. Alexis, in contrast, felt heavy and sunken. He thumped up the steps and stood at the front door for a moment. "It's just a spin of the wheel," he repeated again to himself. Taking another step forward, he tore a long strip of fabric from the hem of his trousers that had gotten snagged on his toe after catching a splinter of wood on the porch. He pushed the door open.

Inside, Marick and Madame Chaussepied were standing at the counter by the cashbox. Alexis entered and looked at the two of them. Marick feigned a blank expression, but then looked away; while Madame Chaussepied cast her eyes at Alexis with anger and annoyance. Yet, before she could open her mouth to ask why he'd come back, Alexis stepped forward and tossed the envelope onto the counter. It hit the cashbox and slid off, falling to the floor. The envelope burst open and the coins rolled off in all directions. There was then silence.

Alexis looked at Marick, then back at Madame Chaussepied. She said nothing, just kept staring while her bosom heaved. Alexis took his gaze off the two of them and looked at the money on the floor while the final coin turned a last circle and the toppled on its face. Tails. Alexis' eyes moved to the corridor. That sandal that had been lying on the floor the last time he had come was no longer there. There was still the puddle of water where it had been. Alexis stared at that corridor for many moments. He trembled with feverish confusion. He looked back at his money lying on the floor. 'Am I really going to get down before these odious people to gather silly coins?' he asked himself, 'Certainly I am not.' Then he said through his lips which were curled up in caustic malice, "Certainly I am not – hear me now!" He then spat at the both of them, turned around and walked out.

Chapter IX

"The Ashes and the Ardor" – decent into the basement...

"A spin of the wheel," he repeated to himself as he walked towards the river, "A spin of the wheel, and we landed on night. A lonesome night, alone in rags." ... "Alone in rags, and such..." ...his words went on as such and such, mumbling again and again... "...a spin of the wheel...spin of the wheel...."

To his consolation, the rain stopped falling and the air began to warm as the night advanced. The sky too completely cleared and the moon gleamed like a silver coin in the darkness. When he came to a bridge crossing the river, he looked out at the lights of the East Station glimmering on the other side. He couldn't decide what to do. He started off across the bridge and stopped halfway to look down at the river.

"A spin of the wheel." And the river waves lapped. "Character is the sum of a man's actions. One word, five steps, a toss of gold, a piece of pride, and that's who you are." ... "I threw away all that I had. What did that amount to?" ... "She never did pay me yesterday, but I threw away all I had. Did that amount to greatness? Certainly not. Not what I had." As his thoughts drifted on like this, he himself drifted on. He felt everything distorted, frayed and truncated. His ideas seemed drunk. Drunk and sleepless and beyond quelling, he yearned for clear thoughts. Standing on the edge of the bridge, he looked down at the dark river flowing rapidly far below. The moon glimmered on the peaks of rocks far off on the banks. They looked like whitecaps – rather, like wet teeth set in the black gums of a canine. He yearned for those sharp rocks jutting up to cut through the fog in his head. Below where he stood, there was only darkness. A black abyss to swallow all. He took a deep breath, looked deep into the black river, closed his blurry eyes and turned around to face the other way. He then leaned back, arching his back on the railing.

"Empty!" he said aloud. He leaned forward over the blank rails where a tram car would eventually come to pass. He crouched down. He dug his hands through his trouser pockets. "Completely empty!" The storm had torn everything from them. No, wait… There was something. Stuck in thready lining of a waterlogged pocket, he found a little scrap of paper. It was damp but he managed to peel the leaves of paper apart and read it. It was a ticket of some kind – a little stub with some numbers stamped on it. "Hmm…what is this for?" Without another thought, he rolled the ticket into a little ball, turned and tossed it off the bridge into the river.

"Ah…!" he let out a sigh, dropped his head back and looked at the moon. "Oh Moon, how peacefully you gaze down on our turbulent earth!" … "*Our*," he repeated, letting that single syllable float in his hollow cheeks, "why *our*?" … "who is this *our*?" … "and how could it be gone?!" He searched through his pockets again. "It couldn't have fallen out!" Oh, no. It hadn't. It had been there all along. He found it. It had been in his back pocket. He forgot to look there.

From the back pocket of his trousers, he pulled out the blue folded-up note and peeled the damp leaves apart. The wet paper tore at the creases yet the address was fully legible when Alexis pieced the scraps together. It was the paper upon which Dominique had written his address on couple nights back at The Rook. Fortunately, he hadn't lost it.

DOMINIQUE SO-AND-SO

31 STRATSNOY BOULEVARD

He read the address over again, memorized it, and returned the torn scraps of paper to the damp pocket of his soiled trousers.

"What is he going to think when he sees me?" he wondered, "I used to be dressed like a prince. He'll mistake me for a beggar. He'll get the wrong idea and...wait! I am a beggar, aren't I? I'm no prince anymore. If I'm lucky, he'll take me on as a servant. If that's too honored a position, maybe he'll give me a job as a servant for the servants. I'll iron aprons for the ministers' maids. Is that lowly enough for a wet and dirty man with no shoes and socks and no money? Well, I ask? What is that, a seagull? No, it's nothing. Some wet garbage is all." Alexis wandered back across the bridge and walked west along the north bank of river and crossed over from the third district to the first. He no longer paid any notice to the fact he was barefoot, walking on a cold and dirty street. He had somehow grown used to it and it seemed now even an appropriate station for him.

"All earthly delights the world can conceive...an address in my pocket, an arm in my sleeve...all earthly worlds, delights can conceive...why won't anyone look at me?!"

It was true, the passers-by all walked with averted eyes when they passed Alexis on the street.

"They think I'm a bum. They think I'll ask them for money. Or, at least they think I'll transmit the germs of a contaminated life by way of my singular gaze. Oh well, they're Great City people. They're as crazy as anything."

"Stranger!" he called out to one passer-by, "Do you know where Stratsnoy Boulevard is?" But the passer-by answered him not. He pulled the lady he was walking with close to his side and continued on quickly, disappearing in the fog.

"Never mind!" Alexis shouted back at him, "I'll find it on my own!"

A little farther up, he came to a hospital. OUR LADY'S HOSPITAL, the sign read. He remembered then the fat official with the lazy eye; and that made him think of the steel pen he'd lost. If only he still had that pen, he could probably trade it for some string plants. He felt a hollowness biting at the lining of his flimsy stomach.

Now he was standing at the widest point of the river. Not far off, there was an immense suspension bridge with giant steel poles. Great Bridge! He decided to have a closer look. Maybe he would cross it. What was the city like on the other side of the river, he wondered. Had he ever gone that way?

After climbing the circular stairs, he reached the elevated walkway that led across the massive bridge and he began to cross it. The view looked out high over the city. On the walkway of the bridge high up he turned a slow circle on the balls of his scraped and dirty feet as the wind whipped through his wet shirt and trousers, chilling his skin beneath. In all four directions, he could see an endless sea of sparkling lights stretching to a barely discernable horizon. "So this is why they call it the Great City," he muttered to himself, "It goes on forever."

And while looking out over the illuminated metropolis as vast as a galaxy of stars, he whispered in a voice of deep melancholy. "And who am I?" ... "After all, who am I amongst all of this?" "All these millions of people trying for greatness. And who, after all, am I?" He lowered his head into a sea of grief and broken dreams and continued on across the suspension bridge. Once on the other side, he descended the circular stairs and came to street-level. He walked over the tram station with the thought in mind that there he might find a map of the city posted up. What would a map serve? Lead him where? He walked a wayward weave beneath the bridge in the direction of the tram stop. It was then he saw a most curious structure. There off to the side of the bridge's base, was a kind of basilica – a small palace of sorts with onion domed spires bound by colonnades. There were about five domes in all, and each were patterned with mosaics of colored tiles and tipped with eight-pronged crosses. The moon cast its beams on the crosses and they sparkled of gold. The moonlight on the domes sparkled with violet light and illustrious hues of yellow, orange and emerald green. Alexis stood in the brick square and looked at this strange palace trying to divine its purpose. He drew a clue from a large billboard that was erected next to it. The billboard stood in front of some abandoned buildings – buildings with broken windows. Alexis studied the billboard while a long chain of tramcars zipped high overhead across the mighty bridge above.

Was it an advertisement? A religious poster? The billboard featured a large illustration depicting four gaunt men walking in a barren landscape. They wore earth-colored robes, were barefoot and had shaven heads. Three of the men were following a forth. Alexis assumed that this forth man, the leader, was a prophet of sorts, and those following behind were his disciples. Above the heads of the men, words were written in an unknown language, in a strange alphabet – nothing Alexis could read. A light from the onion-domed palace shone faintly on the billboard. The upper corner of the illustration was peeling off and it curled over.

"I am like he," Alexis muttered aloud as he studied the prophet on the billboard, "I too am barefooted. I too am gaunt. Barefooted and gaunt..." He pinched the skin on his belly, "…but my stomach is not used to being so barren." He turned around and looked behind him to the shadows, the cached area beneath the suspension bridge. A noise came from some garbage cans where stray cats were hunting for scraps of food. "…And I look behind me and see no disciples. No one follows me. I walk barefoot alone. And I am headed nowhere. Oh, how I have been deceived!" Alexis sat down on a cinderblock in the palace square, beneath the billboard, and put his head in his hands. He studied the darkness with closed eyes. When he opened them, he again looked at the illustration. He remarked that those men had been illustrated by the artist to appear both brave and broken. "Brave and broken," he said aloud, "Courageous men know suffering." And when he said this, a pleasant thought joined the gallery of miseries in his soul. "Yet, I am just as strong. My feet too are bare. They know what it is to suffer. I can suffer like him and I can lead like him. And that prophet is not young. It took him time to earn those disciples. I too can be brave and earn my disciples. I will be even a greater prophet than he!" And so he picked himself up, "I'll show this barren landscape that I can wear it out. I can wear the world out fine!" A smile passed across his face, "By the time I finish, I will reign atop a pedestal of my own building. Yes, I can see it perfectly! I will live and suffer and lead and I will wear the world out!" He clasped his hands together and smiled a smile rich in contentment. "I wonder what that domed house is anyway. Could it be a church? It could be anything, really. For all I know, it could be snow! Ha-ha-ha! … Oh, I'd better keep on, my feet are freezing me!"

And with that, Alexis got up off the cinderblock and walked away from the billboard, away from the onion-domed palace, away from the river. He followed alongside the tram tracks running south beneath the arterial of the suspension bridge and lurched along through the rundown streets of the fifth district of the Great City.

The night was painted dark grey. Street after street presented nothing but textile factories, barred windows and fenced-in loading docks. Empty containers used to transport fabrics lay stacked up on the curbs. "Maybe I'll find some socks," he told himself, sifting through some wet mildew-covered fabrics that were discarded in an alley. He walked on through the abandoned streets. His bare feet were bruised and he was starving. With not much energy left to walk, he accosted a bum who was sleeping in newspapers on a steaming grate. 'Maybe he'll talk to me,' Alexis thought, 'he can't have too much pride to give directions to a traveling man down on his luck.'

"Stranger…" Alexis tried to rouse him.

The bum coughed, and pulled his newspapers over his dingy body.

"Please, stranger," Alexis asked again, "can you tell me where Stratsnoy Boulevard is? I'm looking for Stratsnoy Boulevard."

The bum sat up, looked at Alexis, and jerked his thumb over his shoulder... "Two or three streets back that way."

"Thank you," Alexis replied in a grim tone. Then he added quietly, "...and goodnight."

"Yeah," responded the bum as he leaned back and covered his legs with the newspapers. Then he coughed out in a mumble, "It's the big street...back that way."

Alexis said once more "Thank you" and left the bum to sleep in his cloud of steam and wet papers and turned the corner, heading off in the direction he was told to go in.

Sure enough, three blocks later, there was a big street called Stratsnoy. Alexis looked at the numbered signs above the doorways. "Nineteen...twenty-one...twenty-three...this isn't such a magical neighborhood," Alexis observed, "Dominique said things sparkled where he lived. I see nothing sparkling. Everything's the color of rusted tin. Oh well, nothing can get worse. If Dominique has even a blanket of newspapers to offer me, I'll be grateful. More than grateful...twenty-five...twenty-seven...twenty-nine..."

Alexis stopped outside number thirty-one. It was a soot-covered building of red bricks. The doorway dropped below street-level. A squalid staircase led down to the door obscured by shadows. Alexis started walking down the stairs. A family of mice was nesting in a crack at the foot of the door. Some other kind of vermin scurried away when he almost stepped on it with his bare feet. He could hear roaches chirping in the walls. Alexis made a fist and knocked hard on the door. The door was hollow metal and it resonated when he pounded on it. "Dominique sure lives in a slum," he mumbled to himself.

Alexis knocked again and waited. No one answered. Obviously, Dominique wasn't in. Alexis dreaded the thought of going back out into the streets with his filthy wet clothes, his tired unprotected feet and his empty pockets. 'Back out into the night to find a grate to sleep on,' he thought. Just when he was about to turn around and go back up the steps, however, somebody opened the door.

It was a little man who opened the door. He had clouded eyes and soot stains on his face. He stood in the crack and looked at Alexis with a spooked expression. Alexis looked back at him, and the little man spun around and ran away, leaving the door ajar.

Alexis pushed the door fully open and entered. 'Strange looking man,' he thought, 'Dominique's servant?' He walked through the dismal corridor that led to a pitch-black, musty-smelling staircase that led farther down underground into a basement. He could hear a faint sound coming from far back in the corridor – like someone shoveling coal. As he descended in the darkness, he held tight the railing, taking care not to stumble. So dark it was, so tired and dizzy was he.

At the foot of the stairs, the corridor continued. It was lit by a single bare bulb that buzzed and flickered. Alexis' eyes darted around. At about halfway down the corridor he could see two doors, one on either side, both stood wide open. He approached the doors and stopped. He looked into the room on the left. What he saw was bewildering. There was an immense room with sooty black walls. In it, there were no windows. All the light was coming from the center of the room where a furnace was burning, erupting blue flames. Scattered about the room were long wooden tables; and gathered at these tables were men – roughly twenty-six of them. They were a disheveled group – all with ugly, worn-out faces. They stood hunched over the tables kneading dough. The only one who wasn't kneading dough was a gaunt creature with blistered arms and a sunken face who stood hunched over the furnace, where he slid pans of dough into the flames to cook. And so they stood, as if in a trance, kneading and kneading, shoveling and shoveling. Alexis watched on, studying their faces. He recognized one of them to be the little man who had opened the door for him; but all were strangers. Dominique wasn't among them. "Fancy these are his roommates. He must be farther down." Alexis backed out of the furnace room, thinking to continue on to the end of the dark corridor; but when he turned around, he stumbled upon another strange sight. What he saw in the room facing the one he'd first entered was even more bizarre. An office with papers everywhere. A dingy light bulb hanging on a string overhead. Flies buzzing around it. The smell of old stale coffee. Seated at a desk was a fat man in suspenders with a cigar in his mouth. He was at work pulling stockings up on the leg of a tall, buxom, middle-aged blonde woman. Her high-heeled foot rested on the seat of his chair, in front of his crotch. And as he puffed on his cigar and pulled up her stockings, he slapped her pale thigh, and the flesh of it quivered. Alexis glanced around the room. There were piles of stockings and pantyhose everywhere.

It was then while Alexis was glancing around the office, the fat stocking-maker noticed him watching from the doorway. With an angry face he turned and shouted through his cigar, "What do you want, guy?!"

Alexis took a breath and answered, "I'm looking for Dominique." That was all. He was not in the mood to offer further explanation.

"Do I look like a goddamned Dominique?!" responded the stocking-maker, "Damned if I do!"

Alexis then heard snickering behind his back. He turned around and noticed the dough-kneaders were all bunched up in the doorway across the corridor, eavesdropping on the situation between Alexis and the stocking-maker – all the while snickering behind his back. Alexis turned around to show his annoyance at their behavior, and each time, they stopped snickering and started whistling innocently. As they whistled, they looked at the ceiling and rolled their heads around on their shoulders. The stocking-maker was also obviously annoyed at the snickering and whistling and when they persisted in this behavior, he stood up (setting the tall blonde's leg aside) and walked over to the doorway, brushed Alexis to the side, and lunged across the corridor to swat the gallery of sooty-faced dough-kneaders. "Get back to work, you scoundrels!" he shouted at them, whereupon they scurried off to their furnace like the roaches in the walls.

Relieved of this nuisance, Alexis turned back to the stocking-maker, once the latter was seated again in his chair with the blonde woman's foot once again in his lap... "I'm looking for someone named Dominique. He said his address was thirty-one Stratsnoy Boulevard. That is..."

"Well, that's your problem right there!" the stocking-maker broke in, cutting him off mid-sentence, "This is thirty-one Stratsnoy *Avenue*! Stratsnoy *Boulevard* is in the seventh district! You're in the fifth now. Wrong place, guy!"

Alexis inhaled tiredly and exhaled wearily, preparing to turn around and set off again. The stocking-maker, who by now seemed to have lost all interest in Alexis, returned his full attention the slender leg of the blonde. With his hands gripped around her calf, he slid down the stocking he had just put on, and threw it across the office into one of the many piles.

"Are you a stocking-maker?" Alexis asked suddenly.

The fat man turned to Alexis, slid his chair back and shouted, "Do I look like a goddamned stocking-maker?! Do you want to get smacked in the face?!" Just then he grabbed an object of some kind off his desk and hurled it past Alexis into the corridor. It was apparent he was aiming at a sooty-faced dough-kneader who had come back behind Alexis to snicker. The fat man looked back at Alexis...

"I'm the boss here. And those dirty rogues are my workers."

"What are they working at?" Alexis asked.

"Damn, guy! Can't you see I have a lady here? You came at the wrong time. Anyway, it must be midnight. What do you want?"

"Well sir, I'm sorry...but you can see I'm dressed in rags and have no shoes or socks. But, believe me, I'm not a beggar. My clothes were stolen, and my money too. And now I need a place to sleep and some work. Can you offer me work? I'll do anything, I don't care what the job entails. I'll even wash dishes. Anything!"

"Listen, crumpet," the boss turned to his lady-friend, "Go on for now. I'm going to talk to this guy...what are you called?" he asked, turning back to Alexis.

"Alexis, sir...I'm called Alexis. What are you called?"

"Boss," the boss replied, "but you don't call me, I call you. This here's the Fifth Central Bread Production Plant. I'll be honest, it's not the nicest job and it only pays one sovereign a week. Starting out, you get the dirtiest work – sweeping ashes out of the furnace."

"And to sleep?" Alexis asked.

"There are bunks. All the men sleep in the same room. I don't advance anything. You get one bread roll a day. Eat two and I kick you to the curb. You'll get a bunk. Wash your linen in the sink. Oh, and watch out for the other men. They're all a bunch of rogues. But you've got nothing to steal, so that's not a problem. Next week when you get paid, buy yourself some shoes and socks.

Thus, for some time, Alexis worked, slept and slaved away in the ashes at the Fifth Central Bread Production Plant in the Great City. His work began at five in the morning and went without a break until late into the evening. The work entailed shoveling fuel into the immense furnace and sweeping the soot out of it. While he performed these tasks, the other men stood entranced at the nearby tables, mindlessly kneading dough to make cracknels, batards, and loaves of rye bread. The only sounds came from the repetitious shoveling and the blazing furnace. No one spoke or ever had anything to say.

In the beginning, Alexis' nights were sleepless, spent with insomnia awake on the hard bunk, thinking over the sorrowful road his life had taken. In the workroom, there were no windows; but in the basement bunkroom, there was one tiny window up near the ceiling. It was covered in bars and the glass was covered in soot, yet Alexis could see through it a small obscured white light shining in the night sky which he mistook for the moon. It was actually just an incandescent security bulb out in the alley.

While Alexis remained awake, the other men slept and snored loudly in their bunks. The room smelled stale and musty from the body odour of filthy men. There were bedbugs in the linen.

'How dirty I feel,' he thought as he lay awake on one of the first nights spent in that basement, 'What a boy I was…have been all along…and how I thought myself already a man.' While looking at the white disc of light glowing through the film of soot on the dirty window, he played back his recent past. He tried to retaste every failure, every misery. This, and this alone, brought him pleasure. '…So broken I am…so dirty…so weak. Here, I thought fame and power would come easily. And here I am now, fettered in a cask of ashes – too weak to move. Why now, even if the world came to me offering fame and power on a silver salver, I wouldn't be prepared to take it.' Thus his first nights were spent in this kind of mournful sleepless reflection; but soon, even that came to pass. Eventually, the long days of grueling labor took their toll and he no longer had the energy to lie awake at night. The time came when, as soon as the work was finished in the evenings, as soon as he'd thrown his sooty apron in the corner with the rest of them and had eaten the one bread roll he was issued per day – a meagre meal which he consumed slowly and carefully, offering almost religious gratitude for each small bite – he would go straight to sleep a thoughtless, dreamless sleep on his hard bunk – where, just like the other men, he too snored loudly and filled the room with the stale odour of musty sweat.

He also stopped grooming himself. His face grew a ratty beard. His head itched from the lice that infested all the men there. The soot from the furnace stained his hands, his feet. He began to cough up thick black phlegm. Chronic pain riddled his throat as well as his back. Not having money or energy or the will and desire to see anything around town, he rarely left the basement, and he never left the fifth district of the city – an area made up entirely of textile factories and abandoned buildings with sorrowful broken windows. When he wasn't working or eating his daily bread, he slept. And he slept more than the other men, who usually stayed up for a couple hours after work playing cards and sniffing hearth-cleaning fluid. In the short sleep he was allotted, he found all he really wanted…oblivion.

These other men didn't take an immediate liking to Alexis and rarely spoke to him. Likewise, he didn't trust them and always made sure to stuff his yellow handkerchief in the crotch of his trousers while he slept so no one would steal it. After the first couple days, however, one of the men made a gesture of friendship towards him. The man's name was Chippel. He was a dwarfish specimen. His face bore the scabs of syphilis. He apparently felt sorry for Alexis, having no shoes or socks; and so one early morning just before work began, Chippel left the basement and went outside. A half hour later, he came back with a pair of shoes and offered them to Alexis. They were worn out, of sad leather, and one size too big for Alexis, but he appreciated having something to wear on his feet. He thanked Chippel warmly for the gift and for his kindness and decided that when he received his first pay of one sovereign at the end of the week, he would go buy some inexpensive trifle for Chippel as a way to say thank you. In addition, he would go out and spend at least half of the sovereign on a good pair of socks for himself.

As soon as Friday, the day to get paid, came around, the boss issued each man an envelope containing his weekly sovereign. Chippel was the messenger sent by the boss to distribute the pay. When Chippel came in the bunkroom with the box of envelopes, he handed one to each man – each man except for Alexis, that is.

"But, you forgot me!" Alexis addressed Chippel.

Chippel passed him off.

"Yeah, but Chippel, where's my envelope?"

"Let me remind you," Chippel responded before the audience of the other men, "that you agreed to pay me one sovereign for those shoes you're wearing."

Alexis looked down at the floppy shoes on his feet. What gall, this villain! He looked back at Chippel with angry eyes of disbelief, "For these shoes?!"

"Yes, those," Chippel replied, "You didn't have shoes, and I sold you shoes – one sovereign! These men are my witness that you didn't have shoes…the shoes came from me!"

Alexis huffed angrily while stepping on the heels of the shoes to kick them off his feet... "Then, damn it, take the shoes back! Take them and give me my money!"

"I don't want the shoes," laughed Chippel mockingly, "I have my own shoes!"

Alexis was furious. "Give me my goddamned money!" he demanded.

"Not a chance," replied Chippel with complete calmness, "It's my money. I had to pay for those shoes. One sovereign, I paid. So you need to pay me back one sovereign!"

Then broke in some of the other men who were gathered around. They began to jest, "Did'ya really pay for those shoes?" ... "Huh, Chippel? Did'ya steal 'em, or did'ya pay for 'em?!" they were having a great time. Chippel turned to them and bared his teeth with a proud smile, as though tremendously pleased to be the object of such a jest.

"Oh, I paid for them, boys!" he joked back, "I tell you I paid for them!" Alexis eyed this odious creature and was about to leap for him and tear his ears off. He looked at the other men who were standing in a semi-circle around the two. Judging from the looks of them, they were not going to offer Alexis any support.

"Give me my money," Alexis drew out in a slow and forceful tone, "Give it to me, or else I'll…"

"Or else you'll what?" asked Chippel. And he took a step close to Alexis. "Or what? Or you'll tell the boss?" And as soon as Chippel said this, the other men began to slowly advance towards Alexis. They wore fiercely threatening faces. Some rolled up their sleeves, making fists with their scarred and sooty hands. It was clear how this situation was turning out. Alexis, realized he could not win, and so he backed off and let Chippel keep his week's pay without further protest.

That night, Alexis lay beneath his thin blanket fuming with anger. He was bitterly hungry and had looked forward to having his pay so he could go out and buy a real meal. Now he would have to wait at least another week for something to eat other than a bread roll. While he lay on his bunk, he was kept awake by his anger and by his hunger, as well as by the raucous the other men were making as they sat around on the floor of the bunkroom playing cards. Alexis noticed that on this night, the bottle of whiskey the men passed around was a large one. No doubt Alexis' money had paid for that whiskey. Regardless, Alexis was alone and hungry without money or companions, while the men had all just been paid and so were very merry together and stayed awake drinking and gambling into the night.

After this event, Alexis retreated even more into himself; and not only did he not speak with the other men, as before; but now he also refused to even look at them. He simply continued working as usual – sweeping the furnace and stocking the fuel. With only one bread roll a day to eat, he grew extremely gaunt and his health grew ever more worse.

That was the beginning. After more time passed, Alexis grew accustomed to his role there at the Great City's Fifth Central Bread Production Plant. Not only had he already started to work like the other men, punching the time clock in the same drone-like mechanical way, muttering the same solemn swearwords while bitterly putting on his dirty apron, but he also believed he was beginning to resemble these men in appearance with their dry skin, scaly from malnutrition; their ugly faces, distorted from misery; their long filthy fingernails and gaunt and hunched-over bodies. He fancied he even began to think like them, with their low ideals, their criminal preoccupations, their cynical apathy.

Then came the day that a new man was hired on. He was younger than Alexis, naïve to the type of work, and was given the dirtiest task of sweeping out the furnace. This-upon, Alexis was promoted to the ranks of the other men, and he too began the mindless work of kneading dough, rolling it out to make cracknels, batards and loaves of rye bread. This new position, though infinitely beneath the ideals he'd held for himself long ago at that forgotten previous time of his life, he took on with a relative amount of pride, now able to look with scornful malice on at the fleas crawling in the threads of his clothes. He no longer had to sweep ashes out of the furnace.

This gradual yet tremendous change that occurred within Alexis, the complete evaporation of his desire for greatness and his wish to live an extraordinary life, ran its course without his even being conscious of it. Whereas, in the very beginning, he had made plans to get himself out of this situation, thinking each week he would spend a couple thalers of his pay on cheap but substantial food to supplement his daily bread rolls – while saving the bulk of it to buy suitable clothes to go look for better-paying and more respectable work; in the end, he squandered all and saved nothing – although he did manage to find once a cheap pair of trousers that, though ragged, were not torn to shreds so much as those that he first entered the basement with; he also came upon a pair of decent socks to wear with his floppy shoes one evening while wandering the desolate alleys around the textile factories. In the end, his money ended up being spent in the same way the money of the other men working there at the Fifth Central Bread Production Plant was spent: a few careless thalers here and there on food items, with the rest of it going to liquor rations which he and the men drank every night after work to ease the physical and mental suffering that came with the burdens of life and labour in the basement.

Though Alexis continued to harbor disdain for the other men, and while they never did take a sincere liking to him, they all eventually grew to tolerate each other; and soon Alexis began to spend his off-hours in their company; and every night resembled the one before it. Come eight o'clock in the evening, once the fifteen hour shift of mindless work was over, Alexis would pitch in his ten thalers along with the rest of the men, and one of them would go to the liquor store and come back with a bottle. Each would receive his share and Alexis would sit on the floor and drink while watching the other men's card games.

All introspection vanished from Alexis and he gave almost no further thought to his situation. He rarely recalled his memories of leaving his family and country to emigrate to the Great City, and forgot altogether his initial ambitions. His passions were dead. Gone were the impressions of idle days of yore. Memories, like that sunny afternoon he ate soup on a terrace on Chancellery Prospect with two young charming girls, were gone for him. All this was dead, as if they were someone else's memories. Now, he but lived and worked, slept and slaved away without any thought for the past, present or future.

It was on a stifling morning in summer when the air was particularly stagnant and musty in the bunkroom, Alexis awoke more ill than his usual chronic sickness from alcohol. Sweating in the oppressive heat, sick in the gut and nauseous, he got out of his bunk and went to start his shift along with the other men who were already at their tables, hunched over as they mindlessly rolled out dough. It was at the time when this new young worker had just been hired on. He was an eager lad with ugly crossed eyes. He had rosy cheeks and lips that seemed to be always wet with saliva. It appeared that he was an orphan in the world, and he glued to Alexis from the first day when the latter was assigned to train him for he job. Alexis was annoyed by the stupidity of the lad, always repeating the same questions… "Where again do I put the ashes once I've swept them out?...How again do prep the fuel to put in the furnace?"

On this particular sultry summer morning when Alexis was especially ill and bitter-tempered, he lost his patience quickly when this new worker came to his table early piping his questions. 'I've had enough of the little chicken,' he thought.

"Listen guy," Alexis snapped, "If you start squeaking again today, you're going to be sorry. I'm gonna explain to you once again the furnace. But first, you have extra work to do. You're going to clean the bunkroom, got it? All our sheets are filthy. D'you realize, we have to sleep in that filth at night after listening to you squeaking all day? It's alright, don't look like a dumb lost lamb, just go clean up the bunks. What? Good, I'm glad you like that idea. Wash the sheets and blankets in the sink – powdered soap down below. But pay extra special attention to bunk number eleven – that's my bunk." ... "While the sheets are hanging up to dry," he continued; meanwhile, the young worker stood balancing on his shovel nodding stupidly, "...while they're hanging up, bleach the floors in the bunkroom. Once the beds are made up, return here and I'll show you the furnace. But keep in mind the work's gonna lag on. It'll be a while before you're finished."

The lad eagerly obeyed and disappeared off into the bunkroom to carry out the orders. After he left the furnace room, Alexis turned and snickered with his lip curled up at the other men who thought the whole affair was quite funny as well; then his mouth dropped into its usual empty and sunken appearance, as he resumed his task – hunched over his table rolling and kneading, rolling and kneading, while the listless and dreary hours passed on into more hours, also listless, and also dreary.

None of the men were in the habit of anticipating the end of the work day. There were no clocks on the walls. The signal for the end of the day was the boss's ringing of a bell in the corridor which came at eight o'clock. But no one waited for this or looked forward to it. The end of a work day just meant the beginning of another gloomy evening spent with whisky that was so cheap that it always made one sick, followed by a night of oblivious sleep which would be disrupted all too quickly and painfully at five in the morning when it was time to begin a new day of work. When the end-of-work bell in the corridor rang, the men would awake from their trances, drop whatever dough was in their hands, and march silently to the bunkroom.

It was on the evening of the day when the new lad had been ordered to clean the beds and the floor, that Alexis was stirred from his trance earlier than usual.

"Sir…" came from someone. It was the lad. He was standing wide-eyed by Alexis' worktable.

"What?"

"I'm finished, but yours is bed eleven, right?"

"Yeah. What of it?"

"Well, it's just that I found these on the floor under the mattress when I was shaking it out." He held his open palm out. "I wouldn't want you to lose them."

Alexis looked in the palm of the lad's hand. He was holding his yellow silk handkerchief and a crumpled up piece of blue paper. The handkerchief was soiled and covered with dust. Alexis took these items from the lad's hand with disinterest and stuffed them in his trouser pocket. He then nodded in the direction of the shovel and told the lad to get to the furnace and get to work.

"But you said you would help me understand the furnace," piped the lad.

"I explained it perfectly well the first day you were here," Alexis replied.

"But I still don't understand it."

"You simply sweep," replied Alexis, "Sweep and sweep and when you're done with that, keep sweeping." And with that, Alexis fell back into his trance and continued rolling and kneading, rolling and kneading.

At the end of the shift that night, as usual, the men went into the bunkroom to eat their bread rolls and ration out the night's supply of whiskey.

Seated on the floor, while cutting the deck of cards, Chippel laughed and said to the other men with a mocking smile, "That was sure nice of the new lad to pay double his share for the whiskey, eh gentlemen?" He unscrewed the bottle and poured out doses of liquor into the men's cups who were seated in a semi-circle around him.

"Where is that squirrel?" one of the men asked.

"Ha-ha!" Chippel howled with malicious joy, "We sent him on a little errand, you see, boys! We told him to go across town to the Upper East-End, 'cause it's there where the bottle of whiskey is on hold for us. 'Already paid,' I told him, 'you just have to go to the East End liquor store and pick it up!'"

"But the bottle is here," Alexis said, naïvely.

"Exactly!" Chippel laughed, "and it'll be gone by the time he gets back!…'cause it's gonna take him a while. He's not gonna find a liquor store on the street I told him!"

"Funny as hell!" Alexis laughed.

The other men laughed too.

"Hey, you're alright!" Chippel suddenly said, turning to Alexis.

Alexis smiled.

Chippel continued…"You know, I thought at first you were a complete cod. But you're not at all…you're one of us!" he smiled, "a comrade like the rest of us."

Alexis pushed his cup forward to be refilled with whiskey when Chippel offered. Chippel slapped him with friendliness on the shoulder and Alexis slapped Chippel's shoulder right back. That evening Alexis remained in the circle with the other men. Not as before, an outsider who sat drinking while quietly watching the card game over someone's shoulder, but rather he sat in the circle with the other men, as one of them, and they all drank and played cards together. On this night, there was a copious amount of whiskey and the men got more than usually rummy. Everyone was in a loquacious mood. They talked and told stories; and for the first time on this night, Alexis learned each of the men's histories.

One spoke about his leaving his seaport town in New Scotland, near Halifax, where his father wanted him to be a fisherman like he and his grandfather. But the man, then just a boy, wanted to travel the world, and so he did. He sailed around, saw a few things; and eventually ended up here in the basement.

"And you wouldn't want to find better than this basement?" Alexis asked.

"Well," the man responded, "It's better than prison."

Another talked of leaving Mexico where he grew up in poverty with his mother and younger sister who both worked as prostitutes. He had depended on his sister to feed him. His mother was too old and wasn't bringing in money. Then came the night that he ended up following one of his sister's clients out into the street after he left her room. There he attacked him, beat him up severely and stole his money. With the money, he bought a ticket and sailed across the ocean with ambitions of earning a fortune so that he could return to Mexico and provide for his sister and mother so they wouldn't have to work as whores anymore and his family could be respectable.

"What happened?" Alexis asked.

"That was twenty-five years ago," the man responded gloomily, with a bowed head.

Another man kept wanting badly to tell the story of his life and started and stopped many times but could never get it going. He didn't speak the language well enough. All he managed to explain was that he was born in Portugal and that his mother had been very beautiful and she always smelled like taffy. "Taffy," he said over and over, "she smelled taffy!"

Some of the men asked Chippel to tell his story, but each time they did, he simply laughed and bared his teeth at everyone, saying "Oh, you know boys! Ha-ha! You know my story, alright, dontch'ya boys! Ha-ha!" And the table would be turned to someone else.

The last story Alexis listened to was one of patricide. One of the men explained how he'd killed his father with a hunting knife. After, he ran away to the Great City where he wouldn't get caught.

"But why did you do it?" Alexis asked, "was it simply that you wished you'd had another father instead?"

"Another father?" the man replied in a voice of bewilderment, "Why another father? I would have just had to kill him too!"

These stories filled Alexis with disgust. They seemed to awaken in him a certain kind of thoughtfulness for the past, the present and future that was deeply mournful and melancholic and soon he could hear no more. Abandoning his cup of whiskey, he left his place on the floor and walked over to his bunk. Leaning on the thin mattress, he looked up at the tiny soot-covered window up by the ceiling. He studied the obscured white light coming through the dirty pane of glass. For the first time on this night, he remarked that it was in fact not the moon, that it was merely an incandescent bulb in the alleyway. He had been deceived. The whiskey swirled in his head with floating thoughts and emotions. With his gaunt hand rippled with weakened veins, he reached into his pocket and pulled out the wad of blue paper the new lad had returned to him that afternoon. He uncrumpled it and studied the address written on it in faded ink. "Stratsnoy," he muttered aloud, thinking hard about this word. He then pulled out the yellow handkerchief. It too was worn and ripped and stained with soot and grime. Neatly, with slow methodical and exacting movements, he laid the handkerchief on his bunk where he flattened in out and tried to press the wrinkles out and pinch together the parts that had been torn.

That night, Alexis didn't finish his dose of whiskey; neither did he return to listen to the dissolute stories of the other men's lives, neither did he retreat to his bunk to seek oblivion in sleep. After having heard of the whores, the prisons and jails, the patricide, these impoverished tales of lost dreams, broken hopes and years gone by...after hearing all this, Alexis laced up his floppy shoes and left the basement to take a walk in the balmy summer night. It had been a long time since he had left the basement. He walked down Stratsnoy Avenue, past the rows of abandoned buildings and dilapidated textile factories, and left the shambles of the fifth district of the city. He crossed the river. The streets took him to the closed-up marketplace where he remembered that once, long ago on a bright cold day in spring, he had observed, with such innocent amazement and joy for living, the market scene with the goods being sold, the busy Great City shoppers, the happy vendors, the healthy girls in white dresses carrying flowers. He passed the closed marketplace and continued on west until he entered the seventh district; and there he stopped and asked a stranger for directions.

"Where are you trying to go to?" the stranger asked.

Alexis searched through his pockets. His memory wasn't what it used to be. He looked for the blue paper. "Oh, Christ..." he exclaimed in a feeble voice of great sorrowful regret... "I forgot my yellow handkerchief!"

Chapter X

"A Little Job" – Alexis pays a visit to an old friend...

"You're just in time!" Dominique exclaimed to Alexis when he opened the door, "I have a little job for you. You look like you're in need of a job. Come in, come in! Just look at you, your clothes are shot! And look how thin you've become!" Dominique looked just the same as he did long ago – handsome, clean and well-groomed, he wore a light silk summer blouse. "What have you been doing with yourself?"

The two shook hands and Dominique ushered Alexis into the spacious and airy loft where he lived at thirty-one Stratsnoy Boulevard in the seventh district of the Great City.

"It's been ages. How come you're just now coming to visit?"

Alexis didn't mention the tremendous turn of fate that came from his mistaking Stratsnoy Avenue for Stratsnoy Boulevard. He didn't detail anything about his experiences in the Great City since the two had met. He simply gave a shrug, and followed him inside. Dominique offered coffee, which Alexis accepted with gladness. It had been so long since he'd had the luxury of drinking coffee.

This neighborhood around Dominique's loft, with its elegant white ministerial buildings, its clean, quiet streets lined with manicured parks where stone and marble statues of heroes and thinkers stood on pedestals, was nothing like the grimy textile district where Stratsnoy Avenue was. Here, there were no rat infested basements. Dominique had been telling the truth when he said that things sparkled where he lived. Alexis walked in pessimistic worry as he traversed the neighborhood, clutching the crumpled and faded blue paper in his soiled hand, merely hoping Dominique still lived where he once said he did, that he'd find him, that Dominique would remember him and perhaps welcome him inside for a few moments to talk; or at the very least, burden himself with the favor of letting Alexis wash his hands.

When he found the building, he pushed open the tall gate and crossed into a quaint stone courtyard where a little patch of grass in the back was lit up by colored garden lights. Stone lions guarded the steps that led into a large foyer where tapestries hung on the walls. It was no castle, but still a luxurious affair. While climbing up to the first floor, Alexis wondered what godly wonders lay within these walls, and what devilish humanity it was that had led him to the subterranean nightmare across town on Stratsnoy Avenue. Why to that filth, when a boulevard across town with the same name was the home of such grandeur? "Was it by fluke, or by design?" he asked himself, "And for what that only now do I walk on the hearth of greatness, when I've not a stick of timber to light my way? ... Greatness by fluke or grandeur's design? Oh, who cares about greatness now! Damned be greatness…greatness be damned!" Alexis, who had grown cynical as of late, now climbed the stairs of the building in the elegant neighborhood, quite certain that there he'd find neither greatness nor anyone home. "Outdated or phony address…whatever the reason, I won't find old Dominique here." …Although, to his surprise, when he reached the fourth floor, there was a door with a plaque bearing Dominique's name; and, after ringing the bell, that same young officer who had befriended Alexis on his first night in the Great City, answered and welcomed him into his life once again.

"How long it's been!" he marveled, beckoning the visitor to come inside, "When was it we met in the gazebo that time? If I remember right, it was around the time of that earthquake, wasn't it? Did you feel that earthquake? That the first earthquake to hit the Great City in the last six hundred years. How have you been getting on?"

"Oh, not bad," Alexis lied.

"So, as I was saying," Dominique resumed, once the two were seated on the sofa and had coffee, sugar and heavy cream before them, "I have a little job for you." Alexis watched on as Dominique stood up to feed the carp that were swimming in a large glass tank on a bamboo stand across the room in between two impressive jade plants. As he sprinkled flakes in the water, he explained what was needed. "You remember me telling you I publish a newspaper, right?" He looked over his shoulder at Alexis who responded with a blank expression; and stopped feeding the fish and walked over to the bookshelf by kitchen. "Well, you'll be interested in this, Alexis…" His voice resonated loudly in the immense space of the loft, "it's an underground revolutionary paper." He pulled a copy off of a stack of books and came back over to the sofa to show it to Alexis. Alexis looked it over. There were some feature articles that were translated into various languages across the pages and some propaganda artwork. He briefly scanned one of the articles. It was a high-flown attack on the policies of one of the controversial Great City ministers.

"Looks like good work," Alexis said with measured enthusiasm.

"Come this way. I want to show you something." Dominique had stood and was beckoning him out onto the terrace. Outside, the balmy summer night breeze rattled the leaves of the potted ferns. The sky over the city was starless, a polluted haze covered all. Alexis tasted the sweet coffee on his tongue. It had stimulated his senses and made him alert, but otherwise he felt solemn.

"So, this is where I live!" Dominique's hand swept out across the view from his fourth-floor terrace. "What do you think? If you lean out to the right, you can see the top of Our Lady's Bridge."

Alexis leaned over the rail, and looked right, but couldn't see the bridge. All he saw was a nest of buildings and a few lights from boats on the river.

"But the best part is this," he pointed straight ahead.

Alexis looked out across the boulevard to see a small palace with great oval windows and an impressive courtyard where flags were hoisted on poles, fluttering in the windy night air. In the windows, Alexis could see crystal chandeliers with numerous tiers, which illuminated long draped curtains with creamy ivory light.

"That," he explained, pointing to the palace, "is where the Prime Minister lives."

"Okay. So what is the job, then?" This palace brought him little interest. 'Better for it to live in a fairy tale,' he thought. Alexis, who had grown accustomed to slaving for meagre bread rolls alongside shifty-eyed, toothless criminals, had begun to think with a mind like cold frosted stone – even more so, when an opportunity for ready money presented itself.

"Like I said," Dominique continued, leading Alexis back inside. He expressed worry in a whisper that their conversation might be overheard by the policemen down on the street guarding the entrance to the palace; and his paranoia led them back inside the loft. "Simply like this, Alexis...I print an underground newspaper and I badly need an article."

"You want me to write something?"

"Not exactly. You see, there's a well-known politician who lives in the building across the boulevard..."

"In the palace?"

"No, no...the building next to it. Not the one the police are guarding. This one's unguarded. Anyway, I'm going to take you out on the terrace again, and when I do so, you'll look across the boulevard and see the last window on the second floor of the building far on the right. Through the window, you can see a desk with a lamp on it. Next to the lamp is a brown briefcase. In that briefcase, there are some important papers that leak a great scandal. If I can get my hands on that briefcase, Alexis, it'll be worth a lot to me. It will mean money and power. And if you help me, it will mean money and power for the both of us. The scandal this politician is involved with needs to be exposed. It will change the political situation in the Great City forever. If you can help me get those papers in that briefcase, you will not be short of rewards."

"Why don't *you* go take the briefcase?" he asked, "why do you want me to do it?"

"Because, for one," Dominique replied, "You're physically stronger than I am. I don't know if I could climb up that drainpipe to get to the second story window. Second of all – I'll be frank with you, Alexis – you aren't known here in the city. If you are caught breaking in to that politician's home, at worst they'll charge you with minor burglary and slap your wrists. I, on the other hand, as the known publisher of this famous revolutionary paper, will get charged with political conspiracy. They would throw me in prison for a long, long time. And lastly, Alexis...you need the money."

Alexis inhaled deeply. He then tried to explain to Dominique that he too may get charged with political conspiracy and thrown in prison for a long time, but Dominique insisted there was no chance of that. "It's perfectly safe. The only policemen on the street are the ones guarding the gates to the palace.

There aren't any near where you're going. I'll explain quickly how to do it... There's a back way to enter and exit my place. You go out the back way, down the stairs, around the building. Then, cross the boulevard and go to the building across the street. Discreetly climb over the stone wall. Run across, keeping in the shadows and shimmy up the drainpipe. Once you get to the second floor, edge around on the outside of the building till you get to far window ledge, the one facing my terrace. Then you simply open the window, climb in, take the briefcase; climb out, back down, back through the shadows, over the wall, back across the boulevard, around back, simple as that! But before re-entering my building, Alexis, make sure no one's following you. I'll pay you as soon as you come back with the briefcase and we'll have a drink together. I'm going to give you an old pair of my pants because yours are shot...."

Alexis inhaled deeply. The situation made him nervous. He tried to explain to Dominique that he didn't need the money, but it was a hopeless argument. He did need the money. And so he agreed.

Dominique watched from the terrace as Alexis scurried across the boulevard and climbed over the stone wall and dropped beyond it, out of sight. Dominique then went back inside the loft and drank a glass of brandy with bitters. He then changed his socks and leafed through a newspaper. After this exercise, he went over to his typewriter and ticked out a few sentences. While he was doing so, he was interrupted by a knock at the backdoor.

"Yes, yes..." Dominique stood from his typewriter and went to open the door. Alexis rushed in, out of breath. He was dirtier than before, clothes torn to shreds, he had smudges of grime on his face and blood on his skin where he'd received several scratches. He panted for breath. Dominique helped him to a chair and closed and locked the back door. Resting on Alexis' lap was the briefcase.

"Bravo!" Dominique cried out, "Bravo, my friend!" He rushed over to where Alexis was seated. "Did anyone see you?" Alexis, still out of breath, didn't answer right away. Dominique darted over to the terrace and pulled the curtains tightly closed. In his excitement, he ran about the loft to both find some old clothes for Alexis to wear as well as a tool to pick the locks on the briefcase. He found both. Alexis surrendered the briefcase to Dominique and accepted a pair of sturdy brown corduroy trousers. He took off his own torn rags and put the trousers on. He also took off his shirt and slipped into a brown summer shirt Dominique offered him. That was the last of his father's cotton shirts, and with hesitation, he threw it in Dominique's trash bin and didn't look back. Dominique, all the while, was installed on the sofa and plied the locks with an ice pick. The latches gave and he opened the case and began to sift through the spoils.

Inside the briefcase, there were but three things: a stack of receipts tied with a rubber band – mostly for dry-cleaning, there were also some receipts for take-out dinners. There was a photograph of a pretty girl sitting on a rock next to a totem pole. The third item was leather bound journal. "Within this journal," Dominique exclaimed with great triumph, "is my scandal! You see, Alexis," he tapped the cover of the journal with an immense smile on his face… "This is my article!"

Dominique removed the string around the journal and opened the cover. He flipped through the pages for a few moments. Then, a sunken look came over his face. Were these not the politician's notes after all? The handwriting was strange – big crooked letters, bright green ink. He began to read a some of it aloud: "Someday," was written, "Daddy will come back and we'll picnic together at the Ministereal [sic] Park. We will eat ice cream at the Imperial Gardens and drink peach soda at the Artemis Hotel. I would like to own a girafe [sic], so I can eat all the fruit on top of the trees if I am ever in a jungle of fruit. I'll ride on his head and take the fruit and feed some to the girafe [sic] so he won't die. Then we can run away together and be married and I will bake fruit cakes…et cetera, et cetera, et cetera…."

The journal of a little girl! Dominique didn't know what to do with this find. His eyes darted around the room. "What the hell am I supposed to do with this?" he grumbled, "It's just a damn diary belonging to a little girl!" His eyes searched around the room. A look of great defeat hung on his face. Finally, he reached in his pocket and pulled out a single sovereign and tossed it carelessly over to Alexis. "Here, Alexis…it's nothing but…" Pause. "…Well, keep the clothes too." He sighed. "We'll drink a brandy together and figure out what to do. Oh, I'm in a foul mood!"

"I have to go," Alexis told him, "I have to get back to my job." Another disgusting situation. Alexis wanted to leave as soon as possible. Dominique didn't protest but made him promise to return to visit sometime. Alexis said 'fine' in a cold tone, pocketed the one sovereign, and said a hurried goodbye. Dominique said 'see you soon,' and his words floated down the stairs and into the hair on Alexis' head where they dissolved in the strands and were gone.

It was while Alexis was leaving the building, going down the stairs, that he saw Sidonie coming up. Her eyes were puffy and red. She was crying. On her head was a floppy hat that made her look rather like a sniffing mouse. Alexis didn't know what a sniffing mouse was, but that's how she looked. She recognized Alexis as he came down the stairs and she looked at him with her large red eyes and gasped in a pleading voice, all the while choking on her tears, "Is he in there?"

Alexis, none too interested by this girl, barely looked at her. He merely mumbled something in response and passed by her there in the stairwell. "Odious people!" he exclaimed. He crossed through the courtyard and left the building. Outside he nodded with indifference to the policemen guarding the Minister's palace and headed off down Stratsnoy Boulevard.

Chapter XI

"All Roads Lead Away" – in search of the Acropolis…

"Stranger!" Alexis called out to a figure hidden in the shadows down by the boats that were docked up along the quai of the river "…No, never mind, I don't want any part of you." He continued on his way, grumbling up the river bank away from the seventh district of town. "jokers, swine and thieves…this place is full of jokers, pretty girls, lecherous shifty swindlers. Damnable place! Nope, Alexis, this Great City was not nearly great enough!" He had just left Dominique's and it was getting on midnight. "Not nearly great enough!" The first bridge he came to, he crossed and it took him through the arcade of the National Museum.

"Well, where are you off to now, Alexis?" he inquired of himself. Still he wasn't sure, "but I feel it's time to take a new road." The day had already dragged on enough, he was malnourished and physically worn. In spite of all this, his spirits were enjoying a strange resurgence and he walked along feeling strong. This was the night he decided to leave his dissolute life in the basement once and for all; and now he felt a renewed vitality such as is afforded anyone who has his mind made up to take a bold leap in this or that direction. In spite of all the ugliness that had come to pass that day between he and the thieves in the basement, as well as he and his own thieving for the reward of a sloppy sovereign in the Ministerial District, he felt quite alive. And so, as he chatted with himself on this night, he was more than usually friendly...

"I'll tell you where I'm off to, Alexis my good friend! Ol' travelin' man!...I'll tell you, alright!...I'm off to find the Acropolis, that's where! Ha-ha!" he cheered, drunk on the idea... "Travel! Freedom and travel! No more dry bread rolls... No more cheap whiskey... No more odious heists... No more slaving away... No more sorrows!"

And so, with his floppy leather shoes, his brown corduroy trousers, and his new cotton shirt bristling on his skin in the warm, agreeable summer night's breeze; and with all of a single sovereign at the bottom of his pocket – a pocket sadly empty of that cherished yellow silk handkerchief – gift from his sister – he crossed the Faubourg and the South Canal, traversed the University District, wandered away from the factories of the Textile District, away from the cardboard cut-outs of the industrial suburbs; and soon the city was just a background haze of smog and lights beneath a sky that was ever so dark, and he knew then that he was on the right path. He saw a wooden painted sign with an arrow pointed in the direction he was headed. The sign read: *CHEMIN DE LA BONNE-VOIE*, and he wandered on.

That single sovereign bought him a fourth-class train ride out of the country, and for days he traveled through a range of blue mountains where summer wildflowers bloomed. Through wide expanses and narrow valleys, the train tracked along, tracing the curves of rivers and streams, where immense peaks towered on either side. Alexis rode along filled with happy anticipation. Memories of the Great City were far from him. His was a future in a new far-away place, just as his was the sun-saturated present around him. He looked at the mountains through the train window. "What is this mountain range?" Who knew? Might it be the Atlas mountains, the Urals or the Pyrenees? Perhaps the Sierra Madres, the Alps, or the Carpathians, or the Harz. At one point, the train crossed a steel bridge spanning a magnificent river. "What is this river?" Was it the Danube? The Rhine? The Rhone? The Saône? Perhaps the Neva? Certainly, with that beauty it must have been the Moldau. This he had not seen. Not seen but had heard. Heard but not looked for. Oh, with what beauty that river sang!

His train wound around the arid mountain slopes and descended into a valley where the fields shone golden and fiery below blue azure. After, it chugged up through more and more mountains; and finally it came to a halt atop a vista overlooking a village ensconced in the valley below.

Here the train doors opened and the passengers climbed out to stretch their legs. Alexis got out with the rest of them and walked along the tracks beside the train. He felt the sweltering sun on his face. Dusty gravel crunched under his feet. The sun burned mightily. He passed train workers with shovels who were turning over the hay in the train cars and pouring disinfectant on it. He saw a woman crouched on the side of the tracks breast-feeding an infant. The child was stuffed well up inside her sweat-stained blouse. A few minutes passed before a conductor wearing a pillbox hat came out of the train to tell the passengers that they would be stopped until evening due to an accident on a bridge up ahead. Many of the passengers groaned. The conductor than repeated what was apparently the same message in four other languages, whereupon the remaining passengers groaned. Alexis, all the while, was walking away from the clatter of the stopped train. He was terribly hungry and felt dizzy from the scorching heat of the sun.

He stood atop the vista and looked out, wondering what country he was in. On all sides around him, mountains sat on the sun-baked earth like lumps of golden sugar. After a minute, he started off walking down the dusty trail.

He soon came to a waterfall and stopped to drink. The water was icy cold and tasted good and he drank too much so his stomach cramped up. He stopped to rest on some rocks by the waterfall. All the while he was increasingly hungry. He searched in the pockets of his corduroy trousers for a crust of bread, but found nothing. He decided to go down to the little village that he spotted in the valley below. There, he thought, he might find something to eat.

The village was a nest of little houses built of colored bricks, all huddling around the central structure: a rose-colored cathedral with a tall black belfry that looked like the stinger of a wasp. After a few minutes of hiking down the trail, Alexis reached base of the valley and entered into the village through some narrow little streetlets paved with sandstone. The village seemed vacant and empty and no sounds could be heard, only the wisps of dry plants blowing through the streets when the arid wind came down from the mountains. Then the cathedral bells began to toll. *Dong-dong!* Their ringing echoed through the canyons. Alexis walked along the rows of pink stone houses and dry juniper trees in the direction of the cathedral, while vertigo made him feel ever more faint.

The tiniest of streetlets in the village presented a row of little dwellings, each with a wooden door painted a different color. All was so quiet. No one stirred in the little street and no noises came from the houses. It seemed as though no one was living in any of them. When he came to the last house, he saw the front door was standing wide open. It was a dwarfish little door of pale-green only a meter high. Alexis went inside.

A beam of sun came through the window illuminating a yellow cloud of dust in the dry rustic room. He ducked his head to pass beneath a wooden beam on the ceiling to enter what looked like to be a family's kitchen. The walls were earthen. The ground was covered with straw. Two chickens paced back and forth in a wooden crate, prattling their beaks. Alexis looked around the room when suddenly he caught the smell of warm baked goods.

He looked over to the wooden counter in the little kitchen area and noticed there were breads sitting in a pan to cool. Steam rose from their flakey crusts. Ah, what delights! Giant brioches dusted in creamery butter. No, egg yolks! No, creamery butter! Their golden crusts puffed up and the warm sweet smell filled Alexis' nose and he yearned to snatch one of these sugary breads. He made a step towards the counter but in his dizziness, perhaps caused by the overwhelming hunger, he stumbled and braced himself against the wall to avoid falling. Then he looked around and his eyes again returned to the breads. Then while spying these baked goods, he also spied past them to the back corner of the house where there was a small room sitting empty. 'What a curious little room…' Alexis made some steps towards it to have a look inside.

The room had rustic wood beams supporting a thatched roof. At the far wall was a little window. Below the window, stood a little bed. The bed had a mattress stuffed with straw, and the straw gleamed fool's golden yellow with the reflected noon sunlight coming through the window. Alexis spied that bed feeling oh so tired. Was there no one around? He backed out of the room to go back to the kitchen. Gazing again at those sweet loaves set to cool, he licked his lips. Mmm…what a delight! Suddenly his stomach was full and his lips were caked with sugar crystals and creamery butter. He yawned and stretched and felt with his hands what he was lying upon. It was the little stuffed straw bed in the little corner room beneath the window. Had he been asleep? He must have. It felt like he had slept an hour at least. He no longer felt tired or hungry, he yawned and stretched and looked up and across to the open door. Still, as before, the little house was empty. The open front door of the little house let in beams of the sunlight that illuminated dry dust clouds coming in from the hot baked empty street outside. The only sounds came from a single cock and hen chasing each other around on the straw floor of the kitchen where those breads had been set to cool. Alexis yawned once more, and stretched his neck out the little window above the bed in order to feel the sun on his face.

This back window over the bed in the corner room of that little house looked out into a large village courtyard built of stone. Alexis squinted in the bright light of the sun and surveyed the courtyard. The ground was cobbled with golden stones. Lining the courtyard were some more stone houses with thatched roofs, but most were taller, and some even had four or five storeys. These buildings were neatly packed together to form a great barricade around the village square. From many of the high-up windows, clothing was hung out to dry. A light breeze flapped through a sheets of cloth while a singular bird fluttered down from the one of the rooftops and landed in the middle of the courtyard to peck at some crumbs of food that were being dropped by a small crowd of people, men and women, who were gathered in the courtyard to eat together.

This crowd struck Alexis very strangely. They appeared both wild like gypsies, and rustic like pilgrims or mule drivers; the women were hairy and wore colorful handmade dresses and the men wore plain brown robes. They held clay bowls in their hands and while they sat cross-legged on the hot stones in the courtyard, they silently ate grains from these bowls. It appeared to Alexis that there was a central figure in this group; that all these gypsy-like folk were gathered piously around one individual: a man with long brown hair the color of dry soil, and a lanky body. This specimen had a gaunt and meager face with pronounced cheekbones and deep-set blue eyes that darted around at the others in his group as he ate, scooping grains with his fingers into his bearded mouth. At one point, he turned to a woman seated on the ground beside him and addressed her. The woman was a plain creature, built like a well-fed mare with a full rump in a gypsy dress; her hair was long and braided with colored threads. The bearded and gaunt man spoke to her in a voice that, in spite of its soft tone, resounded loudly across the arid open courtyard…

"Shalea, take some more lentils please. Yes. That is good. There is enough to go around. One must eat to be strong." He passed the largest clay bowl around so the other women in the circle could serve themselves to the cold lentils. They each thanked him respectfully, calling him 'Yeshalem.'

Alexis was watching curiously from the window as this group shared their meal together when, suddenly, he heard a clang of gate opening from the far left side of the courtyard. He turned his gaze to watch two figures entering the square. They were two men dressed like soldiers or official guards. They carried swords and wore helmets, and walked with the sound of iron chains falling on a prison floor as they approached the pilgrims.

"You must move on!" bellowed the voice of the smaller of the two guards.

The eaters did not respond. A couple of them looked up momentarily, but quickly returned their eyes cast downward, burying their faces meekly in their grains. Yeshalem, their leader, also looked up briefly, and then also dropped his head to resume eating.

"Who is your leader?" demanded the little guard.

No one responded.

"I asked you…" his voice rang out.

"I am their leader," Yeshalem said quietly, firmly, while setting his bowl aside, "and we are eating. Leave us to eat."

The guard rested his palm on the handle of his sword and addressed Yeshalem directly, "You cannot eat in this courtyard square. It is a private square. You are not from here. You must move on!"

Here there was some commotion among the pilgrims. Some made frightful gestures and scurried to gather their blankets and belongings. Others seemed more annoyed by the interruption and huffed as they looked to their leader. Yeshalem, however, remained passively seated and slowly waved his arms in an effort quell the commotion. "No, we are not from here," he told the guard, "We are traveling through. But now we've stopped to eat, so leave us to eat."

Here, silence swept over the hot courtyard square. The two guards looked a each other. The larger one lifted his helmet to wipe the dust and sweat off his forehead. He then walked over to one of the men in Yeshalem's group and took his bowl away to examine the contents. The man surrendered his bowl with the meek look of a frightened dog who cowers beneath his master's fist, and waited for his meal to be returned to him. The guard's nostrils dilated as he sifted through the grains in the bowl with the tip of his sword, eyeing them suspiciously. While this was going on, the small guard addressed the group again…

"All of you… *pilgrims*, or whatever you are…you must move on immediately – understand! Leave the square!" The guard tapped the handle of his sword with his right hand. In a house on the other side of the courtyard, an old man appeared at a window and begin to watch the scene that was arising.

"You there!" The small guard walked over and grabbed one woman by the wrist and dragged her to her feet. "Leave the square!" As he pulled her up, her robe tore. She looked around at the men in her group for help.

"Let her go," was Yeshalem's simple, but firmly articulated, response.

The guard turned from the woman to face Yeshalem and asked him while grasping the woman by the nape of her neck, "What is your name?" The woman remained passive and limp, drooped in the grip of the guard like the stem of a wilted flower.

"Yeshalem."

"And her name?"

"Shalea ... She is my wife."

The larger of the two guards who now up until this point had still been examining the contents of the men's food with his sword, threw the particular clay bowl he was holding across to the far end of the courtyard where it hit a step and shattered, flinging grains and chips of clay upon the stones. The group clamored and the commotion increased. Alexis watched with great interest.

"She is your wife...Eh!" The small guard lifted his chin, looking at Yeshalem, "Well, I'd advise you to leave the square and take your wife."

"Yes, let's go," came the light voices of two of the female pilgrims, "Let us continue our journey." They set down their bowls and picked up their cloth bags as if to suggest leaving the square.

"No," called out Yeshalem. "No!" His eyes darted around with a suspect look, and his arm stretched outwards to signal to these two females to sit back down. "We've walked all this morning. We are tired. Now it is time to eat. We will not leave the square." Yeshalem then signaled to the guard while addressing his group of followers, "Can't you see this man is afraid of his own image?"

Silence swept anew.

"Afraid of my own what?!" The guard stopped to consider what had just been said. He knitted his brow beneath his helmet and unhanded the nape of Shalea to approach her seated husband.

"Come, Yeshalem, let's go!" one of the females pleaded. The males in the group sat motionless and did not speak. Yeshalem soon began again. Looking directly at the small guard, he addressed him thus... "You, soldier, had better hide yourself behind your broad sword, lest your image be that of a watchdog with a snarled tooth."

"Stop, Yeshalem," his wife implored, "Let us move on!" The others in his group appeared to want the same and were apparently waiting for Yeshalem to give his approval to depart. After all, he was their leader.

"No, Shalea," he turned to his wife, "this man is afraid of his own image."

The man he was referring to was watching him all the while with a steady eye.

"And if I were to beat you?" the guard asked, "would *you* then too be afraid of my image?" His mouth twisted in a mocking smile. His eyes brightened. It was clear he was beginning to enjoy the scene that was taking place.

"No," Yeshalem responded firmly, "I would not be afraid."

"And would you fight back?"

"No, I would not fight back."

"You would not fight back!" the guard repeated, giving a little chuckle, "…even if I were to beat you!" While saying this, he flicked the sandaled foot of Yeshalem with his heavy boot. "If I were to beat you, you would not be afraid, but also you would not fight back, is that correct?" The two guards looked at each other and laughed.

"Yes, that is correct," affirmed Yeshalem, "I – unlike the dog – do not fight."

"And they," asked the smaller guard, pointing around the courtyard at the rest of the members of Yeshalem's entourage, who all had their sandals on and clutched their cloth bags in hopes of leaving the square as soon as possible, "would they fight for you?"

"No," answered Yeshalem, "they also are not dogs."

"So then you won't fight, eh?!" The guard was entertained by this notion. "You won't fight?…even if I beat you?! Well, then," he asked, taking a step towards Yeshalem's wife, grabbing again the nape of her neck. "what if I were to beat her?" He jerked her head back, which made her chin raise and exposed her pale fleshy neck. Then he raised his hand as if about to slap her across her face. The others in the party gave a sudden start, yet then sank back down motionless and gazed at Yeshalem to see what he'd do.

"I will not fight," Yeshalem repeated his words firmly.

"Yet, even if I beat her?!" the guard was astonished. Meanwhile, Shalea quivered in his grip, "but she is your wife, is she not?" Shalea looked down at her seated husband with a trembling lip.

"Yes, she is my wife. And you will do what you will. But I will not fight."

A merry chuckle came from the small guard as he raised his large hand and brought it down with a crack of the knuckles across Shalea's face. The sound rang out in the courtyard. Shalea squealed and her face flung to the side. Her lower-lip was pierced by her teeth and a clot of blood flew down on the stones of the square. She bowed her head while tears and blood dripped on the sandy stone floor.

Seeing his wife being beaten, Yeshalem finally jumped to his feet. The other men and women in his group darted their eyes around, trying to make sense of the scene that had arisen with their leader and his wife.

"You are standing now!" The small guard said tauntingly to Yeshalem while keeping one hand on the nape of Shalea's neck. "I just beat your woman, and now you are standing. Then, are you ready to fight?"

"Let her go!" demanded Yeshalem. While Shalea's tearful, bleeding face was lowered, she looked up imploringly at her husband, from the very tops of her eyes. She dared not raise her head, lest she be beaten again. "Let her go!" Yeshalem repeated, more firmly, more loudly.

The guard asked again, "Then, will you fight?"

"No, I will not fight."

Upon this answer, the guard looked back at Shalea. She jerked in horror and let out a groan. The guard again raised his hand and swung it around, smacking her on the side of her lowered face. He beat her again and again, and on the third blow, her two front teeth were knocked out. They fell like pebbles on the ground and bounced a few times, leaving spots of blood on the dusty stones. Still, Yeshalem did nothing. He merely watched on with calmness and inertia, as though expecting a god to intervene.

"I see he'll watch his wife being beaten by another man and won't even lift a finger to help her!" ... "You, why are you shaking?" He cracked the woman again with his knuckles. Yeshalem looked past all this, calmly gazing up at the cloudless sky burning with fiery hotness overhead. Meanwhile, the guard went on beating his wife. The other pilgrims watched on trembling. Their eyes darted back and forth from the bleeding woman, back to their leader, Yeshalem the pacifist, who did nothing. Alexis all the while felt deep disgust as he observed this scene from the window. He felt revulsion and hatred for this feeble Yeshalem. Stupid, feeble Yeshalem. He reached outside the window and found the shutters and closed them to not further have to observe the odious scene.

With the shutters closed, the sounds of the guard's beatings and the cries of Yeshalem's wife could no longer be heard, and it was as if that party of pilgrims and the two guards no longer existed. Alexis, now alone and awake in a strange room, seated on a mattress stuffed with straw, looked around. He was about to leave when a woman entered.

She was a round and stumpish woman with silver hair. She wore an crisp apron and came in carrying a tray of breads. She didn't seem to be at all surprised to find a stranger in her home. Moreover, she looked at Alexis as though she were expecting him to be there. She set the tray of breads beside him. "A man cannot have courage if he doesn't eat," she said smiling, "You must eat to be strong and not get sick, young man! You know, we women too must eat to be strong, But you, men…oh certainly! A man's stomach is a palace, they say. Well, did you sleep well?"

"Huh? I don't even remember sleeping," he rubbed his eyes and squinted at the silver-haired woman in bewilderment. He added, "But how did you know I was sleeping here?…I mean, I'm sorry, I just mean to say I found this bed alone. I'm afraid I was tired and dizzy, and so very hungry and I saw the door open and the breads cooling on the counter, and so I came in just to eat one little…then there was this bed and, well, you can see…"

"Oh-ho!" laughed the woman heartily, "You couldn't have possibly seen the breads cooling on the counter! I just took these breads out of the oven a moment ago. I'm afraid you hit your head and had a strange dream, young man. You don't remember, do you? A neighbor found you lying unconscious in the street. He said he saw you fall when you were walking past the church. Probably from the heat. We talked about what to do with you. He suggested putting you in his bed. But he has so many dogs and chickens in his room that his bed has lots of fleas and mange. So we carried you here. You slept soundly for several hours. Here, eat some hot brioche…it just came out of the oven."

Alexis was thoroughly confused but didn't say anything more, neither to the woman, nor to himself, lest he confuse himself even further. He just silently took a brioche from the tray and stuffed it into his mouth. Chewing it up and swallowing it, he licked afterwards the sugar crystals and creamery butter from the sides of his mouth. The woman watched on satisfied, apparently by the return of his health, his good appetite, and his delight in her breads. Alexis munched silently, staring straight ahead. Then he gave a sudden start…

"You said…" he jumped up, "that I slept soundly for several hours?! But my train! I must go!"

"No, no, sit down," the old woman said in a purring voice, "you cannot go. You must get some strength. Eat another brioche."

"No, I can't. I must go. My train will leave without me!" And with that, Alexis tossed the remaining half of his third brioche on the her little tray, bowed to the woman, gave her a glance of appreciation for her hospitality as well as acknowledgement of his obligation towards her and an apology for his sudden haste, and ran out of the tiny dwarfish house, bumping his head on the squatty little doorframe on his way.

Outside, the golden sun, still quite warm, was reposed behind a stone house lining the small cobbled street which led uphill into the mountains. Evening was in commencement. Alexis passed the cathedral and the village and soon he was back on the trail. He hastened, fretting he'd missed the train, climbing the switchbacks. He passed the waterfall and soon he was high at the vista point and the village could only be seen as a small stack of rose-colored stones far in the distance, with a black dot in the center – that was the cathedral.

Alexis ran up from the vista and found the train tracks. To his relief, the train was still there. He had come just in time. The last of the passengers were reboarding. The accident on the bridge up ahead had cleared and the train would soon be moving on again. The conductor helped an old crippled woman get onboard. She was jabbering something about being an immigrant and wanting someone to look at a sore spot in the crevice of her eye. Alexis followed her into the car, took an empty seat on a wire bench by an open window. The whistle blew and the train began to chug off again, coursing around down through the mountains.

It passed great expanses of burnished red fields and valleys of scorched grains. The inland country seemed interminable. Every few hours, the train needed to stop so the hay could be turned and the cars doused with disinfectant. The people took water and stretched their legs outside. Alexis noticed at one point stopping in the grain fields that the warm wind that blew into his face was swifter than before. It was salty and humid. He heard gulls in the distance. The ocean was near.

A few hours later the train terminated at a station near the piers of a port city. There, Alexis managed to get free passage on a flagship. The boat coursed the shoreline for days and the went out into the deep where it sailed o'er crystalline waters of blue, reflecting the infinite hues of the sun. Come one evening, the ship arrived in the dark harbor of a foreign seaport city built into a hillside. Alexis deboarded the ship with rest of the passengers and trailed behind, wandering slowly along the docks.

"What country is this, we're in?" he inquired of a dockworker who was tying the ropes on the ship.

"Thrace," replied the dockworker, "we tie the ropes three times in Thrace!"

"Thrace?" Alexis wondered, taking leave of the dockworker. He said the word again, "Thrace," letting it roll softly off his tongue – a tongue which was bumpy and tasted salty from the air in the harbor. He stopped and looked at the twinkling lights of the houses stacked on the hillside. The sun had already set behind those hills. Behind him the sea was an abyss of blackish blue. His head drifted farther back. Above him there was sky – plenty of creamy dark sky, laced with more and more stars.

Strolling along the docks, he found a fisherman tending a quiet line.

"Stranger," Alexis addressed him.

The fisherman looked up. Alexis approached him and struck up conversation. The fisherman made room for him to sit down beside him and he offered him oil and bread to eat. The fish splashed in the gentle slapping of the quiet nighttime sea.

"Where do you come from?" asked the fisherman.

"The Great City."

"Indeed." He cast his line out again. "And what are you doing in Bulgarie?"

"Bulgarie?" Alexis asked, "But I thought this was Thrace!"

"Thrace!" exclaimed the fisherman, "There's nothing Thracian about Bulgarie!" He cast his line out once again.

Now Alexis was confused. He decided to go ahead and ask... "Do you know where I might find the Acropolis? ...I was told that that ship I came in on would drop me off not too far away."

"The Acropolis…" said the fisherman, breathing in a smooth flow of syllables, "the Acropolis… You can get there in a day or two if you head straight for the Pleiades."

"The Pleiades?" Alexis asked.

"There," the fisherman pointed. He pointed up at the sky where the horizon and the far shores of the beach merged in darkness, "The Seven Sisters, they're called."

Alexis looked at that patch of sky. Nested within it, six great glimmering stars made way for a minor seventh.

"Beneath that little constellation," the fisherman declared, "lies the Acropolis."

Alexis remained a while on the dock and filled up on oil and bread. He listened to the fisherman talk about the store he was planning to open up in town with his brother. Music could be heard from the patio of a bar on the main street near the beach. He eventually said goodbye to the fisherman and wandered away from the docks and went up to see on what was going on, on the patio. There he saw couples drinking. Some children danced playfully together while their parents ate at nearby tables. The musicians were men in white tunics and they strummed wildly on instruments of gourd, while women in flowing dresses turned circles and flipped their hair. Alexis wished he'd had money to have a drink on the patio with these people. The air was warm and smelled of brine. The sky was a nest of stars. And then, there were those hills.

After some moments near the patio, he walked off and wandered down along the harbor, southwards, away from town. There, near the dark crashing waves, along the rocky beach, he met a tan-skinned boy with about twelve or thirteen years. The boy was pulling his nets in from the sea. He had caught some mussels and a crab. Alexis walked up to the boy and asked him whether they were in Thrace or in Bulgarie. The boy laughed and said they were in neither.

"This is not Bulgarie, then?" Alexis was bewildered.

"No, this is Macedonia," the boy assured him. He threw his nets out again, "Is it your first night here? My mother rents a room if you need a place to stay." He pointed up at some dark houses with tiled roofs that were built into the sides of the cliffs overlooking the harbor. "That's where we live."

"No," Alexis thanked him. Anyway, he didn't have money to rent a room for the night. "Actually, maybe you can help," he turned back to the boy, "I'm headed for the Acropolis. Is it possible to get there from here?"

"Of course," said the boy. "just walk straight that way." He pointed at the sky, "...straight towards the Seven Sisters. Eventually you'll get there."

Alexis smiled feeling reassured. It seemed no one agreed about what country they were in yet everybody believed in those sisters; and so Alexis decided it was good advice. He thanked the boy and walked his way down the beach in the direction of those stars. He walked until he found a deserted place where there was a patch of sand without debris or rocks. There he slept. The moon was new and growing.

The next morning Alexis awoke with mighty thirst. He dusted the sand from his clothes emptied out his floppy shoes and went in search for water – strange sensation to be next to an ocean of water and have no way to remedy thirst.

He wandered awhile inland through rocky fields and plots of dry ground and eventually he came to a pasture. It was lush and green. He looked for the source that was nourishing this green vegetation and eventually he found it in the form of a fresh stream. He drank and washed his face. The golden sun glimmered like warm amber berries in his wet eyelashes.

By noon, he was hungry and tired from walking. He came to an orchard. Though it was no orchard, the trees were barren of fruit. He tried to eat some olives off of an olive tree, but they were too bitter. He renounced the tree and hunger both, and stretched out in the shade beneath the bows to take a nap.

Then came the sound of a bleating goat. "Sir..." came a voice. "...wake up, sir!" It was boy and he was standing over Alexis tapping him on the foot with his walking stick. Alexis, stirred awake, sat up and looked at the boy. It was a dark-haired youth with bronze-colored skin. He was shirtless. He had been leading a goat, and held a rope tied around the goat's neck with his left hand. With his right, he tapped Alexis' floppy shoe with a stick.

"This is my orchard you're sleeping in," said the boy.

"I'm sorry, boy," Alexis replied while sitting up, searching for his senses, "I didn't know anyone owned this place...an orchard, you say? Why are there no fruit on the trees?" He looked at the boy's hands and saw he held a sprig of grapes. The boy was feeding the grapes to his goat. "Where can I get some of these grapes?" Alexis asked.

The boy told Alexis that they came from his house. "If a meal is what you want," the boy said, "you'll be able to eat well if you come and help with my father's work."

Alexis wanted very much to eat, as well as to work. In this new and strange place, there wasn't anything he didn't want. His eyes were open to all. "Who are you, boy?"

"Well, as you can see, I'm a goatherd."

Alexis stood up and with the sun burning overhead, he walked on through the orchard with the goatherd boy.

"When we get to my house," the boy told him, "don't bother trying to talk to my father. He won't understand you. He speaks only the old language. In fact, best if you avoid him altogether."

Soon the two came to a little spread on the hill. It was a house surrounded by trees – plentiful trees where fruit grew and were indeed ripe. The house on the spread had a plaster roof and a fenced-in pasture where many goats were grazing. The boy led Alexis around the side and into a covered area. The roof was supported by wooden poles. There was straw on the ground. Inside this covered area, cheese was being cured with salt. "If you're hungry, eat this." The boy gave Alexis a single thin, dry, grey-colored cracker to eat. He then showed Alexis a barrel in which there was fat.

"Stir the fat," the boy told him. "Just like this." He put his stick in the fat and began to turn it. Alexis watched the instruction. In his hunger, he ate half of the grey cracker right away, but set the other half aside for later and began to stir the fat.

A good hour went by, and Alexis was alone doing his work when a small tanned and toothless old man came hobbling into the covered area. He was mumbling some incomprehensible words. He had an upset countenance and took Alexis stick away from him and began stirring the fat himself. Alexis took this to mean that he had been doing the work wrong, and so after watching the old toothless man for a few moments, he nodded his head in a polite manner, said okay, and attempted to take the stick back to resume stirring the fat. When he did this, however, the old man huffed and stamped one of his bare feet. He then slapped Alexis' wrist three or four times and began again grumbling in that strange language. Alexis stood there confused. He once again held out a hand as if to accept the stick and the burden of the work. The old toothless man then spit through his gums at him and ran out of the covered area. Alexis looked out after him, shrugged his shoulders, and picked up the stick from where it had fallen and stuck it back in the fat.

A moment later the old man returned with the goatherd boy at his side. The man was spitting angry sounds while slapping the boy's arm. The boy's eyes seemed to be concealing something. They darted back from Alexis to the man, then back to Alexis. Finally the goatherd boy explained to Alexis, "My father was not supposed to see you working." He then turned to the old man and spoke in some incomprehensible language to him. The old man nodded, then shook his head, then nodded again and looked around the place before finally settling on Alexis with a questioning glance.

"What?" Alexis asked.

The old man simply let his jaw fall down; and, while his mouth hung open, one could see he did indeed still possess one single tooth, and it dangled from his gums like a rock hanging on a string.

"My father doesn't want you doing the work," the boy finally said to Alexis, "You need to go."

Alexis understood clearly what this was all about.

"Fine," he said with angry calm. He took the remaining half of his meager little dry grey-colored cracker and walked quickly out of the covered area to go off on his way, neither looking at the father nor the boy as he left. Behind his back, he could hear the two of them arguing in that strange language. Alexis spat on the soil outside and walked quickly and he got a fair distance away before the boy finally caught him up and called out to him, "Wait, wait!"

Alexis turned to the boy and asked with malice, "What?!"

"Listen," the boy said, "You can stay and eat with us. I promised you a meal for working. I'm sorry. It will be ready soon."

Alexis said nothing for a moment. He didn't want the company of the young boy, nor of his old father. Still he was famished and needed badly a meal, and so he accepted the invitation to eat.

The golden sun dropped below the hilly landscape where that goatherd boy and his father lived on the spread of land where vegetables sprouted from the soil. There the three sat down to a meal at a table outside beneath a canopy of olive trees.

Alexis ate quickly, dipping his flat bread in the oiled rice with avarice. Throughout the meal, the father spoke in the old language to his son. At one point, the boy turned to Alexis, "Father says you can work here in return for food…" then he paused… "Just so long as he never sees you working. You'll have to hide when he comes. I'll bring your food around to you."

Alexis simply ignored the boy's idiotic talk while continuing to eat with great appetite.

The father then spoke in direct address in words that were easily understandable to Alexis, "You…?" he asked, "Where do you come from?"

Alexis set his bread down and turned to the boy, "I thought he couldn't speak our language?"

"He doesn't know more than fifty words of it. Practically nothing at all."

Alexis looked back at the old man. "I'm from a city," he told him, "the Great City."

The goatherd's father nodded. A bit of rice was stuck on his worn leathery lips. "Me…" he said, "I know nothing of cities. You… *dye…damyata!*" the father rambled off mumbling something in the old language and his son translated. "Father says, 'cities are poison and they are built from nothing but the blood of those who fail and the bones of those who succeed.'"

'The blood of those who fail and the bones of those who succeed,' Alexis repeated this in his own mind. These words put fabulous images in his head. His mind wandered back to the time of the Great City – 'Yet how far away all that is now!' He thought of the clean and smooth white color of the buildings there 'How beautiful they are, those buildings made from the bones of those who succeed!' Then he pictured the gutters in the streets of the Great City flowing in torrents and trickles, now with streams of brackish drain water, now with streams of the blood of those who fail … all along past the great white buildings built from their holy bones. These images gave such a beautiful smell to the city.

'Ah, the past! What a glorious thing that we are allowed at times memories of the past!' With his flatbread, he scooped up spiced herbs and olives dripping with oil into his mouth, and ate.

A moment later the goatherd's father scratched the bristle on his old chin, "You…!' he demanded of Alexis, 'What is it, this city you come from?"

Alexis dropped his bread on the table. "I'm truly not from the city," he told the boy's father. "I just lived in the city for a while. Truly, I'm from the Great Northern Woods. It's a place far from all cities. It is a place like this, except the sun burns cold and the trees have moss instead of fruit." Alexis went on then to describe his home while the boy translated his words for his father to understand.

"Then we are the same," the father said, "we are the same…" he repeated, following his sentence with some words in the old language… *"Filotêsi'an propi'nô…dya, dya!"* He then made a gesture as if to get up from the table. He looked at Alexis, but seeing Alexis didn't react, he sat back down.

"What did he say?" Alexis asked the boy.

"He said, since you are the same and since you come from similar places, that he can drink with you before you go. Before, he didn't want to."

'Before he didn't want to,' Alexis thought. He looked around at the little house with the loosely sewn patches of soil and the rolling hills on the perimeter, dotted with fruit trees and grazing goats. "Yet, we are not the same," Alexis turned back to the boy's father, "You have your land here, and are tied to it. You are tied to it at least till next harvest time. And even after autumn you will wait until your boy has grown. And even after that, you will probably remain here for the rest of your life, and you will die here. Me, I'm a traveler. A voyager. I belong to the road. So, while we do come from similar places, to similar places we do not go. And me, I must hurry. I cannot stay to drink. If I drink I will want to sleep. I have eaten and now I must go." He looked around himself as he pulled the sleeves down on his shirt to cover his forearms. He saw a goat peeling the bark off the trunk of a thin wispy tree with his teeth near a fence. The sun was enlarged; and as it sank in the sky, it touched the leaves on that tree and they began rattling like coins of jade in the evening breeze. Something about the rattling of leaves…Alexis stopped to consider a moment. He then said quietly to the father… "No, we are not the same. We are not the same, however, good old man, I will happily drink with you before I leave."

The boy relayed the message, and the father looked strangely at Alexis. Then he stood and went inside and brought out a corked bottle of clear liquor. He poured two glasses. The men lifted them and drank.

The three sat at the table. The boy's father and Alexis drank. The increasing blow of wind cooled the air, but the liquor flushed Alexis' head with warmth. "Do you know?" Alexis asked the two, "if we are in Thrace, or Bulgarie or Macedonia?"

The boy didn't know the answer and the father couldn't understand the question and the boy didn't know how to translate it.

'Hopeless,' Alexis thought. "Then do you know how I can get to the Acropolis from here?"

"That road down there," the boy pointed, "Follow it and it will lead to the Acropolis."

Alexis wondered if not the boy was lying as he had been. He surveyed the eyes of the two. The father turned and looked over his shoulder at that dusty evening trail and nodded to Alexis, mumbling something in that strange language of his.

Alexis sighed and looked at the road.

"Father says you can take his bicycle if you want. To go to the Acropolis. It will be faster."

Alexis looked at the old man with a questioning glance. He knew better than to take the boy's word for anything, lest he get slapped on the wrists again.

"Bicycle," the old man said. He stood and walked to the side of the house and dragged out a rickety old thing with broken spokes and a dusty seat. He wheeled it over to Alexis.

"But if I ride your bicycle to the Acropolis," Alexis said, "Then I will have to ride it back to return it to you."

The father shook his head and mumbled to his son.

"You don't need to bring it back," said the boy, "it's not my father's. He took it from the acropolis to ride home one day, so it belongs in the Acropolis. And so when you get there, just leave it somewhere."

'A sound idea,' Alexis thought. "Okay, thank you."

Meanwhile, night had fallen on the quiet land. Alexis and the boy's father had one more drink of the clear liquor together; then the father suggested Alexis sleep on a mat in the covered area and leave in the morning. Alexis thought this a good plan. He suggested he finish stirring the fat in exchange for the meal and the bicycle, but the father insisted that that was work for his boy to do. Alexis tucked himself away on the mat and fell fast and sound asleep. The next morning, he woke early to the sounds of birds in the trees. He looked for the boy and his father and found them working in the vegetable patch. Alexis bid them farewell, expressed his gratitude to the father and said that he

hoped his vegetables wouldn't get eaten by locusts. The father offered Alexis a
hat but it was worn and not very handsome and Alexis refused it. The boy gave
Alexis a brick of salted cheese wrapped in cloth. Alexis ate some and stuffed the
rest in his pocket and rode the rickety bicycle off down the dusty morning-lit
road.

Ô, the summer sun and gentle dawn, and all that comes does go along... Alexis
rode his borrowed bicycle on and on along winding roads, while the day proved
bright, pleasantly hot, and full of promise. After the morning riding, a glimpse
of the blue ocean emerged in the far distance. If the boy's direction were
correct, this glimpse of the ocean meant that he was not far off from the
Acropolis.

Hours more passed. The road wound on and on.

"If I remember right," Alexis told himself while peddling along, "Once,
long ago, I said that as a 'man of the world' I would no longer spend all day
traveling down long dirt roads. Didn't I? Yes, back in Krüfsterburg, I swore I
would only ride trains from then on, like a gentleman does. What little I knew
back then. I'm quite happy to be traveling down this long dirt road about
now...

"I honestly thought," he continued on with his soliloquy while
descending a slope on the rickety machine, "that when I first left home, within a
month's time I would be a king. That I would have dozens of servants to drive
me around in a seat of plush velvet with gold in my pocket and gems on my
fingers." ... "Now," he laughed, "look at me here! So long a time after, and
here now I am dusty, with no money, driving my own's self on a flimsy bicycle
down this sunny road in a strange country...

"And yet how far I have come! Then, I was where I didn't want to be,
going towards where I wanted to be. Now I am where I want to be, going
towards where I *will* want to be. Just as I was before, thus I am now: on a dirt
road. But now things are altogether different. My body is different. My mind
is different. What has changed? Well, I wouldn't say I have more memories
now...for then, Alexis, you were full of memories too, smaller memories,
though...memories of a more limited scope. *Memories* is a pretty word. It's like
shimmering. Or like *mirror*. *Mirrories*. Shimmering *mirrillories*. ...Regardless,
it is strange how life does not go the way one imagines it will go...how one's
fantasies describe it...how it is dreamt up with such grandiosity by the young
knight with his tin sword, and then later by the stripling with the light down of

a beard on his chin at the tale-end of boyhood; yet nonetheless, life expands incredibly, should one let it. It grows and soars to immense heights, expanding with greatness and great humbleness intertwined; and all the while in its humbleness, things turn out even more impressively than any boy could imagine. And just to think: if this glorious moment here was in store for me then and I didn't realize it then…then what will be in store for me later, which I don't realize now? Could I just answer that? Of course I can't! Oh, how happy I am!"

Chapter XII

"Time in the Garden" – Alexis' arrival in the Acropolis...

Alexis peddled merrily along that sunny afternoon until the time came he arrived at a fork in the road. He stood with his feet planted in the crabgrass off to the side of the road and looked at the sign that was posted there. One arrow pointed left. Below it, a sign read: ACROPOLIS CITY-CENTRE. He looked at the arrow pointing right. Below it, read: ACROPOLITAN PALACE.

"City-Centre?...or Acropolitan Palace?" he asked himself, "Well, which way?" He stood there spinning the front wheel of the bicycle with the toe of his floppy shoe while trying to decide where to go. "Well," he finally decided, "If a palace goes right, then Alexis too goes right!" And with that, he left the fork and started peddling the right way off down the road.

After an hour of riding, Alexis saw himself coming up upon a guardhouse. Signs were posted all around with words on them written in many strange languages. Of the words Alexis recognized, he read: ACROPOLITAN PALACE: ALL VISITORS MUST REPORT TO GUARDS.

'All visitors?' he thought continuing to travel along, 'well, I'm no visitor. If there truly is a palace up ahead, I might just stay forever!

'...That is,' he added humbly to this thought, 'if they'll have me.' ... 'For remember, Alexis, as you learned from your time in the basement, the world doesn't give a damn – at least not intrinsically. And it doesn't owe you any favors. Your laurels aren't going to come on a silver salver when you snap your fingers!'

Alexis kept peddling along past the signs; and when he passed the guardhouse, he smiled at the guards baring his teeth as he thought appropriate. They seemed to pay him no mind though, probably just assuming he was another local peasant farmer with the dust on his face and in his hair, and with his dirty brown trousers and rickety bicycle. Peasant farmers often passed on that road.

After the guardhouse, the road was paved with stones and lined with hedges and it wound uphill. The sun came through the cypress trees growing alongside, and the wind on his face was warm. He passed groves of fig trees. He passed vistas that looked out over the Acropolis – a singular landscape of ancient ruins embedded in a pastoral scape where rivers ran like frayed blue string and the mighty azure ocean swelled beyond far rocky cliffs.

Brittle pods of carob trees lining the lane crackled in the heat of the summer sun; while the birds, they twittered and hopped gaily from branch to branch. Alexis rode alongside the rockeries and the great manicured hedges with lacquered leaves until he reached the garden.

"I have found it!" he exclaimed letting his arms sweep out. "What?" he asked, rolling up his sleeves... "Arcadia!"

Arrival at the gardens of the Acropolitan Palace: Alexis dismounted and walked his bicycle up the paths. He looked around at the numerous treelets with little colored clumps of fruit planted on sunny berms, gentle bushes with their roselet buds. Brooks and streams ran here and there, with little white wooden bridges to cross them, joining into little garden paths. Coming from behind a wall of hedges, Alexis came to see the palace itself. What a sight to behold!...with its stone arches, its colonnades, latticed balconies and spires. On the far side, two castlesque towers concealed what appeared to be small fortified village. And there in the center, all of the sparkling streams and stone-paved paths converged at a garden square of flourishing petals and leaves that formed the palace's grand columned façade, held like a maiden of honor holds the bride's bouquet.

"An Arcadian palace, an Arcadian dream," Alexis muttered, lost in awe and revelry. He walked towards the palace, and he simply sighed and looked on ahead. Then, while a charm of finches fluttered down and swooped by yonder palace gates, he again simply sighed and looked on ahead.

It was there on the path, he felt something stinging his calf. "Aye!" he cried. "Snakebite!" He turned around and saw a little girl walking behind him. She'd been following him, swatting his leg with a branch that she was playing with. Her knees were all scratched up. She wore a little dirty yellow dress and had great big eyes.

Alexis smiled at her and asked her to whom she belonged. She pointed to the palace, and said she belonged there. She said she wanted to ride Alexis' bicycle but didn't know how. He tried to teach her. He lifted her up on the seat, but her feet wouldn't reach the peddles, so he ended up pushing her around the garden while she steered. She laughed the whole time.

This little girl was the daughter of the Head Cook at the palace. When he came out and found Alexis playing with her, he was very impressed. "She likes you a lot," he laughed. Alexis offered her the bicycle, "A gift for you! Don't worry, you'll grow into it." She stood there with timidly pursed lips, too shy to accept, but happy nonetheless. She looked up at Alexis shyly and fidgeted with the soiled hem of her yellow dress. The Head Cook tried to persuade Alexis not to give such a gift to his little girl – "It's a largess!" he said; but Alexis would have none of it. That bicycle needed to settle down with someone. The Head Cook thanked him while his daughter hid behind his leg. Alexis asked him who was living in the palace.

"The Governor," replied the cook.

"The Governor?" Alexis inquired. "…of the Acropolis?"

"The Governor of the whole region!" he said proudly. His daughter by this time had drifted from her father's leg to Alexis' leg where she now hung affectionately while her father patted her head.

Alexis thought this a good opportunity to ask the cook if there wasn't any work for him in the kitchen.

"I'll see what I can do," said the cook, "maybe there's some work for you." Yet the decision wasn't his to be made. He'd have to ask the Kitchen Supervisor.

Alexis remained in the garden with the girl and her bicycle, while the cook went inside to speak to the Kitchen Supervisor.

He came out a minute later with a disappointed look on his face… "There's no work to be had in the kitchen," he shook his head. "Wait! Hold on a second…." And with that, he disappeared again.

A few moments went by.

"You're in luck!" the cook said, coming back outside, "there's no work in the kitchen but you can work in the garden if you want. I just spoke to the Head Gardener. He said he can use an extra hand. Would you work as a gardener?"

'Work as a gardener?' Alexis thought, 'What an idea!'

The cook introduced him to the Head Gardener who wasn't as friendly as the cook, but pleasant enough. He was firm and gruff man with an oily mustache and dirty blue garden pants. He gave Alexis a tour of the palace gardens and told him where he could sleep. Alexis accepted the job with gratitude. 'Clean air, plants and sunshine,' he thought, 'much better than opium smoke at the House of Sevres, or crooks at the Bread Production Plant…Christ! That's a memory to forget altogether!'

Alexis was given a small rustic room in one of the stone castlesque towers on the west side of the palace. The floor was of packed earth, the walls were of sandstone. There was a cream-colored mattress of muslin and a little desk of dark wood with a drawer full of candlesticks. From the window which, having no glass, was rather an arched hole cut out of the stone, Alexis could look across a little open-air foyer, which served as the entrance to the fortified village on the left, by way of an large square behind the palace. Just past the foyer, on the other side of the entrance, he could see into the arched stone windows in the rooms of the second tower that was connected to the west wall of the palace.

Here, in his room in the tower, Alexis spent the evenings reading. The Head Cook had a brother in the village who was a scholar and owned a great many books to read. The work in the garden was gentle and ended at sundown – a time when Alexis enjoyed a brief, private promenade through the warm fragrant evening garden before he put his tools away and went to the kitchen to get his dinner from the cook. The cook liked his fellow palace staff members and took pride in making something that tasted good for them to eat in the evenings.

Then, back in his room, Alexis would sit alone on the earthen floor and eat this well-prepared, albeit humble, meal from an earthen bowl that was his own. He'd then go and let his food settle while lying down on the mattress of muslin, reading by the light of the candle burning on the sill carved out of the stone wall. There he'd read about the histories of far away places. He read novels – stories of lovers and travelers, tales of cities and countries.

Sometimes, in his room in the evening time, he would go and stand at the little arched window and look out across the dark foyer. A couple of goats were kept tied-up by the door built into the second tower across the way and they made all sorts of noises. From his window, Alexis could see into the room of the man who lived in this other tower. This man, an old hunchback, stayed up evenings painting large canvases. He painted fantastical pictures of heroic gods warring and making love. The hunchback dressed himself like a monk, in a brown hooded robe of burlap; and as he painted, he munched grape leaves stuffed with rice. His easel faced the window, and Alexis had a clear view of it; so at the times when Alexis finished a part of a book or tired from reading, he would go stand at his window and look out across the foyer; and there the hunchback would be standing at his easel, dabbing color on one of the flowing robes of his gods or adding a tinge of gold to a tresslet of hair. He liked to take a peek at least once an evening to see how his paintings were progressing. When Alexis slept at night, the muslin mattress was comfortable, and he slept well.

The work in the garden was gentle and began at dawn. He worked in the sunshine, in the clean southern air, tending flowers, pruning plane trees, trimming the vines of grapes.

"Ah, what a better life this is than that of a basement dweller in the city!" he rejoiced one clear morning while digging up earth in a grove of olive trees where he had intended to plant a rose bush. Charms of birdlets flew in playful chains overhead. "This, oh life, is sweet perfection!...

"...Yet maybe," he stopped himself with doubt, "maybe there are yet better lives to be had. What life would I have if I had chosen another place to live?...say Damascus, or Guadalajara, Alexandria or Yekaterinburg? ... Could it be better in one of those places? Perhaps elsewhere, instead of being employed in a garden, I would be the owner of a garden. I would be lord of all gardens, even. Yes, lord of all gardens!"...And on his thoughts went as such and such.... Shovel, shovel, pick, spade, dig... 'Yet, this is a good life, no doubt. Better than a basement! Let me just lie beneath this olive tree and dream a minute....'

"No you don't, young man!" came the voice of the Head Gardener from out of nowhere, "You've work to do! Get out from under that tree and go tend the flowers!"

Later on that day, Alexis was tending flowers on the other side of the garden, by the bye. The Head Gardener was working beside him, watering lavender. "These are beautiful flowers," Alexis said to him, "We don't have these in the north."

"They're for the Governor's daughter," the Head Gardener replied through his oily brown mustache.

"All these flowers?!" Alexis looked around the immense garden at the abundance of blooming colored petals on the infinite array of stems sprouting from the fertile soil.

"Yes, all these flowers. All are for the Governor's daughter. This is the Governor's garden and all the flowers are for his daughter."

Alexis looked around, quite impressed.

"You see, Alexis," the Head Gardener explained, "it is you who tends the flowers. Another employee picks them – one large bouquet's worth per day. Another removes their thorns and washes their leaves. Still yet another person on the staff arranges them. While a subsequent one inspects the arrangements to ensure that they are beautiful enough to be presented to the Governor's daughter. And there is yet another who finally presents them to her – one large and beautiful bouquet every morning when her highness wakes up!"

"When she wakes up!" Alexis repeated. His eyes brightened thinking of the tremendous ceremony involved with the daily presentation of flowers to one important man's daughter. "...And who, may I ask out of curiosity, presents the flowers to her every morning?"

"Horace," replied the Head Gardener, "hunchbacked old man, second cousin of the Governor."

"Hunchbacked old man, you say?" Alexis rubbed his chin "...second cousin of the Governor? ...Very curious!"

With that, the Head Gardener left Alexis and the watered lavender to go supervise the other garden workers elsewhere around the palace. Alexis finished up his work while whistling a happy song.

Early the next morning, whilst Alexis was working away on a sunny berm near the foyer that separated the gardens from the village and the square, he heard the loud bleating of the goats tied up outside the hunchback's door. He set down his spade and looked over and saw one of the garden workers whom he didn't know standing before the tower knocking on the hunchback's door. The worker was holding a great bouquet of flowers – roses and honeysuckle. The goats were trying to eat the roses and were sneezing loudly while doing so. The garden worker fended them off and the hunchback soon opened his door. He hobbled out and took the bouquet from the garden worker, said 'good day' and 'thank you.' Alexis paid particular attention to the hunchback's voice when he said this – it was a curious voice, a squeaky and crotchety voice. After the worker gave the flowers up, he turned away and disappeared off through the foyer in the direction of the village. The hunchback then headed off with the bouquet for the side door leading into the palace. Alexis looked on and smiled as he retook his spade. He smiled because those were the roses and honeysuckle flowers that he had tended. With pleasure he smiled and looked on as they disappeared through the west door of the palace in the hands of the hunchback, second cousin of the Governor, off to go be presented to his daughter as she awoke in her bed.

After the sun had flit over the earth and sunset came with its golden hues, Alexis took his usual after-work walk through the garden; yet as he did so this time, he left the principal gardens and went out to the quiet environs. There he gathered up a bouquet of wildflowers, not as pretty as the roses and honeysuckles such as had been delivered to the Governor's daughter that day, but oh so very fragrant! He then picked some ambrosia, a sprig of valerian, another of passionflower and a bit of chamomile. All this he took to his room and put in a vase of water on the sill next to his candle.

That dinnertime, the Head Cook prepared a nice dish of peppers in oil, salted cheeses, breads of different kinds. Alexis filled his bowl and went off to his room where he ate and read until he was tired enough to sleep. When he got up to blow out the candle, he looked out the window across the dark foyer. Horace could be seen in the glow of candlelight at his easel with a quiver of brushes, his palette dabbed with oil paints and his plate of grape leaves stuffed with rice. Alexis watched him from his own darkened room for some time. He recognized on the canvas a scene from one of the books he'd been reading. It depicted Penelope waiting for Ulysses. Longing for him, she sewed buttons on one of her robes. The strap of her sandal was torn, as was the yellowed lace of her bra. The old hunchback lingered on the strokes of her lower lip, while her wandering eyes gazed out the window. Whence he placed the canvas aside, he resumed work on another – this one of warring gods. He then worked on his painting of what Alexis believed to be Aphrodite making love to a mortal – a man bound to a bed with his wrists tied. She kneeled over him with her maidenly hips, rubbing red oil on his body. As Alexis stood sleepless at the window, he looked now on at Horace across the way, now at his own sill, at the wildflowers he had taken from the garden that afternoon, the flowers he had arranged with his nimble fingers. Pollen was caked on these flowers and they emitted a great fragrance so strong that it entranced Alexis and filled his mind with notions of dalliance.

In the small hours of night, after having had eaten a great many grape leaves, old Horace, letting out a groan, set his canvas aside, abandoned the easel, and went over to his bed where he lay rubbing his belly in pain. Alexis watched with great interest from the window. When finally he saw that Horace appeared to be sleeping, he took some of the sprigs of flowers from the vase on his window and went outside into the dark night.

Outside, the foyer was silent and empty. When Alexis approached Horace's door, the goats began to sneeze. Alexis fed them some ambrosia and they quieted down. He stood then by the window and peeked inside. A bit of rumpled snoring could be heard coming from Horace's bed. Take care, Alexis! – he pushed open the door and crept inside.

The hunchback was asleep in a cotton nightgown. His hands draped over his large belly, he snored in gashes – faintly, heavily, faint. Alexis creaked the door closed behind him, making every effort not to wake the sleeping man; yet when the door was shutting, it snagged a rock on the packed earth floor and made a scraping noise. Thereupon, Horace choked on a snore and it just about roused him; but before he could wake up, Alexis, who had tip-toed over to his bed, laid the sprigs of valerian, chamomile, and passionflower under his nose. The fumes from the flowers drifted up and old Horace then went far, far and deep into sleep, snoring louder than ever before.

With the hunchback in the background, Alexis crept over the dresser aside the easel and opened one of the drawers. From there, he took out one of his brown burlap monk's robes. He pushed the drawer closed again and dressed in Horace's clothes. Now in disguise, Alexis surveyed the room. He then tip-toed over to the bed and, careful not to let the flowers fall from beneath Horace's nose, he took the pillow out from beneath his head. The hunchback kept snoring and didn't stir in the slightest. Alexis clutched the pillow and looked down at the sleeping man and held it above his face. Another look at Horace, then again at the pillow…then he wondered something…

'Will it be enough?'

'Yes,' he told himself, 'It will be enough…'

…And so with that, he lowered the pillow. He stuffed it up underneath the burlap monk's robe; and there he kept it, so as to give the impression that he too had a hunched back.

Now it was done. Alexis had become old Horace – old Horace the hunchback.

Following these exercises, he pulled the hood up from the burlap robe to cover his head and crept out of the room, crossed the foyer past the lulled and tranquil goats, and returned to his own.

Back inside, Alexis lay down on his bed to wait. He folded his hands over his chest. The lump in his back was pushed up against the stone wall.

The hours of night passed and once the blae light of dawn seeped in with softness in the sky; once the stars lightened and the first birds began to whistle in the trees, Alexis got up from his muslin mattress and went over to the window. He took a breath of the thin air of dawn and noticed the silver stars were fading quickly as the sky grew evermore light. He tied the cord of the burlap robe around his waist. He went to the bed and put on his sandals. He practiced hunching over as best as he could, and feeling quite convinced of his own disguise, he returned to the windowsill and took the bouquet of wildflowers from it.

He then left his room.

He looked left towards the square, everything seemed quiet and abandoned. He hobbled across the foyer in the fashion of a hunchback. He saw a gardener he knew dragging a rake over one of the berms nearby in the gardens. Alexis' nimble hand pulled the hood well over his head to cover his face. Tip-toe, tip-toe…at Horace's window he peered inside to check once again. Sound as lead, asleep with flowers under his nose! Those pesky goats too were quiet. Alexis hobbled around the side of the palace to the same door he had seen Horace entering through the day before with the roses and honeysuckle. Skittishly, he looked left and right, opened the side door, and then once in the corridor, he shut it behind him and was gone.

The stair was dark. Grey stone circular stairway winding upwards. Alexis mounted swiftly the two flights of steps. At the top, he came to a long, clear hallway that led apparently to the east wing of the palace. Far at the end, there was a balcony. Beyond it, he could see the sun had risen over the hills. Its light flooded the hallway like golden wafers of scattered coins. Alexis hobbled horacely along, clutching his hood on his head as well as the bouquet of wildflowers. When he came to a door on the left, he opened it: a dining room table set with crystal dishes, attended to by elegantly upholstered chairs – not a soul belonging to a person. He closed the door and hobbled up ahead. He then passed a grand carpeted stairway that led downstairs to an anteroom. Sniff, sniff, he checked the arrangement of the flowers he held and passed the stairway quickly. Then he came to a door on the right. He turned the knob slowly and opened it to peak inside.

The young lady's bedroom was spacious and airy. The fragrance of lilacs, the room of a maiden. Lace curtains were pulled open and the early light poured in from the balcony; and the summer morning breeze that came in from the open terrace was mildly warm and fresh. There, in the middle of the room sat a small bed made up with pink rose-colored sheets. And upon this bed was a sleeping girl – spread out across the sheets, dressed in a gown, the light cream light of dawn cast lengthwise across the curves of her silently breathing body.

Alexis hobbled horacely over to the nightstand by her bed. He stood above her and watched her body rise and fall with its breaths. There beside her on the nightstand was a vase – empty and half-filled with clear water, just waiting for the new morning's flowers. There in that vase on the nightstand beside her, Alexis set the bouquet of wildflowers, and as he did so she stirred slightly.

Oh, sweet girl in the presence of spring. He looked down upon her, on that head of hair, a tangled nest of weaves thrown upon a sleeping face. Her eyelids gripped each other in their struggle with a fleeting sleep…now thin, now deep. Alexis-as-Horace adjusted the flowers in the vase; and as he did so, their pollen flaked from their stems and their perfume filled the room. It was then, with this, that the sleeping young lady began to stir. She arched her small back in a stretch and yawned.

Alexis grew nervous. "Why are you waking, little one?" he whispered, feigning the squeaky voice of crotchety old Horace. The young lady stirred even more. She sniffed with her nose again and again, and opened her eyes, and stretched and yawned.

"No little one," he whispered, "don't stir." But while she stirred and sniffed she looked about her; and when she looked at her nightstand, she said in a sweet sleepy voice… "Oh, Horace, these flowers you brought today… they are so more fragrant than usual…and so more beautiful!"

Alexis turned quickly now, pulling the hood farther down over his eyes, and like a hook-nosed bandit with that pillow stuffed up the back of his burlap robe; he, in his hotchety way, hobbled off towards the door to leave.

"But where are you going, Horace?" she called from her bed, "Old Horace, you big mole! Come back and tell me a morning story!"

Here, the imposter stopped at the door and turned his nose to the left side. He glanced at the girl from the corner of his eye.

"But Horace," she called out, stretching again, "You've grown younger!" She glanced down at his bare calves visible beneath his coffee brown robe.

"You've turned into a boy, Horace!" The young lady sat up in her bed, "...or else you aren't him at all!"

Alexis stood still and petrified by the door. The Governor's daughter, thereupon, climbed out of bed and wrapped her rose-colored sheets around her body. Alexis didn't move. The girl then ran towards him in a trail of sheets, and when she reached him, she yanked the burlap hood from of his head. He turned with urgency to her. His cheeks appeared painted like a masquerade doll, his nose resembled a beak. He looked at her. She looked at him, at his blue eyes and golden temples.

Then, she giggled.

But why was she giggling?

The young lady was about to burst into laughter; but before she could do this or any other thing, Alexis flushed with shame and ran out of the room. Without looking back, he ran down the hallway and the down the stairs and out the palace door.

That day Alexis worked as usual, tending the flowers in the garden; though he felt horribly panic-stricken. A knot of fear burned in his stomach. But he kept fastidiously at his job, spading soil around the tulips and chrysanthemums. He paid much attention to the roses and tended all the pretty flowers that day, avoiding wildflowers such as those he had presented to the Governor's daughter early on that morning. Spade, spade, spade...oh, what horses galloped in his gut! Why had he done that? Terrible wildflowers with their potent fragrance! Surely a madness had been boiling in his brain. Now he was certain to lose his job. First sight of the Head Gardener, it was sure, Alexis would be shamed and sent away from the palace forever.

Thus, he avoided the Head Gardener all day. He didn't take lunch, but kept on working on the flower berms far removed from the palace façade. Late in the afternoon, however, he needed to find the Head Gardener to have his spade sharpened. "Better just get it over with," he told himself. A certain relief came knowing that he could at once put an end to the uncertainty, just simply by taking his spade to be sharpened. Still, he was rueful and gloomy nonetheless. He'd grown fond of his job, fond of his little room in the tower with an earthen floor and sandstone walls; fond of the foods prepared by the Head Cook and the books loaned to him by the scholar who lived in the village. He'd grown fond of lying on the muslin mattress on the warm nights, reading by the glow of a candle, and waking to the pastel light of the predawn and the songs of the young birds. He'd grown fond of his life at the Acropolitan Palace and he didn't want to lose it. 'But things terminate and a man moves on,' he understood this well by now. So, dragging his spade behind him, he walked across the gardens to the Head Gardener's shed to have it sharpened and get the matter over with

Alexis imagined what the Head Gardener would say: "Sharpen a spade? You don't get a sharp spade, you!...entering the Governor's daughter's private bedroom while she's sleeping to present her with ugly wildflowers! Get away from the palace grounds! You are lucky not to get hanged! How would like to be hanged today?! Huh? We could easily arrange that!" ...Yet the Head Gardener said nothing of the sort. When Alexis came to him, he simply took Alexis' spade and sharpened it for him.

Still the unsettling feeling didn't cease, the torment didn't subside. Alexis knew it was only a matter of time before the Governor himself, upon whom he'd never laid eyes, came in person to have him arrested for entering his daughter's chamber. And so, before the day was over, when he could bear the dread no more, he went and visited the high office of the Governor himself...

"What are you doing here, young man?" the Governor asked Alexis when he entered his office. Guards stood perplexed behind Alexis who had pushed his way through carrying a little tin garden pail.

"I came to offer you my services in any unpleasant task you wish, your Honor. What I am doing now is too easy, too pleasant, not at all fitting for a strong young man such as myself. Tell me, sir, is Horace alright? I haven't seen him for days."

"Oh, Horace is alright," the Governor replied with a distracted wave of his hand, "...stuck in bed with a belly ache. But tell me, son, how do you know Horace? Who are you? And what is the work you are doing now?"

"Why, I am Alexis, sir, employed in your gardens!"

"Well how should I know this?! I don't know the people employed in my gardens. But if you are supposed to work there, get back to work and leave me to my important matters. And if I find some unpleasant work for you, I will be sure to let you know – good day!"

After Alexis was dismissed, the guards followed him down the stairs and out the side door of the palace. Once they left him he went back to the garden shed to get his spade to resume working. It was while he was doing so that he saw the Governor's daughter coming out of the palace towards the gardens. She was wearing a dress and ribbons in her hair that were fitting for a young lady of decent age. She didn't see Alexis, but rather looked at the Head Gardener who was raking a patch of soil not far off. In her hand, she held a bouquet of chrysanthemums and tulips. "Hey you there, with the rake!" she called out to the Head Gardener in a haughty scolding voice, "Hey, rake man!" The Head Gardener dropped his rake and ran obediently to the beckoning girl.

Alexis went back into the shed and took his spade. He then crossed a little wooden bridge over a stream on the eastside of the gardens, where some crocuses needed attention. He was only back at work a few minutes before the Head Gardener came and found him.

"Alexis!" he shouted in an angry voice.

'Oh, no,' Alexis thought, 'It has come!' he dropped his spade and looked expectantly at the Head Gardener. All the while, a fierce burning seared his stomach.

"Alexis!" the Head Gardener shouted angrily from afar, brandishing a bouquet of chrysanthemums and tulips. When he reached Alexis he stopped to catch his breath. He then continued in a quieter, yet still angry, voice, "The Governor's daughter sent these back. They are wilted. How dare you tend wilted flowers?! Wilted flowers must be thrown away before the Picking Gardener picks them! You'd better watch yourself, Alexis. If you ever allow wilted flowers to grow in this garden again, you'll be sent away. Sent away, I tell you!" And with that, the Head Gardener stomped off and Alexis was left standing alone, holding the bouquet of rejected flowers sent back by the Governor's daughter. He inspected them closely. Wait! They were not wilted. No, they were not wilted at all, but there was a note inside. A note tucked in the flowers, written on rose-colored paper. It read simply:

BOY! COME TO THE TERRACE TONIGHT AT THE TWENTY-SECOND HOUR.

...AND MUST I REALLY TELL YOU WHICH TERRACE??!

Alexis folded the note, kissed it, and put it inside the breast pocket of his shirt. Oh, joyful life and the coming of spring! Throughout the rest of the day he worked and whistled and had a mood so happy that it could not be believed. Even the sun burnt twice as bright and twice as warm. Everything smelled clean and perfect.

After work, he skipped dinner and had a bath. He then went for a walk in the garden to kill time. He anxiously strolled down the paths, scattering gravel absentmindedly with his foot which upset some of the flowerbeds he'd spent the entire day tending, but he paid no notice. He crossed the footbridge over a stream and found a patch of meadow where some dandelions were growing. 'The perfect thing!" he exclaimed, and picked a few sprigs. With the bouquet of dandelions in his hand, he headed off for Horace's room.

The old hunchback was lying on his bed, rubbing his sore belly when Alexis knocked and entered.

"Horace?" Alexis called, "I brought you some dandelions. They'll help your stomach ache."

"Oh...oh, thank you," old Horace moaned in a squeaky and crotchety tone, "who are you?"

"Alexis is my name. I work in the gardens. Dandelions are the best cure for a bad stomach, I tell you..." his eyes darted around the room, "we're all worried about you, Horace!" As he said this, his thoughts were elsewhere, "The laundress said to give her your clothes and she'll wash them." He spied the dresser drawer.

"Oh...okay," Horace squeaked, "She can take my clothes, just let me rest a while, I don't feel so good."

Alexis insisted he'd give the clothes to the laundress personally. He opened the dresser and took out one of Horace's hooded burlap robes, "I'll have her bring your clothes back clean when she's done." Without waiting for a reply, he flew out of the room.

Back in his room, he began to change into the robe and ready himself. Then, realizing it was still too early to go to the terrace, he stopped and headed back to the gardens to kill more time. The sun had just set and the sky was a blooming deep violet. Nightingales began to flutter to the tree bows, while his own stomach began to flutter with aches of nervousness for his meeting to come. He went to the kitchen every five minutes or so to check the time on the clock – half past eight o'clock seemed to linger forever.

Finally, as often occurs with time, the fateful hour arrived. The violet of evening seeped into the horizon to make way for the night – a clear moon like a silver coin hovered between wisps of clouds in the crisp dark sky. At the twenty-second hour, Alexis – dressed in Horace's coffee brown burlap robe with its hood pulled up over his head (this time with no pillow stuffed up the back) – passed through the gardens and arrived beneath the terrace that was known to belong to the fair young lady. There he climbed the rockery, climbed the lattice, up the limbs of a fig, then swung his legs over the marble rail and entered onto the balcony of the Governor's daughter.

When Alexis appeared, the young woman was seated alone at the table outside on her terrace. She wore a white silk coat. Tea service was set before her and slices of fruit. Her gaze rested on the ivy vines that climbed and clung to the lattice walls of the balcony. The moon shone on her face, glimmering on her eyelids and lips.

Alexis came from the far end of the terrace, crossing through the shadows stealthily, with nothing of nervousness in his strides. The Governor's daughter appeared to be lost in thought as her fingers played with a piece of ivy that had come unhinged from the lattice; she didn't notice him at first. Halfway across the terrace, he raised his hand and pulled the hood from his head to fully reveal himself. It was then the seated miss heard that he had come, and she turned to him.

This lovely daughter of the Governor turned and looked Alexis carefully in the eyes. She looked carefully…there was a slight pause, then… then she gave a yell…"Ah! What are you doing here?!"

A startled Alexis took a step back. The girl made another little scream. From her chair where she sat, she swatted at him. Swatted him away as if she were swatting at a horrible winged insect. Who was this intruder! Her face had the look of shock as if Alexis' presence on her terrace was the most absurd thing on earth. He, meanwhile, was so startled that he almost tripped over a footstool while backing up; had he done so, he would have certainly toppled over the railing and fallen down to the gardens below. Having caught himself, he reached for the railing, as if to climb back over and hide himself.

The girl screamed again.

'But why is she screaming? What is she doing? Someone might hear her!' Alexis backed farther away. By now, the Governor's daughter had come to her feet and was pursuing him. And as she pursued him, she swatted at him with her small lovely hand. There was, however, no loveliness in her expression.

"What are you doing on my balcony?!" By this time, Alexis was truly worried that someone had heard her, and although he found the railing of the balcony he'd been groping for, he dropped it and ran up to her so as to cover her mouth so she wouldn't make any more noise. And as soon as he made this lunging movement towards her, she stopped swatting and calmed peaceably down.

"But you asked me to come!" Alexis voice was beseeching, as if all that he hoped for in the world was that the young miss would not scream anymore. He looked into her eyes, "You asked me to come." ...and she into his. And here she let her hand fall on her breast that was heaving from the excitement and she calmly looked at back him and said, "Oh...so I did." Her reply was expressionless. She calmly turned and walked back over to her chair at the table, where she sat back down. Alexis remained standing, hoodless, looking at her, half expecting her to scream out again.

"Well," she said to him in a calm and reasonably pleasant voice, "come, sit down."

Alexis looked around him suspiciously, and then walked over to the table and took the empty chair beside her.

"There is tea," she offered, "I'm sorry if it's cold. Tea is served at eight. The maids are in bed asleep."

Alexis didn't reply, but just sat and sipped his tea, relieved and grateful that the girl had stopped screaming, and glad that she had finally realized that he came because he'd been invited.

Now close beside, he looked at her. How earthly beautiful she was. Now as she had been in her bed. Impossible beauty. More so now here, in noticing a delightful imperfection, an almost imperceptible dark fleck in the white of her eye. She lifted her hand to drink. Around her wrist hung a light gold bracelet thin as a thread of gossamer.

"You probably wonder why I asked you to come," she broke in suddenly, taking the silence.

No, he wasn't wondering. He thought he knew why.

"I just wanted to know where those flowers came from…the strange ones you brought."

That was why?!

"…Their perfume was so…well, where possibly did they come from? Anyway, a lady enjoys flowers but she likes to know from whom they come."

"From your garden," replied Alexis, as though stating the obvious, "they came from your garden, miss, and if you'd like, I can show you…" …and here he used the familiar 'thou' and the Governor's daughter interrupted him with a stern and haughty voice, "Listen, boy! Neither 'miss' nor 'thou' should you be calling me. 'My Ladyship' is the proper way for you to address me, for I am after all the Governor's daughter." The whole time during her speech, she addressed Alexis in the familiar 'thou' herself. "…And do you really think I'd let you show me where the flowers came from? Are you delusional? Do you think I would go out into my gardens at night?! First," she continued, "you sneak onto my terrace – onto *my* private terrace! – and then you try to get me to follow you into the garden? Are you mad?!" She took a breath and calmed down a little, "…besides," she sighed a haughty sigh, "there are snakes out there."

The Governor's daughter took a sip from her cup and cast her eyes upwards at Alexis, "No. First I will finish my tea. Then I will sleep. And you," she flashed her eyes at him, "you, garden boy, shouldn't be here. You should be out killing snakes and other night creatures." And then she leaned close and whispered in his ear. He could feel her hot breath on his lobe; and with this hotness came a dampness, and a sweet scent like acacias and clover flowers. "And do you know," she whispered to him, as he trembled with the sensation of her full lips close to his skin. He leaned forward closer towards her, yearning for that mouth with its hot damp and sweet breath to touch him… "you could be hanged for coming onto my balcony at night."

Just then, Alexis heard a stirring in the other room. It sounded like a door flying open. Then the sound of the footsteps of several men. "Oh, it's nothing," the Governor's daughter said, leaning back in her chair and laughing slightly, "Just the wind blowing through the door," but Alexis gave a start. He did not want to be hanged for accepting the young lady's invitation to come to her private terrace. His eyes darted around and he made as if to stand and leap off the balcony.

"Oof!" she huffed in annoyance as he stood up, but it was too late. He was now on his feet looking over the balcony to where he thought he should leap over to. He could leap to the bow of the fig tree, he thought. Meanwhile the Governor's daughter sat calmly sipping her tea. She winced at the bitterness and reached out to take a white sugar drop from a plate in the center of the table. She stirred the sugar in with her rose-white finger and gave a funny look to Alexis, observing with amusement what he was doing as he was halfway over the rail, trying to reach out to the limbs of the fig tree with his leg.

During this exercise, the young lady stood up and walked over to Alexis and took a hold of the burlap cloth of the robe he was wearing and tugged it, urging him to stop his attempts to flee and come back onto the balcony. She pulled on his robe, pulling him towards her, and he heeded her gesture and swung his leg back around. 'So it shall be!' He climbed down off the rail and went back to sit at the table. 'Let them come take me if they will' he sighed in surrender. The two remained seated quietly a moment. Then the young lady leaned close to him as if she wanted to say something else to him. The curtains of her balcony doors swept in the window and Alexis looked past those doors and could see into her bedroom at the tidy bed, well made up with rose-colored sheets. Alexis looked back at the young lady. He decided to be bold then and speak freely. Her hand which had dropped from the cloth of his robe, fell into her lap. Her eyes remained looking at him – eyes dark and glossy – black like obsidian. She leaned towards him and her lips parted. These lips slightly swollen, slightly damp, soft and red like the seeds of a pomegranate fruit. And here Alexis grew bold... he leaned close and began to...but...

"But now you really must go," she said first, before he could say or do anything.

"But wait!" he said to her, trying to draw her near, but she was unwilling. "But maybe there is a way..." His voice was somewhat imploring, somewhat firm and confident, overall hopeful. "Maybe there is a way that this doesn't have to be our last meeting..."

She didn't interrupt.

"...Maybe the Governor's daughter would like to meet this flower tender in the noontime, in the sunshine, where he could take her for a walk in her gardens...."

To this, she tossed her head back and laughed quite loudly, obviously amused by his earnest request. "Boy!" she exclaimed, "the garden is for you. The high palace room is for me! And from the balcony of my high palace room, I can already see well, well beyond that garden where you want to take me; well beyond the palace gates even!

"...And besides," she continued, "though you may be able to protect me from the snakes who slither out there – for you are a garden boy after all – you are still just a boy all the same. What interest would I have in a boy?"

"But I am no boy!" he exclaimed, "You..." (he now addressed her formally) "Perhaps you can see beyond your palace gates from your balcony. Perhaps you can. But have to ever traveled beyond them? No? Ha, I thought not. Well, I have, my dear. I have traveled through cities and countries far and wide, you can be certain," and here he resumed addressing her as 'thou,' "and anyway..." with a loss of more to say "...anyway, I am not such a boy. My body is that of a man, my age is that of a man,, my chin and cheeks are rough, not smooth...."

"Enough!" the Governor's daughter waved her hand in haughty contempt, "Enough of this smooth and rough. Smooth and rough, these are the words of a boy! To be with the Governor's daughter, you have to be a man. I can teach you many things, garden boy, I can teach you about women, but I cannot teach you to be a man."

Here, Alexis searched in his quiver for an arrow to aim back at his opponent. Having none, he said nothing, while the Governor's daughter continued her speech with vehemence, "...Anyway, you will find nothing of the sort within these palace gates, my garden boy, I speak of manhood, so I suggest you go back out there, out beyond the gates which I see all too clearly from my high palace room, and out there become a man..." then she recoiled, took a breath and added calmly, "...and then come back to me with your proposals."

There was little else Alexis could do or say, though he remained a few moments searching for words that likely did not exist, or perhaps they existed but could not be ordered rightly around one another; all the while the Governor's daughter stacked sugar drops on top of each other on the plate. It was then that a sweep of wind blew the bedroom curtains aside. Alexis, startled, looked back over his shoulder through the doorway to the Governor's daughter's balcony and back into her room, and there he saw clearly the figure of a man standing, peering through a crack in the door – the door leading out to the hall – it was the Governor! Her father, he had come. And he appeared to Alexis like the king from a playing card: a jeweled man with a fiery heart, a spade and club dangling over his head. Ah, the Governor! Alexis leapt to his feet.

As Alexis stood and backed away, the young lady's black jeweled eyes darted back and forth questioningly across his face – as if she too wasn't finished with their meeting, with their careful and reckless game, this scrimmage of rook and queen. But, alas!, it was the end of the meeting. Alexis wished to say goodnight, oh he did so, to kiss her hand once soft, but he had not the time. And watch the way the daughter stirred when he backed away, it was as if she too were worried for him, for the fate that would arrive him – either in the palace or out in the world. She stood from her balcony chair and pulled her white coat tightly around her, while Alexis – with a final glance at this King of Clubs standing beyond far chamber's door, while looking in with piercing eyes – turned and swung his legs over the railing, took hold of the sturdy branches of the fig tree, and descended by way of that tree into the shadows of the night garden, off the way he had come. He snuck quietly through the foyer; and, removing the burlap robe, he folded it and set it on Horace's windowsill. He then crossed to his own room and took for the night to his muslin bed with fiery dreams and romantic plans.

In the days that followed, Alexis learned that the Governor's daughter's name was Sophia. Sophia learned that Alexis' name was Alexis. The two, however, did not see one another during this time. Alexis was not invited to visit anymore terraces; and, anyway, he was too busy preparing to leave the palace, to go on her mention to become a man.

'Haven't I been doing that already?' he wondered, tossing the idea around in his head. 'What has all this travel been? What was that basement about if not to make me a man? And how piercingly her father looked at me!' his mind went on as such and such while he tended the flowers in the coming days. Alexis was certain that when he'd been on the balcony, the Governor recognized him as the one who had come to his office prior to offer himself in unpleasant tasks. 'But how would he remember me? He, Governor and Lord of the city and country…and me, but a knave and garden hand…no certainly, oh but he did remember me!" … "Well, Alexis, my friend," he inquired of himself, "where are you off to next?"

Yet by this time, he felt a strangely happy indifference to everything. Of course, on the first morning following his nighttime visit with the Governor's daughter on her balcony, he awoke fearing that it would be only a matter of minutes before the Governor's guards came to imprison Alexis for his intrusion. "The gallows are being built as I blink my very eyes!" he told himself. But to his surprise, the day passed and no punishment came.

On the second day, this punishment seemed even more inevitable. When Alexis inquired casually about the name of the Governor's daughter to the scholar in the village that afternoon when he came to return the books he had borrowed, the scholar seemed to have a knowing look of pity. And the air the Head Gardener took in dealing with Alexis that day was nothing short of apocalyptic. Still, Alexis was abuzz with the joys of love. There was something even heroic about the idea of being hanged for meeting that noble beauty on her private terrace. "I will die a legend! She will keep a tress of my hair, with which to ward off future suitors, she will lock herself away." For all this, he didn't hasten to leave the palace as quickly as he maybe should have. Still, the second day passed by and no punishment came.

It was on the third morning after his meeting with Sophia, that Alexis was roused in his bed before dawn to the shouts of two officers knocking on loudly his door.

"Wake up and come outside!" they shouted.

Alexis leapt with a shock. "No, already!" Now that it had come, his indifference and love of heroism vanished. He was suddenly mortally afraid. 'But it can't come like this!'

"Wake up and come outside!" the officers yelled again.

Alexis hurriedly pulled his trousers on and slipped into his shirt; and, with a terrified racing heart, he ran to open his door.

When he got outside, the guards were gone.

Alexis stood there a minute.

"Wake up and come outside!" they yelled again. But this time they were yelling it to someone else. They were standing by a door leading to a little house in the village a little ways off past the square. Alexis squinted and saw that the guards were passing by all the doors in the vicinity, rousing all the garden workers and all the village dwellers. They hadn't just come for him. By each house they stood as by the one before it, knocking on the doors with solid fists yelling, "Wake up and come outside!"

'What is the meaning of this?' The only thing Alexis could think of was that this was going to be the lineup to spot the person who had intruded on the Governor's daughter's balcony three nights prior. 'Of course!' Alexis realized with terror, 'the Governor recognized me, but he doesn't know where I live, so these soldiers are bringing everyone out so the governor can come personally identify me – then they'll erect the gallows in the foyer and string me up!' Oh, what caustic horror chewed his gut.

"Wake up and come outside!" the officers yelled again on the far side of the square passing down the lanes of the little village from house to squatty house. As they made their rounds, people of all sorts emptied out of their houses into the streets – some clothed, others wearing sleeping dress, others nude – to see what the commotion was about. Some had fear-stricken faces. Others, looks of confusion. Still others looked simply tired.

Then the officers yelled… "All young men must report to the Grand Plaza for the conscription of the troops!"

"The conscription of the troops?" Alexis exclaimed, "Fancy that!" Suddenly the fear was swept from his stomach. It wasn't just about him after all! With the tenseness relieved from his body, he casually buttoned his cotton shirt and brushed his hand through his sleep-tousled hair. Just then, one of the armed officers who had come to make another round of the area by the foyer, returned and grabbed Alexis by the arm and squeezed it hard… "Hurry up, you!" the officer bellowed in his ear, "Report directly to the Grand Plaza for the conscription of the troops!" Then he looked Alexis square in the face and added with a knowing wink of the eye, "And beware, my young friend…the Governor hasn't slept well for three days and he's in a fiery mood!"

Chapter XIII

"The Conscription of the Troops"

The rising sun peered between the cypress trees flooding the Grand Plaza with yellow matinal light. The backside of the palace overlooked the plaza with balconies supported by two tiers of colonnades and was framed on each of the three other sides by columned façades of buildings constructed from marble and stone. This plaza was the pride of the acropolitan village that served the palace. It was separated from the foyer where Alexis' window overlooked simply by a tiny lane of one-storey village houses.

On this morning, the young men belonging to the palace and the village were lined up in the Grand Plaza for the conscription of the troops. Among them: kitchen workers and gardeners, young tradesmen who lived in the village, as well as farmers from the fields surrounding the village. There were also young men from the Acropolis itself who had been brought in for the conscription. A few women had joined in line too, palace laundresses and maids, but the officers quickly dragged them off by the earlobes, telling them to get back to work. For some reason, a few very old men also joined in and stood in line, waiting to be selected to go into military service for the Acropolis; but they were quickly rejected. The soldiers dragged them off by their elbows or by tufts of their thin grey hair and ordered them not to further disrupt the conscription.

So there Alexis stood, lined up with the other young men in the Grand Plaza while the officers walked back and forth, up and down the line, selecting men to go into battle. Quite a bit of time passed before the actual selection began. There was some chatter amongst the officers. The young men awaiting conscription, though, remained silent. Some stuck their chests out and clenched their jaws to make their faces appear like stone in hopes of making a more favorable impression; while others let their chests drop and appear sunken, and let their faces droop to repel the officers. Alexis did neither. He simply stood straight and gazed up towards the second balcony, where, standing among the crowd of officials, lords and ladies, he saw the Governor. The Governor was overseeing the conscription and was half obscured by one of the fluted columns. Alexis surveyed this gallery of noblemen gathered on the balcony. All were dressed in handsome suits; their ladies dressed in robes of cream or gowns of color. They were drinking aperitifs as if at a garden party. The Governor, however, drank nothing and didn't chat with the others. He stood soberly watching over the conscription with serious eyes. Alexis could have sworn that the Governor was looking right at him. 'Ah, those eyes!' he remarked, 'those piercing eyes!' While he surveyed the crowded palace balcony, he thought he saw Sophia too. He looked hard to catch a glimpse of her; but then the guards passed in front of him and his gaze was torn away. The selection had begun.

Almost all of the young men were chosen and given rifles. They were then told to wait in a group until the signal would come to march through the plaza in a ceremonious departure. They would go down the lane, past the foyer, to where they would cross the gardens, leave the gates and march down a road that would lead to the train that would take them to the front. Almost all the young men were selected, with the exception of one cross-eyed youth, another stripling who was missing a leg; a little boy of four or five years old, and Alexis. When the little boy wasn't chosen, he burst in to tears and had to be carried off by his mother. So at the end, all of the officers were walking away from the lineup to instruct the newly conscripted troops and poor Alexis was left alone standing in the center of the plaza.

He called to one of the officers… "What about me?! Aren't you going to choose me? I am ready to go to war for our Governor!"

The officer looked back at Alexis, looked him up and down, "Very well, come along," he said, returning to fetch him.

So Alexis was chosen but he wasn't given a rifle, only a dull sword. Yet he took that dull sword eagerly and ran to join the other new soldiers who were marching out of the plaza carrying issued rifles. All of those young men walked so proudly.

This whole time, the Governor's daughter, Sophia, had been watching the procession from a high up window in the palace; and when Alexis marched below her – he with floppy shoes and a flimsy sword, lagging behind the other soldiers who wore black polished soldiering boots and carried rifles – when he passed below, she leaned out of the window, called his name, "Alexis! Alexis!" and threw him a flower. It was a fragrant wildflower. He caught it and looked up at her and waved. She blew him a kiss and beamed him a radiant smile.

"The Journey to the Front"

The train was packed with soldiers and smelled of feces mingled with hay. Alexis marched behind the others through the foyer, through the garden in which he was hitherto employed, and on past the palace gates to where an arid road led to the cargo train that would take the new soldiers to the front. Once the doors were closed and the train departed, Alexis was pressed against a wall in the crowded car. His sword was slipped through his belt loop and he clutched his cherished wildflower – gift from Sophia. The air was stifling in the train car. The men were sweaty and were pressed together and it was dark, though there were cracks where one could look out at the changing landscape. Some men tried to hoard these cracks and pressed their mouths up to them to breath clean air, but each in turn was pushed aside as everyone demanded a turn to look out and taste clean air.

This landscape outside changed from green, lush and hilly, to a dry, flat and golden brown. One of the men Alexis talked to informed him that it was the Hungarian landscape they were traveling through. Though he talked to another after that who defended it was Serbia. Another swore it was the Andalusian countryside. One man said it was Mongolia. Eventually Alexis' turn came to look and breath through a crack in the train, and he looked on with fondness at the strange landscape passing, although he didn't know to whom or to what it belonged.

None of the men slept on the journey. Some, like Alexis, were too excited for what was to come. Others were too fearful. No one in that train car had ever seen a war.

The Acropolitan cargo train coursed southward along the perimeter of the front. As it did so, vivid scenes of battle and heroism erupted from view through those cracks in the car. The train made regular stops; and a few at a time, the young soldiers were called to leave the train to join their new company at the battlefront. Each time it was the same. The train would slow to a halt. The doors would slide open, and the men would take desperate breaths to inhale the fresh air that suddenly filled the stuffy foul-smelling train car. Then the officer who had opened the door would yell something like, "Numbers fifteen to twenty-five!", whereupon eleven men would deboard. Following, the train doors would close, the train would start up again and build to full speed to continue on. Many countless hours passed and soon Alexis found himself alone on the train. His number, thirty-seven, had never been called. And so he stood in the now empty car with his floppy shoes full of hay, clutching his dull sword, and occasionally petting the petals of his wildflower. All of the cracks in the train were now his and he kept his mouth pressed to one of them to breathe clean air.

"I have been forgotten," he mumbled over and over.

When eventually the train came to the end of the line, it slowed to a stop and the watchman began making his rounds – opening each cargo door to check inside. Alexis, hearing this, stood poised clutching his sword like an eager knight.

"What are you doing in here?!" the watchman demanded of Alexis, when finally he came to his car and slid the door open. The guard reached in his holster for his pistol.

"I have been forgotten," Alexis answered with solemnity, setting down his sword.

"Well this is the end of the line," the watchman grumbled, putting his pistol away, "So I guess it's your stop." He paused, then added in a louder voice, "So go on, you! Out of the train!" Yet, by this time, Alexis had already left the train and was off walking away, so the watchman's words were actually directed at no one. "Hey wait!" the watchman called after him, "Don't forget your sword!"

Alexis found the only trail that led away from the train tracks and began to walk down it. It was a narrow path, overgrown with dusty dry weeds, and it wound through fields dotted with black trees and sewn with the bleeding light of the red setting sun. 'Night will be here soon,' he told himself. He kept on walking and the trail passed through a small canyon. He heard rustling sounds. 'Wolves,' he thought. When he passed through the canyon, the terrain flattened into plains of sand and dry grass. The trail came to an end. Up ahead, he saw a camp. He saw smoke and smelled wood burning. He crossed the dry grass and approached the camp and there he found a man, a soldier who was all alone, crouched down building a fire.

Chapter XIV

"Warriorhood"

The soldier's name was Perfory. He was a man of thirty-nine, maybe forty years of age; of uncertain origin. He had ruggedly handsome features, a face covered in dark whiskers that was worn by the sun and marked by battle. His eyes were light and grey and brilliant and radiated kindness and gentleness, as did his voice; though everything else about him – his face and body, his gestures and mannerisms – suggested masculine strength, suggested power.

"I'm glad you came," he greeted Alexis, tossing aside the sticks he'd been throwing on the fire in order to shake the newcomer's hand, "I've been asking them to send another man for weeks now." Alexis, who had been cautiously holding the handle of his sword since he first came upon this stranger in the wilderness, now let go and it dangled in his belt loop and flapped against the side of his leg.

"Yes, glad you came," he repeated, smiling warmly at Alexis, "It gets tiring guarding the 33rd Turkish front for months all alone. I've even started speaking to the crickets!"

"Crickets,' Alexis thought, looking carefully at the stranger, "This is the front, you say?"

"Indeed it is," Perfory replied. He looked around himself at the landscape with a bewildered expression, as though he were seeing it for the first time; though he later explained to Alexis that he often looked at it in this way. Following this exercise, he threw up his hands and crouched down to resume throwing brittle sticks on the fire. Alexis stood there silently; and while silent, Perfory resumed chewing on his long blade of grass and speaking to the fire as if he were all alone and Alexis had never come.

"There you go flames...yes, yes...burn, burn...rise, rise, rise...good wood!" He then turned and smiled at Alexis, "A charming fire we have now!"

Alexis simply stood there observing the soldier a moment. There was something about this character that struck him profoundly. The tone in his voice; his manner of ease, resting on the sandy soil coaxing the fire and speaking to it as though he were a gentle god creating a world. He had the way of a snake charmer. It seemed to Alexis that this man could command a wild cobra like he commanded those flames. More than a cobra, if the all men of the world were coiled up in woven baskets, Alexis imagined this soldier would be more capable than anyone of blowing a flute to make the men dance. Many secrets were contained in that being. Was it just his voice or the look in his eye? Perhaps too the great benevolence in his smile. Maybe it was all of this. His smile contained both innocence and experience, pride and humility, curiosity and wisdom. Yes, there was something about this character: a king seated on a sandy throne, a man in a world of children, dressed in the clothing of a soldier. Never before had Alexis encountered someone whom he admired so greatly in the first instance of their meeting. Now Alexis thought if only he could learn this power, if he could learn to have this effect on other people, he believed it would be the greatest of possessions. And so while Perfory crouched down and continued feeding the fire with sticks, Alexis looked on with a great desire to know who this man was and where he came from.

A chilly wind swept across the plains. Alexis pulled the sword out of his belt loop and tossed it on the ground and went to take heat from the fire. Perfory remained crouched, skinning bark from sticks, tossing them on the flames.

"This front, you say..." Alexis inquired after a moment of silence by fireside, "A Turkish front?" ... Then he jested to himself, 'Turkish front...It might as well be Patagonia!'

"Turkish front it is indeed," Perfory replied. He then dropped the sticks, stood up, and walked over to his rolled up sleeping bag and picked up the rifle that was lying across it. Alexis watched his movements carefully. Perfory took his rifle, walked a few steps, and facing Alexis, he raised the gun…

"It is the Turks we are fighting, so…" He then bent down and drew a line in the sand with the barrel of his rifle. "Here is Greece – the side we are on." … "And over there," he pointed to the ground on the other side of the line, "you have Turkey."

Alexis looked across at the Turkish side. That carved line divided them from a great expanse – sand and dry grass rolling away, off to a darkening horizon smudged with purple dusk.

"That's Turkey?" Alexis asked, astonished by the distance he had traveled.

"Yes, that's Turkey," Perfory confirmed. Then he added in a jest, "…although, I tell you, it might as well be Argentina!"

"Yes, might as well!" Alexis agreed, "or Uganda, even!"

"Uganda or Iceland!" Perfory laughed. He then gave a great smile that revealed teeth that were ivory-colored and slightly chipped. They shined like glass from his swarthy sun-browned face. "Or Scandinavia!" he added, "Why not Scandinavia?"

'Why not?' Alexis thought. Scandinavia, Serbia, Greece, Turkey…so many conflicting stories. When he had been on the train, he believed they were off to fight the Moors. He was sure he was passing through Portugal. Yet some of the men on the train swore they were nowhere near Portugal. They thought they were going to fight the Indians. One man insisted that it was the Visigoths they were going to battle with. Alexis had never heard anything about being in Greece before. This was new news to him.

"Yes, it's an old story," Perfory said as he assisted the sticks that were charring on the fire. "Greece here, Turkey there. Do you want to eat something?"

"Gladly."

Perfory handed over a bowl filled with food – some kind of cooked beans seasoned with salt and dried peppers. Alexis devoured it with great appetite and set the bowl aside. The two sat by the crackling warmth of the flames. "Yes," Perfory muttered again, "I've been alone at this front for a while now. I'm glad they finally sent me a companion."

'A companion,' Alexis thought. "And you've seen many battles?" he asked with great curiosity.

"Oh, I have seen battles. I have seen many battles."

Pause.

"...But none here. No, not at this front. This has been a very quiet war." ... "And you?"

"Never," Alexis shook his head in regret, "And I'm afraid I won't be of much use to you in battle. I have no rifle. Only a dull sword."

Perfory smiled, "Only a dull sword, you say. Well throw your sword away. I have an extra rifle. A good one." And he paused, "Let's, you and I, get some sleep. In the morning I'll show you how to use it."

Perfory gave Alexis his extra sleeping bag and the latter rolled it out. The two then lay quietly by the warmth of the folding fire. Soon, the fire died and eternal darkness flooded the sky ... a darkness littered with light – light from swarms of still and flickering stars.

Alexis dreamt of Sophia that night. A woman bathing in a nest of wasps. He dreamt of war. Dagger wounds and running blood. He dreamt of lovers. Lips glistening wet from rose wine and anisette. A naked man and woman swimming in the crystalline waters of a lake – a blue lake in a golden sandy dessert. He dreamt of marble gods eating grape leaves. He dreamt of Constantinople.

The next morning, Alexis woke at dawn as was his custom. He stretched and sat up to find the sky overcast and the air cool and crisp. Perfory was already awake. He had built a fire and had coffee cooking in a pan. The two made up their camp, ate breakfast and drank the coffee. Perfory gave Alexis the rifle he'd promised. It was a handsome rifle. He spent the morning teaching him how to clean, load and shoot it.

"Where are you from?" Alexis asked him at one point in the day.

"Here and there," Perfory rubbed the whiskers on his chin, "Here and there."

"How long have you been a soldier?"

"For the Greeks? About six months now. Before that, I fought for the Italians. And before that, for the French."

"But you are not Greek?" Alexis asked.

"No, I am not Greek. But it doesn't so much matter. I am fighting for them. I'm as much Turkish as I am Greek, but I'm not fighting for the Turks, I'm fighting against them..." ... "and you?" he asked after a minute, "Do you know about this war?"

"No," Alexis bowed his head, "I know nothing about it."

Perfory explained the situation. "Simply, we're here to guard this front." He pointed east, out over the quiet plains. "When they come from there," he said, "we'll fight."

"And why do we want to fight these people?" Alexis asked.

Perfory paused a moment, as if searching himself for an answer... "The best I can say, Alexis, is that the lines in war are hazier for the soldier than they are for the civilian. In the cities and villages, one reads in the papers that So-and-so is fighting against Such-and-such a country and everything seems so simple and clear. They say, 'for the sake of our people, let our soldiers conquer the enemy!'...but for the soldiers it isn't always clear who the enemy is. One has a general and fights for that general..."

"Where is our general?" Alexis interrupted.

"He doesn't come down to the 33rd Turkish front. He is up fighting beyond those hills." Perfory pointed with his rifle barrel at the ridge of mountainous land yonder lit by the rosy sun and continued, "...So the soldiers fight for their general and the general gives the orders of the sovereign. King or governor or what have you – in our case, the sovereign is the Governor of the Acropolis. But one never sees the Governor."

Alexis thought of the Governor of the Acropolis – that King of Clubs with his royal face and those piercing eyes that stared into his on that balmy night back on Sophia's bedroom terrace.

"Yet although one never sees the Governor," Perfory went on, "our general's orders come from him. Or rather, the objectives of the war come from him and the general interprets these objectives and translates them into battle plans." He picked up two hefty rocks nested in the dry grass on the ground, "So there are these two influential men," he said, setting the rocks down firmly beside each other. Then he picked up a handful of loose gravel, tiny pebbles, "...and then there is us." And he tossed the pebbles over to the Turkish side of the line to where they scattered and vanished amongst the others in the sandy soil. Then he picked up some of the blood berries that he had gathered on a spread-out piece of oilcloth. He stuffed the berries in his mouth and bit into them and the dark red juices ran down the side of his chin and he smiled with a joyful smile, "To be honest, who knows exactly why we are fighting these men! Although…who knows why men do much of the things men do, except for the reason that they are important to do and we know they are important to do, and so we do them and don't ask ourselves too often why."

He ate some more berries and the juices ran down his face and he offered some to Alexis and Alexis took some. "Once, Alexis, I remember…" …this and that, Perfory rambled on, recollecting his memories while the sun revolved around the sky…

"In the desert once there were sandstorms. Grains of sand as vicious as bullets, they wore the skin off your forehead by day. By night, the cold winds would whip through and freeze the bare meat on your face. It was a damned, waterless place. Many of the men there died of thirst. When finally we did find water – it was a stream beyond the desert, in the highlands – we drank and there were some parasites in it. About half the men developed bubbling lesions on the skin…they bloated up like dead whales… Later we had a fire show in the hills and the sick men couldn't fight. They kept on the ground in the trenches. A couple of them were in such pain that they shot themselves. But the ones who were still standing, were standing and fighting. And, let me tell you, Alexis, when men are fighting for you, and you for them, it's beautiful. They become your brothers. You say, "for the sake of our sovereign, let us conquer the enemy!" and together you charge forward and it is beautiful…

"Other times it is sad," he said ruefully biting the nail on his thumb, "Sometimes you are fighting for your brothers, and they for you, but your general will turn on you. It may be that he is wicked, or is fighting for a sovereign that is wicked, or else he just has a toothache or is a plain coward; and at those times it is necessary to stop fighting – to desert or to change sides. These things are never talked about in the patriotic papers they read in the cities and villages.

"But when you are fighting truly," he went on, becoming more spirited and animated, "and when you are fighting well, it is the general and sovereign you love, your governor and your brothers you love and must love. When you watch your brothers fearlessly climb the trench and run before you, in front of you as you too climb the trench; and as they are ready to catch a bullet that could easily pass them and hit you – killing you instead – this is beautiful and it makes your heart cry. And for this, you too will run before them, ready to catch a bullet that will hopefully not hit them, but will hit you instead, if it is necessary to hit anyone – and this too is beautiful and makes your heart cry. In battles like this, these are all who exist: you and these men, you and your brothers against a veiled, faceless, soulless enemy…

"Yet should this enemy reveal his face, as sometimes happens during war, you will still kill him, though he ceases to be faceless and veiled. But should the enemy reveal his soul – as also may happen in war, then he will cease to be an enemy, he will become your brother, and you will not kill him. If you were to kill him, you would cease to be a soldier and would become a murderer. But the soldier only sees the soul of the enemy under the rule of a bad general or corrupt governor. And in these circumstances, if he is not weak, he deserts. This is not treason, it is true warfare, what the citizens never see."

"And is our governor corrupt?" Alexis asked.

"No," Perfory replied, "this is a good war."

Alexis sifted the sandy soil with his fingers and looked at the bold and fiery sun now beginning its descent in the sky. "Will you always go on fighting?" he asked Perfory.

"Of course not. Only young inexperienced boys and corrupt men go on fighting when it is not time to fight. No, Alexis, I have a wife at home. And, I just learned she gave birth to a girl recently. My daughter. No, when it is time to stop, I will stop. Happily, I will stop!" Perfory's face brightened, "With more gladness and joy then you could know, I will stop. I will stop and go home to hold my wife and my first child. …Just think of it, a little daughter! It's a pretty thought isn't it?"

"Yes." Then… "You miss your home?" Alexis was not really thinking about what he was asking, moreover, he wanted to know where it was Perfory was from.

"I just miss my wife," he answered, taking the question as it came, "and I want to see my daughter. My home is just a place, like here or like anywhere…Oh, how I want to meet that little girl…" And his voice trailed off in melancholic longing while his fingers trailed across his stubbled chin and the early evening sun trailed across the sky and lit amber specks in his light grey eyes.

"Why didn't you leave when you heard she was born?"

"Because then I would be a deserter." … "No. There is a time to fight and time to stop. As long as one is fighting for a noble sovereign, one must continue until it is time to stop. That way, provided one lives through the battles, one returns to a wreath of laurels and a newborn child. Of course," he added, "if one fights for a dissolute king, one returns to a life of isolation and private nightmares. ...If one doesn't stop, one is lost.

"...But I will know when it is time, Alexis. And, God willing, I will live till that time and I will be rewarded thus with seeing my wife and child. But now is not yet the time. I cannot explain why."

"I hope I will know when it is time for me to stop," Alexis said after the two were silent for a moment.

"And you," Perfory turned to him, "what did you leave behind?"

Alexis suddenly remembered those old orders: 'Speak nothing of us to those you meet.' He smiled upon remembering this. So had time eroded them. Life and time and distance had changed so many things. "What did I leave behind? Nothing I guess." Alexis paused. "My mother is dead."

"Mothers die," said Perfory, "That is their nature. But she would have been glad that she died before you, her son."

"And I left my father behind. Though he did not die. I left him behind." Alexis face took on a look of solemnity.

"Did you make peace with him before you left?"

"Yes," he said, "I think so."

"That is good. Who else?"

"I left my little sister behind."

"Does she look up to you?"

"Yes."

"That is good. What else? Did you leave a lover behind?"

"Perhaps," Alexis thought of Sophia, "Perhaps, I left one woman behind. One who might be waiting for me."

"And is she what occupies your thoughts?"

"Yes."

"That is good. And does this cause you to suffer?"

Alexis paused and bowed his head and answered, "Yes."

"That is also good," Perfory put his hand on his companion's shoulder. Then he asked another question, "And have you known travel?"

Here Alexis' head lifted, his eyes grew wide and his face brightened. "Oh, yes!" he replied, "I have traveled! I have seen cities and countries like I never thought possible!"

"And this gave you pleasure?"

"Yes!" Alexis replied with a happy smile.

"And this made you suffer?"

"Yes!" he said without hesitation, laughing the matter off, "oh, yes, did I suffer!"

"This is all good," Perfory told him, "This is all so very good. Sounds like you are ready for battle, my man!"

It was that night, while Perfory and Alexis were seated by their glowing fire, cooking the food they would eat before going to sleep, that a rumbling sound came from the far-off hills. Both, startled, turned and looked at yonder hillsides. The hills were dark silhouettes against a sky alight with violet flashes. Perfory leapt up in alarm and ran over to the fire and tried to extinguish it with his boots. No avail. It kept sparking and reflaming. He grabbed his sleeping bag quickly and stuffed it on the fire to kill the flames. The sleeping bag smoked, smelling of charred wool. Perfory then returned to where he had been sitting while the fire had been going. They both sat silent in the darkness, while the hills behind their back rumbled. Both knew what was happening. Neither of them spoke.

The wind blew in over the dark plains. With no fire, Alexis began to shiver. Even with his sleeping bag to cover him, he was still freezing; but didn't want to tell this to Perfory who lay across from him on the bare ground with no more sleeping bag of his own. Alexis offered up his sleeping bag but Perfory refused it. Perfory had an extra coat for himself, but this didn't seem to be enough. He was shivering as well. Still, there was nothing to do. Without the fire, they would have to just bear the cold night through. Other than the clattering sound of chattering teeth, Alexis kept silent. Meanwhile, the rumbling sounds in the hills grew louder. Soon the explosions were close enough that the sky became brightly illuminated with intense flashes of magenta light.

An hour or two passed. Finally Alexis spoke…

"Whose bombs are they?"

"God only knows."

"What can we do?"

"Wait here and hope they don't fall on us," Perfory replied.

"What does this mean?"

"It means the war has reached the border and it is time to move on. Tomorrow morning we march on for the Turkish city of Adrianople."

"What will we find there?"

"God only knows."

Chapter XV

"For Conquest or Conquer" – the march on Adrianople...

Morning time. Perfory and Alexis abandoned their camp and began the journey to Adrianople. Perfory dismantled the mortar and left it behind as it was too heavy to carry. The two started off towards the hills where the explosions had been hitting the night before. Now, the activity in those hills had stopped and no sounds came from the distance.

Perfory carried a pack with rations and a rifle. Alexis carried the sleeping bag and his own rifle. The clear sky that had brought forth a chill the night before allowed in the heat of the sun once the day had broken; and by noon, the weather was scalding hot. Once, out of the plains, when the terrain turned to mountainous slopes of rocky soil, the two climbed steadily. Heat and fatigue kept them silent. After the summit, they began to descend a steep narrow trail. They found a stream and drank. Alexis thought of Perfory's stories and worried that lesions would grow on his body from parasites in the water; but he drank anyway and the cold water tasted good. It was refreshing and put them both in a cheery mood. As the two hiked along, Perfory hummed a little song...

Off to our death, or off to our birth,

whichever it is, we'll praise the great earth;

no time for sorrow, no time for mirth,

off to our death, or off to our birth.

"What's that song called?" Alexis asked.

"'The Song of Perfory'!" Perfory replied.

The two continued on.

The trail led uphill again and led to another summit. There, while the sun was at its hottest, the two found shade beneath a tree and ate their lunch. Alexis told Perfory the story of his life at the palace where he worked as a gardener in service of the Governor.

"Where were you before that?" Perfory asked.

Alexis told Perfory then about his life in the Great City.

"Really!" Perfory lit up, "I've spent a bit of time there. I tell you, Alexis, my most favorite thing when I was there was to look out over the river at night from Our Lady's Bridge. Or to stroll through the Imperial Gardens early in the morning. I used to love that! The statues of the old queens in the gardens. One nice thing about the Great City, is that one can be alone and among people at the same time."

It seemed to Alexis that Perfory had been everywhere and had done everything in his life. An ageless man who had lived forever. Alexis asked Perfory how he met his wife.

Perfory told him the story...

"It was while I was traveling through the countryside in the north of Italy. I had just finished laboring on the construction of a new Winter Palace in Budapest and I had money. It was spring. And I had come from the rainy Hungarian countryside and was now in Italy where the sky was blue and it was pleasantly warm...

"On the road, I saw a young girl wandering alone. She was wearing a light summer dress and was carrying a small suitcase – a pretty girl. I asked her where she was going.

'To Rome,' she said.

"'Rome is a long ways away,' I told her. 'I'm going there myself, but you'll never make it dressed like that – and not on foot.' ...I was on my way to Rome to live a life and spend my money. The girl decided to follow me...

'Why do you want to go to Rome?' I asked her.

'To find my father and brother. They went to Rome.'

'Where do you come from?' I asked.

'There,' she said, pointing to the eastern horizon, where one could or could not see, depending on how hard one squinted, the signs of a tiny village far off in the distance. 'That's where I come from."

'Well, you should go back there,' I told her.

'No,' she says to me, 'we will go to Rome. You will help me. I have to find my father and brother.'

I walked on longer down the road with the young girl in the summer dress.

Later we came to a railway station. The girl had no money to buy a ticket and, though I had money, I couldn't have taken this girl with me.

'Little girl,' I said, 'I will take you back to your village.'

'No you won't!' she answers me in a bratty voice, 'I am going to Rome. If you won't take me, I will go on my own!'

'Do you have money?' I asked her.

'No,' she said.

So I asked her if she had a home in that village back there.

'Yes,' she says, 'we have a nice home ... except my father and brother aren't in it. They are in Rome!'

'And who is in your home?' I asked her.

'My sister and my mother.'

'Listen,' I suggested to the girl, 'Let's go back to your village. We will buy an automobile there and take your sister and mother to Rome.'

'They will not come,' the girl told me, 'That is why I am by myself.'

'And they let you go alone?' I asked, dismayed.

'I left in the night,' she replied.

'Of course you did,' I said. Then I decided to trick her. 'Well listen, miss, we will buy an automobile in your village and drive to Rome ourselves – just you and me.'

'There are no automobiles in my village,' the girl told me, 'There are floods everywhere.'

'Floods!' I said. Well, you can imagine, Alexis, I didn't know what to do with this girl. After a while I said to her, 'Come, little girl, we will go back and get you some clothes. I will ask your mother and sister to come. And we will travel to Rome by train to find your father and brother. I will pay the tickets.

'Okay,' she said to my great surprise, 'let's walk.' And she took my hand and started leading me off in the direction of the horizon where she had pointed out her village a little while before. You can believe how relieved I was! And so off we walked, hand in hand, towards the far horizon...

"By nightfall, we arrived in her village. 'You can wait here in this square,' she said to me, 'I'll come right back.' Sure she was coming back! I had my doubts. She left me there and disappeared between two buildings that lined the empty stone square. Nowhere was there a sound. It was true her village had been destroyed by floods. But the waters had receded. There were dead rats everywhere and sewer waste lay in the gutters of the cobblestones. The old buildings were decrepit. The night was thick and nowhere was there a sound...

"I waited in that square a long time. I was certain the girl wasn't coming back.

Finally, I heard some footsteps coming from the alleyway. Then, beneath the only lit streetlamp in the square, two girls appeared. One was the little girl who had brought me to the village. The other was an older girl. They held hands and walked shyly. The little girl led the older one and I could tell by their similar faces, as well as by the way the older girl walked with such protective hesitation, looking cautiously around her, that she was the girl's older sister.

"...The two girls approached me in the square. 'Mama says you can sleep with us tonight,' the younger one said to me. After this, the sisters turned around and started walking away. The older girl turned her head back around a couple times and glanced at me, strangely, timidly. I began to follow them and was led through the alley and down another street where we entered a small ground-floor apartment. I was led inside, into a room where an older woman (their mother) brought me tea. The mother bent down to set the tea-tray on the table and whispered to me in a hushed voice:

'Her father and brother are dead. They were killed by the floods while trying to save others. No one is in Rome. I thank you for bringing her back. You may stay here for a night or two. You are welcome.'

And here the mother gave me a kind smile and left me in peace to drink the warm tea and go to bed for the night.

"…The next day I took a walk with Maria, the older of the two sisters. I made her laugh in spite of the fact that no one in the village was in the mood for laughing. Maria was the most beautiful thing I'd ever seen. I fell in love with her immediately, though she kept distance, used caution, and was torn by grief…

"A few days later I rented a room down the street from where Maria lived with her mother and little sister. It was cheap. I had to sleep on a hard mat. The room had been hit by the flood and smelled of mildew and sewage. The floor, which had once been brick, had become soil, mud and loose rock. It was cold at night, but how joyful I was as I drifted to sleep. My only thoughts were of Maria and how I wanted to be with her, and only her, for the rest of my life…

"'If I only accomplish one more thing in my life,' I told myself, 'no matter how long it takes, I want that one thing to be her…to be Maria.' And so I stayed in that little destroyed village and made it my home.

"…During the days I helped rebuild the houses that had been hit by the flood, and during the night I slept like a stoic on my mat; and once a week, in the evening time, I took a walk with Maria and tried to make her laugh.

"…They began to call me Saint Perfory in the town. *Santo Perfory, Lo Straniero.* Some thought I was actually a saint and that I was sent by God to this remote village to help them rebuild and erase the signs of the dead and the miserable. I told the children stories in the square and, though there wasn't much food, the women often brought me bread. I helped rebuild the town and helped the men rebuild their homes and everyone called me *Santo Perfory, Lo Straniero.* It was quite something.

"…Sure, many thought I was a saint. But I was no saint. I was just a man. A man in love. And what I did, I didn't do on behalf of God, or on behalf of the village. I did it on behalf of Maria. And eventually, after two years of hard work and two years of courting her, she agreed to be my wife.

"…We married the following spring and the entire village attended the ceremony. We moved into a house on the outskirts of the village and lived a passionate and tender romance for several years. Later I was obliged to leave to fight a war in my home country. But our love remained strong even through our distance. She is the greatest thing to me, and now she has just given me a baby girl."

Alexis listened to the story and wanted to hear more. Perfory, however, was silent after that.

The two continued on.

At night they stopped to camp and Perfory built a fire.

"Oh, good fire," Perfory said, warming his hands over the flames. "My most charming fire." The wind howled over the plains, blowing across the two men's ears. It swirled the ashes in the fire pit, provoking the flames to grow wild. "It's a real pretty thing, this life," Perfory muttered, settling back on his army coat to sleep. "It takes no more than a camp fire in the wilderness to remind one of this." Alexis looked out over the dark plains. He saw shades traveling among the black bushes far off. Perfory's voice seemed to drift out of his body with complete lightness… "Yes, a real pretty thing." The stars revolved in the sky, one by one dropping down like pins of light to pierce the black membranes of sky. And through these holes in the night, the darkness drained out and clear white light seeped in to stain the landscape with morning.

Alexis stretched and looked around himself. Perfory was already awake, changing into his spare white undershirt. The ridges of his brown ribs showed through the skin of his chest. Over his clean shirt, he put on his green army coat, picked up his rifle and jumped up and down a few times. He sang to Alexis… "Off to our deaths, or off to our births!" He smiled cheerily, kicking a little sand around with his boots. "Whichever it is, we'll praise the great earth!" Alexis smiled back and stood up to gather his pack. Only Perfory, he thought, could make one feel at ease, or even excited, about going off to an enemy city where perhaps death was awaiting. If not death, than a gruesome battle – a battle to end in death, in torture, or terrible wounds. Perhaps imprisonment or execution. But these possibilities didn't worry Alexis. He was taking the course of a man. He was standing up, standing and following after Perfory who had started off across the plains, towards the hills. Perfory who floated effortlessly over the rough landscape like one of those shades of night. Perfory, who drifted seemingly effortlessly though life, in complete harmony with life, and for this the world offered him no resistance. Life, it seemed, was a banquet where

Perfory was the distinguished host. And he welcomed Alexis in to this opulent feast like an honored and esteemed guest… "What is this little wilted wildflower you keep with you wherever we go?" Perfory asked his friend. Alexis started to answer but Perfory just smiled the broadest of smiles and slapped him on the shoulder and the two started off… It seemed to Alexis that Perfory was the happiest man alive, and it was hard not to see the intrinsic beauty in the world when around him, even if you *were* marching off to your death.

The hills sloped from arid valleys to jagged mountainous ridges, to round crests of lush green land, and back again. Two more days of traveling passed. On the third, Alexis and Perfory came to a particular trail in the hills that looked out over a wide expanse of pastures and streams, an expanse which led onto more hills; hills Perfory assured him, which would lead unto the city of Adrianople. Signs of the city were yet out of sight. Perfory led by means of a compass. The trail continued on. It was narrow and ran alongside a tiny brook that took water off down the slopes of hills. In the valley below, the brook emptied out into a wide river. Alexis stopped to drink. Perfory washed his face and filled his canteen. The two men sat to rest awhile on the edge of the trail. From the vertical hills rising up to the sheer peaks on either side came a few rocks tumbling down. A hawk with black tips on its wings flew in circles overhead. Those steep rock formations quivered as Alexis looked at them – heat rising off their surfaces in viscous waves.

"Keep silent, Alexis. Look over there," Perfory crouched down and whispered while pointing down into the valley at the base of the trail towards which the two were heading. Hundreds of meters below, on the other side of the river, one could see a dozen or so little black spots that Alexis recognized to be horses and men. They were gathered at the far riverbank. The horses were corralled and the men appeared to be sitting, though every few moments a few of them would move, resembling tiny black fleas crawling in a carpet.

"Are they soldiers?" Alexis asked.

"They are soldiers."

"Are they Turks?"

"Partisans," Perfory replied, "Turkish partisans. I see about six plus a horse for each man. Is that what you see?"

"Yes."

Alexis climbed back up the trail a few steps and lowered himself to the ground beside the rocky face of the hill, blocking sight of the valley. There was no where else for Perfory and Alexis to go except straight down into the valley, into the group of men. For there were but two routes they could take: either down the hill, across the river and forward on the trail towards their goal, the city of Adrianople; or it was back up the trail, through the hills, and again into the wilderness from which they came. That would be a retreat and a retreat was out of the question. Adrianople was their goal. And so, they would go down.

"We will wait here," Perfory whispered almost inaudibly, aware of the echo his voice might have in the rocky canyons surrounding the trail, and so he let his words simmer out like the wind itself. He knelt beside Alexis and the two crouched down, trying to not let the rocks crunch beneath their feet and knees. "They outnumber us. Although we have the advantage of being uphill from them, the amount of distance we'd have to travel to get down to where they are would tire us, and they would win right away. Besides, there is a river between us and too much open space between the base of the hills and that river. If we were to attack, their group would take shelter and wait until we are in the water fighting against the current, then they would advance and kill us…

"No, we will wait here until they move," he continued, "If they go off in another direction, following the river upstream or down, we will simply go around them and be safe. If they cross the river and climb this steep trail coming towards us, we will wait and surprise them. They will be forced to fight an uphill battle and we'll stand a very good chance of winning, even if we are outnumbered three to one. It's too bad we didn't bring the mortar. We could shell them from here."

Alexis and Perfory waited silently on the trail in the hills, ducked behind the rocks of the canyon. In the late afternoon, when the sun was no longer overhead, the partisan group left the riverside, having rested and gathered canteens of fresh water. They saddled their horses and led them across the river. They then mounted them and began to ride them up the trail in the direction of Perfory and Alexis.

It took the half dozen men almost an hour to get close to where Alexis and Perfory were hidden in the canyons of the hilltop. Alexis poised himself and waited for them trying to kindle a fire of courage in his belly. He had based himself off the side of the trail at the top of the hill in a small trench where the rocky precipice defended his back. The rifle in his hands defended his front. He held it pointed at the point where the last leg of steep trail met the summit.

Perfory had instructed Alexis to lead the assault. Perfory was based on the other side of the trail about ten meters farther back from Alexis. Alexis was to fire the first shot. From where Perfory was positioned, he would see the men first while their horses were still engaged in the uphill climb. When the first man came into view, he was to raise his rifle. That would be the signal that they'd arrived. Alexis dug himself into the crevice, settling his weight on his lower back so he wouldn't tire too quickly.

So this was to be the battle. His hands shook on the trigger and his palm sweated on the barrel of his rifle. He had much fear and focused on keeping from trembling, while his glance passed back and forth, left to right…left eye to watch the movements of Perfory, followed by right eye for any movements on the trail. He felt a wave of heat pass over his backside and the tremor of a tiny seizure in his limbs. As the moment of crisis neared, however, his fear numbed him and his finger held firmly, almost like dead flesh, against the spring of his trigger, while his right eye peered down the length of the rifle barrel.

The six partisan soldiers mounted the hill in a single file line. Alexis felt the rush of heat turn to a cold shiver as he felt the moment approach. He looked to the left and saw Perfory lowering himself farther down behind the pile of rocks that was to help shield him. As he did so, he raised his rifle. Now Alexis knew the first man had come into view.

Alexis' eyes darted back and forth between the figure of Perfory and the summit that met the hidden trail. Loud were the sounds of rocks crunching under the hooves of horses. Along with the fear, he felt another emotion, a foreign one. Something akin to power accompanied by a taste of dry salt on his lips. The moment had come. Perfory's rifle had raised. A figure came into view. Alexis ceased to think or be afraid. He simply acted.

Four of the six horsemen had come into view. The soldiers drooped over their horses' saddles, dark brown garbs with packs and rifles, bobbed up and down on their walking beasts. Alexis took aim at a man and fired. Crack and a whistling shot buzzed across the air. A plume of smoke blew from his gun barrel. The sound rang out through the canyons of rock. The panic of horses whinnying. Scampering left and right. The horsemen guided the reigns to control them. Drew their rifles. All but the fourth man. He went down with his horse at the dispatch of Alexis' swift inaugural bullet. This opening bullet missed the man. The horse, though, had been shot in the neck. That was the fourth. The two enemies in the rear, yet unseen, immediately galloped off with their riders up the side of the hill. There was a small switchback that mounted to the top of a precipice several meters over the trail, towering above the trench of rocks where Perfory was crouched down. A moment after Alexis' shot heralded the battle, the barrage of fire came from the ambushed partisan group as they scattered; as well as came from Perfory, hidden off the trailside. The two leading enemy men shot the sky while struggling to control their panicking horses. The third in line aimed at Alexis, fired and missed. He cocked his rifle again, aimed back at Alexis, and was sniped from the side. Perfory took him down with a shot to the head. He fell off the saddle into the pulp. His horse galloped away. The second enemy man now saw clearly Perfory's position as he poised to shoot. He leapt from his horse and ran for shelter on the far side of the trail, in a trench of rocks. Alexis fired towards him but couldn't tell if he hit him or not. What followed then were several moments of chaos.

Shots fired from all around.

Rocks tumbled from the canyons above where Alexis stayed crouched and one stung him on the head. He felt the warmth of wet blood. Another moment, Perfory leapt out of position to fire. Alexis tried to shield his companion with shots towards the scattering horsemen, but they were well obscured from Alexis' view by a cloud of rifle smoke. Alexis heard someone running past him. He crouched down further to shield himself behind the rocks. Another shot rang out and Alexis heard the cry of a man somewhere off to the left. Then he heard nothing. A movement. He cocked and fired and was then enveloped himself by a cloud of smoke. The first man's expert rifle fired towards the banks which Alexis and Perfory had entrusted to keep them safe only moments before. Another two shots. Rocks crumbled down. A string of fire and a fallen horse. Alexis saw a flash of metal. One man on a ledge, aiming clear for Alexis, the black barrel of the gun and he could feel the shrapnel exploding in his brain; he drew his rifle and fired. His shot went astray, and another shot came. It was Perfory's and it took the man in the side, and a flash of red and the man tumbled down off the rocks. Then there was quiet.

The smoke wisps rose and drifted out of the silent summit at the peak of the trail in its nest of rocky canyons. Only did sounds come from a single man. Everywhere else lay the dead and silent. The last enemy man that appeared to be alive was the one who had been first pinned beneath his horse when Alexis had killed the horse with the first bullet fired. The man's leg was crushed beneath the flank of the steed, and like a wounded insect, he squirmed in the gravel of the trail while he struggled to raise himself up to cock his rifle and make a last stand. Alexis' eyes darted left. Across the trail he saw the clear whites of Perfory's eyes gleaming like sugar drops, they were set like predator on prey, upon this man pinned beneath the horse. The man struggled to raise his rifle and fire at Perfory. It was then, Alexis looked up and saw at the peak of the precipice two new horses. They were saddled but had no riders and they stood at the top of the rocky ledge and neighed, pounding hooves on the loose rock.

The rocks crumbled and rolled down the face of the ledge. Perfory, meanwhile had fired unsuccessfully at the man pinned beneath the horse who had successfully hoisted himself up and cocked his rifle to shoot Perfory down. Perfory fired another shot. Empty. He was out of bullets and threw his rifle aside. Here, the injured man rallied his rifle, cocked it and prepared aim. It was then that the empty-saddled horses on the ledge disappeared, were pulled backwards by their trailing reigns, and two enemy men appeared in their places. Their bodies eclipsed the afternoon sun passing over the crest of the precipice and they appeared like two black shadows, desert beasts, short-legged lizards; they kneeled and took aim at their own enemies not yet killed.

Down below, Perfory had thrown his empty rifle aside and drew his serrated fighting knife from its sheath on his leg. He gripped the knife tightly and charged the injured man. If only he could stab him before he himself was shot...

The partisan trapped beneath the dead horse, laid the barrel over the meat of the steed and took aim on the warrior Perfory. He had a clear view of the large and nearby target that was his chest – a chest that swiveled and pounded as he charged the injured man, with arms swinging like muscular pistons, in a sprint like a fierce beast in gallop, he charged with fighting knife drawn, while his chest stayed in clear view of the fallen man's rifle. Beneath the faded green army jacket, Perfory's shirt shone white and bright and ready to receive, it was well in the rifleman's sights.

A whirl of visions passed by Alexis' eyes, He saw that white disc of Perfory's chest as it closed in on the shaking barrel of the stranded enemy man. And he had seen the two enemy men engaging themselves with their own rifles on the ledge above. They too took aim on Perfory. But before their injured comrade managed his desperate trigger to fall the charging host, Perfory took to flight and leapt like a deft carnivorous cougar. He came down upon the man – death by blow – the man received the serrated blade in the side of his neck, and there much blood was spilled.

A clean kill, Perfory's body draped exhausted over the man's corpse, if just to rest a moment. If there to only rest a moment, he mistakenly thought the battle over and won. But, alas, there was the click of a rifle cock, while Perfory lay face down in plain sight over the fallen man, where he caught his breath, meters above him the remaining two enemy soldiers pointed barrels and prepared to finish the event themselves.

All but for the suns rays like shards of glass, here Alexis made to act. Abandoned shelter, he leapt into view from behind his rocky barrier, sprinted across the battle trail while the enemy's cocked their guns. Three rifles drawn, he charged the precipice, caring nothing but for two bullets he hoped would swiftly fire. While he charged the precipice and aimed at one of the men, the other aimed clearly at Perfory's mortal back; yet though he had a clear shot of Perfory's spine, Alexis came to pass in front of his friend, thus eclipsing the target, so that Perfory was not at risk. And in the moments that followed, the exercise came to an end...

From where he lay on dead man's back, Perfory's swung his head around, realizing that the battle was not yet won. But the storm of motion was too quick. He was too confused. He did not move. He couldn't see Alexis, neither the other men. All he could hear were the three shots ring out. One. Two. Three. Three crisp shots with clear reports, echoing in the canyon. And there, with Alexis between he and the enemy, did he catch a spray of blood.

Terminus: three final shots, the first came from Alexis. He had fired a bullet that went upwards and inserted itself beneath the right eye of the first enemy. His body fluttered downward from the precipice like a brittle bird. Alexis cocked. The other fired. Then, while Alexis was falling backwards, he fired the third and final shot. Oh, happy death! This last effort managed to pierce the last man with a clever charge, neatly taken in the breast. And with his surcease success, a bloodstained smile passed over Alexis' face as he tumbled backwards, spraying blood of his own on the cheek of Perfory – Perfory whose body gave Alexis a tender resting place.

Smoke billowed up in smokelets from the trail, from the rocky barriers and sheer precipices, and the surrounding forms of the landscape were now changing colors with the twilight. These smokelets lifted up into dusky sky, streaked with a broad ribbon of faint violet light which seeped into the horizon as the sky grew quiet and darkened into the black of after dusk, absorbing the smoke, absorbing the light, absorbing all and bringing forth the stars and the moon – and thereupon it was night.

Perfory, exhausted and confused, held his fallen companion. Alexis' body lay upon him. His consciousness lay elsewhere. Taken on an excursion through deathly dark mountain trails by a poisonous bullet. Perfory ripped the cloth from the chest drained of life and blood. He searched for the source of Alexis' bleeding and laid him down on the trail to get the breathing going. A lot of blood was lost. The patient was thrown into terrible shock. Fortunately, the wayward bullet had merely pierced the shoulder. Unfortunately, Perfory had seen other men die after suffering lesser shocks, and with more blood remaining.

Perfory tied a strip of torn, cloth around Alexis shoulder and twisted it. Alexis struggled for consciousness finding it now and again.

It was late in the night when he fully awoke. Perfory had lit a candle and was searing the wound with a knife, when that wound began to register pain. Alexis jerked and began to shudder from the intensity of the injury sickness. He vomited on the trail. Perfory washed Alexis' mouth out with his canteen and made him drink. Alexis squirmed while the wound was being treated. He tried to look around him, but, unable to see, he lay back. Once Perfory had finished with the wounds, he too fell asleep next to where Alexis lay quiet.

The next morning, the golden light of a new day fell fresh to illuminate the earth on the trail where Perfory and Alexis slept. The same ground where the six dead enemy men lay. Where they lay, and would remain until to seep into the ground – a ground that would accept and hold them, all the while being stirred by thousands of storms, being rumbled by thousands of earthquakes, over the centuries to come.

Nearby, the living horses of the dead men remained in the places where their masters had abandoned them. Now and then, they whinnied and scuffed their hooves, looking around for fresh grass to eat. They hadn't understood that they had just fought a battle, that they had just lost a battle for their masters; and now all they wanted to do was to eat grass and continue on their journey – to wherever it was they were going.

When Alexis awoke, the light of morning diffused itself and he felt nothing, neither sleepiness nor pain. He was swept upwards, the light grew brighter and the sound of birds, golden birds, rose to a crackling crescendo; and thereupon he was lifted onto a golden chariot, flung about, until another flash and things began to darken. Where was he? He looked around. Was Perfory around? His vision was gone. Blind and his body kept rising upwards, turning itself around. There was a moist, warm dampness, the comfort of soft fleece like cloudlets of the heavens engulfed his weightless body; and then, when he could rise no more, he began his descent. He fell deeper and deeper, down to the depths. All heavenly sensations were gone. He tumbled down and dug his face into its resting place, a bristly brown sepulcher that smelled of a horse's mane.

When Alexis awoke again, it was night. The clear sky overhead presented a moon that resembled a chipped tooth floating in the sky. He found himself draped over the back of a horse, dressed in a fleece coat, his cheek bouncing on the bristly neck and mane of a horse that tiredly bore his weight as it sauntered along behind another horse up ahead. Alexis' body felt unburdened, as though soaking in warm saltwater. He felt a physical well-being. The realization that he had not died from his injury sent tingles of euphoria through his bones. He wanted to laugh. He sat up in his saddle and looked around, wondering where Perfory had gone. There, up ahead, a dark figure was drooped over a horse. This rider wore a brown cloth wrapped around his head and was leading Alexis' animal by a rope tied to their bridles keeping them together.

"Compass is broke, but I know where to go…compass is broke, but I know where to go…" The rider was Perfory and he mumbled this phrase over and over through his head-covering, in a tired monotonous drone, as he rode along…"Compass is broke, but I know where to go…compass is broke, but I know where to go…." His horse continued on in the northeast direction. Alexis' beast followed a few feet behind. The two rode on the moonlit night, towards the bright steady stars of Ursa Major overhead.

"Compass is broke, but I know where to go…" came again and again from the drooping rider, speaking to keep himself from falling asleep.

"Hey, Perfory!" Alexis called up to him in a refreshed and cheerful voice, "Why's the compass broke, Perfory?"

"Somebody shot it," Perfory replied in a low trailing voice.

Then a pause.

"…Is that you, Alexis?" A little more life came into his voice.

"Yes, it's me, I woke up!"

Perfory slowly turned his head around and looked at Alexis through slits of closing weary eyes visible through the cracks in the cloth wrapped around his head. The horses kept on at their steady pace. Perfory pulled back the reigns on his own and it heeled to let Alexis catch up. Soon, the two were riding alongside each other.

"Good to see you're better. I knew you wouldn't die. How's your shoulder?"

"I can't feel a thing, Perfory. But, I feel great, like a new man!…"

Silence.

"You sound awful, Perfory. When was the last time you slept?"

"I'm not sure. Long time ago, I guess."

"Well, you need to sleep, Perfory."

"Can't sleep, gotta lead. Somebody shot the compass."

"Well, let's stop and make camp for the night and start again in the morning."

"Nope. Too hot to ride in the day. We should ride in the night and sleep in the day. It's okay, Alexis, I'm fine. Just wake me up if I fall asleep. But tell me about your shoulder."

"I feel great!" Alexis pulled his coat tightly around him. A short stab of pain shot through his neck and shoulder and he winced, yet it quickly went away and immaculate numbness returned. He buttoned the coat, wondering where it had come from. "But really, Perfory, it's strange how good I feel."

"Well, the pain will come around again, Alexis, but don't worry. I'm drifting off. Just wake me if I fall asleep...."

Alexis, noticing that Perfory was carrying two extra packs on his back and two extra rifles, interrupted him to ask where they came from.

"Same place the horses came from," Perfory replied, "Our friends, the Turks."

"Well let me carry them, I'm in good shape tonight."

"Oh, it's all the same," said Perfory, "I'll just carry them. If I try to get them off my back now, I'll just fall over and sleep where I land. Just keep your eyes out for camp fires up ahead. If you see any fires burning, it'll probably mean we have another battle ahead of us."

"Fine by me!" Alexis said, "I'm ready for another battle!"

"Well that last one wore me out," Perfory responded, "wore me clean out. But on we go. Have to get to Adrianople. Off to Adrianople...Adrianople...October's the opal...Off to our death or off to our birth. That's the 'Song of Perfory,' you know?" Perfory was getting more and more rummy from fatigue. "That's the 'Song of Perfory.'"

"I know it!" Alexis said. "What should the 'Song of Alexis' be?"

"Well, I'll tell you, Alexis, you deserve a song...hell, you deserve an anthem after that battle you fought. Saved my life. That bullet you took was meant for me. And if it had hit me, it wouldn't have been the shoulder. It would have been the head. Oh, my tired skull. No, but you saved my life...fought like a great warrior. You deserve a song of true greatness."

Perfory's horse began to wander off to the right and Alexis snagged the bridle to bring it back in line. "Let me see..." Perfory continued, "The 'Song of

Alexis,' 'Song of Alexis'... In the hills, the warrior fought... treasure, honor, glory sought... the bold Alexis with eyes alight... Alexis the...no, wait..."

"Wait?"

"Alexis?"

"Yes, Perfory?"

"Do you really like that name, Alexis?"

"What do you mean?"

Perfory slowed up on his horse pulled the cloth down from over his mouth in order to speak clearly. "I mean, do you think the name Alexis fits you?"

"It's the only name I've ever known."

"Well, it's just to say that to me it's a name fitting for a boy. But you are a man now. You cannot be more of a man. You see this? I mean, you have traveled and you have lived, and now you have fought your battle, and heroically so. I should rather call you by your full name, Alexander. I prefer. What do you think? It is a stronger name than Alexis. It's the name of a man..." Perfory's voice here trailed off as his horse drifted behind a few paces. He gave it a light kick of the heel and it again caught up with Alexis' horse.

"But I'm serious," he said a moment later. "It sounds silly to you, but to me it's important – and I think it could be important to you. I'd like to call you Alexander from now on if you don't mind."

Alexis stayed silent and didn't speak for a few moments.

"It doesn't sound silly," he finally said.

The two kept quiet for a bit.

"But I don't know..." Alexis added finally, not wanting to drop the matter.

"Well, I know," Perfory kept on, "It's not schmaltz. It's a serious thing."

"Schmaltz?"

"...Yes, I mean it's no small thing to fight a battle like that. It's no small thing to grow up either. To grow old. It's a great thing. I think, well...think of Alexander. It's the name of a man." Perfory started becoming spirited in his talk despite his extreme tiredness. "Think of Alexander who fought with Perfory against six armed horseman and prevailed. Alexander who, in his first battle, saved Perfory from death. Alexander the great warrior who is now a man. Put your youth aside, my friend. Put it aside gladly. With pleasure take on the life of a man."

"I'll think of Alexander," said Alexis. A pain grew in his gut. "And so it will be Alexander," he said then, this new man, Alexander, as he took the young Alexis by the nape of the neck, and tossed him behind on the dark trail. He touched Alexis' cheek with the palm of his hand before he did so. He looked affectionately into his own eyes for just a moment, but at this moment, the new man Alexander tossed that young Alexis back like an object no longer needed. He threw him from his saddle and let him lie in the night on the plains of his boyhood, away from which he was headed. Thus he put Alexis away forever and the two of them, Perfory and Alexander, continued on their way.

"A pretty thing to be a man," Perfory said, "A real pretty thing." The two trotted on silently for some time beneath the white chipped moon. Perfory remained drooped wearily over his horse. His companion rode alert, now watching the stars overhead to memorize their route, now watching nothing, but just thinking, thinking over life – the life gone past and the new life at present. Every now and again, he checked on Perfory to see how he was doing. At times, Perfory's horse began to veer off to the side. He would then call over to his friend to make sure he wasn't sleeping.

"I'm awake," Perfory jolted. "I'm awake." He looked overhead and at the horizon. A creamy band of predawn light ran like scar tissue across the charred sky. "Soon it'll be day and we can camp. But you know as well as I when it is time." And soon it was time. The night expired. Hour overtook hour. The sun had risen and its heat tore across the land. And the two men dropped from their horses and tied the beasts so they wouldn't wander away. They then fashioned a tent from their rifles and the cloth in their packs to shield them from the sun's rays – and there the two soldiers slept through the heat until the cool of afternoon.

"Are you awake?"

"Who's that?"

"It's me."

"Who me?"

"Alexander."

Perfory turned over, "Is it time, already?"

"It is time. Let's go. It's cool enough to travel on. Anyhow I can't sleep anymore. The pain has come back to my shoulder."

Perfory turned over on the ground, rolled the sleep out of him, and sat up, rubbing his eyes. He then said he knew the pain would come back. He looked at his comrade's shoulder. The cloth was caked in dried burgundy blood. "...Yes, let's move on. When we find clean water we'll change the bandages. I have some alcohol to clean it." Perfory managed to get to his feet. He stood beneath the late afternoon sky and arched his back in a great stretch and yawn, "Dear God, I feel good!"

Alexander turned to him and smiled.

"I was getting a bit delirious last night I think. That long sleep did me exceptionally well. I can think clearly again. Oo-la!" Perfory stretched again and Alexander heard his back crack. "When did we finally go to sleep?" He turned to his friend.

"Oh, early morning."

"I don't remember a thing about making this tent. Did I help?"

"Yes, you helped."

Perfory paused. "Hey, are you still Alexander? ...Or Alexis?"

"Alexander," replied Alexander, "No more Alexis."

"Good," Perfory smiled with those great white teeth that shined against his rough sun-beaten and stubbled face. "It's a more fitting name. Hey, check in the left pocket of your coat!...Oh, I forgot your shoulder. Well try anyway. No, you can't move that left arm at all? That'll go away."

"Perfory? Where did these come from?" Alexander reached down and rubbed the dust from the toe of some shiny black boots that were now on his feet.

"From the same place our horses came from," Perfory laughed. "...from the men we shot! Those floppy shoes you were wearing weren't going to get you far. The Turks have good soldiering boots. Look, I swiped myself a pair as well!" Perfory lifted up his foot to show his friend his own pair of shiny black polished boots laced up tight half-way up his shins.

"When did you get them on my feet?"

"When you were sick, of course." ... "Also the reason I got those two extra packs from the Turks. I took their clothes. We might need them." ... "Here," he tossed a long brown scarf at Alexander, "Oh sorry, your arm again.

I'll help you wrap that scarf around your head when it's time. Anyway, these brown fleece-lined coats. These we wear to Adrianople. You see, when we enter the city, I don't know what we will find there. It is possible that the city has been taken by our friends, the Greeks; in which case we will toss these Turkish clothes aside when we get to the gates of the city and ride in proud and unafraid." ... "We will keep the Turkish boots though," he added with a smirk, "because they're good boots." ... "But it's also possible that Adrianople is still under Turkish control – in which case we will be riding into a city where everyone is our enemy and everyone wants us dead. If it is so, we'll keep the brown coats on and the scarves to cover our faces, and we'll ride through the city with our heads bowed, wearing the dead men's clothes, carrying the dead men's rifles. We will not look up. We will not speak. And when our horses have passed through the city, we will continue on, we will leave the city and go towards the far horizon and we will not turn back – for if we turn back, all for us will be truly lost."

The two silently started crossing the plains on horseback, off into the direction of the hidden city which lay somewhere behind the horizon. During twilight, they stopped at a stream to let their horses drink. Perfory helped his friend change the bandages and treated the wound with alcohol. It appeared that it would heal fine with little risk of infection. Alexander washed his hands and knelt over the stream and looked at the slow-drifting water. In the diffused light of twilight, he could see glimmering of flakes of gold at the bottom of the stream. He reached his hand in and stirred the water. The gold flakes mingled with the alluvium and made a dark cloud in the stream. Once the alluvium settled and the gold once again reappeared, the surface of the water cleared and showed Alexander's reflection. His face had grown rough and blackened by the sun, dark stubble grew on his chin. Like Perfory, he now had brown lines that ran from the corners of his eyes. He looked for a long time at his distorted reflection as the light dimmed on the plains. The sky was a funnel where pure black night was pouring through, ever so slowly, seeping into the great cloth of sky stretched over the landscape.

"Do you think we should drink this water?" Perfory asked his friend, "It tastes strange." Alexander dipped his hand into the stream and touched his wet finger to his bottom lip and licked it. It tasted brash and gamey. Alexander shook his head. "Let's keep to what we have in our canteens. We'll drink when we find a cleaner stream."

"It's as you say."

Perfory went to remount his horse. There was something new in the way he was treating his companion. After the battle in the hills, the two had exchanged few words; but there was something more meaningful behind the expression of the words they did share. Something strong and subtle, carried in small part by the words, moreover in the tone and by the look of the eyes. It was clear to both what had happened. Perfory had lost his apprentice. Lost him and gained an equal. He now spoke to his friend as though the two were just as old, just as wise, just as much men. For Alexander and for Perfory both, there was something very beautiful and very somber about this.

Later, in the night, the two stopped to eat. They rested, but decided not to sleep.

"We could sleep for a moment, but maybe we shouldn't," said Perfory.

"Better that we don't," Alexander stated, "It won't be safe to build a fire, and it's too cold to sleep without one. Let's continue on."

"There is a little more bread," said Perfory.

"Yes, thank you." Alexander took the hunk of bread, tore off an end with the crust and handed the rest back to his friend.

"Hey, Alexander," Perfory smiled, washing his bread down with a swig of water from his canteen, "Reach into the left pocket of your coat with your right hand."

Alexander looked at him questioningly for a moment, hesitating. "You know, I think I can reach with my left hand as it is. My shoulder isn't hurting much now." Alexander felt in his left pocket with his left hand. There was a heavy piece of metal inside. "What is it?" He pulled it out. It was a watch. A silver pocket watch on a long chain. "Where did this come from?" he asked, smiling a great happy smile. "Wait, I know, don't tell me. The same place as the horses! ...Is this for me?"

"Yes, yes, it's for you...I got a couple gifts of my own from their pockets!" Perfory pulled out a knife with a bone handle and held it up laughing. "I'm glad they didn't live to stick this in me!" Then he pulled a little brass ring out. "I found this tied on a string around one of the men's necks. It will be a present for my little baby daughter." His chipped white teeth shone brightly as he held out the ring for Alexander to see.

Alexander sat looking at his watch as he rubbed the etched silver with his thumb. A watch lost and a watch gained. Alexander felt a foolish tear come to his eye. "How did you know I'd lost my watch?" he asked Perfory, opening the cover. The inside silver was engraved with intricate patterns, flourished oriental designs. He found it more beautiful then the wristwatch he'd lost long ago to the pawnbroker in the Great City.

"Which soldier did it come from?" Alexander asked.

"One of the last two that you shot off the ledge…

"You know, I still don't know how you managed to shoot two men at the same time."

"I don't either." Alexander sat on the bank of the stream where the gold flakes rushed, and touched the silver of the new timepiece. He thought about those men he'd killed. He wondered who they'd been. What were the histories of their lives. Where they had traveled to. Whom they had loved. When he saw that he had killed them, he remembered feeling nothing but triumph and success. The glory of life saved for he and his brother at the expense of a veiled soulless enemy. Let the ground dissolve their bodies, whoever they once were. Alexander inspected his new timepiece. There on the inside cover, he noticed a curved line carved into the silver, it resembled a snake and looked like it had been scratched in by hand with a nail. Alexander grabbed his rifle and took a pin out and begin etching his own mark into the cover of the watch. He finished the lines on the snake to make the letter 'S.' Then, next to the 'S,' he carved the letter 'A,' deep and bold…"Woman and Man," he smiled to himself, "War and Travel. Conqueror and Conquered. Cities and Countries. Birth, Life and Death." He took another look around him, at this bank where he was seated; and at his silver watch, this shoal of time. He gave one last instance of thought to the men he had killed whom time would bury. He thought again and again of the woman he hoped was waiting for him to return from the war. He thought of Perfory, his companion, his former master, his friend. He looked at this friend who lounged on the bank of the stream with a pack stuffed under his head for a pillow. He was humming a song and had a long piece of brown grass in his mouth that he chewed on. His gaze moved back and forth across the sky, reflecting the light of the stars. He then stopped humming and yawned a great yawn. He picked another piece of grass beside him and started chewing that too. Alexander smiled at him.

"After all, maybe we can just sleep for an hour or so."

"Yes I'd like to."

While they napped on the river bank, Alexander dreamt of Sophia. He dreamt of her lying waiting for him on her pink rose-colored sheets. He dreamt of her and he dreamt of Constantinople. There in Constantinople, he lived in an airy room of amber stones, where the eastern sun came through in a bright beam. There in Constantinople, he was seated on the packed earth floor of this room, eating spiced bread and drinking sweet coffee out of a golden kettle. There was a cobra in his room, and he was teaching it to fetch a giant ruby. He'd toss the ruby across the room, the cobra would slither majestically over, take the brilliant red stone between its teeth, and slither back to return it to its master. It was a pleasant dream. Both of the dreams were pleasant. Both of Sophia and of Constantinople.

He awoke to Perfory rousing him. It was the night's milieu. The two started off riding again, mounting slowly the darkened slope that led to a plateau.

"Perfory," Alexander said at one moment during the ride.

"Yes?"

"My arm hurts."

"Bullets do nasty things to people."

When the two men reached the top of the plateau, they continued their slow ride across it. Once it ended and they came to the downhill slope, they stopped to look out across.

"Let's get off our horses," Perfory suggested.

The two stood at the edge of the plateau and looked across the small barren valley. The moon shimmered on the little streams in the valley and in the darkness these streams looked like spilled oil. To the left, beyond the valley, was a set of closely knit round hills. To the right, there were sheer canyons and low-lying mountains.

"It's a beautiful, landscape," Alexander said, while looking out.

Perfory drank from his canteen and ate his half of the last of the bread. "It's beautiful, this earth," he smiled, "It's an old story for me, this landscape, this country. I've come through here before. But I was alone and on foot. Now is a better time." He handed Alexander his own bread and the latter took it and ate.

"What's beyond those hills?" Alexander asked, pointing off to the leftern horizon.

"Adrianople," Perfory replied.

"And beyond those mountains and canyons?" he asked pointing off to the right.

"Constantinople."

Alexander looked out at those mountains and canyons that obscured Constantinople. 'I wonder,' he thought, 'I really wonder.'

"Come on," said Perfory then, stirring Alexander from his revelry, "It's time to disguise ourselves."

He handed his friend the brown cape he had taken from one of the dead Turks. He helped Alexander wrap a tan Turkish scarf around his head. "It is not so far to Adrianople," Perfory insisted, "We will make it there by mid-morning." He then fixed his own scarf around his head and over his green coat he put on one of the Turkish brown coats with the fleece lining. Alexander had on his own Turkish coat. "I don't know what we'll find in Adrianople." Perfory paused. "It could be good...or it could be very bad." He was fidgeting nervously with the brass ring that he was saving for his daughter, flipping it on the piece of string around his neck. He then reached through the brown coat and put his hand in the inside breast pocket of his green coat and took hold of something. He pulled it out and handed it to his friend.

"Take this, Alexander – another gift." He thereby handed his friend a medal. It was a gold medallion on a black, red and white striped ribbon – a decoration for honorable military service. Alexander received it, turned it over in his hand. The moon reflected off it with shards of white and yellow light. He looked then at Perfory. Perfory looked strangely at his friend. He said nothing but swallowed and Alexander saw his Adam's apple rise and fall as he did so. "I want you to have it," Perfory finally said. "I don't know what we'll find in Adrianople." His face took a gloomy expression. "It could be bad. So I wanted to give it to you before." Then he made a great effort to cover his gloominess with a happy grin, but it appeared forced and therefore more solemn than it had been.

"An award from Perfory to Alexander. An award for bravery in battle. An honor of the highest order." Then he dropped his shoulders. "No, but you fought well. You saved my life and took a wound. You deserve it..." He then paused, and nervously scratched the whiskers on his chin while looking at his friend. Alexander spoke not but looked now at the medal, now at Perfory, now away to hide the emotion he felt. Finally Perfory began again to interrupt the silence. "It's alright, Alexander. Keep it. I will not need it. I have a new and different kind of honor." With his finger he touched the brass ring on the string around his neck, he then took the ring and tucked it inside his shirt so it was no longer visible. "Just make sure for the time being to wear your medal on the inside of your green coat," Perfory said, helping Alexander to pin it on.

"…Because if you wear it on the outside and the Turks see it, they will shoot you – worst case…best case – we get to Adrianople and there are Greeks there – you will lose the medal when we throw our scarves and overcoats away. So you'd better wear it on the inside!"

Alexander felt more foolishness building itself in his eye while he touched the medal a final time before fixing the button on his brown coat to cover it up. He looked away from Perfory, on at the horizon. Perfory, seeing his friend's gaze that moved from the hills on the leftern horizon to the canyons and mountains on the rightern, said to him, "Alexander…"

"Yes?"

"I know about your dreams. I know about your dreams, but I urge you not to travel on too much farther. Think not to go to Constantinople. Of course, you are a man and you will do as you do. But just consider going back to the Acropolis after it is over. Ask for this young lady's hand. You know," he winked at his friend, "with your medal of high honor, even a Governor's daughter will be impressed!" He reached out to slap Alexander on the shoulder, but remembering his injury, he patted him on the chest instead. Alexander said nothing but just looked at Perfory. He had mentioned neither Sophia nor Constantinople to him. He had said nothing.

"By mid-morning, you say, we will reach Adrianople?" Alexander asked, mounting his horse.

"By mid-morning," Perfory confirmed. And the two rode on.

Chapter XVI

"Meeting the Firing Squad" – arrival at Adrianople...

Perfory and Alexander rode through the final hours of night, coming out of the valley beneath a sky that swirled with violet wisps of clouds. Their horses cantered through the final hills and the dark sky lightened and flooded with creamy blue as a magnificent sun emerged on the horizon, lighting the poplar trees, lighting the road where their horses took to a slow trot as they approached the great fortified city. Above the stone walls in the near distance, the domes of mosques and their pillars gleamed with jeweled light. They heeled their horses to walk slowly, hooves stepping on the sun-baked and cracked earth of the road leading to the gate – the gate that stood open, leading into a city where all appeared to be empty and silent.

Alexander, with his good arm, secured the brown scarf covering his face, so only the slits of his eyes showed through. Strange for the city to seem so quiet. He held the reigns and approached with trepidation, rifle at his side. He glanced at Perfory who rode beside him and Perfory turned and looked back at Alexander through his own brown scarf that covered his eyes and mouth. Alexander could not see the expression on his friend's face, though he was sure it was also one of confusion. Had the city been abandoned? Perfory, held his own rifle discreetly at his side while his other hand looped through the horse's reigns and secured the scarf over his own face. The two went according to plan, and began to ride into the city quietly, alert and prepared,

There were snipers stationed at the gates of Adrianople atop the city walls. Obscured from view, they followed Alexander and Perfory with the barrels of their carbines as the two entered the city, riding languid horses. Once through the gates, the road turned from sun-cracked earth to a street of loose cobblestones.

Back in the hills, before entering the city, Perfory had told Alexander that one of three situations would likely present when they arrived in Adrianople. The city would either, he explained, be experiencing a battle, or it would have had already experienced a battle, or else it would be undisturbed. If a battle were underway, the plan was: the two men would discard their Turkish disguises and join the Greeks in the fight. That was if there were a battle underway, yet, having now arrived, it was obvious there were no battles in progress.

If their arrival concluded a battle already past, the city would be torn and possibly destroyed and the victors would be building walls and standing behind closed gates to claim and maintain possession of their secured polis. That was if a battle had passed, yet, having now arrived to a city where the streets were empty, the buildings intact and the gates wide open, it appeared that no battle had been fought and won.

If the city were undisturbed, Perfory and Alexander's arrival would be an arrival into hostile territory, an arrival into a city under Turkish rule. And in such case, this most feared of situations, Perfory and Alexander would be the only two on their side, and they'd advised themselves to ride in discreetly with Turkish garb and heads bowed low, and hope they weren't noticed, for such would mean a swift demise.

Now at the city of Adrianople, the situation the two soldiers feared most appeared to be the situation at hand; and so the two rode in with heads bowed, nervous fingers resting on their hidden rifles. Perfory and Alexander now intended to continue riding through the city to the far gates, and leave as quietly and quickly as possible. Though unbeknownst to themselves, as they rode in, snipers hidden atop the city walls had carbines following their every movement.

Cloudlets drifting in the sky now passed in front of the sun, casting shade on Adrianople, while these guards nested in the city walls watched the languid horses carry their riders with drooping covered heads. In addition to these guards, there were snipers on each of the roofs of the buildings lining the cobbled streets at the city's entrance; and they too were aware of the strangers' arrival. On the streets near the entrance, all was quiet. A few chickens pecked at some crumbs on the arid sandy sidewalk. At the end of the first street, a group of men were gathered, talking amongst themselves. Their conversation had begun idly, but soon turned joyous and there were intermittent outbursts of boisterous shouts. Alexander looked through the slits in his scarf from the corners of his eyes as he and Perfory passed these men, hoping to go unnoticed. It was then, however, the group took sight of the newcomers. Six men in all, they turned to foreign horsemen...

"You there!" one shouted, drawing his pistol from its holster, "Dismount your horses!" He pointed the firearm at Perfory. Two others drew their pistols and pointed them at Alexander...

"Off your horses and drop the rifles!"

There was a clack as the rifles fell and landed on the cobbled street. Without any resistance, Alexander and Perfory climbed down from their horses and put their hands on the tops of their heads.

Two in the group searched the pockets of their trousers for weapons. The four others kept steady pistols at their heads; while, all the while, the snipers on the rooftops kept a protective watch on all with the aid of mighty carbines.

"Against the wall!" one of them yelled. Alexander felt a strong hand grab his neck and squeeze it as his face wrapped in cloth was pushed against the stone wall. The men raised their pistols. Perfory as well was thrown up against the wall. Alexander tasted blood from where his lip was cut by his teeth when his mouth was thrust into the stone. He felt the pulsing hand of the man who stood behind him, gripping his neck. Both he and Perfory remained silent. Soon the men released them from their grip and stood back a couple steps. Perfory and Alexander didn't move.

Hadn't this end a better way?...A fiery sickness burned in Alexander's gut, fears of the ugliest sort. The group of men stood around Perfory and Alexander, whispering in hushed tones. The captured soldiers, meanwhile, stood trembling with their faces pressed against the wall. Hereupon, two of the men in the group pulled back the hammers on their pistols to get ready to shoot. The firing squad stood about five paces off.

"Have you anything to say at the moment of your execution," the first man with his pistol raised called out. Alexander felt a wave of vertigo, a flush of heat and cold. Perfory gritted his teeth and spoke slowly and clearly: "Soldiers…must we greet our execution with our backs turned? …Facing a wall?"

"Not at all!" the soldier laughed with sardonic pleasure, "Not at all! Turn around, if you prefer to greet the bullet with your eyes!" this-upon the other men laughed. Alexander knew there was something wrong with all of this. Perfory slowly turned around, face still enshrouded with its brown scarf. Alexander too turned around to greet his own death and his fear intensified to a climax, where it dissolved into another feeling. A feeling of hope came, and for why, he was not sure, but as he looked through the slits in his shroud at these men with their pistols pointed at him and his friend, ready to execute them, a lightness and hope mingled with his heavy despair. A feather from a startled rooster caught in the wind and fluttered upwards…strange disjointed thoughts and images passed through his mind: he saw his sister wringing out a rag at the window in their kitchen, cedar wood burning in the Great Northern Woods. The march of a band of coyotes. The hope of a life of greatness. It could not end here. A cloudlet passed before the sun over the city and cast a cold shade over everything. The firing squad stood poised, hammers pulled back, barrels raised, darkness fell, it was night. He saw his father seated at the table of planks, picking his teeth with a splinter by the light of a crackling candle flame, his eyes changed from lead to iron, from copper to bronze. He was alone now, an adult, a grown man, lying in a small stone room on the ground floor of a tower. He read a book bound in calfskin. *Commedia*, the cover read. Sophia was gathering flowers in a garden. She wore a white hat with a broad brim. He felt like laughing. He smiled and wrinkles branched like train tracks from the corners of his eyes. There in his hand was the small hand of a young girl. In her other, she held a piece of glazed bread. Upon it was spread golden jam. She was asking him to help her climb the perforated trees. It was night. Then he heard another sound like the striking of gun metal, the pounding of an industrial hammer on a leaden anvil. A shot. Then there was a burst of light.

A burst of light as a cloudlet had been blown away to unblock the sun; and the sun's bright hot rays came down upon the city of Adrianople, reflecting off the jeweled facets of the metallic dome of a mosque across the way, and this concentrated light reflected from the dome and shot into Alexander's eyes, and here there was a burst of light and he awoke from his numb reverie to see again the reality before him: six executioners standing around him, ready to kill this sunlight for him forever and send him into unholy darkness. Yet, with this reawakening, Alexander looked on at his executioners and realized that he would not – that he could not – die. A strange smile betrayed his despair and curled the corners of his mouth. Perfory, who stood beside him, spoke again...

"...And the soldiers will execute Perfory and Alexander?" His voice was steady and firm. His covered face turned back and forth around at the men standing there with their coal black eyes and ready pistols. A buzz perpetrated Alexander's head. He wasn't even concerned about the answer that would come to serve Perfory's question. He merely stood and looked on at these men who ceased to resemble men, but rather green lizards, large iguanas that danced around, leaping on crickets. Oh, how the sun overhead burned hot!

So, these men, the veiled faceless enemy before them, wore no veils and their faces were pale...white skin and green soulless eyes fixing on their own veiled and faceless enemies: one Perfory and one Alexander – two men enshrouded in their death masks of fibrous, earth-colored twill.

'...And that death should come in mid-morning!'

Alexander heard a crack.

'...And that the life of greatness should be but a myth, to lead me from one slippery stone to the next, until I reach thy far lying bank, where tadpoles swim and the alluvium flows, all as meek as I; though I, for the most-part, for I have sought and have been deceived...but oh, to have lived! Oh, to have lived, and beneath such a gentle sun, whose rays come fierce as a kiss – soft the boneless gums of a babe and the withered skin of an aged man, that death should come swift from the dancing lizards with shining chests of white...green coats...green coats...green coats...but something is wrong with all of this, God and bride, father and sister, ach! I taste blood in my throat!...'

Perfory asked again, more loudly this time: "So the soldiers will execute Perfory and Alexander, here at the gates of Adrianople?"

"Yes," was the reply, "the soldiers will execute." They raised their pistols higher.

Perfory's voice grew stronger... "Well, gentleman..." His voice concealed not the smile that played across his lips beneath the brown scarf wrapped around his face. Alexander heard the smile in the voice of Perfory, felt the joyous mockery in his friend's discourse, and his own joyous smile shone through a crack in his own shroud.

"Gentlemen, let us take off our scarves first. Let us take off our coats. I'd like you to see the resemblance our underclothes bear to yours."

Here the man leading the execution fell silent; the other men in the crowd gathered around, and one who had hitherto remained silent, began to laugh like a jesting fool, "Yes, prisoners, take off your clothes!" And he waved his pistol in the air, the barrel fluttered at the sky. "Take off their clothes, men! Let's send these Turks out of the world the same way they came into it – as naked as their mothers made them!" He laughed and shot his pistol in the air. With the shot, the other men stopped and looked around. The attention was raised of the guards on the rooftops and the snipers on the city walls with their carbines. There was general confusion. The men in the group of six fell silent. Many lowered their pistols. Alexander and Perfory looked at each other through the cracks in their wrapped scarves. The man who had laughed and shot his pistol in the air even fell silent, and looked around at the others, waiting for someone to speak.

Finally, the leader of the group of six, the more sober among them, took on a neutral expression and waved his pistol twice towards Perfory and Alexander in a gesture to signal that the two disrobe.

Alexander and Perfory careful raised their hands to remove their scarves. The foolhardy of the six men raised his pistol again at the two. The prisoners dropped their scarves. There were some smirks among the group of men. Two of them returned their pistols to the pockets of their green army coats. Alexander and Perfory unbuttoned their brown coats and let them drop to the cobbled street. One of the men laughed. The others mumbled something and the sober leader put his pistol away and walked up to Alexander and Perfory, who stood silently, seriously with their backs against the wall, faces unmasked, each with their Greek green coats on, and white undershirts underneath. The leader stepped towards them and said without any humor in his voice, in all seriousness, "And you were going to let us shoot you?!"

Here there was laughter from the other five in the group. Boisterous laughter crowned by the sound of the pistols of the foolhardy one and one other who joined him in shooting at the sky. These pistol shots alarmed the snipers on the roof who drew their attention around and scanned the streets below looking for activity. The sober leader didn't seem to find so much humor as the rest, and he seemed annoyed that the situation hadn't been cleared up earlier, but he too eventually made a small smile and signaled to Perfory and Alexander that they come with the men and walk a bit.

Alexander was still confused. Slowly, the realization crept in that he was not going to die. He was almost afraid to smile, though, lest a bullet come to mock his joy. He was almost afraid to look around with these, the eyes of one newly born to the world, lest this foreign city be a stillborn's lair…had he really been saved? No, he would live. And the pleasure was both lessened and made greater by the realization that his life could not – would not – have ended thus, like that. Of course he wasn't to be shot, had he been a fool to think these men had been his enemies? Had he been foolish to confuse an execution with a welcome ceremony? Oh, to be a fool! To be a fool alive beneath the shining sun!

Perfory and Alexander were led along by the six men down the quiet streets at the entrance of Adrianople. They all kept quiet and none made further jokes or comments about the scene of execution. Their way led through a long arcade, and when the arcade ended and emptied out into the city's inner-ring, the arrivals looked around themselves and saw that this inner-ring was a whole new world unlike the quiet environs near the city gates. Here, Adrianople was bustling and lively – a city captured by their fellow men. In the streets there were Greek soldiers, foreign allies, men like themselves dressed in the same green coats, the same stolen boots, faces like those Alexander had seen on the train to the front, or back in the Acropolitan village. Honor was secured – Alexander felt the medal in the inside pocket of his coat to make sure it was safe. Perfory walked close beside him. Pistol shots rang out. Boisterous shouting came from some groups of soldiers gathered on the crowded street corners where the men were talking, laughing and drinking. After being led through three more narrow streets, they arrived at a mosque.

"This is headquarters," the sober one said to the two. He led them up the steps into the mosque.

"What happens here?" Alexander asked Perfory in a whisper.

"I'm not sure," the latter responded.

Just then, a man ran up and grabbed Perfory by the arm…

"Perfory!" the man cried out, "Old, Perfory! Hell if it's you!"

Perfory turned to the man, not recognizing him for a moment. Then, his eyes brightened… "No!" he laughed, "Is that you, Petros?!"

"Yes, Petros! Ha-ha! Look it's Perfory, old dog!" He remained gripping Perfory's arm with great friendliness and the two embraced and greeted each other with much brotherly warmth. Alexander stood back and smiled at this unexpected event. The six men who had led Alexander and Perfory up the steps to the mosque now faded into the background as Petros came forward … "Bring your friend and come along!" he told Perfory.

Alexander, Perfory and Petros all started off down the steps. Those six other men remained behind.

Together, they headed off through the streets surrounding the opulent mosque. Perfory was happy to see his old friend. Likewise, Petros laughed the whole way and kept slapping Perfory's shoulder. He shook Alexander's hand five or six times but was so caught up, he kept forgetting to introduce himself. He led them on into the very center of Adrianople. The streets were hot and bright and the Greek soldiers gathered around happily laughing, talking and drinking in the vibrant warmth of the early noon.

"How are you old friend? You just arrived, I hear?" But without waiting for an answer, Petros kept on talking and pointing around the city... "Look you two, we are painting the city! This will be the new Athens!" Alexander looked around himself. They passed a group of men gathered on the sunny sidewalk. The men were drinking from gourds and laughing. Occasionally, a man shot a pistol in the air. Here in the city-centre, there were no snipers on the roofs and no one became alarmed if the men shot bullets in the air.

"Look around, old boy!" Petros pointed about the scene, "Greek wares being sold. Greek shops with Greek signs…even there are Greek women here!" Petros gave the tour of the heat-filled streets where tawny faced soldiers sat at folding tables on sidewalks drinking and laughing and playing games of Tavli. Chickens in wooden crates pecked at seeds. Vendors sold breads and shirts, as well as ammo for the soldiers to shoot at the clouds in celebration. These vendors were neither Turkish nor Greek civilians, but were entrepreneurial Greek soldiers who had taken up free enterprise in their new and happy city. A city which had been theirs for less than a week. All the victorious men were catching their breaths from months of long battle, and now was the time to live the sweet life, the newfound life as rulers of the city. Food, wine and liquor, supplies, and women were being brought in on trains from the Acropolis. The soldiers' wives and girlfriends were arriving. Soldiers' daughters and sons. Unmarried girls came to entertain and congratulate the victorious heroes. The war was over. The war had ended and everyone was encouraged to transform the city into a paradise for the victors. "The city is ours, men!" Petros repeated over and again, "Trains come in full and they leave empty. Anything you want, you can have. Anything one can find in the Acropolis is being brought in. We are remaking the city." Alexander looked around with intrigue and excitement. The sun shone brilliantly, and happy was he. Perfory followed along with the group with a more serene and calm happiness. The three walked on through the cobbled streets where colorful victory streamers flapped in the warm calm winds that came and stopped and came again.

Petros led the two men into a little café in the city-centre. The old screen door swung open and the three entered. Inside, ex-soldiers in civilian dress played games of Tavli and drank. Petros explained that the café was being run by a hefty lieutenant by the name of Costas. Costas had stormed the café on the siege of the city, shot the Turks who were inside and made it his base. He then cleared out the dead enemy soldiers, hung up his uniform on a hook in the kitchen; took an apron off another hook, and began cooking and pouring out ouzo, which was arriving in Adrianople of supply trains by the hour due to the constant demand of the city's new inhabitants who needed things to do and things to drink in this unusual and pleasurable time. Petros, Perfory and Alexander all sat down at a table inside and Costas brought over a bottle of ouzo as well as some little dishes he had prepared.

The three toasted glasses. Alexander liked the taste of the clear liquor. Petros said it was drinkable but that better stuff was supposed to come on the next train. Perfory took long draw and expressed appreciation to be drinking something other than stream water. The three settled back into their chairs.

"How are you, old boy?" Petros asked Perfory, "It's the first time that I see you that you're not shooting bullets at something! ...And the first time we can have a drink together without fear of someone else shooting bullets at us! Who is your man here?" He signaled to Alexander who then introduced himself and stretched out his hand and shook strongly with Petros.

"Ah! Now we are a merry group! A merry group of victorious men!" Petros exclaimed.

Just then, a group of revelers passed by the window of Costas' café. They were marching down the sidewalk beating drums and singing songs. Perfory, Petros and Alexander, inside all turned to watch. Behind the revelers followed some girls who danced to the beat of the drums. They were dark-haired Greek girls with tawny skin and flowing skirts.

"You see," said Petros, "Not just a merry group of men. We have women too! They have come just for us...just for us conquering soldiers!" Petros' cheeks began getting red from drink and his joyous ramble continued on.

"Well," Perfory smiled to his friends, "If a general wants to keep a captured city, he has to bring in women, that's for sure!" Then he laughed, "but Alexander should know that more than any of us."

Alexander had understood the joke and laughed too.

"Yes, it's good to have a whole city to ourselves," Petros sighed, pouring more drinks.

"Where are the Turks?" Perfory turned to his friend, "...out of curiosity."

"The Turks?!" Petros repeated. He took a drink and yelled back into the kitchen in a loud voice, "Hey Costas!...where are the Turks?!"

"Just a second!" big Costas replied, "I have something's gonna burn...wait!" and he came around with a steaming pan in his hand to the table where the three men sat. He began piling fried aubergines and grilled tomatoes and onions onto a plate in the center of the small table where the little dishes the men had been eating from were. "The Turks?" Costas bellowed, scratching his chin. He turned to Petros who was stuffing the oily aubergines into his mouth and washing it all down with the cool ouzo.

"Yeah, Costas," Petros said, "we were killing the Turks. Didn't you know?"

"I thought it was the Syrians we were killing," Costas replied, "The Turks I thought were the good guys! Oh, who knows about these things...Wait, hold on! I have some more food coming." And with that, Costas left the table, and ran back to the kitchen where the sounds of popping grease could be heard from the pans on the flames. Some of the other customers got up from their table and emptied their pockets of change for some tips for Costas. Petros asked his friends if they wanted to play a game of Tavli.

"Oh, I forgot," Petros said apologetically, "You just arrived in the city, I bet you're tired from traveling. Do want me to show you to your quarters so you can nap a bit?"

"That might be nice," Perfory replied, rubbing his forehead.

"When was the last time you slept?"

"Well," Perfory turned to Alexander, "What did we..."

"We got an hour of sleep last night, I think right?" Alexander said.

"Yes, an hour, or so...."

"Well, after a game of Tavli. Just one game," insisted Petros. One could read on his face that he really didn't want this joyous lunch to end. "One game and a little green ouzo. It's Costas' specialty. He won't tell anyone what's in it, but it's green and it wakes you up… Whad'ya say?" Petros eyes bounced back and forth to Alexander and Perfory, awaiting a response.

Perfory smiled and so did Alexander, "Yes to the game, and to the green ouzo," Perfory said.

"It's been a long time sleeping out in the wilderness," said Alexander, "eating berries and pointing rifles at shades…I say yes to both."

"Hey Costas!" Petros yelled back to the kitchen, "A half carafe of your green poison!" he got up and grabbed a Tavli board.

"Pointing rifles at shades," Petros laughed, "where did they have you stationed?"

"At the 33rd front," Perfory told him. We rode in when we saw the bombs in the hills."

"Yeah, those were our bombs!" Petros exclaimed, "They were all our bombs!" He turned to Perfory, "So you saw no fighting this go-around?"

"Oh, sure. Alexander's exaggerating…we saw a gorgeous battle. He won it for us. Otherwise, I wouldn't be alive to be here to see you, old friend…No, I wouldn't be here…" Perfory's voice took a solemn tone, but Petros quickly lightened things again…

"Ah well, all the fighting and all that is behind us. Now we are the victors and we are going to drink this mighty green poison and play a game of Tavli. Ever play?" he turned to Alexander. "No? Well I'll show you." … "Your piece there. My piece here" … "Ah-ha, *Plakono!* One piece on top of the other. *Plakono!* One city on top of the other! *Plakono!* Let's toast glasses, men…"

"*Plakono!!!*" the three men yelled in unison and chimed glasses, and so loudly and so merrily that the other men in the café all yelled out and raised glasses and shouted *Plakono!*, while a few tossed plates and what-not on the ground.

Just then, three young girls ran giggling into the café. They were black-eyed Greek beauties. Young sweet girls. The first one caught her cotton dress on a metal nail on the door as she ran in and the fabric tore and part of her thigh was revealed. The men in the café laughed and one sitting by the door pinched her thigh and she blushed and ran out. The other two girls continued to run around the café, pinning little ribbons on the men's shirts and hanging wreathes around their necks . They kissed each of the men's cheeks. Alexander got a wreath of large white flowers and two honey-sweet kisses on his cheeks. After all the men had been kissed and decorated, the girls giggled and ran out.

"Ah," sighed Perfory with happiness, "It's a charming life when you have your countrymen and countrywomen behind you."

"Oh yes," agreed Petros, "It's almost no fun to take a city if you don't have pretty girls kissing your cheeks afterwards!" The three men laughed at this, crossed arms in a toast and drank.

Alexander remarked that Perfory had been rather quiet and to himself during that time in the café. Must be just tired, he decided.

"Okay, let's finish this game up," said Petros, "then I'll show you your quarters." He turned to Alexander this time, whom up till now he hadn't said much to, and started in with great animation, "Alexander, good man, you should see the amenities here. You and Perfory are going to like where you're staying. You see, they left us soldiers an entire city to play with, and naturally the officers get the best. Me and Perfory can have whatever we want...and since you're our comrade, Alexander, you can serve yourself as well...Oh, and I forgot, your rooms look out onto a splendid square..." Petros then turned and yelled back to the kitchen, "Hey Costas! What's the name of that square down that way where I'm staying at?" He turned his chair back around, "Oh I don't think he knows, and I forget. Oh well, we'll rename it. Maybe it will be named after me. 'Petros Square' is nice...or maybe 'Perfory Square,' yeah that's it...hey Costas! You don't mind if I take that square over there, do you? After all, you got the café!" Petros was merry and slightly drunk and Costas too was slightly drunk. He whistled while he cooked and collected tips from the men; and after Petros paid for the three's food and drinks, Costas came out to shake the men's hands and every one was happy and laughing and Perfory and Alexander left the café with Petros in very good spirits, although they were both very tired as well.

In the street, the sun fell down and flooded the ancient city. A group of soldiers in handsome uniforms were parading along singing, while amorous girls followed them giggling. Petros strode gaily with one hand in the pocket of his trousers – in the other he held a bottle of ouzo he'd taken with him from Costas'. He began to explain the lodging... "There are nice baths there. And you two will have three big rooms to yourselves; and as I mentioned, the balcony overlooks a square – did I mention that? – well, get some sleep you guys...but not too much! There are festivities this evening and a great feast tonight." ... "Perfory," he turned to his friend, "there's the Officer's Bureau set up at the mosque, you can arrange affairs there when you wake up," he leaned then over to Alexander and whispered about what a great hero Perfory was, what a great soldier and how many battles he'd won back in the day when he fought alongside Petros. It was then the three men came to a tiny stone arcade that preceded the square Petros had told them about.

The arcade had a little rockery with a fountain in the center. Some soldiers were playing flutes and girls were dancing around. Petros veered off to take a handful of water from the fountain to wet his mouth and one of the flute players stopped playing to sprinkle a little fountain water on his head. He laughed and tossed water back at him, and the front of the flute player's shirt got all wet, and everyone in the plaza seemed to be in great spirits. Petros ran back over to where Perfory and Alexander were standing and grabbed the two by the shoulders and pointed to the young girls in the colorful skirts who were standing together by the fountain, attempting to dance to the musicians' flutes. They wore colored streamers in their hair and shook their hips back and forth. "Hey, look at these girls here!" Petros pointed and laughed, "You can tell they're virgins by the way they dance. Look at their hips. That one doesn't know whether to put it left or right! Ha! I'll show her where to put it! Oh, that feast is going to be great!" Petros, laughing, peeled a strip of sealing wax off of the neck of the bottle he'd been holding in his hand and tossed it at one of the young girls. She turned around and looked over her shoulder at Petros with her dark eyes and smiled nicely.

"Oh, this feast is going to be great!" he continued, leading his friends away from the arcade, "...The first big – I mean really big – celebration we'll have had since the capture of the city. A real bacchanal! Starts at nightfall..."

While Petros had been talking and the three men were walking down the narrow lane that led to the square, Alexander spied down at the bases of the stone buildings of the lane. There at foot-level, on the sidewalks, were little square windows cut out of the stone that led into the cellars. Those windows were covered in bars. Behind the bars was darkness. And within that darkness, Alexander spied the hands of men and women that were stretched through the bars, groping for the gravel in the cracks of the sidewalks. These hands touched with just their fingertips the yellow flood of daylight sun which poured down from the sky upon the city.

"Who are they?" Alexander asked Petros, signaling down at the hands reaching up through the bars. Petros looked down. He stopped laughing and turned to Alexander and said with almost sober solemnity, "Those are our captives. Our enemies, Alexander. Let's walk on."

Alexander peered back down at these enemies beyond the dark holes of windows cut out of the stone. Amongst the dirty hands gripping the bars and the sidewalk, he saw dark-skinned faces looking out – faces that saw no light and felt no heat, just the damp cool and musty air of the prison squalor. He looked down and his eyes met with the eyes of one of the prisoners. It was a man, like Alexander, about the same age. Their eyes met and upon the prisoner's face, Alexander read suffering. His eyes seemed to speak clearly to Alexander, asking for pity, "Oh, why was it we who were captured, why was it our city that was conquered, why wasn't it you? And now that it was us, what will you do with us now, oh prevailing ones? What will you do with us?"

"We will do as we please!" Petros roared with joy, but not in response to the squalid look of the prisoner whose gaze Alexander had finally broke with, but rather to the gaiety of the sunny street that was emptying out into a beautiful opulent stone square of immense size. "...We will do what we please in this city," Petros repeated, throwing his hands out, 'Look at this beautiful place, and it is all ours! Look Perfory, look Alexander, it is all ours and we will do what we please!"

"We will do what brings us pleasure," Perfory said, in a wise and quiet tone.

"Yes, we shall...And hopefully we will also rest a little," Alexander added to the conversation as he gave a great yawn. Perfory agreed with him that getting a little rest would be the greatest of all pleasures and that it would please him very much and Petros thought that that was a good idea since his two friends looked very tired and they had had a heavy meal and more than a few drinks; but fortunately they were now already at the square, and the three walked beneath the arch to enter the marble hall where an interior stone staircase led up to a mezzanine that continued on to a top floor where Perfory and Alexander would be staying during their time in Adrianople.

Petros had the keys and gave them to Perfory and led them through a spacious series of rooms: three bedrooms with stone walls, decorated with tiles and tapestries; each with its own separate bath, a large stone basin where one could soak in the steamy water that poured through ornately-carved copper pipes. Beyond the rooms and the baths, an immense sunny balcony overlooked the square. All was of stone: the balcony tables and chairs, the meter-high vases in the corners where blooming flowers were planted. Petros led the two to the balcony and pointed across the square at another palace across the way where he said his own quarters were. "If you need anything, I'm just across the way. We'll see each other around nightfall for the feast. I think I'll go lie down awhile as well...the heat...you men get some rest!" Lastly, before Petros said goodbye and left, he showed them the closets where his friends could help themselves to new clean clothes. It was evident that before the city's capture, these palaces had been the residences of high nobility. In the closets were beautiful silks, long white robes of fine satin, as well as simple shirts of sandy linen and blouses of white cotton. There were also linen trousers and cotton trousers. Petros found the bathing towels and gave them to Perfory and Alexander and said goodbye and kissed both on the cheeks. He asked again to make sure that Perfory had taken the keys, and Perfory confirmed that he had gotten the keys and Petros left with all his usual jovial warmth and friendliness – although he too was yawning at the end. As he descended the stone staircase that led back outside into the afternoon square, he could be heard singing and whistling his funny songs.

Alexander took one of the rooms and one of the baths and bathed and oiled his hair with the fine scented tonics that were provided. He felt the cleanest he had in a long time. Halfway through the bath, he got out of the stone tub and shaved himself in the glass in the steamy room. He splashed cold water on the mirror to clear it and examined himself. It was a long time since he'd looked in a mirror. His face, he noticed, had grown older, more mature. He was no longer thin as he was in the Great City. His muscles had filled out. His chest was baked brown from the sun and dark hairs had grown on it. His face too was brown and his eyes and teeth sat in their rows of glimmering pearls as he washed them and spit the froth in the sink basin and finished by rubbing tonic on his freshly-shaved cheeks and chin. He then went back to immerse himself in the warm steamy bathwater. His muscles were tight from the journey on horseback and the bath softened them. When he caught himself falling asleep in the soapy bath, he stood and dried himself with a towel and walked into the adjoining room and climbed into the giant soft bed and fell into the mounds of silky white folds, and here he fell briefly but heavily asleep.

He only slept an hour or two, but when he awoke, he was strangely refreshed. The water had cleansed him and the brief dreamless repose had purified him. He dressed in a pair of cream linen trousers and buttoned up a loose white cotton shirt and went to the closet to get his green army coat so that he could take his golden medal. He put the medal in the pocket of his linen trousers and found some bathing sandals in the closet, slipped them on his feet and went out to the balcony.

Perfory was already on the balcony when Alexander came out. He too was wearing fine white clothes. Around his neck was the little brass ring on the necklace of string. His own face was shaved and his own hair was oiled and rubbed with scent. He looked different to Alexander now that his nails were cut and his fingers were clean and he had brushed and oiled hair and clean clothes, though his face still had the shadows of whiskers. He had shaved but there appeared to be a permanent stubble on his chin. Alexander studied him carefully. "How do you feel, Perfory?" he asked.

"The bath was good. The nap was better." ... "It's a most charming place, this villa. One could be very happy here." Then after a moment... "I'm going down to the Officer's Bureau. I'll be back in a bit."

Alexander wished him a nice walk and sat down on one of the balcony benches overlooking the square. The stone was hot from the sun and it took a minute before the sting of heat went away. Perfory gave a little salute and left the balcony. Alexander remained seated.

A minute later, a knock came at the front door... 'Must be Perfory, forgotten the keys,' thought Alexander, as he crossed through the series of rooms to answer it. It wasn't Perfory, however, but a little Turkish boy who had been sent to bring refreshments to the men – grapes and spring waters. This boy had been spared the prison to become a servant. Around his ankles were loose shackles which allowed him to walk but not to run. Alexander took the tray of fruit and iced waters and sent the boy away. He carried the tray to the terrace and sat down on the bench and turned his face to let the sun fall on it. He was still sleepy and gave a yawn. He felt the weight of his medal in his pocket. He took it out and pinned it on the breast of his white shirt. The gold of the medal glimmered with great luster in the sun, Alexander pulled some grapes off one of the sprigs and put them in his mouth. He chewed them and the juice inside was cool and it tasted good. He chewed some of the tiny seeds inside the grapes and spit the rest over the railing of the balcony. Then he returned his face to catch the sun and closed his eyes.

He must have had slept a while. When he opened his eyes it was late in the afternoon, the sun had cooled down and a partial shadow was cast over his face. From far off, he heard someone turning the key in the lock. A moment later Perfory appeared on the balcony.

"I'm glad," Perfory said, looking at his friend. He was holding something in his hands.

"Why?" Alexander asked.

"Because you're wearing your medal. It looks good on that white shirt. Wear it to the feast tonight."

Perfory sat on the bench near Alexander and thumbed the two envelopes he was holding in his hand. They were thick envelopes, sealed shut. He handed one to Alexander. The other he slapped against the stone table, smiled and put in his pocket. Alexander looked questioningly at Perfory and then started opening his envelope.

"Banknotes," Perfory said, "I got you to officer's status. They pay us for fighting these wars, you know." Alexander flipped through the large stack of notes in the envelope. An unfamiliar currency. Perfory said it was a fair amount of money. Alexander smiled and put his envelope in his pocket. Perfory continued speaking but before he did so he took some grapes from the sprigs on the tray and chewed them up, so when he then started speaking, he spoke through the little grape seeds he was grinding in his teeth.

"Tomorrow I hear there is supposed to be a great parade," he told Alexander. "...a parade that will fill the streets of the entire city. A giant celebration. Everyone's talking about it at the Officer's Bureau. The soldiers will march and the women will throw them flowers, they say." He poured himself a glass of spring water from the pitcher on the table and drank from his cup.

Alexander thought of the prisoner's he'd seen crammed in the cellars on the way to the square, and he asked Perfory if Perfory thought it was good to have a parade and a feast. Perfory answered him, "You are a hero now in this city. Also, you are a hero back in the Acropolis... So, Alexander, smile and be joyous and celebrate. Be happy to be alive on this great earth, and think of me tonight when you wear this medal to the feast...not the whole time, but at least once. And think of me once when you march in that parade tomorrow." Perfory's voice had turned serious – half mournful and half joyful, but overall serious and contemplative.

Alexander simply laughed.

"Yes, Perfory, and you too think of me when you feast tonight and tomorrow when we march together in the parade. He patted Perfory on the shoulder and reached for some more of the red grapes from the center of the table, which he pulled from the sprig and put in his mouth and ate. Here Perfory stood up leaving Alexander to sit, and leaned out over the ledge looking at the square.

"But I will not be feasting tonight, Alexander...and tomorrow I will see no parade."

"But I don't understand. Are you ill?"

"On the contrary, my friend. I have never felt better." He paused and looked at Alexander with steady eyes, "...but it is time."

Alexander understood what Perfory meant. Now the battle was fought and won and only the feasts and parades remained. Perfory did not need this glory. He didn't need this feast, neither did he need the flowers thrown by the amorous girls – these girls whose homes and villages had been saved by the flow of blood and bullets of the men who had fought. Perfory did not need these amorous girls. He did not need this glory. He had experienced it many times before. Alexander, however, had not and he needed it. Without it, the fighting would just have been fighting and it would have made no sense to Alexander; but with the glory, the world was just and the war was just and everything was in order. But for Perfory things were different.

"You see why it is you who wears the medal now?" He asked.

"Yes. I do," replied Alexander with solemnity, for now he knew the consequences of this moment: his friend would be leaving.

"You reap your glory here. I will find mine with my wife and newborn daughter. Stay here as long as you think is right. Enjoy yourself and your life. I hope you will..."

Pause.

"...I hope you will enjoy yourself here, Alexander. But when I think of you in the future – as I assure you, my friend, I often will – I'll like to imagine that you'd have returned to the Acropolis soon after to rejoin with this young lady who is in your thoughts and in your dreams ... to think that you went back to join with her, to be hers and let her be yours."

"You may think that, Perfory. I will do that." Alexander said this and he meant it. Perfory smiled a soft smile and stood still a moment. His features that had always seemed so rugged and masculine to Alexander, so chiseled and strong, now seemed to have a softness. His face had relaxed. His skin under his eyes sagged and became supple. His mouth seemed more gentle, more delicate. He smiled once more and abandoned Alexander on the balcony again to go inside to pack his sack and put on his boots. He then returned to the balcony, shook hands with Alexander. Alexander stood and embraced him. "But you will not stay until after the feast, at least?" he asked his friend, "You may be hungry on your journey. At least stay to fill your stomach."

Here, Perfory's strong voice became more feeble. Alexander heard a slight quiver in it. "I cannot eat anything, my friend. I am too nervous and too excited to see her again. To see both of them. You understand. I have to go now."

"I understand," smiled his friend with genuine sincerity, "I understand. Go on, my friend Perfory, and good luck."

"You are a great man, Alexander,"

"You too are a great man, Perfory."

And here the two parted ways. Alexander, still watching as Perfory disappeared behind the door of the balcony leading through the rooms turned to look down out from the balcony over the square where he saw Perfory moments later walking in the shade down the narrow stone lane leading out of the square. He walked down the lane wearing his white clothes and black boots, over his back was slung his old pack. Alexander watched him, but Perfory didn't look back, but just continued on down that lane – the lane that would lead to other lanes, through and away from the inner-ring of the city, and off to the train station where soldiers and supplies were coming and going, and soon Perfory's figure was small and far away and eventually it disappeared altogether in the nest of people and houses in the busy street, and Alexander sighed and turned away. He looked once more at the medal on his shirt, and then turned back to the happy procession moving through the square, where he watched the golden evening sun turn amber and orange and fall in a flood of jeweled light behind the palaces, houses, markets and mosques of the city of Adrianople.

It was twilight when he awoke again, on his stone bench on the balcony, leaning against the railing. He had been more tired than he'd thought. He yawned and stretched and poured himself a cup of the tepid water from the pitcher on the table and looked down at the square where lights were beginning to be illuminated. The festivities in the square were picking up, but he didn't feel he needed to take part in the festivities for the moment. He felt good being alone. He missed Perfory already, but it felt good too to be alone. It was the first time in a long time that it was just he with himself. On all his travels through all the cities and countries that he'd seen, he had been alone. The other people who had adorned his travels had just been superficial furniture on a stage where he and only he was acting out a divine and personal dance. His private drama…comedy or tragedy, he knew not which. But these were just words and all that had passed in his life was too private and too personal even for words and couldn't be truly shared even if he wished it…Yet, Perfory hadn't been merely superficial furniture. He had come to join his dance and act a part in this drama and in doing so had taught him many things. Alexander felt he still had things to learn from this man. He asked himself if it wasn't too soon that Perfory leapt away from his life. 'But it was not too soon,' he decided, 'It was time for him and it was time for me. Now I will keep and cherish what this man gave me and continue on in my own private drama. Perfory showed me what it is to be a man. What it means to surrender that which belongs to the world of a boy, and happily embrace the life of a being a man…and how far I have come! If I had known what I would come to do and learn, back in those days so, so long ago, when just a youth living in the Great Northern Woods…'

It was while Alexander was reflecting on these things that a knock came at the door.

'Perfory!' he thought, and jumped up to answer it.

When he opened it, there was a man there in the doorway, leaning his weight against the doorframe. It was Petros. He was drunk and merry and was laughing. His sunburnt face radiated great joy.

"Alexander, good man! The feast is beginning…come on! Are you ready? Hurry up and bring Perfory and come to the feast…do you know," his loquacious words skipped over one another, "…do you know how to get there? It's in the Grand Courtyard. What you do is go down to the square, walk down the lane until you pass Costas' Café…" As he spoke he leaned forward with the appearance that he had the half-drunken urge to tug on Alexander's elbow as he spoke but for some reason did not. "…and pass behind the mosque. Behind it there is a large courtyard where many tables are set up. That is where the feast is happening. Bring Perfory and come on…"

"Perfory has left, Petros," Alexander informed him.

"Oh, great! He is down there already? I walked right passed him then! Well come on, let's go find him…"

"No, Petros. He left. He left the city. He's gone back home. Didn't he tell you?"

"Oh, no!" Petros threw his head to the side, shrugged and smiled. "But that's okay. He never tells anyone anything when he leaves. I'm surprised he told you! But I'll see him again. I always do. Either in the next battle or after the next victory."

Alexander didn't tell Petros that he thought there would be no more battles for Perfory – at least not the kind fought with rifles. He didn't tell him that he was a father now and had a new life to live. He didn't speak to Petros anymore about Perfory. All of those things were private and didn't belong to Petros. Alexander simply smiled and told him he would come down to the feast in a few minutes. Petros, leaning against the doorframe, woke as if from a daze, smiled back and Alexander and slapped his shoulder and departed amicably in a merry romp down the stone staircase singing drunken songs away.

Alexander shut the front door and went back out to the balcony. He sat on the stone bench and drained the waters from the pitcher and finished the last sprig of grapes. He reclined back against the stone railing. Down below in the dark square, illuminated by festive torches, crowds were passing by on their way to the courtyard, all singing songs of victory. But these sound drifted away and on the balcony there was quiet and Alexander leaned against the railing and thought... 'Sophia ... She too has not been mere superficial furniture in the procession of my life thus far lived. I once believed the strides of a man's legs were as vast as the world. Now I... No, Sophia especially is holy to me. I wonder how she has been occupying herself since I left the Acropolis. I fancy she has been becoming a woman, too. No, probably she was already a woman when I knew her. I wonder what trials a girl must go through to become a woman. That, I will never know, but it doesn't so much matter. It's enough for one life for a boy to learn what must be learnt to become a man.

"But still, Sophia, sweet Sophia..." His voice languidly hung on that name as the last violet streaks of the crepuscule lent its color to the square and sunk down Alexander's brow where he drifted backwards, farther backwards, repeating her name, and rested his head on the railing. Still exhausted from his travels with Perfory, from the long time spent at the front; that physical exhaustion met with another, deeper exhaustion – one that began to take root long before the Acropolis – in the Great City perhaps. And this profound exhaustion took Alexander there into sleep – a deep sleep where dreams were scented and flowed aplenty.

Chapter XVII

"The Bacchanal" – reveling in the conquered city...

When Alexander awoke, it was well into the tail-end of the night. Gunshots were being fired by drunken revelers staggering back to their beds through the square below, and Alexander was startled awake on the bench on his terrace. He awoke with a start, worried he had missed the feast, he jumped from the bench and looked out at the night to discern the hour. The air drifted across the balcony, thin and fresh, cool, no longer balmy; and dawn seemed not so far away – its blae light being pulled in on a string. There was a moistness in the air. Yes, dawn was approaching. Alexander leapt from the stool horrified by the thought that the feast had passed without him. Why had he slept? He ran inside and fixed the belt on his linen trousers, splashed some water from a marble basin by the front door on his face and left, running down the steps, past the mezzanine, and out the door.

He passed along the right side of the square and went down the cobbled lane where the prisoners' hands still grappled through the bars despite the late hour. He hurried down the streets that led past Costas' café. Broken pots and trash filled the gutters. A soldier ran past him, drunk and shooting his gun. Another was hunched over in a passageway, vomiting, while some rats scurried out into the street. As he neared the mosque, the streets were more crowded. People sharing bottles of wine lingered on the stone steps, and Alexander slowed down realizing the feast had not ended, though it was clearly waning as many were passed-out sleeping on the stone benches around the mosque and the courtyard.

At the Grand Courtyard, behind the mosque, tables were set up under the nest of faint stars fading in the lightening sky. The tables were full of revelers draining goblets of wine...what a relief the torches still burned! Colored lanterns hanging from strings glowed above the tables. The prisoner-servants with clanking shackles on their ankles walked up and down the rows of tables serving food and wine from trays and bottles mostly drained and picked at. Baglamas players gathered in the back and strummed the strings and sang their bellowing tunes. Drunk soldiers danced with the young ladies. Others kissed them on the benches. The musicians too were drunk, and even the young girls who were dancing playfully together, twirling their partners in their lighthearted feminine ways of glee, had had their share of wine and their cheeks were all red.

Alexander quickly found Petros seated at a table in the back of the courtyard. He was throwing back ouzo and laughing at a joke another officer was telling. Alexander walked up to him.

"Ah, ha! Alexander...so glad you finally came! I didn't know why you'd want to miss a feast like this!" he jumped up and embraced Alexander and kissed his cheeks in drunken gaiety... "Look over there," he pointed to two girls who were skipping by, laughing as they fled from a hungry young officer. "...The prettier one, the light one... she's for you, Alexander, I've been saving her for you!" ... "Do you want something to drink? Of course you do! Come sit down. Here, take this chair! No, take that chair, this one's got a bit of a broken seat. Ivankor was jumping on it. It was wobbling. He was leading the girls in Ring-Around-the-Rosy. Their breasts were full of posies... ha-ha!... Posies! Here, no, take this chair! What have you go in your eye?"

It was just an eyelash that had got in Alexander's eye and was causing him distress, but he quickly got it out and after rubbing the lid for a moment, he sat down next to Petros and tilted over an empty glass wondering where there was something to drink.

Petros snapped his fingers in the air, "Here, here!" A prison boy in white serving clothes came over to pour him a hearty glass of wine. He filled the glass while keeping his submissive head bowed low, loose iron shackles on his ankles. Alexander quickly drained the glass of wine in order to join the spirit of the other men, and waited for his plate to be filled. He was very hungry after sleeping.

The servant boy heaped warm food on his plate. There were pickled cheeses and grape leaves dusted with powdered spices and sweet syrups. There was rice stuffed with other kinds of rice, stuffed in turn with minced fillings. There were flatbreads with bubbling brebis creams inside; fermented beans with spiced avocados and thin strings of sweet onions. There were dishes of plums and blushed potatoes drizzled with pomegranate and lime juices. There were various steaming cakes of seasoned peas laced with seeds of hot chilies, wrapped and fried in paper-thin flakes of golden dough that crackled in one's mouth when eaten; and Alexander chewed and savored all of these tastes and dainties and smiled with lips gleaming from all the oils of the food. Under the palely lit sky, his teeth shone as opalescent pearls and he drank too. He drank and laughed and told stories with the other drunken revelers. He danced too, and he walked around the courtyard, drinking with people and watching the flirtatious games played by men with the soft-faced girls sitting at the tables, and with the other girls spinning dances in the courtyard with their festive skirts, they appeared as colorful crêpe streamers flowing in the breeze.

Aurora, the dawn came on. The stars slipped into the sky, the bottles and goblets were drained, and the dregs of the feast came unfurled. Alexander found Petros once again. He was crooning to the single slow ballad of one wayward lyra hymn. On the lawn nearby, men and girls lay entwined in fantastic displays, wanton orgies, feasts of flesh. One man had torn the blouses of two women and tied them together, and while these women laughed, he snaked between them like a milk serpent drinking from their happy breasts.

People still ate, despite the late hour; but as the members of the party became too full on rich foods and wine, they dispersed to lie on the lawn in the courtyard. Many of the very young girls left to go to their beds to sleep. Some of the men as well. But most remained, and drifted over to the lawn to play amongst the flesh. Alexander too had had much rich food and wine, but the long sleep that night on the terrace had refreshed him and his thoughts were extremely clear. He too went to lay on the grass with the others, but he resisted the orgies, and rather settled in on the serenade of a single string player. The musician began with a song of Dionysus, and as he sang, the girls on the lawn laughed and leapt like lionesses upon the men. Then, when his song changed to a ballad of Aphrodite and Anchises, his voice became rueful and melancholic and Alexander's eyes drifted to the sky. He looked at the moon – like a drop of wine in a crystal pool, this silver moon in the morning sky. It was a Turkish moon. He mused on how many different moons he'd seen in his life... "I've seen the moon of the Great Northern Woods; the Great City moon, a bashful little speck. Remember those arid mountains where my train ran through?...and those lush pastoral valleys...and oh!...those harbors where the fishermen threw their glistening nets out...that moon was the most charming moon of all! A charming moon, Perfory would've said, 'a most pretty and charming moon'...oh, sorrowful sorrow, it's too bad Perfory's not here to drink wine with me. We would have so much...no, back to you, Ô moon... I've seen the moon of the Acropolis, remember those nights I watched it pass over the garden? Sophia's flower garden...that flowered garden... gardens and springs, gardens and springs, gardens and springs, no... onward, thoughts!...then there was the moon at the front, the moon of the plains, the moon of the beast and the gathering, the moon of bloody hands and shoulder...hey, my shoulder doesn't hurt anymore! More moons...look! Now there's this moon traveling across the sky – tumbling like an orchard disc...an orchard disc? What is an orchard disc? Oh, moon overhead, from where did you come? The oriental moon reigns the occidental sky...the sky reigns the, Christ! What the hell are these people doing?!"

It was while Alexander had been talking to the moon in his nostalgic reverie that a great commotion began to stir. Most of the guests in the courtyard garden were exchanging games of love and joy. Some like Alexander, were involved in private drunken soliloquies as come commonly after a war, but a few ornery officers who had drunk their share, were looking for disputes. It began when one such officer spotted a shackled servant sneaking a drink of wine from one of the bottles left on one of the tables. "Look there!" the bellicose officer shouted out, "a filthy prisoner stealing our wine!" His shouting cut the laughter of his friends and some ran to his side. The servant who had taken the wine couldn't understand the language that was being spoken, and thus didn't know that the officer was shouting about him, or was even watching him, or that anybody was, so he remained taking his few tiny swallows of wine. So here, our ornery soldier walked over to the table where the shackled servant stood and gave him a swat on the back of the neck. When came the blow to the nape, the surprised servant choked on the wine left in his mouth and coughed and even spit some wine from the recess of his mouth onto a plate of olives that was set on the table. This only enraged the officer further, as apparently the olives at this feast were of great concern to those remaining present at dawn, and so when the servant returned the bottle to the table, which he did so hurriedly, all the while looking shame-faced at the youthful officer from the corner of his eye with his head cocked in the fashion of a scared hound who's about to receive a whipping – here the officer commenced to beat the servant savagely. Did the shackled servant really think he was entitled to a small swig of wine after serving the victorious army so dutifully and respectfully all evening and night? After the second blow to the neck, the prisoner-servant bowed his head as low as possible, obviously praying that no more would come. After the third, he began to tremble. Following the fourth, which came down upon the back of his head with a violent sting, his body collapsed the stone floor below. The officer was triumphant. He shook his nimble fist in the air and looked around with gleaming teeth at the intrigue of his spectators. Upon seeing this confrontation, the soldiers who had been sitting with the officer before this, jeered and whistled. The people farther away on the grass simply stopped their previous laughing and lovemaking and fell silent as they watched. All the while, the servant in his soiled white serving clothes shook on the ground like an injured salamander, clutching the back of his neck as he whimpered and whined. The assailing officer wasn't through with him yet. He pulled the servant up to his knees and pushed him on the banquet table. One of his friends drew his pistol and raised it; but the first officer told him, "Not yet, not yet!" He then pulled his belt from the loops and the servant upon hearing this sound poised to receive the slashes. All the while the other shackled, chained up, brown-skinned, white-jacketed, servant men and boys, grew very nervous and began to clear the tables with great haste and sweep the stones with the utmost promptness and attention paid to not upsetting any more of the drunken Greek soldiers who were ready for new kinds of amusement in the waning night.

This event signaled to Alexander the end of the feast. From his lawn where he'd been having his private commune with the moon, he stood, dropped the leaf he was holding, and looked on with disgust at the drunk officers occupied with herding the servants, and with distaste at the others who laughed about it, and at the girls who continued singing in spite of it. He stood from his lawn and he left these men and he left these girls and left Petros and the courtyard behind and he wandered out past the silent mosque and out into the street that branched into all directions, and he squinted his eyes to see clearly and to remember which one led back to the place he was staying.

After wandering alone the tiny streets at dawn for some time, Alexander arrived back at his quarters. He was drunk and tired and didn't have the strength to cross through the series of rooms to the bed where he'd slept the day before, but instead, fell onto the first bed he came to, clothes and all, and gave himself up to sleep. It didn't come easily though, his head spun for a while. There was a bad taste in his mouth. Eventually, he felt himself drifting surely, albeit slowly, to sleep.

Then a knock came at the door.

"Ugh!" he exclaimed, pulling himself out of bed. He got up annoyed and headed for the front door to respond. The knock continued. "I'm coming, I'm coming!" he shouted, fully tired of everything, sick of being awake, aggravated that someone would come knocking at such an early hour. That ugly conclusion to the feast had put him in a foul mood.

He opened the door and saw a small servant boy holding a salver with water.

"Master Petros sent me to see if Master Alexander is in need of anything."

"No, thank you. I have water," he told the boy.

"Does Master Alexander need a woman for the night?"

"No, he just needs to sleep."

The door closed and Alexander then returned to bed and fell hard and fast asleep.

It was about noon when he awoke again that day. A loud commotion was coming from outside and he walked out on the balcony to see what it was about. On the way, he washed his face and drank a cup of water. He checked on his shoulder and saw the wound was healing nicely. It didn't hurt too much, and otherwise he felt pleasant and happy, despite the liquor and wine from the night before and the short amount of sleep.

Outside, the balcony was steeped in warm, soft yellow noontime light. The sky was a creamy blue, spotless of clouds. The day seemed promising. Below in the square, throngs of people were gathered. Musicians were playing and singing. Men in military dress were marching. Men in costumes, colorful masks and feathers, were prepared for the parade. Wine bottles waved in the air. Alexander bathed and washed his hair and dressed in a new change of clothes – again, linen pants and a white cotton shirt. He pinned his medal of gold on his chest and shaved. He drank a pitcher of spring water and left his quarters to go find some breakfast and see the parade. After going downstairs, he gave thought to the envelope of banknotes he'd slipped under the armoire in his bedroom the evening before, and he went back upstairs to reassure himself that he'd locked the doors leading to all the rooms.

252

Down in the square, Alexander saw the same girls with colored streamers in their hair beginning to dance again. Some clever young man juggled pistols while another blew fire. Many had started drinking already, but everyone seemed a bit tired from the night before and no one was too rowdy. A couple men were chasing each other around like boys in the fountain in the square. It was starting to be a hot day, and the fountain tempted a lot of people.

Alexander found an older officer who was handing out pamphlets. He asked him where the parade was supposed to be.

"It'll run through town and terminate at Eski Square," said the pamphleteer. "Eski Square, the main square in the city, about a mile down that way." He pointed down the lane that led to where the mosque and the Grand Courtyard was. Alexander thought of his stomach, and left to find a meal.

While walking down the cobblestone lane, towards the mosque, he noticed that the doors leading to the basements where the prisoners were kept were open. The prisoners' hands no longer reached out through the bars in the little dark holes cut out above the sidewalks. Now the basement doors stood open and Greek soldiers were leading the prisoners out in little groups. The soldiers held the chains that dragged on the dusty ground; these chains led to shackles around the prisoners' wrists and necks. Alexander passed by and looked at these prisoners: gaunt, dark-skinned men with bald heads – women as well, some children, but mostly men. He looked at them with curiosity, but none looked back at him. All were either looking at the ground or up at they sky, which they evidently hadn't seen for sometime. Alexander turned from this sight and hurried off in the direction of Costas' café.

Outside the café, crates of live chickens were stacked up and the fowls were squawking. Two old men were seated at the outside table drinking ouzo and playing Tavli. The sun was cooking their bald heads. When Alexander entered, he found Petros sitting with another man whom he'd never seen before. Petros was wearing his green coat over a white undershirt, as Perfory had dressed during their time on the front. The other man was dressed like Alexander, in a light linen summer suit.

"Ah, it's good you found us!" Petros said, standing up to shake Alexander's hand, "We have all this food here we can't eat." Petros introduced Alexander to the other man in the white suit, but Alexander forgot the man's name right away.

"Have some of this," Petros insisted, pointing around to the dishes on the table

Alexander helped himself to the platters filled with food. Their were little toasts covered with green olive paste and chilies; and spinach pie seeped in olive oil. He nourished himself and Costas brought over some lime salad and juice to drink. Costas seemed tired. There were a few children in the café. One of the soldiers was seated with his wife and his three children that had arrived that morning on a train. Apparently the city was safe enough for children. Still, with prisoners shackled up in chains all around the city, it seemed to Alexander a strange place to bring a family. The wife was talking about a hat she wanted buy. The children were playing with their napkins and chattering.

Petros suggested the three men start thinking about going to watch the parade. "They say the Governor himself is going to make an appearance," Petros told the others. This statement perked Alexander's ears.

"Which governor?"

"Which governor?...Why, The Governor!" Petros said, "...the only governor, the Governor of the Acropolis!"

The nameless man drained his glass of juice, "That's what they say, but it doesn't look like a place for a Governor." The three men turned and looked out the window at Costas' café. Outside, sinewy men with painted bodies were dancing down the street. Following behind them, armed soldiers were leading gaunt Turkish prisoners by their shackles and chains. These prisoners were all nude except for dirty loincloths worn around their waists.

"Nope, it doesn't look like a place for the Governor," Petros affirmed. They're leading all those prisoners down to Eski Square where they're tying them to posts...ha!" and then he paused, "...but it's just play."

Alexander continued thinking about the Governor of the Acropolis. Petros was busy paying Costas for the meal. Alexander had pulled a banknote from the envelope back at the room and he offered to chip in, but Petros refused. Outside, the street was getting more and more crowded. "Look there, Alexander," Petros pointed, "that may be the Governor's procession. His figure fell on a group of soldiers riding past in the street on horseback with black helmets crowned with scarlet plumes. Behind them, a dozen soldiers marched in unison, with rifles balanced on their shoulders. Two men trailed behind with flags. Alexander squinted to see in between these soldiers, but he didn't see anything resembling a governor or a governor's daughter.

Now, outside of Costas' café, Petros, Alexander and the third man looked down the crowded street, deciding which way to head. Alexander peered on after the procession of marching soldiers who'd vanished around the corner, thinking there was a small chance that the rumor about the Governor's presence in the city was true and that he might see him. He thought of Sophia. Petros lit a cigar.

The street was getting more and more full. Alexander and the two others in his company joined the procession that was headed towards Eski Square. In front of them, a group of men beat drums. Behind them were more soldiers just like them. Alexander wore his medal on his chest and girls threw him flowers from the sidewalks. He caught flowers in his hair and Petros too caught flowers in his hair, and one older woman broke through the line and kissed him on the mouth.

"Oh, sweet victory!" he laughed to Alexander joyously.

'It's becoming madness,' Alexander thought to himself after the three had gone a few streets away from Costas' café. The closer to the square one got, the more the men in the crowds became unruly. Also the more numerous became the basements, with their little dark holes covered in bars lining the sidewalks, where the bony fingers of the remaining caged prisoners reached out to feel shards of the sun's rays. Small groups of armed soldiers were busily running down the basement steps to open the bolted doors. They'd disappear inside for a few moments. When they came back out, they held in their hands the chains attached to shackled hordes of naked captives. These prisoners mounted the stairs in abject and quiet submission. They passively accepted all that came, and as they reached street-level, they were thrown into the crowds where they were then dragged through the stone streets on their bare feet and shins. One soldier had a whip and was giving lashes to the boney back of prisoner who had refused to obey. He was an exception though. The other prisoners obeyed.

When the parade reached Eski Square, the marching ended but the drinking and drum beating continued. It was an impressive square – three or four times the size of the square that Alexander's balcony overlooked. In the center, stocks were being built and presentation scaffolds were constructed…platforms, apparently places for political and celebratory speeches to be given. The soldiers had amassed a great number of prisoners and they all stood naked in the center, in shackles, head bowed low in shame, while the ruling-party revelers gathered around them, singing and dancing. The ones who had been drinking most threw rotten vegetables at the prisoners.

All the streets led to Eski Square and all the streets were crowded with soldiers and women and marching bands and shackled prisoners; and as they all emptied into the square, the square became tightly packed with people, so that there was very little room to move. Among the hordes of prisoners were children captives – young Turkish boys and girls; but they were quickly grabbed up by the soldiers and led back to the prisons in the cellars.

Once the children were gone, the prisoners' heads were put in stocks. There weren't many stocks, however, so most prisoners remained simply corralled in chains. A few of the women prisoners were led back to the cellars along with the children, however, most were kept in the square with the men.

The afternoon was in full force and the sun was scorching. The already packed square became more and more crowded. Like a great river's delta empties into an ocean, so did those city streets pour its people into the vast Eski Square and Alexander soon felt his body being crushed as it swayed along with the ebb of the wave of people. Alexander threw his weight hard against the drunken soldiers who were pressed against him so as to earn himself a little space to breathe. Then there was a loud explosion.

"Hoorah!" the crowd boomed. Alexander looked to the source of the explosion. It was a building near the square. A bomb had been detonated for the sake of spectacle and a large plume of smoke rose up from the carcass of the building where flames poured out of the glassless windows.

"Hoorah!" another explosion was heard.

Two more empty buildings around the square erupted plumes of smoke when bombs were detonated inside. Within the square, the pressure of people lightened as some of the crowd backed out into the surrounding streets near where the buildings were on fire. In spite of this, the square remained impressively packed with people for all the while to follow. One man threw a wine bottle and it shattered on the stone floor, sending broken glass and red wine flying everywhere, but he was not applauded and one officer even boxed him in the ear for this. Many others, however, continued throwing food and other objects at the prisoners. The scaffold that had been set up, which as of yet had no function or purpose, also received the mockery of thrown vegetables.

Sooner or later, one of the head generals mounted the platform in the center of the square. He met with great applause as he looked out over the heads of all the soldiers gathered there. He saluted the crowd with a yell, and they returned the salute and their voices boomed and echoed across the square as they did so. Alexander looked into the crowd trying to spot Petros but he couldn't. He had lost him. Many of the men in the crowd were shouting hoorahs for the army and for the Governor. Others were shouting for more bombs to go off in the nearby buildings. When the roar of the crowd in the immense square died down, the general on the wooden platform began to speak.

He called for one of the prisoners to be led up to the platform. The word in the crowd was that this prisoner he was asking for was a certain prisoner who was being kept under special guard for trying to incite a prison revolt after the capture of the city. This prisoner was a leader of men. His men, however, were imprisoned and could no longer be led. The general on the platform, he too was a leader of men; yet his men were in power, so when he called the prisoner to be brought up, his orders were obeyed and the prisoner was brought in chains up onto the platform. While the prisoner-leader mounted the stairs to the platform with two armed soldiers holding him on either side, the serious men in the crowd shouted violent political phrases. The sillier ones threw crusts of pies and rinds of fruit.

Once the prisoner was on the platform, a group of soldiers lifted the scaffold up and wheeled it to the middle of the platform. "Ah, it's just play!" one of the men next to Alexander kept saying over and over. "Cowards!" another yelled. "More bombs!" some of the men shouted.

The soldiers leading the prisoner-leader lifted him up on the stool and made him climb the scaffold for the mockery of all. The general stood beside him and looked at the crowd with a white-toothed smile and a look of pure power. Contrastingly, the prisoner stood like a feeble heap of jaundiced flesh. His eyes were grey and their gaze fell empty towards the boisterous crowd. He offered no resistance, but fell like sand into the cupped hands of the general. Now, on the platform, the noose was brought out and wrapped around his neck.

"Oh, we're not going to hang you, pitiful one!" the general cried, "We are not going to hang you!" But this promise from the general changed nothing of the prisoner's despairing expression. Not even a fleck of hope registered on his pathetic face. As the prisoner stood on the scaffold, the general leaned in close to him and said again firmly in his ear, "We are not going to hang you."

The general called out to the armed soldiers in the crowd and ordered these soldiers to make sure the prisoners were put to where they could see their leader standing on the stool on the scaffold. Once the crowd was quiet and all the prisoners were watching, the general readdressed the crowd.

"You see what happens to those who fight against us?" He pointed at the neck of the prisoner around which the noose was wrapped. "You see what happens to those who incite revolt? This is our city now. This is our city!

You..." he pointed at the hordes of prisoners, "...you are the servants!" One of the general's sidemen handed him a whip and the general cracked it while the prisoner-leader on the scaffold trembled and shook.

"Bastard!" cried a man in the crowd.

"Vile!" cried another.

"Kill him!" cried a third.

The general then looked directly into the hordes of shackled men and women and asked them...

"And what do you say to this? What do you, the prisoners, say?!" But they said nothing. The prisoners kept their heads down and said nothing.

"You see!" the general laughed at the mass of shackled captives. He raised his head triumphantly to have his speech resound through the entire square. Then he turned to the silent and meek prisoner-leader who stood placidly on the scaffold. "You see, pitiful man, your people have nothing to say! ...while mine say 'Vile!...Kill him!' ...Why," he asked, "when my men say this, yours stay silent?"

But the prisoner did not reply. He stood still, body visibly trembling – the color running out of his skin. His head bowed low. The general raised his whip and lashed the prisoner one time. He lashed him again, but the prisoner did not react. He simply quivered silently in tearful anguish under the pain of the whip. It was then the general stood up on the scaffold and tugged the noose on the prisoner's neck to ensure that it was tight. To this, the crowd gave a loud cheering applause.

Eski Square dimmed for a moment as the sun went behind a tiny cloud. That cloud lit up with bold silver light and a light breeze fell in, cooling at once the stifling air of the square. Then, with a gentle kick, the general let fly the stool out from under the feet of the prisoner on the scaffold. The loose rope of the noose became taught. The stool tumbled. The platform shook. The scaffold bent and the prisoner's body dropped and snapped with a jerk. A short shiver passed up the prisoner's body. His head passed from pale to flush red then back to bluish pale and sank on his shoulders while his lifeless body swayed in the rhythm of the beating drums and clapping spectators.

"Tell the newspapers," the general recited in well-flown and carefully articulated words, "that the hanging of the rebel leader was carried out with grace and elegance. All future threats to the new rulers of Adrianople will meet a similar fate."

A man with a tablet jotted down the general's words and the audience stirred. The dead prisoner remained on the gallows, rocking back and forth. Alexander looked on with astonishment, abhorrence, interest, disgust, curiosity and wonderment. He then turned and began heading out of the square. With this sight, he had seen enough. He followed the narrow dusty and sunny streets spiraling away from Eski Square until he reached his quarters. On the way he passed groups of boisterous men who had gotten a late start for the parade, and were just now heading to the square. He passed more Greek soldiers leading more and more shaven-head prisoners with bare feet and shackles, who were to be taken to the square to meet with some fate or another. He passed some Greek children sitting on a sidewalk cracking open a melon on some bricks and eating the red flesh and the seeds inside. He came to the little square where his rooms were and began to climb the stone stairs. The building was empty. He stopped at the mezzanine and looked around. Not a soul, the whole city was outside gathered in the streets.

Alexander remained in his quarters for sometime. Outside the sun burned red and its heat fell like swords. Outside, the prisoners were continuously being led barefoot across the baked stones of the streets towards Eski Square. They had brown skin like leather hides, gleaming wounds, golden sweat a-sparkle.

A curious thing then happened after the hanging of the prisoner-leader and the two bombings of the nearby buildings. Not long after Alexander left to return to his room, a wave of furious energy passed over the soldiers and free civilians assembled in Eski Square. Those who had before been the happy revelers in a victory parade, those who had, the night before, been the joyous revelers at a midnight bacchanal, now turned into a horde of cockeyed barbarians that ran about the square and its environs in a ravaged and highly-fueled pursuit of the next splinter to burn and the next spine to split.

The general who had hanged the first man, in his deft leadership, now funneled the remaining mob in Eski Square off into the nearby buildings. These men carried torches. They carried explosives.

"Smyrna has been burned! Conquerors were we! Now we burn Adrianople! Onward, men!" The general's words exploded, shot fumes, his arms pounded into the air as torches were raised and gunpowder laid.

The crowd dispersed outwards. Their shackled prisoners – all horribly trembling with fear – were then led off by their armed and drunken shepherds to various places in the city. Some went right to the chopping-block. Some were taken to the river. One prisoner was carried by two men up atop a fluted building overlooking Eski Square and from there he was flung off. Once he landed, his corpse was tossed onto a heap of other prisoners, who, by the gallery of soldiers in the square, had one by one been strung-up, hanged, and cut-down and tossed from the gallows to the gutters.

Even the women and their suckling babes were all either hanged or herded into the basements of the buildings around Eski Square which were then barricaded and burned. Then, in some kind of phenomenal brilliance of leadership, the clever general managed to guide the mob to all split up in even numbers and head off in even directions away from the burning square, and on into the rest of the city in a swiftly executed and most eloquent massacre.

From the balcony high up in his luxurious quarters, Alexander stood and leaned on the stone railing, and looked down at the fountain square where scourges of men passed, tearing apart what they could on the way. He neither acted nor reacted, but simply watched. He watched as the bombs blew in buildings nearby, smoke billowing up in the afternoon sky, the ground rumbling, shots being fired. He watched the mobs of men as they looted the houses and shops around the square. Over the rooftops, he could see the top of the central mosque, and it too was blown by explosives.

"The fools," Alexander said as he watched all this pass by his eyes... "...The fools! Those were our shops they're looting. Those were our buildings they're burning. This was our city!"

He knew it would only be a matter of time before his own building burnt too. The drunken mob worked senselessly, indiscriminately, spreading and burning, decapitating whomever, moving on.

"Perfory said this is what happens when a general has a toothache! Now, Alexander, my friend, it is time for you too to move on." He leaned over the railing, inhaling deeply the air of the massacre. "It is time to stop. Now the glory is over and it is time to go."

A vast plume of copper smoke hung in the sky over the ruined city of Adrianople. It slowly changed shape with the changing winds, now appearing like a mushroom, now appearing like a fighting cock. A few explosions could be heard intermittently detonating in the city below; and with each one, a new plume of smoke rose into the sky and grew more vast and endless the farther up one rose.

Chapter XVIII

"Leaving Adrianople" – Alexander's return to the Acropolis...

Bronze-bellied clouds hung in the sky over the destroyed city; and in the ether above a funnel of birdlets spiraled up seeking the sun, a fiery red and setting sun, one that illumined a singular train departing the city in the westward direction. Through the valleys of scorched earth that stretched out from the city like the arms of a star, or the gums of a weary mouth, or rather like the ridges of bones on a broken back, the train continued on, puffing smoke in a charge towards the frontier line, and on that train was the passenger, Alexander.

The train was a conquered train. It had belonged to the Turks. But now it belonged to the hills of Thrace and the men aboard were not Turks but were Greeks or the allies of the Greeks. They were people who were going home, and they were docile. Alexander sat in the plush seat in first-class in his white linen summer suit, the golden medal pinned on his jacket. The train attendants brought him such delightful things as cream cakes with sweet frost and fruit juices with grated ice and he tipped them each a couple of small bills from the envelope of banknotes he kept in his pocket. They brought him pillows when it was time to sleep and they gave him newspapers when he awoke. These newspapers told of the successes of the soldiers fighting for their sovereign, of all the fortunes that were secured for the Governor of the Acropolis.

The last day of the voyage came to pass, evening cast itself aside and the train chugged into the night through the Arcadian hills where the moon fell broad and wanton, lighting the fields with silver light, now glimmering emeralds, now glittering with the diamond light of dawn. It was barely morning when the train came to arrive in the Acropolis.

Peacetime in a city of civilians absent of soldiers and guns, absent of prisoners in chains – moreover morning time. Alexander walked through the early streets where vendors were starting to bring their wares to be sold in the stalls. There, he found a driver to take him out of the city-centre, through the pastoral outskirts, until the Acropolitan village. Upon reaching the village walls, he walked on his own, on down the sunny path passing poplars and sweet-smelling cypress trees. When he arrived at the Governor's palace, the gardens were empty and quiet. The workers apparently were still sleeping.

He traversed the familiar garden and climbed the rockery. He scaled the lattice and the fig tree to reach the terrace belonging to the Governor's daughter. He had no fear, only happy excitement. So much time had passed and changed everything. A warm wind was blowing. On the abandoned terrace lay a bowl of grapes and figs and a plate with sugar drops. Alexander peered into the daughter's empty room. He saw the large bed in her room with peach-colored sheets, unmade. Some clothes lay on the chair beside. He sighed and smiled to himself that she was already awake on such a promising day and turned and left the room and left the terrace and climbed back down the tree and ivy-laced stone and lattice to the garden below.

From a sunny berm where celosia flowers bloomed, Alexander cast one last look at the terrace belonging to Sophia and turned and walked on through the empty garden, towards the little footbridge he knew of beyond the acacia trees. On his way he stopped and bent to pet the velvety petals of the wings of a butterfly resting on a sprig of clover. Then came a sweet laugh from behind. Alexander felt a hand on his shoulder and a gentle kiss on the back of his neck.

"Alexis! Oh, Alexis, you came back!"

It was Sophia, and she was standing behind Alexander when he turned around. She wore a pale peach garden dress and white sandals and she smiled at him, bouncing slightly on the balls of her feet in excitement. She was playful now. She seemed changed. Alexander smiled back at her and when he did, she leaned forward and kissed him on the cheek, then she leaned back and smiled again, "you came back, Alexis, you did!"

"Yes, I did!" Alexander replied with joyous delight. His eyes shined wet as her lips were full, "And what a beautiful greeting after where I've come from." Even his nervousness was delightful now.

"You must tell me all about it, Alexis…You know, Alexis…!?" She looked at him, now questioningly, now not at all; then she tipped her head slightly to the side, playfully, while crinkling her nose, "You know, Alexis? Oh, you!…let's walk together." She took his hand. "You look nice! You're limping though, what happened?"

"I am limping?"

The two walked on through the garden where the tended poppies grew, where the wild dew on the grass sparkled. Sophia held Alexander's hand, and he hers; and they walked through the parts of the garden where snakes slithered in the night, yet Sophia was not afraid, and she led him down a path, and into the dark parts of the garden where canopies of trees blocked the light; and here she picked a sprig of salmon-colored berries from a bush and not even Alexander knew what kind of berries they were, though he'd been a keeper of that garden for quite some time; and after they passed by a creek and crossed the bridge they came once again out of the dark shade and into the fresh open sunny and flower-filled garden, and here Sophia stopped a moment and looked at Alexander and he again at her, and then she asked him to come drink coffee with her on the terrace. He accepted with gladness and the two went around back.

"Shh!" she asked him to be quiet ascending the stairs as the maids were waking up. Alexander sat on the terrace while Sophia went to get coffee. The light lacquered leaves on the overhanging trees rattled in the light fresh sun. Alexander rested with the warmth on his face; and when he looked over his shoulder, he saw that she had hastily pulled the peach-colored sheets up over her bed. He smiled about this and turned around to wait for her.

She soon came out carrying a little tray. Upon it were two cups of coffee and the sprig of berries she'd picked in the garden. She set the tray down on the table next to the bowl of figs and grapes and picked up some sugar drops from the plate on the table. Alexander didn't want sugar. Sophia took two. They drank their coffee and talked for a while. She had put something in the little pocket sewn in her peach cotton dress when she had gone inside to get the coffee. She now told Alexander about it…

"Alexis, I have something for you…you know, when you went off to war, I told myself that if you came back here I would give this something to you." Her hands fumbled with what was in her little pocket. It was a thin bracelet of pure gold, a single thread of gossamer. She undid the clasp and put it around his wrist. She looked at him to see what he thought. He was happy and she was too. He smiled with hope and a great lightness came over him. He felt light and she did too and she admired him with her bracelet on his wrist, while he admired her; and all the while, the trees and everything kept rattling in the warm morning wind and the sun played softly with the clouds, and all was gentle… Until Alexander had to go and become so serious…

"Sophia, listen to me." He squeezed her hand lightly. The bracelet slid down against the base of his thumb and palm, "When I left here before I was practically still a youth…hardly more than a boy as you yourself said. …Well, Sophia, I went to war. I fought for the Governor, your father…for you. I killed and was almost killed. I have become a man, Sophia…"

"No, but…"

"Yes, yes…"

"No, but wait, Alexis…" she tried to interrupt but managed not.

"…No, but you wait, Sophia."

He paused. She waited.

"…Remember what you asked before on this terrace. Well, I did as you asked and I went away and now I've come back for you, and I want to be with you now, Sophia. I want you for my wife."

There was a long pause amongst the two of them. A cloud caught and wound itself around the sun and a shade passed over the terrace. And everything then on the terrace had a cool glow diffused with a soft peach light. Sophia looked into Alexander's eyes with infinite tenderness.

"Oh, sweet Alexis," she held his hand warmly. "Sweet, poor Alexis. My poor, sweet, sweet Alexis. Listen to me, Alexis. I see how great you've become. You've been gone a long while. You now wear this medal of gold on your chest…" then she laughed with soft eyes, "like a real proper officer!" He noticed again the lovely dark fleck in the white of her eye, "…a true handsome officer!" She laughed a tender laugh covered in nervousness, and as she did, the sun came back and she shielded the light from her eyes.

"…Yes," she continued, "I admit I wanted the same thing back then when I threw you that little flower from the window. I can admit I wanted this

... for you to go off and come back as a man and have it be just like this. There was something beautiful about you even then." She paused. "Oh, Alexis, I see that you are a man, now. And this gold you wear on your chest is more precious than the gold of my silly little bracelet." Here she pulled back and sighed with lowered eyes, "Yes, the bracelet is rather silly. It's the bracelet of a girl."

"Not of a girl..." Alexander said, not wanting her to devalue her gift to him, but she wasn't interested in that; so she continued on along with her own course of thought...

"But me too, Alexis, I have gold now too."

Alexander didn't understand. She could see that and so she continued... "I am no longer the girl who sleeps in the little bed with pink sheets. The girl who takes her tea at eight. I have my gold now too. Gold more precious than all."

She then coughed and cleared her throat and stirred her coffee with her peach-colored finger. "...You have noticed my ring, haven't you?"

He had not.

"I have already been a bride already, Alexis. I am the wife of another...."

She stopped a moment and there was silence.

Alexander didn't know what to say for the sake of the hurtful knot in his neck, and so he remained.

"Oh, poor Alexis!..."

Here the sun fell behind a cold cloud. Here, he hurt, and here he wanted to change the way the light had altered with whatever foolish words could be made. "You have gold now, you say? Well, I too am changed. We are both, so..." then he put his forehead into the cup of his hand and shook it once. "We are both so..." he picked his head up again and reached into the pocket of his jacket and pulled out his watch. "See this watch?" Foolishness. "No, don't turn away, look at it. The S is for Sophia and Alexander is the A. ... Oh, yes, I am no longer Alexis, so you know," he put the watch back in his pocket and spoke with unfeeling directness in his voice, with despairing numbness and calloused fear, 'but why would she say this? And be it a lie, oh it must be, it...' "...is Alexander now... My name... I've changed it." He looked up at her and straightened his back. A pain crept up. "...Alexander suits me better. Can't you see...I..." his words trailed off as he turned his face away from Sophia to conceal his emotions from her – wet as all beginnings...

"Alexander," she said the name. There was gloominess in her voice. "Yes, I like it better..." And whatever she said after that went unheard. He didn't care anymore and so stopped listening. He looked to the trees for the presence of birds, but they were empty of sounds and flutters, of fruits and all green blooms. He looked beyond those trees, to a sky where a country's worth of cloudlets sailed along by...

Now Sophia looked at him and he looked away and she took his face with her hand and turned it back towards her so as to say something, but all she said was that she liked his new name better, but he neither cared nor understood why she thought it important to say this. He wanted her to invent words of a different nature. He wanted his own script of speech to be written now. 'Why must the morning pass so? And this, my hero's return!' ...with his face turned back to hers, she continued on speaking thus... "It was a few months ago...my wedding, that is...My husband, his name is Peter. Did you ever meet him? We were married last spring. It is his gold I wear. He is wonderful to me..." "Oh," she stopped, "...but Alexis...no, I mean Alexander, but why do you cry? What is this tear in your eye? ... But it isn't nothing. It's something. You're crying, Alexander!" She took his hand and with her other, she took the tears from his eye with her little finger and kept them on her dress and saved them there, and after that was done, he lifted his face from her shoulder where it had lain while the two remorsefully embraced. Then the two separated and looked again at each other.

You know, Alexander... strange Alexander... There is something about you so more... so more... Well, there is something very unusual about you. I thought so the very first time you snuck into my room. You were someone, well..." she smiled, "seeing you again, I almost regret it. My wedding, I mean. I almost regret that I was married. No," she frowned and pouted her lips, "but I do not regret a thing. Yet still, I am solemn...

"...In a fairytale," she went on, pressing her hand against his knee, "...in a fairytale, it would have been another way. You would have returned from the war as Alexander – Alexander my shining knight! – and I would be all in white as I would have waited for you – sewing and unsewing robes, as they say, fighting off suitors as they come my way – I would have waited for you...me, the King's daughter, and you the shining knight; and we would be married, us...

"…But life is somehow different, Alexander. It cannot be like a fairytale. Yet still I feel that how things went and how they are, are somehow in accord and in harmony with the course of life and the ways of the world. And it is sad. I am sad. But I can never wear white for you and I am with another now. I am with another for now and for my life…" She backed off and smiled, glancing aside, to lighten the situation for them both. Alexander was thinking at that moment that he wasn't sure if things were also in accord and in harmony with the course of life and the world as far as he was concerned, but he realized that they were what they were and thus had to be…in harmony and in accord. Yet, he too was sad. Though now he felt sadness was not the worst to bear. He looked at this woman's full lips as the wetness of them shimmered in the sunlight, and for a moment he mistakenly thought those lips belonged to him.

"But still wear my bracelet, please," she coursed his wrist with the nail of her little finger, "wear it as a symbol of your heroic homecoming, as a sign of our friendship, and sit with me a while longer."

Sophia then picked up the sprig of salmon-colored berries from the coffee tray and pulled some of the berries off and put them in her mouth.

"Look, Alexander, you can eat these berries. They're sweet. I would have never thought to pick wild berries and eat them before I was married, but now my life is different. I think differently. Oh, but I'll stop talking about that, I see that it's making you sad. But, Alexander, you're crying again!" … "Oh, now I see that you're not. I just thought for a moment you were crying again but now I see you're not."

The two sat silent for a moment. Sophia started and started again to speak but finally kept quiet.

"Where is he?" Alexander eventually asked.

"He is out with my father. They left early this morning to go hunting. They'll be out till late."

More silence ensued. Unpleasurable silence for Alexander, but he was aware that any words from him now would be futile, for rest assured Sophia knew already who he was; and who she was, and what each one of them wanted. Yet words were not valuable to Alexander at this moment, for had he the means to coerce her to him, through trickery or clever charm, she would still be in the position she was in. They would still be distanced by earthly things, those of the spirit and ideas; and anything achieved would amount to many things lost and would merely be the fruits of trickery or clever charm.

Sophia too rested clean in the silence, having also no use for words; as all there was to tell had been already said. And anything more, no matter how sweetly put, would only tarnish and tear that which was too delicate to touch and should be left undisturbed.

Neglecting their coffee, the two nurtured a gaze. Alexander wanted to separate from Sophia, to go quickly and as far away as possible; yet while they sat ensconced in each other's eyes, no eyes did wander, no thoughts did travel; but rather the two drew closer. And each time they broke themselves apart, they only returned to draw close again. Sophia seemed to want to flee and once pushed Alexander away. She turned her face from him and he recoiled, only to return again. And as he returned, so did she. Then, at last their bodies fell together, clean as flowing water, not again to come asunder. And the last words destroyed themselves and their flesh drove them on.

Ô, grace that the spirit is the sap of the tree; the spirit is the blood of the flesh, and the wind on the hills. And grace that the body is the leaves of the tree, is the lips of the flesh, and the wind in the skies. Here now, nothing was holier than these two bodies moving not by thoughts; two bodies that yearned not to disperse but to remain wholly one flesh and one spirit; and where their arms remained enlaced, their cloth cast away, a drop of gold and the clasp of time; his chest, her breast, his groin upon her womb; and this, their first and only kiss saw many things – it saw the sun revolving in the sky and passing beyond the distant hills, and the moon's coming forth, tumbling through the heavens. And though it was only a crescent, it illuminated their two bodies huddled together in a long communion of breath and dreams.

When they awoke, first Alexander, then Sophia; their bodies were woven together, glimmering with sweat in the light of the moon, upon the bed in the balmy room – still but for the warm breeze coming through the open patio doors...the sounds of yelping dogs could be heard not far off. Alexander heard the dogs and stirred. He opened his eyes in the night, and upon them fell the silver-blue cast of the early moon; he opened them to look at she who lay beside him. And he felt one more time her gentle palm, and one last time the contours of her uncovered body – clinging strongly as though needing him even while she slept, thighs and breast like the folds of flowers – no, greater than flowers, for they were the curves of woman – and he lay on his back and breathed in rapturously. If only he were to die right then, not a moment longer, but right then, so happy and willingly would he go, but it would have to happen right then, but right then something else happened. It began with the yelping of the dogs.

Sophia awoke while the dogs were yelping. She rolled over – about, it seemed, to kiss Alexander; but then she stopped. Her eyes grew bright and wide with remembrance and fright, and she pushed him away and leapt from her bed. Again the dogs did yelp.

"They've come back!" she exclaimed, and ran to find her clothes. Alexander too stirred while Sophia fluttered to find the dress she had thrown thoughtlessly from the bed before their coming there hours before. Alexander searched for his own clothes. All the while, below in the yard, the Governor and Peter, Sophia's husband, were traversing the gardens with a team of hunting dogs. The two carried rifles and a string of slain rabbits. After the gardens, they stopped at the backdoor to take off their boots before going inside.

Up in the room, Sophia straightened her hair and smoothed down her dress. "Alexander, hurry, go down from the terrace and then come around back!" he was fighting to get his shoes on his feet. "But hurry!" ... "Quickly, you!" ... "No, not here" ... "Yes, there, down there!" and she held his forearm as he swung himself over the stone wall and descended the fig tree and the wall, rockery, lattice and all.

"Don't forget to come around back!" she had whispered at last upon his descent. She then turned, fixed her hair a final time in the mirror and left the bedroom to go downstairs to greet her husband.

In the quiet evening garden, Alexander crouched and laced his shoes. He stood by a cypress tree waiting to catch his breath. He looked a last time up to the terrace where beyond it in the room Sophia could not be seen, only imagined. The light was out. All was dark, but for the moon. All was quiet, but for the gurgling water in the garden brook where the golden carp were swimming. The dogs had stopped their yelping; and there beneath the moon dripping light, Alexander started off for the back entrance of the palace.

When he appeared around back, strolling calmly with his hands in the pockets of his linen trousers, he was first spotted by Sophia's husband, Peter. Peter was unlacing his hunting boots beneath the overhang of the back entrance. His rifle was laid over his knee. The Governor was admiring the rabbits on the string as he hung them up by the back door. Peter heard whistling and the crunching of twigs underfoot and turned to see Alexander approaching from the garden.

"Where are the guards this evening?" Peter asked the Governor, speaking through his mustache. He turned towards Alexander, stood erect on the balls of his feet and made sure his rifle stayed by his side in case of need, "You there!" he called to the stranger, "Are you supposed to be here?"

Peter was a slickly-groomed and handsome gentleman of medium height with a thin black mustache and curling lips that made him look devious, slightly sinister – a quality made more enhanced by his unflinching and dubious stare and the featherlike hair on his head that furled at this moment he saw Alexander come near. He poised himself like a fighting cock and called out, "You there!" to the approaching stranger, "what are you doing here?"

Alexander had not yet answered. He was about to, but Sophia appeared then from behind the backdoor. She had descended clenching her dress at her thigh so as not to trip the lace.

"Hello, Papa," she greeted her father who was busy stringing up the rabbits by the door. She caught sight of the Alexander approaching and acted her part: "Oh, Alexander!" She beamed him a smile, "You've come after all" Then more calmly, turning her face to her husband, "Hello, Peter," Sophia stood on the balls of her feet and kissed him affectionately, "How was the hunting?" Her voice was cheerful. She waited not for an answer, "Peter, Father, this is Alexander. An old friend. He just came back from the war. I invited him to visit the house once you both returned. I thought it would be…" Here she silenced herself and swallowed the next words that were about to leap out of her mouth. Peter turned and gave Alexander a short bow, full of disinterest and coldness. The Governor seemed tired, but turned and raised his hand in salute. Peter then set his rifle down on a step by the door and lifted his boot up to unlace it.

"Well, that's good, my girl," said the Governor, putting his hand on his daughter's shoulder, "You see the hunting went well." He pulled up one of the rabbits by the nape to hang it, "…Your old father shot his back out. But I'm happy to say your young husband can pluck a hare in the eye at fifty paces without any trouble."

Peter smiled wryly at his wife and twisted his mustache with his fingers, "Indeed Father is being kind. Yet as far as my shooting goes, I'd say seventy-five paces with ease."

"That's nice, Peter." Sophia turned to her father who had left the last rabbits for Peter to hang, and who was now dusting off his jacket to go inside. "But father, please stay and greet Alexander. He is a hero, you know? Look at his medal. He fought in the war. He was at Adrianople and he was shot in the shoulder and is wounded and tired and…" here the Governor turned to Peter, as if seeking an easy way to unburden himself. Peter saw this, and while Sophia continued on telling her father about Alexander, Peter interrupted her… "Well in that case," he said, glancing only halfway at Alexander in a way that suggested he was either fulfilling an obligation, a duty, or that he just wanted to hush an excited wife, "…In that case, my good sir, come inside, repose yourself, have coffee and desserts with us. Sophia, darling, tell the cooks to prepare something." Sophia turned as if to run inside.

"No, no, I won't be staying," replied he who up until then had remained silent as the others spoke, "I thank you but I won't be staying. I'll be traveling on. I just came for a moment…just to see one last time the palace…to see the place of my old home." His eyes drifted down to Peter's rifle set aside, and then to the ring on Peter's finger – band of gold catching the unclasped light of a drifting moon; he scratched his wrist which suddenly itched. A brittle leaf from an overhead night tree fell… "I used to live here, you know…" he addressed everyone present, "I used to live right behind, in the tower across the foyer. Over there," his voice was becoming slow and dreamy as he lost himself in a sort of verbose reverie, "near the village, the gardens, the nightingales…" Every word and every thought he uttered further left new sweetly melancholic impressions on him and he savored this feeling and continued on… "having again these trees and flowers, their fragrances, it is, well…" a pretty feeling he was having. He realized now while looking at this place that was once his home, that quite a bit of time had passed. It had been a different body that tended this garden. A different spirit. And how long even before that it was when he first traveled to this place – when he'd come across the pastoral landscape, meeting a goatherd and his father and eating with them, sleeping in their orchard. And before that when he arrived at the port of that fishing village, where the dark waves lapped in the nighttime sea, and was shown the stars by the fishermen; and before that even, his life in the Great City. Oh, the Great City…he'd forgotten many of the people he'd met there, the names of the streets he'd walked down.

'What a long path it's been,' he mused to himself, 'And so this has been my life.' He looked now at the Governor, at this venerable old man who ruled over a land so foreign to what he was brought up to know, a land where he now stood so comfortably. And at his daughter, whom he had chanced to know completely and whom he was about to cease to know at all; whom he would guard as a memory in the gallery along the passage of time through the cities and countries that belonged to him. He looked at this woman, at her husband;

he looked at the gnats that flew into the burning lamp in the backyard; and all of it was a pretty feeling. He was painting his own drama, his own love affair, his own tragedy. And his laconic words, he strung together in a long chain and ran away with them, galloping languidly away with them, as they draped behind him like streamers in the wind...

"...Yes, I used to live just over there. By the Acacia trees. Next to Horace. Old Horace..." Then his eyes fixed on a nondescript object on the ground and, putting the nails of his finger and thumb together, he touched them lightly to his lips and looked steadily down as if trying to think of something that was lost – something particular and very important. Then, he continued on, no longer aware of those around him. He saw not the worried face of Sophia, nor the expressions of her husband and father.

"...Yes, it was before the fighting. I was employed in your gardens. I read at night, beautiful books. They came from the scholar in the village. At night it was nice with the candle glow. In the day I tended the gardens. From ivy and mushrooms grew fruits at once of golden hue. Now and..." ...then before he slipped completely, he found himself and realized the reverie he'd fallen into was deep and he suddenly turned his face upwards to look at the Governor who had all the while been standing before him and noticed that this exalted figure was actually looking at him as though he'd been listening with great interest all along. Alexander then added... "I was given this decoration when I marched on Adrianople." He touched the medal on his chest and it reflected shards of moonlight, "Well, enough. That is enough about me. Thank you for listening. I won't be staying for coffee and desserts. True, I am tired but I'll be traveling on regardless." Here he looked at Sophia and her alone and said in a voice very steady and very quiet, "It is time for me to go back home."

Another voice, just as steady, but much louder and more firm and agitated, came then to interrupt this self-imposed drama...

"Well, okay then! Good luck to you in your travels!" Peter spit these words towards the ground while casually hanging up the last of the rabbits. "Looks like we'll be having hare tomorrow, Dear," he added touching his wife lightly on the wrist. The Governor gave a huff and a couple last pats against his velvet hunting habit to shake the dust off. He muttered a brief and respectful goodbye to the stranger who had once been employed in his garden and went inside.

For a moment longer, the other three remained outdoors. They stood silent for this moment, Peter, Sophia and Alexander. Sophia looked at

Alexander with a look of question, with a look of longing, a look of understanding and of misunderstanding. Peter's eyes darted back and forth at the both of them, trying to form an idea of what was happening between his wife and this stranger. Then Alexander, knowing the moment between them had begun to turn, and would only wither and expire with moments to come, took one step forward and said, "Farewell, Sophia." He asked to kiss her hand. He felt her delicate skin on his lips for just a touch of time. Peter was ready for this stranger to go. And Alexander, well aware that he among the three was the stranger, would always be the stranger, said farewell.

"Farewell, Alexander," Sophia returned to him.

He bowed politely to the both of them, turned and left the palace grounds.

He left the palace grounds and the Acropolis and walked along the dark nighttime rural road that led away, well away; and after a while of walking, head bowed low in thought, he turned to see if the Acropolis or the palace, the city or its ruins loomed over him – but it was too dark to see and nothing loomed; or at least it hid as it did so. Neither houses nor the outlines of trees were discernable on the horizon. Only the crescent moon accompanied. Alexander wondered why the moon didn't stay with Sophia but followed him instead. But he decided that she needed no moon. She had the palace. She had her husband, her garden and all. She might have even had her husband's child growing inside her. If not then, then soon enough, he knew. No, the moon she didn't need; but he didn't need it either and perhaps he would have preferred to be alone. But no matter. Along he walked down the road, not caring that it was night, nor where he was going. And the moon it followed – that is, it followed until it cached itself behind some trees that came to emerge along the path. Then a whiteness seeped up from the edge of the sky to overtake the purple midnight.

So, on he walked, with autumn at his back and winter on his brow – having then what only experience allows; and he, one singular person, felt it alone and knew it alone, and spoke not a word to himself, save to give a solitary toast to his love gone away. And on he went, and on and on, down the summer path, a path to lead on to other paths, to lead on to his winter home.

Chapter XIX

"Alexander's Homecoming" – the return to the great family...

What happened that night, was that Alexander kept going without caring to where or by which way, although he knew exactly to where and by which way. And eventually at dawn he arrived at a railway station far in the north that served trains to the villages around the Acropolis; and having his share of banknotes, he bought a first-class ticket north, and waited the morning out in the empty station until the northbound train arrived.

Exhausted from the night of walking, from the morning spent on the hard benches at the train station, Alexander fell into a great sleep when finally his train arrived. He was given his own cabin on the train with excellent accommodations, pleasant cushions on which to sleep. Attendants brought him food and coffee when he rang for them. They bowed respectfully, for he was an officer wearing a medal, and a gentleman – though he needed a shave. When he awoke on the first evening of traveling, he realized that his keepsake of Sophia was gone. The thin gold bracelet she had given him was missing from his wrist.

But when had he lost it? He searched his memory for artifacts of events, and then he recalled that it was in her room, in the bed... "Now I remember," he exclaimed, "'a drop of gold and the clasp of time'...that was it!"

He recalled that in the wild searching of hands, it had snagged on her finger and the clasp broke and it slid from his wrist. "That was the drop of gold and the clasp of time...that had been it!" Then he startled himself, "but the time!"...thinking fearfully a moment, "If that was the drop of gold, then what was the clasp of time?" ... "The *tick* of time? No, not that! But it couldn't have been that!" He searched his pockets in fear. Oh, luck!... his fear proved wrong. The watch was still there. That had not fallen out. That was still in his jacket pocket. The clasp of time was something else. Only the bracelet had gone – the sacred bracelet...oh, but he would let it go. To all the bracelets he would lose...to all the bracelets he would lose, let them go. Let them go like the sound of the train passing over the railroad tracks with a *clack, clack, clack, clack,* and be gone.

Through the Arcadian hills, the train traveled on. It left the southern lands where the fig trees grow and the sun burns warm even in winter, and traveled on through the subtropical seaboard. At one point an older man came and joined Alexander in his cabin. The two had a couple drinks together and talked. The man was planning to travel by boat from the same port where Alexander had arrived in that country long before. He asked if Alexander would be joining him, but Alexander said that he would remain on the train. He'd be taking a different route this time. He wanted to travel around the great archipelagoes, to see some of the unfamiliar outlying countries that lined the coast between he and his destination. At the train station of the town closest to that fishing port from which the passenger ships disembarked, the older man said goodbye to Alexander. The two wished each other luck on each own's odyssey and parted ways. Alexander ate a silent dinner in his private train cabin and slept the night through.

The next days were spent covering a seemingly endless terrain of marshlands. At one point, a layover was necessary to change trains. Alexander waited on the platform for the next train to arrive. The air was still warm and balmy and Alexander knew he was still relatively far to the south. On this next train, there were no private cabins. Alexander found the first-class car and took a seat on the left side so he could watch the ocean and tiny islands pass as the train went up through the archipelagoes. Everyone in the car was well-dressed and appeared affluent. Most were middle-aged. Some were businessmen, studying papers. Others were officers in uniform. There were a few elegantly dressed gentlemen, obviously traveling on pleasure, who sat beside ladies wearing hats.

There came an evening late during the journey when Alexander was dozing in his seat, that the train chugged and slowed and came to a jerking halt. The abrupt jolt and noise stirred him awake and the other passengers too were awakened and began to make a commotion. A moment later, a group of men in olive green jackets, carrying rifles, came on board and demanded everyone's papers – customs officers. Alexander looked through his pockets to find his envelope with the banknotes. The customs men had come from the third-class cars in the back and were now working their way forward.

In front of Alexander, a lady was seated wearing a light blue veil and a hat with a flower in it; beside her, there was a gentleman – apparently her husband. The lady began to complain about the delay. Her husband explained that they had just entered a country that was experiencing a civil war of sorts. He wasn't exactly sure of the political situation, but he explained all of this in a way that made him appear quite intelligent and well-informed before the lady.

Eventually, the customs men made their way up to the first-class car where Alexander was seated. They were dragging with them a large pockmarked woman whom they had in handcuffs. As she was dragged along, she protested, swearing wildly in some language or another. An old bow-backed woman and a child followed behind her both waving their arms. The old woman had but a single tooth in her head. The child was pigeon-toed. The old woman was yelling at the customs men. The child was crying.

Once this scene had passed, and the two women and child had been removed from the train, the few straggling customs officers glanced over the papers of those in Alexander's cabin. Everyone's were in order. When they came to Alexander, he showed them the military discharge notice that had been included in the envelope of banknotes. They gave it a cursory glance and handed it back. They then deboarded the train, the passengers settled back in their seats and resumed carefree conversations, and the train began chugging on forward once again. They were on their way.

A few hours later, many of the people in first-class were asleep. Alexander was not. Neither was the couple seated in front on him. They were awake and talked quietly amongst themselves. The lady with the light blue hat was interested in the country they were passing through. She lifted up her veil and fastened her eyes with childlike curiosity on the window where a dark oceanside landscape passed by. The train then veered away from the ocean and went through the inland hills. Occasionally, the train passed a little nest of lights scattered in the darkness which signified a city. Alexander had no need of sleep at that time. He was wide awake and thoughtful, and looked out curiously at the landscape as well. At one point, the lady with the hat in front of him turned to her husband.

"Edgar!" she exclaimed, "do you think they're fighting right now? I hope nothing gets close to our train."

"No, Dear," her husband patted her hand that was gripping the satin of her dress. The two peered out the train window. "Don't worry, Dear. Any fighting going on now would have to be way up on the hillside."

"Oh, gracious!" his wife exclaimed as she turned back around to face forward. She blew a puff of air that flitted through the veil covering her face. "I don't hear any guns. Do you? Some civil war!" She seemed thoroughly disappointed.

After the train restarted, her husband once again patted her hand and told her that in two hours, the train would be passing through the capital and that it was a sight she had to see.

"Really Edgar," she said to her husband, "I shan't be awake for two more hours. It is so late as it is!" Here she yawned, putting her little hand with its light blue satin glove over her mouth to cover it. "Surely, it can't be such a spectacular sight, this capital…Anyway, it will have to do without me looking at it." She then turned back to peer out the train window to see what she could amongst the darkness.

Alexander had overheard the conversation between the husband and wife and wondered with interest about this capital city that the train would be passing through in a couple hours. The civil war, however, didn't interest him and he gave it no thought.

Coming on two hours later, the lady with the gloves as well as her husband were fast asleep, as were the rest of the passengers in the first-class train car. Alexander, however, was wide awake and full of thoughts. The memory came to him time and again of when, still just a youth, he rode the train from Krüfsterburg to the Great City. The way he thought at that time, he was convinced that one who wants to live a meaningful life must never return to where one started. That to achieve greatness means to always move forward, onward, farther into the world. When, in aspirations of becoming a man of the world, he said farewell to his fatherland, back at that time, he never gave consideration to the idea that returning home again was a means of going even deeper into the world. He considered such an enemy of progress, a 'mental swing-set,' he used to tell himself. "Life shouldn't go in circles!" But now he knew that life *couldn't* go in circles, it couldn't no matter if one wanted it to or not. Even to return to the home where he was raised, to the very yard where he played, to the very cradle where in chaos he was born, would be merely a visit on this unwavering, deeply sloping, sublimely curling and impetuous road moving forward. He was going forward and onward whether he liked it or not, was prepared for it or not; and along with him, went his life.

The train car stayed silent. All of the other passengers slept. There was just the low, steady rumbling of the tracks and the vibrating of the window against which Alexander's forehead was pressed as he sat thinking. Outside, the lights of an approaching city were becoming more and more numerous. Alexander wanted to have a look at this foreign capital that he'd heard the couple talking about. He got out of his seat and walked back to the platform in between cars. When he slid the door closed behind him, he immediately felt a warm, thick wind. He heard the *clack, clack, clack* of the train running over the railroad ties, sounding loud and rhythmic. Here, amid the steel joints and cables connecting the cars on the windy platform sailing through the darkness, Alexander felt better. No longer did he feel alone. Here, his thoughts had company. The very air and darkness, the beating against the tracks and the distant city-lights were with him – stood by him. He kneeled down and sat on the platform and watched out at the city skyline. He inhaled deeply. The air smelled spicy and humid. The train then began to slow as it mounted an aerial bridge to pass above the city. It cruised over a grid of dark factory roofs in the outskirts. When it came to the centre of the city, it passed over a network of canals and narrow vacant streets paved in cobblestones. On these canals below, numerous little skiffs were roped up and were rocking. Along the banks, trees bowed over, dragging their tendrils across the dark slow moving waters. The trees were abloom with white subtropical flowers. Here and there, tiny specks of people could be seen walking back and forth across little wooden bridges. Others sat on the canals' embankments, on benches beneath the light of steaming gas streetlamps. Alexander's eyes drifted upwards to the skyline of this city that stood now well-lit before him like an altar of vibrant jewels encrusted in the hollow of a dark cave. He studied the rooftops curiously laid with orange and yellow tiles that appeared like rough animal teeth. These rooftops, covered in a film of wetness, shimmered in the moonlight, in the starlight. It was apparent that it had rained not long before. The buildings had walls like old grey chalk. Nested between their clusters stood numerous white stone pillars with surfaces like polished bones – bones crowned with zinc domes, rubble and stone. 'A strange city, indeed,' he thought to himself. It was a civilization of many impressions that betrayed one another. From the towers like ancient citadels, pillars to deities long since interred, to the quaint little boats rocking on murky waters where arched wooden bridges spanned them, one had the impression that here all of the gamey strangeness of life was on display in all its fieriness and untamed beauty. Through scores of narrow passageways, crumbling squares appeared, eerily revealing themselves for brief moments before being cached as the slow-moving train continued across the tracks.

When the aerial bridge started to descend. It passed through some buildings and then came out to hover slowly over a boulevard a couple storeys above street-level. Alexander looked down below and could see clearly three people walking along. It was a man, a woman, and a little girl. All three were laughing and holding hands. Alexander watched as the man leaned over to kiss the woman. He held her tight against him for a moment before turning his attention to the little girl. He squeezed the girl's hand and she giggled and then let go of his and started skipping away. She swung her arms happily as she jumped over puddles in the street. Alone, the man and woman stopped and stood close to one another, embracing each other, arms laced around their waists. When Alexander's train approached, they looked up to watch it travel across the bridge. They smiled at the train and the woman pointed. Alexander fancied they were smiling at him. He fancied an entire life for this couple: Before the rain had started, the man and woman were walking along holding hands while the little girl hung to the hem of the woman's dress. When the storm commenced, they hurried down a narrow passageway to take cover. In the violence of the storm, the man was separated from woman and child. He looked for them in the parks and squares, in the narrow passageways lined with closed-up shops and rathskellers, seedy inns and drinking dens. He saw madmen creeping through the shadows, derelicts hiding in darkened doorways. He saw soldiers of the civil war patrolling the bridges with guns, and he worried for the sake of his lover and child. Running through the streets looking for them, his mind was filled with terrible visions. He imagined the little girl had been stolen – taken on a gondola across the dark waters of the canals. He imagined his lover tempted by a scarf of silk – the silk of time. She left the city and crossed the steppe on a midnight sledge; was led by blade to Afric's shore – only there to be ravaged by barbarous beasts. A flute played a mournful song as the water lapped on the banks of time. The gondolier docked the boat and tied the ropes, while the little girl was led off by Death to a dirty tenement hall. There the two sat on a crate of mice, and played games while the girl's life swam away to the tick, tock, tick…but what is this, complete madness?!

In search of his wife and child, the man wandered drizzling, worried streets, until the despairing rains ceased and the clouds parted for the emergence of the hopeful moon. And with the calm and clear, he found them once again.

The woman opened her eyes wide and dropped her hands. The two embraced. He kissed her long and hard. Her mouth was damp with oils and rain. She took his lips between parting lips. The little girl who had been frightened to tears, ran to cling to her father's leg for a moment. He kissed the top of her head, her damp little head, and she laughed and let go and resumed skipping down the boulevard, jumping over puddles as puddles came along. Just then Alexander's train came passing on an aerial bridge overhead. The couple turned to look, and smiling with happiness they pointed at the train as it passed on by.

'Strange imagination!' Alexander thought to himself, 'Strange life for us all. Great wanderers, are not we all?…errant, happy and lonesome wanderers in the midst of the world with open wounds!...maybe I'll go try to get some rest now. Still, I really must return to this city. A strange and holy city, I don't want to have to imagine you. I will return. I'll return just after…' lightning struck in a far away cloud and Alexander's train picked up speed and went higher up in the air on the aerial bridge that wound around over the urban landscape, leading over more and more canals. Gradually the city lights faded, the monuments became fewer and the train made its departure. "Yes, I will come back here," he decided, "Someday, I will. But first… Home."

With melancholic joy and pleasant thoughtful sadness, he left the platform and returned to his seat in the quiet train car where he took his place among the other passengers who all slept soundly. Soon after, the train stopped at a depot in the outskirts of the city but no passengers boarded – at least not in Alexander's car. Neither did anyone get off. The lady in the blue hat never did wake up to see this capital city her husband had told her about and Alexander was glad. He was glad he didn't have to hear her tell her own impressions of the city and have them interfere with his. He was glad that city remained private for him, and that he had the lives of that man, woman and little girl as his private memory from a city he where he spent what seemed to have been a century that passed in the flash of an eye. With his memories of the canals' gamey odors, the spicy scents of subtropical winter blossoms, the visions of dark cobblestone passageways and fizzling steaming gas lamps, Alexander fell asleep and dreamt on a train that *clicked* and *clacked* along the rails all through the night and throughout the dawn.

Days of travel passed over stretches of coasts and inland territories where the winter wind was thick and mild, and eventually Alexander entered the northern countries where the air was thin, brittle and brisk. All oceansides were long since passed. The train spent days traveling through damp winter pastures, over which the sun set each evening with the post-harvest magenta light.

It was said that they had traveled through Northern Italy. Throughout this leg of the journey, Alexander kept his eyes fastened on the window, looking at the cold pastoral fields flooded with winter light. He looked out the window as the train slowed to pass a rural settlement. A mist hung low in the air and it appeared to be not yet dawn judging from the dimness of the sky; though dawn had passed long ago and now it was just before sunset and the large red sun dipped down through the misty fog over the winter field like cold smoldering embers in a fire. Little wooden houses passed by the window, farms and pastures. Alexander looked amongst them. Then, his eyes fell on something. Passing this settlement, he spied from the train window a young beautiful woman holding a baby. She was standing in her yard, which was separated from the railroad tracks by a thin wood fence strung together by rope. Her baby was wrapped in a cloth. She held it in the cradle of one arm while with her free hand she hung clothes up on a line to dry. Seeing the mist in the air and the damp appearance of the marshy ground on which she stood, it didn't appear as if the clothes would dry; but she hung the clothes on the line regardless, while far off in the settlement, amid clusters of little brick and wooden houses, some church bells tolled. Alexander's eyes stayed on this woman and her baby until they were out of view, and for long after they had gone he kept that scene clearly in his mind. Near the yard where the beautiful young mother had stood hanging up linen on a clothes line, there had been a little wooden house. And in this house, Alexander fancied, had been Perfory.

Low below a moon slender as a curtain, the express train curled across a landscape dark and smudged with night. The seeds of sparks crackled in the fire of dreams in Alexander's head while he slept on the train. The hearth was also cold, as winter had come, but that and the two chairs quickly warmed once the kindling caught. And that fire it blazed as one empty chair rocked back and forth. There in the picture, Perfory was leaning on the hearth, throwing brittle sticks on the fire, while its warm and tender glow sent happy light across the little room; and his wife, Maria, sat in the other chair nursing her child, watching her husband with loving eyes.

Many more days of travel passed, nights of dreams and sleepless thoughts. On one of the days, Alexander had a bad headache. He complained of his beard. The attendant brought him some medicine as well as razor to shave with. In the bathroom at the rear of the train, he cleaned up his clothes, shaved and splashed lotion on his bare chin. He then returned to his seat and waited for night to come.

The announcement of the layover at the next stop came in the middle of the night while Alexander was sleeping. He awoke to hear this announcement and took the news with an absent air, as though it meant nothing to him; however thoughtful, he could not sleep afterwards, and so remained in his seat where he recollected his last dream. He looked around the train car. There were few other passengers at this time. A couple curled up together sleeping up front. Far behind him, a man was reading a newspaper.

After a while Alexander started humming quietly to himself, making up phrases here and there... "A hole in my shoulder...a train for a bed...tracks for a pillow...a dream in my head..."

Pause.

"Da da da, dum dum..."

A train attendant came pushing a cart carrying food and drinks down the aisle...

"Da da da, dum dum, and tracks for a bed...a train for a pillow...some wine for my head...

"Steward!" he called to the train attendant, "A glass of wine please."

The steward set an empty glass in front of Alexander and poured out some red wine. Alexander paid him and asked if the announcement had been correct. The steward confirmed it. Alexander turned his attention to the glass which he tilted in his hand, watching the wine's viscosity as a sanguine film rose to the rim and vanished. He took a slow sip. A southern varietal, it was warm and spicy. "Oh, good wine," he leaned back in his seat, "my most charming wine. Charming wine...that's how Perfory would say it." He looked out the dark window and tried to imagine the emptiness beyond with a wind howling over the midnight hills. Inside, there was only the rhythmic sound of the passing tracks. "So it is true, then," he mused, "the announcement had been correct. Layover for the night in the Great City. Going north again. Snow storm in the Great City." He repeated such phrases over and again, 'So, the Great City is the next stop to come...to think I'd be going back there! How tired I am from this little drink of wine. Do I mind such a fate? Could that, that should come, just come quickly? Or not. Anyhow, such a layover could be interesting. See my old home in the city again...

"...Wait, I never had a home in that city! Oh careless life...careless and beautiful life. How I'd just like to travel on through...it will be a long time yet before I see them again." Sleep eventually seduced Alexander and held him until morning when he awoke with his cheek pressed against the cold window pane. Outside, there was a hailstorm…hailstones pelting the window, it was impossible to see outside – just eternal whiteness. As the train went farther north, the hail turned to soft dry snow. Around noon, the passengers gathered themselves and their luggage to prepare to deboard for the layover in the Great City. When they reached the southern industrial outskirts of the Great City, there was a thin covering of snow upon the concrete, the bricks of the factories and the junkyards. The sky hung over like a heavy ceiling of lead.

The train terminated at the East Station in the fourth district, south of the river. Alexander deboarded and checked the time when he was supposed to return the following morning to re-board. He then went out to the street – once again in the Great City.

Outside, a frigid wind whipped cold and dry, like an onslaught of iced needles, piercing his light linen summer suit, freezing his skin and bones. He pressed his sleeve to his mouth to keep his chapped lips from hurting. The snow on the concrete cracked under his feet. The bones of his ankles were frozen. He knew where he had to go. He squinted through eyelids that burned to see his way. In the streets grey figures in heavy coats and fur hats with arms full of market goods in bags passed like apparitions, disappearing through the doorways of meat-markets and worm-rotted station-side tenements. Alexander walked coarsely and briskly suffering in thin clothes. He passed a pawnshop. He passed a chemist's. He passed a cheese market with papered windows. He then found what he was looking for – a place to buy a coat. The sign said: FINE CLOTHES - BUY & TRADE. Alexander crossed the street between tramcars that raced noisily by and hurried up the snow-packed steps. When he opened the door, a bell on the doorknob jingled.

Inside the shop, it was only slightly warmer than outside. It was apparent that winter had newly arrived in the Great City and the citizens were not yet used to keeping the furnaces going. The shopkeeper was a stately plump man. His face had a bluish pallor, while his nose jutted out like a red sprig.

"How can I help you, sir?" the shopkeeper asked courteously.

"I need to trade in these clothes."

"Fine." The shopkeeper looked over Alexander with slight bewilderment.

"You see," Alexander gave as way of an explanation, "I've been traveling up from the south. Otherwise I wouldn't be dressed like this in this weather."

"That's alright, I'm quite used to travelers. Let's see what you've got." He helped Alexander remove his jacket.

"I have money too if the clothes aren't enough, but I need a warm coat and trousers."

"This is a fine jacket," the shopkeeper said, "where did you get it?"

"Turkey," Alexander replied, "I believe it's linen with a silk lining."

"Indeed," affirmed the shopkeeper, "oriental bark silk."

"Will it be enough for a coat?"

The shopkeeper brought out a black frockcoat for Alexander to try on. It fit well and felt quite warm.

"It's a good one. Thirty percent cashmere," the shopkeeper told him.

"Oh, I believe it's a good one."

"And for the trousers…" the shopkeeper brought out a pair of grey woolen trousers to make an even trade for the white linen trousers Alexander was wearing. They too were warm. Alexander traded in his brown shoes and brown traveling case for a black pair of shoes and a dark leather satchel that matched the rest of his outfit. He then paid a few banknotes in addition for a nice pair of black gloves made from goatskin. He admired himself in the mirror – quite elegant, he was pleased. The shopkeeper added a grey wool scarf to the deal. "After all, it's cold outside," he repeated several times. Alexander had taken the medal from the white jacket and pinned it discreetly in the inside pocket of his new frockcoat. He then thanked the shopkeeper who thanked Alexander in turn, and the latter left the shop, wrapping his scarf around his neck to protect from the bitter winds.

He had some time on his hands. A new coat, warm clothes, the cold winter weather no longer bothered him. He decided to walk. He headed off towards the fifth district. His sense of direction was keen and he vaguely recognized the area. This had once been his city for a time. Still, he had no desire to visit the places he had known before. While wandering the streets, however, he chanced upon the avenue where the bread factory had been, where he'd once been employed in the basement. With distasteful memories he turned away and headed north. It was mid-daytime and bright with the snow. Tramcars splashed through snowdrifts as they raced beneath cables showering sparks. The city looked forgiving, even submissive with its blanket of snow. Now that Alexander had money and warm clothes, now that he had good shoes, the city was submissive. 'Warm forgetful snow,' he thought, 'good winter…good clean winter.' He kept on thinking how bizarre it would be should he run into Dominique after all this time. He imagined him in his fancy clothes, though grown older, stomping along in the snow with that girlfriend of his hanging on his arm. Or should he meet the woman whom he worked with at the House of Sevres – that opium smoker he had fallen in love with…he could no longer remember her name. He wondered what fate she had met with. 'Ah, strange to think…' Alexander smiled at his past naïvety. He kept on with his head down to block the strong northern wind a-blowing. When he looked up, he saw he'd come to the quai on the river's edge. He walked west along the riverbank until he came to Our Lady's Bridge. It was a familiar sight, that immense suspension bridge with its braided cables and steel poles reaching up to brush the low grey shelf of winter clouds. He headed towards it. Then, before reaching the bridge, he came upon a strange building: a multi-colored palace with onion domed spires capped in white snow. 'Curious,' he thought to himself, 'a Russian orthodox church. I vaguely remember this church. Wasn't it here…?' He looked at the place with wonderment while opening up his coat. The wind had stopped, the air was steady. He wasn't used to the coat yet and he wanted to make sure his medal was still in place. 'Good proud medal.' A few snowflakes began to fall from the slate grey sky. Looking at the church, Alexander's eyes drifted up to a billboard beneath the bridge. There pasted on the billboard was a large advertisement. A streetlamp shined on it. The upper corner of the advertisement was peeling and curled over. When Alexander approached the billboard to study it, he realized where he was standing.

'This had been the prophets!'

Now he remembered what this church was. He remembered this billboard. Yet now the advertisement showed a different scene. No longer were there barefoot disciples following a prophet through a barren landscape. No more words were written in strange alphabets. Now, the poster showed this scene: a family seated at a dinner table, husband, wife and children – boy and a girl. They were feasting and smiling happily. Outside, snow was falling. Inside, the room was lit by a warm glow. The bowls on the table were steaming. Above the figures of the man and woman, and the boy and girl, it read in large letters: GOLIVA'S HOLIDAY SOUPS.

Alexander left the place beneath the bridge by the church, and headed southwards. Before he had stumbled upon the church, he had had the desire to cross the river and walk north, perhaps to find the old tavern where he met that strange official; or to find Chancellery Prospect where he remembered he had once squandered his money with two young frivolous girls. How, at that period in his life, he had been at the mercy of everyone and everything around him. After his first few days in the Great City, he recalled, he was reduced to a level of poverty of the kind where only a miracle could've raised him out. 'That is youth,' he thought. Yet eventually that miracle came, 'or rather it was simply the passage of time...' When one is that age, he realized, one should welcome such suffering, such blows to one's dignity, with open arms. A tingling in his arm, he scraped his elbow against the bricks walking along... 'One thing I should very thankful for is that I learned what failure is early on. Glory that I learned what failure is very early on. Now times are different...'

And they were. Alexander had enough money in his pocket. If he wanted to, he could start up a life for himself in the Great City. How as a youth, he had almost idolized the citizens here for the mere fact that they had lives established in this illustrious capital of the world. Now they represented no more than just grey shades in woolen coats passing through urban winter streets, They were no greater than he, they were no greater than the citizens of Krüfsterburg, or the woodsmen of the Great Northern Woods for that matter. Alexander watched these people huddled up, passing from doorway to doorway, sidewalk to tram station, and he had wanted to walk north to visit the Prospect or find that tavern, but after seeing the billboard pasted up by the church, something in his mind changed and now he wanted to walk south and find a new part of town.

After passing the square at the National Museum, he came to the Faubourg, a long two-lane road winding through a snowy arboretum, and followed it west. From the Faubourg, he crossed over a bridge on the South Canal and entered a narrow street that led through a small quaint island district of houses built in the old style – with wooden beams and tall slanting roofs. Here there were pubs and taverns and little inexpensive restaurants for students of the nearby university. When Alexander came to a café that looked decent enough, he went inside and sat at an empty table by the window. The glass was steamed-up from the heat emitted by the crowd gathered in the café. All, without exception, were people younger than himself – students taking respite on the cold snowy day. They sat in groups engaged in heated conversations while drinking coffee and liqueurs.

Alexander ordered a heavy meal of potatoes and cheese with bread and ate everything. Still hungry, he ordered soup – tomato with fresh cream and pickled mushrooms. The prices were low and the food was tolerable. He wished he had looked for a better place, and decided he'd treat himself to a nice dinner someplace more expensive in the evening – somewhere with candles and a tablecloth, where he thought he'd first buy a newspaper and then go and sit and read in between courses. Or maybe he'd just sit without a paper, enjoy a five course meal and a bottle of wine – a couple long white candle sticks. Alone, he could think to himself, reflect on his life of past and his life to come. He wanted so much to take the time to sort things out, to fathom everything as best as he could. He felt a thought creeping around in the distance. A thought that wouldn't yet let itself be thought upon. Each time it began to emerge, it cached itself again. Otherwise, besides this elusive thought, Alexander was happy and contented.

A second crowd began filling the café and soon practically all the tables were consumed. Alexander cleared the steam on the window with his glove and peered outside. He could see the streetlamps were turning on. Evening, he thought. The sky was still fairly bright from the reflection of the snow. Now in the café, more and more crowds of young students were entering. Inside, they drank spiced wine and laughed and smoked cigarettes. Alexander sat turned away from everything as he finished his soup and bread. He could overhear some of the conversations around him: some spoke of mythology, some spoke of politics; others, of art. There was a group near him that was engaged in a heavy debate about how the city had changed a great deal over the years, and consequently, life there could no longer be as it was. This part interested Alexander but he couldn't quite understand what it was they were insisting had changed. Now the café was filling up to the walls, and the atmosphere was evermore smoky and boisterous.

After Alexander's plate and bowl were cleared, he moved to a table farther away from the crowds, the only empty table left, in the corner of the café, by the window. There were a few empty chairs around him. He ordered a coffee from the waitress and a glass of heated spiced wine. He wasn't anxious to go back out in the cold. Looking out the fogged windows, he could discern only faintly the cobbled streets lined with wooden houses that led on to little arched footbridges that crossed the nearby canal. No, outside seemed brittle cold. The café was quite warm and felt good. New crowds kept coming in, and soon the people were pouring over from the nearby tables into the empty chairs around Alexander's table and this bothered him. One young student was telling jokes while leaning back in his chair. He kept his balance with one hand on the edge of Alexander's table and Alexander was about to shove him off when the youth stopped on his on accord. At one point, someone asked Alexander if he had a match to light a cigarette. Alexander had no matches, and pointed to some others who did and got up from his table deciding to leave. Leave, not only because his thoughts were demanding his entire attention; even if he were looking to start in on conversation, it would not be with these people. He felt far from these people. He was a stranger among them. He felt then what it means to achieve one's desire. He was a man of the world now, far removed; and with its romance and glory there came some loneliness. But what of it? He decided then to leave.

He paid his last coffee and the spiced wine at the bar and went in the back to use the restroom. There was a girl standing in the hallway when he went out. He stopped next to her and stood beside the two paintings that were hung on the walls of dark wood. The girl was quite young, about seventeen or eighteen. A thin and fair girl with light freckles on her lips. Alexander asked if she were waiting to use the bathroom. She answered silently by way of raising a limpid hand in the direction of the closed door leading to the bathroom – along with a slight tilt of her head. Her face gave no expression. From beyond the bathroom door, the sounds of running water could be heard. 'I guess that means yes,' Alexander thought. The two stood quietly in the small hallway, side by side, for many moments. Whoever was in the restroom was taking quite a while. Alexander desired not to have interaction with people at this moment, however, finally he asked, for he was curious…

"Are you from here?" he turned to the girl.

"I was born here," she replied in a flat voice, without turning to look at him.

"I just ask because I'm curious to know what's changed in the Great City over the last seasons." He was thinking of the conversation he'd overheard earlier while he was eating. Specifically he asked about the time between then and when he'd lived there. The girl looked at him blankly. Obviously she didn't know when he'd lived there. "It was the time of that great earthquake," Alexander added by way of an explanation. "I think it was the first earthquake in centuries to hit here…anyway, has anything much happened since then? They talk of great change."

The girl shrugged her shoulders as a way to brush him off. She turned then towards the bathroom door and sighed as if annoyed that the person inside was taking so long. This behavior insulted Alexander and he raised his voice to reproach her for this. "Listen to me, young lady," he snapped in aggravation, "you must learn how to treat other people. I addressed you with a question – what has been happening in the city? – it was not an inappropriate question, neither was it meant to offend or disrupt you; therefore, you are to answer me, or else attempt a polite response as to why you do not wish to answer. Have you not even this basic etiquette?"

Here the girl started trembling. She was shaken nervously from being called so directly on her behavior, she looked up at Alexander with submissive and fearful eyes and responded meekly: "But sir...it's just that I don't know...I...I know which earthquake you mean, but I was so young then, I hardly remember...What's happened in the city? Lot's of things I guess..." The girl at this point was trembling all over. She bowed her head in subservience. Alexander took a half step away from her and lifted his open hand in a simple gesture of apology for upsetting her.

"I'm sorry," he said to her, "my misunderstanding." It was then the door to the restroom opened. The young student who had been inside came out with dripping hands and passed through the hallway, back into the café. The girl then looked submissively at Alexander and proposed in a tone of respect that he go in first to the restroom. "No, of course not," he waved his hand, "Go on ahead," he was sorry he'd scared the poor girl. She hid her eyes and went into use the toilet. Once alone in the hallway, he asked himself, "What is the matter? What's wrong, Alexander? Was it the little glass of wine that made you irritable? No, of course not. You know what it was. It was that thought. Yet why *that* thought? Is there something interfering with the happiness that is entitled to you? Is life anything besides a well of happiness where you may serve yourself until you are full? Do you not, after all, cherish your own life? Yes, I do, of course... It's just something here... And with these people, it's... Alright, what would you change then? Nothing, of course...nothing. It's nothing here... it's just what's up ahead... what's over there. Oh, I should just take a walk and sort my thoughts out. I feel strange tonight." And here the girl came out of the toilet and flashed Alexander a quick glance before going back out into the café. The light was left on. He went in and splashed some water from the tap on his face. When he came out, he passed straight through the café without looking around and went back outside into the cold neighborhood where a light dry dust of snow was falling down on the grey packed icy concrete streets.

The sky was glowing pink. Alexander pulled his coat and scarf tight around him and walked down the narrow lanes beneath wooden pub signs. Every time a door opened, smoke poured out with laughter. He came to the canal that was covered in large floating slabs of ice. He walked alongside it for a moment. He went and sat on a bench and looked out to the far empty banks. A small boat was navigating through the ice. On the other side of the canal, yellow smudges of lamplight glowed in the frozen fog.

"The life of a boy is passed for me," he told himself. "...Fortunately, though," he passed upon, passing... "...if like a boat, oh, how so many thoughts are passing, and to just keep one. But I know what I want. And that which belongs to the realm of man. Oh, good life it is...and for all its arid moments...to trade or to stop...or to leap onto the other...realization that even if this world is but a draining vase, the realization that such moments of beautiful reflection are possible makes it a world...a chalice overflowing. Adieu, old life. I will never again live those days. Happily, I go on. Adieu Acropolis. Goodbye, Great City. I will learn of one more urban hotel room, one more night of metropolitan dreams, and then I will go. I will go back to see my dear father and sister Lise and tell them where I've been."

Taking a late walk that evening around the neighborhood of the hotel where he had booked a room for the night, Alexander passed a wine-seller that was open late. He looked in the window vitrine. It was lit-up with tinsel. There were some expensive bottles of plum wines, pear wines and holiday packages on display. It was there in the window vitrine, Alexander saw a bottle of Seraphome – that red, sanguine liqueur in the voluptuous bottle with a cork and sealing wax. Around its waist, in the display, slipped down like a skirt, the little burgundy velvet bag with the golden cord. Memories of his first arrival in the Great City, of drinking this liqueur in the rathskeller with Dominique, these old memories suddenly flooded him. He opened the door to the wine shop and went inside. The price of the Seraphome was dear. He bought a small bottle, then left the warmth of the wine shop and went back out into the cold streets. Unusually absent of traffic and quiet they were with snow on the ground. Alexander thought of Krüfsterburg. The innkeeper, he recalled...Viktor was his name. He thought he'd pay him a visit on his way through and share a glass of this Seraphome with him. The rest, he'd save to offer to his father. The two could have a drink together of this fine bitter liqueur and muse on life. Alexander would tell him of all that he'd done. One man to another. He smiled to himself thinking how soon all of this would be happening.

The next morning, his train left early. He took a first-class couchette, thinking he'd catch up on sleep, but there was no tiredness in him. He had great anticipation for what was to come. "It will be a happy moment," he told himself, "Oh, it will be!...but then, Alexander, what was that fear?" He was thinking of the day before in the café, among those young university students, about that solemn tension he'd felt. He realized now what it was. He realized it when he pictured seeing his father and sister again. He now pictured his father to be an old man. This was the image he feared. He imagined a weakened body, a face struck by advanced age, withered and sunken. That now Alexander would be physically stronger than his father, was a thought that frightened him, that saddened him and brought him worry. His sister, on the other hand, he pictured the same as she always was. He could not imagine that she'd grown or changed in anyway. It was just the image of his aged father that brought him pain and sorrow.

"Yes, to see them again," he affirmed, "will require all of the courage of one who faces the realities of life and time. Yet, all men must have that courage. All men must."

It took less time to reach Krüfsterburg than Alexander had anticipated. "Life is not shy about moving along, is it?...What is this quaint little train station?" He deboarded the train in the small industrial city. The air was still and cold; and, like in the Great City, snow lay on the ground. Here it was heavier. Here, he was in his native country, his fatherland, and everything had a strangely old and familiar appearance. The light in the sky, the blue smoke pouring from the winter chimneys, the old smells, everything was new and what it used to be. He traded currencies at the station and was given a fresh stack of crisp local money. He then walked through the grey streets beside the sooty factories topped with snow. It was just midday. There were a few things he had to take care of. He found a barbershop and went in to get a shave and a haircut. He wanted to look nice when he arrived back at his old home.

Snip, snip, the barber went to work. "You don't know, off chance," Alexander inquired, "a man named Viktor, runs an inn? He has three daughters. I forget his last name."

"Viktor," the barber said, lathering Alexander's cheeks and neck, "Not sure. Does he come in here?"

"No, I don't think...Well, I mean, he could. It's just that I thought since you live in the same city...."

"This is a big city, sir. I can't know everyone in this city!" The barber swiped the blade up and down, removing the stubble from Alexander's neck.

"No, certainly you cannot," Alexander responded calmly, "Certainly you cannot know everyone in the city." He made no further inquiries but sat and let himself be shaved. He thought it strange, though. It didn't seem like a big city. Not anything compared to the cities he had seen.

After the shave, the barber splashed menthol tonic on his skin and the fumes flooded pleasantly his nose.

"Is that close enough around the ears?"

"A little closer," Alexander answered. He almost wanted to mention to the barber how important it was that he look good, as he was about to see his family again for the first time in a long time, but he thought the better of it. It wasn't the barber's concern.

Alexander took the envelope of money from his satchel and paid the barber, tipping him three crowns. He then left the shop and crossed the entire length of the city. It did not take long. He passed smokestacks and factories. He passed Franzelsplat's market selling sausages. He passed the place where Mrs. Brundel's fried pie cart had been. He passed the house on Tritzel Street where he thought he would find Viktor's inn, but now there was no inn. He looked on at the house, and at the roof which he helped to lay with shingles once upon a time. The shingles were covered in snow. A gust of freezing wind came. 'Oh, well,' he thought, 'let it remain in the past,' and turned away. He scratched the back of his neck. His hair was trimmed short and felt nice. He breathed deeply and felt a lightness come over him. He then decided to delay things no longer; to leave Krüfsterburg right then, and head off on foot down the road that would take him towards the Great Northern Woods.

"Oh, now I remember this road," he muttered aloud as he walked along with his black leather satchel swinging at his side. "I remember it being very long, this road. Leads to that village where I stayed with the widow and her daughter. What was her daughter's name? It was a funny name. Gretel, I think. Yes, it was Gretel. Anyway, I'll find their inn and offer them some of this Seraphome...Ha!" he laughed, "it'll burn their throats right off and send them into spins!

"...That is, if I make it there. I might have to drink all of the Seraphome myself on the way in order to stay warm. Night will come eventually. Christ, if I have to sleep in the snow on the side of this country road, that's going to change things...I'll get filthy and wet. I want to look nice when I see the two of them."

To Alexander's great fortune, however, by late afternoon a cart passed along the road and the driver offered Alexander a ride the rest of the way to the village. Alexander accepted this with gladness. The driver was with his son, a stripling youth in a heavy coat. The father told his son: "Hop in the back to let this gentleman sit up front." Alexander said it wouldn't be necessary, that he would be happy to ride in the back of the cart, but the old man insisted and had his son ride in back.

The ride was pleasant and they traveled quickly, though once the wheel got stuck in the snow and all three had to push the cart out. Along the way,

Alexander counted his money. He thought he'd offer some to the old man in return for the ride. He put the envelope back in his satchel for a moment and felt the velvet bag with the bottle of Seraphome inside. It was yet unopened. He thought then of the good food he'd get to eat when he returned home. 'Finally!' he dreamt of, 'good black bread. Beet soup, turnips with sheep cheese. Oh, to be home again if just for the food!" He cinched the cord on the velvet bag and buckled the satchel. The Seraphome, he was planning to drink with just his father. He then recalled his last meeting with his father. It gave him second thoughts about offering him Seraphome. The last time they were together, they shared in a vodka ceremony. One of the singular events in Alexander's life he would never forget. It had been a holy evening. His father had made him drink from a glass with a broken rim. Now, was he to come offer him Seraphome after that? Silly Seraphome, after all? He decided that a gift of this foreign red liqueur would only add pettiness to their reunion. No, no Seraphome. Their last meeting was sanctified by a drink from a holier chalice than this one tied in a soft velvet bag.

When at nightfall, they arrived in the little village, Alexander thanked the driver and offered to pay him. The driver refused money, saying the pleasure was his and no payment would be accepted. On impulse, Alexander reached in to his satchel and pulled out the bottle of Seraphome. He handed it to the driver. "It's a good liqueur," he told him, "I got it in the Great City. It will keep you warm on the rest of your journey."

The driver was appreciative about the gift and thanked him. He admitted to Alexander that he enjoyed a drink now and again. Alexander shook hands with the youth and again with the youth's father and turned to head off into the village.

Back, in that village – back in the first place Alexander had stopped to stay when he first began his journey long ago: Night had fallen with a cold clear sweep of flaky stars. Thick, quiet snow lay on the ground. Alexander walked down the narrow cobbled streets, tired and needing a place to sleep. He passed the rows of quaint houses with barren winter flower plots on sills with shuttered windows, tall triangular roofs jutting up the sky, frozen weathervanes atop. He passed the church, with its belfry, with its more pronounced triangular roof, and no weathervane.

'It was right near this church,' he remembered. He was certain about it. "Why can't I find it? It's not like this village is any bigger than a pea patch." He walked the quiet little streets looking for the inn where he'd stayed at with the widow and her daughter. He remembered how upon leaving he had mocked them, saying he would never ever return to this...what did he say?...to this 'gangly little speck on the side of nothing?' Something like that! Now he was back and would find that innkeeper and her daughter and tell them what a foolish lad he had been at the time. Now he was happy to be back in their village. It meant he was almost home. So where was their inn and did they have a room? He would pay well and be grateful for a place to sleep on this cold, tired night.

After walking around the circular maze of streets of that tiny little village over and over, Alexander started worrying that the inn was gone, or else it was on a street he just kept missing. He wasn't sure, everything looked different now with the snow than it did back when he had first passed through in the springtime long ago.

The only place in the village where Alexander could see there being any sign of life was at the tavern. Everyplace else was closed and silent. Most of the lights were off in the windows of the houses. The tavern, however, had all its lights on and Alexander could hear men talking inside. Glasses could be heard clinking and the windows were warm with yellow light. He walked up the snow-packed steps and pushed the heavy wood door to go inside.

There in the tavern, village men and local peasants were sitting over their mugs of beer. Heavy planks of wood served as tables. The customers were about a half dozen men of middle age and two men that were quite young. The only woman was the barmaid. She was standing on a keg reaching for some glasses on a shelf when Alexander came in; and at this moment, all the men looked up at the stranger and hushed their talking. Alexander tapped the snow off his shoes and approached the bar. While he crossed the room, he surveyed the men at the tables. One in particular, whose heavy brown beard was full of beer froth, was gawking wide-eyed at Alexander, and as he did so, he clicked his tongue.

'Of course, a man such as myself coming in here,' Alexander was thinking, 'being a stranger in this little village, dressed in fine city clothes...should I be less than a spectacle?' When he approached the barmaid, she climbed down from the keg and set her dishtowel down. The men in the bar resumed their conversations, but now it clear from the few isolated words he did overhear that the conversations were now about him. It was an uncomfortable feeling. He asked the barmaid for an ale. She was a rough, peasant-looking woman with narrow bony shoulders and a pale face. She looked at him blankly, then nodded and turned away to fill a mug. After pouring the beer, she scraped the foam off the mug and set it before him on the bar. He looked at her expectantly.

"Two crowns, please," she said.

Alexander paid her three. Then he asked if there was a place to get a room for the night in the village.

"Can you wait a few minutes?"

He nodded silently and took his glass and went to sit at an empty table. There, he kept to his beer. When he looked up, he noticed the men looking curiously at him. Some met his gaze with silenced lips, others broke away and began talking louder in their conversations.

The beer was warmer than the weather outside and it tasted fresh and nice. It tasted like his home country, good heavy dark barley. After a while, the two young men in the bar started singing a drinking song. An older man near them became upset by this and told them to stop singing. Alexander remained seated in the corner where he finished his beer and sat thinking over an empty glass. Eventually, the men began to file out of the tavern. The largest group – four large types with beards, all seated together – climbed out of their chairs and headed for the door. Two shouted merry words of goodbye at the barmaid, one passed behind the bar quickly to slap her on the rear. She punched him on the elbow in defense and his friends laughed. They all grabbed their hats which were hanging on hooks by the door and turned to give the stranger, Alexander, a last look. After, the two young men left. They thanked the barmaid in polite drunken slurs on their way out. One promised and then repeated three times after that he would come the next day to fix the tap for her on the kegs. These boys raised their hats respectfully to the remaining men in the tavern as they left, including Alexander. After they closed the door, one of the customers, a middle-aged man with an yellowish beard, threw a handful of walnuts at the door and cursed them as being wastrels. The barmaid sighed with annoyance at this and took the broom to go sweep up the nuts. She then said she was closing and asked Alexander to come with her. He picked himself up and followed her to the back storeroom where there was a wooden trapdoor with a staircase leading down to the storeroom.

"I can give you a bed in the cellar for the night. It'll cost seven crowns."

"That's fine, thank you."

"Just one night?"

"Yes, I'll be leaving first thing in the morning."

"We don't make it a practice to rent beds. We used to have an inn in the village, but it's gone. No, here in the tavern we don't rent beds, but we keep an extra mattress down here in the cellar..." While she was saying this, she stretched a sheet over a single mattress on the floor that was crammed between some boxes. A kerosene lantern was burning on a box next to the mattress. The barmaid sheeted the bed and fluffed up a pillow. "...We keep an extra bed for those times a gentleman has had too much to drink and needs a place to sleep it off," she laughed, "Or sometimes he simply won't want to go home to his wife, so he'll pay a few crowns to sleep here. Oh, they're never too angry, the wives. They know their men aren't out with mistresses – only sleeping it off at the tavern. Here you go! A relatively clean bed. I'll wake you for breakfast in the morning, it's included in the price."

Alexander thanked her. She told him to not forget to blow the lantern so there wouldn't be any fires and said goodnight. She climbed the rickety staircase leading back up to the bar. Alexander took off his frockcoat and folded it, folded his trousers; he lay down on the mattress and blew the lantern.

When Alexander awoke the next morning, he looked over to see the barmaid sitting right beside him, staring at him. He sat up quickly, a little disoriented, and looked for his clothes. She had come to bring him breakfast. There was a tray with some toast and mint jam, a cup of coffee, a boiled egg, and a single round bread roll. Alexander pulled his trousers on. The barmaid asked him if he took sugar in his coffee because she had already added some. He said that would be fine, and she told him to call upstairs if he needed anything. He sat in the cellar and chewed his bread roll in silence. There was no need to light the lantern. A little window was up near the ceiling of the cellar and some daylight was coming in. Alexander could see that there was still snow on the ground.

The coffee cleared his thoughts and brightened his mood. As he drained the cup, he realized what a short distance separated him from his family. 'Ah, what a day this will be!' he thought. After finding his satchel and straightening his clothes, he went up the staircase and pushed on the wooden trap door – it wouldn't budge. He knocked on the wood. No answer. Finally, he heard a sliding sound and the barmaid opened the trapdoor to let Alexander out of the cellar.

"Sorry," she said, "I accidentally moved a keg over the door."

Alexander thanked her again for the night's sleep and wished her well. He left the tavern and stepped outside. The sun flashed off the snow with cold white brightness the moment he opened the door, pleasantly blinding his eyes; and off he went down the village street in the direction of the road that would take him to his home in the Great Northern Woods.

Chapter XX

"The Winter Path to the Vernal Home" – a late evening arrival
in the northern woods...

Alexander walked out of the village and came to the same long country road that had first introduced him to the world. Looking to the right, he saw the road curl down through snowy pastures and white hills until it met the horizon where it was crowned by a range of white-capped purple mountains. Looking to the left, he saw the road snake uphill, on through other pastures, also snowy and also accompanied by white hills, until it met its own horizon where it disappeared meekly into an immense forest of trees – a forest, it seemed, even more immense than those sheer purple mountains in the opposite direction. "That," he told himself, "is the Great Northern Woods." And so in that leftern direction he went, crunching snow underfoot.

By afternoon, he reached the beginning of the forest. Off on either side of the road were thick meshes of pine trees. Along the way, he saw a winter fox run across the road. He thought of his sister and father and was happy to be returning. After not too long, he came to where a path met the road and led off into the forest. 'Already!' he thought, 'I remember it taking longer to walk this road. Oh, everything takes longer when you're young and in hurry to get out in the world!' He started off down the path. After walking only a few minutes, however, he realized it was the wrong path. He remembered now that there had been a wooden fence separating the path from the road. He went back down the path and resumed walking along the main road.

By early evening, he arrived at another path, and this one was separated from the road by a red painted wooden fence. 'At last!' he started off down the path. This new way led through a nest of white birches and pines with thin trunks; as it progressed, however, the trees became greater, the forest darker, and the path more narrow. He could feel night was not far off and hoped he would reach his home before it got too late. Alas, however, after another good while of walking, that path ended all together. He could go no further. There at the end of the path stood a large stump of a tree immersed in a snow drift. Behind it, frosted thorns and sticker bushes led down to the abyss of a frozen ravine. There was no where to go but back. Having taken the wrong path yet again, he only hoped now he would find the right one before night came on fully. Now it was dim and the shapes of the forest were hardly discernable. The carpet of dusky snow showed no depth of vision and a few times Alexander stumbled and fell to his knees. It had been a long time since he'd walked in the woods at night. Finally he found the main road again. When he passed around the red-painted fence from the thick snow of the path to the road, he was surprised to find it still relatively light outside. The forest had merely been dense. Now, with the snow on the road reflecting the crepuscular light in the patterned quilt of clouds overhead all was alight with an eerie pink diffused and ghostly glow.

His way continued. Soon, the real onset of night began to envelope the Great Northern Woods with a shroud of crisp blackness. The pink glow in the sky remained, but it darkened to a red violet color so deep and eerie that it seemed to swallow even one's eyesight when looked upon. Only the snow shone white and brilliantly. Now, with night in tour, Alexander came to yet another path leading off into the forest. This path too was separated from the road by a fence – a fence painted dark blue that was all in shambles – rotten, crumbly wood. Oh, he hoped this was the right path. He climbed over the broken fence and started back into the forest.

As Alexander walked this new path, it started getting narrower and he worried that he had again turned off in the wrong place and he'd be forced to return back to the main road. But end, it did not. Through the evermore densening forest, it continued up a slope. After a while, the trees became greater in size and were spaced farther and farther apart. Silence rested in the forest, rested in the frozen petrified trees and the skirts of snow draped on their roots. The snow had gotten thinner. Here it had melted and refrozen, for a hard shell of icy frost covered the surface of the powder and it crunched under each of Alexander's footsteps. His eyes were alert to the shapes of the unfamiliar forest; and just when all could not have become any more unfamiliar, Alexander found himself in a part of the forest he recognized. "There we have it, Alexander," he smiled to himself at his chancing not to make another mistake in finding the way.

Now he was at the familiar summit of the path. Within eyeshot up ahead the path forked into two smaller paths. Sighing with relief, he stood a moment and rubbed the muscles in his calves. It was night. He had been walking all day. The forest was still and silent, hushed by heavy snow; and between the black sticks of giant trees, the ghostly sky now peeked at him, now cached itself. Everything was coming clear.

"I know this territory well," he said to himself, "If I go right, in less than two-hundred paces, I will come upon the grave of my mother." He looked then to the left. It was the path that would lead directly to his home. "First, I want to see the living. There will be time enough for the dead." This-upon, he took that leftern path so as to go straight home.

He walked now fast, with a pleasurable rush of joyful thoughts of seeing the faces of his family again; now more slowly, as a fearful hole seared his gut. Soon he felt a steady sickness of worry in his stomach and he stepped ever more slowly so as to put off the fateful moment. He had been alone for so long in his life. Even when he had been with others – with friends or with women – he had been alone. Part of him had always remained privately hidden away. Now, that he was to see his family, he was going to open up the part and allow those two a place in it, and he would no longer be alone. He wasn't sure if he was ready for that. But he was. Still, it made him nervous, and so his stomach burned in pain and he walked ever more slowly.

Feel it now carefully...feel the stillness of the forest...feel its dark, clean silence – still and yet shuddering, shuddering crystals of ice picked up by a smooth winter wind passing like a gloved hand over a voluptuous carpet of snow. Scents of cedar wood smoke came from not far off, passing between the trunks of trees with its nostalgic musky perfume. Alexander knew that just yonder, beyond a few more trees, was his home. He inhaled the cold night air. Then, there came another sound along with the crisp crunching of the shelf of snow underfoot. There came the sound of someone chopping wood. The sound of an axe. Then the sound of an owl.

"Imagination," Alexander muttered to himself. He kept on and there he could see far off the tiny form of his house nested in the distance, a little glowing light in the window – so far off – it was like a firefly ascending in a moonless sky. That was his home. There inside was to be his father and Lise.

As he approached the area of snowdrifts and trees surrounding the yard belonging to his old home, he came upon a man who was alone in the forest chopping wood in the snow. Alexander squinted to see him closely as he walked towards him. The man was dressed in hunting habit. A stocky figure, looked neither old nor young. His hair that appeared black and abundant was concealed by a knitted hat. His eyebrows were bushy. He wore a beard. He wielded an axe.

"Good woodsman," Alexander called to him as he approached.

The woodsman turned to him and stopped chopping.

"…Won't you cut me one piece of wood? A single log will do. I'd like to bring it as a present to my sister and father. They may be cold."

The woodsman, hearing Alexander's words, stood upright, let his axe rest on his shoulder and eyed Alexander strangely. He then turned his head away from Alexander and spit through his beard onto the snow, and the spit turned to ice. Then with a swing of his axe, he finished splitting the piece of timber set before him. After, he reached down and picked up a piece of the split log and handed it to Alexander. Alexander took it in his gloved hand and thanked the woodsman.

"But tell me, stranger," asked the woodsman, "where are they now? These people of yours? Your sister and father? For there aren't so many cabins in the whole of this region."

To this, Alexander pointed past the trees, across the dark yard, to the house over yonder sitting in the snow with one window lit. The woodsman turned around to look, and the snow crunched under his feet as he did so. He looked to where Alexander pointed. He looked a moment longer. Then he looked back at Alexander. He looked once again at the cabin far off and scratched his black beard. He rubbed his bushy eyebrows and scratched the knitted cap on his head. He turned back to Alexander. Saliva glistened on his wet lips.

"If it is so," said the woodsman, "then you must be Alexis." Here, his voice that had been gruff and heavy turned light and friendly. He smiled, revealing cracked and worn teeth through his heavy beard. His eyes grew tender. His face beamed. He dropped his heavy axe in the snow.

The woodsman looked at Alexander and drew forth as if wanting to embrace him, but in his awkwardness, he didn't manage the embrace. Alexander stood firmly planted and stared cautiously at the strange woodsman. He did not step forward, and so the woodsman settled for fastening his hands on Alexander's shoulders. "Aye, it is so!" he said in a brotherly way.

Alexander was thoroughly confused and remained still. Here he was almost knee-deep in snow and the bottom of his black frockcoat draped in sharp contrast over the white immaculate ground like a mourner's veil falling down on pale skin. Alexander remained perfectly still. He tossed the log he'd been handed aside and, looking more and more suspiciously at the woodsman, said nothing.

Finally, the woodcutter spoke again… "Come with me. Oh, do come with me!" He then bent down and picked up one piece of cut timber in his gloved hand, he left his axe in the snow, and he turned and began to tread off in the direction of the cabin. Alexander remained where he stood and watched mistrustfully this woodsman as he began to walk away.

This woodsman took great strides, plunging his legs deep into the snow, yet every other moment, he turned to assure himself that Alexander was following him. After a moment, Alexander silently began to follow him. But he wasn't actually following this woodsman, he was merely walking towards his home, but it was insomuch as the same thing.

This strange meeting in the dark forest at the moment of his homecoming was not a welcome novelty for Alexander. Alexander wanted to return to his old home and reunite with his family in privacy, not at the lead of some hired woodcutter. And who was this hired woodcutter? 'Father has not become too old to cut his own wood, has he?' Alexander thought to himself, 'Impossible! Father will have the strength of four men for as long as the trees in this region still stand.' But why was this strange man who knew the name that Alexander went by as a youth, why was he here at night, chopping wood in the forest?

When Alexander reached the yard of his home, it was already too late to ward off the unwelcome woodsman. The woodcutter had already gone so far in his eagerness that he was standing on the porch. With one gloved hand, he was reaching to open the front door of the cabin, log tucked under his arm; with his other hand, he was beckoning to Alexander to make haste. Alexander swept across the white packed snow in the yard and stepped onto the porch of his home. The woodsman opened the door and entered the house as if it were his own home. Alexander followed behind as if he were a mere guest.

Inside the cabin. Besides there being the light from the kitchen, pouring through the room illuminating the cedar walls with an amber glow that cast itself on the leather seats of wooden furniture, too on the heavy table of planks in the dining room where lay a plate of black bread and salt, two cups of broth, and an open book to read; besides the steam from the stove where a pot stood simmering, and the smells from the oven where a turnip pie was baking; besides a cooling empty hearth awaiting the cut and gathered wood for burning; besides these and other things, there were they: three figures propped in the hallway. He, Alexander, like a firm stone statue, face white from the cold and from traveling, his body draped in a black frockcoat. And she, his sister, wide-eyed with tousled fair-hair, draped in a nightgown. Her lips quivered and her body shook with the sight of he who'd just arrived. Her fingers fumbled in the tissue of her nightgown while she bit her lower-lip. They were they. Then there was the third.

This third person, the strange woodsman, held the single log in his gloved hand, and watched on at the reunion of brother and sister with rapt attention. Lise stood eyes fixed on her brother for many moments, as he too fixed his eyes on her. The woodcutter faded to the background. Back by the hearth he stood, fidgeting with the log he'd chopped and brought in, brushing the snow from its bark. Lise caught the distraction out of the corner of her eye and turned to him with a look of annoyance – a look that said to Alexander that she too was upset at the presence of this man during this sudden reunion of brother and sister.

"Henrik," she said to the woodcutter. Her voice was stern, betraying nothing of her impatience. "Will you put the log on the fire?" She took a breath and dropped her shoulders. She then added more gently, "Please...will you put the log on?" It seemed to Alexander she was stalling things by directing words at this stranger. Certainly it was not cold in the room. Moreover, her demands that the log be put on seemed to be made more out of a relief at having someone other than her brother to direct her attention to. This man seemed to serve as a crutch for these moments when her meekness didn't allow her to speak to her brother.

The woodcutter obeyed and knelt to prop the freshly cut timber on the slow and dying embers. He lit dry kindling and pushed it beneath the log and soon the log caught and the sap started crackling and a new glow met with the lamplight of the room, and the walls were washed with light. Fire being lit, Lise turned full attention to her brother. They remained several paces apart. She tried to speak time and again, but words didn't manage themselves. What a surprise for him to come…this sudden arrival late in the night – he, her dear brother – and how much time had gone by!

When Alexander heard the demand to put the log on the fire – "it's beginning to get cold" – he was struck by how different his sister sounded. Hers was no longer the voice of a young girl, no longer the voice of the childish sister he remembered. Now hers was the voice of a woman – a voice smudged by time, riddled with experience.

Henrik, having successfully lighted his log, now stood up again, dropped his winter gloves on the hearth and turned around to face the brother and sister who stood across the room, near one another, in frozen silence. Alexander in his turn searched in Lise's eyes. A scratching sound came from the roof. He looked up at the rafters. He looked back at his sister with confused eyes. He then flashed another impatient look at Henrik. Now inside, the woodcutter Henrik no longer seemed the gruff man of black-bearded virility that he had when Alexander first came upon him out in the snow splitting timber in the dark. Here, he looked thinner, his beard was lighter, less copious, he too seemed nervous.

"It's good to see you, Brother." Lise raised her shoulders and finally managed a smile. "This is Henrik," she pointed to the woodcutter, "my husband."

She turned to look at Henrik; and as she did so, the flames in the hearth set aglow her face and nightgown, distinguishing the shadows made by her cheeks, her breasts and her soft round shoulders and belly. Henrik, having been finally introduced, abandoned the fireplace and crossed the room complacently in order to shake Alexander's hand. He removed the knitted cap from his head and clenched it in a wad.

"It is good to finally meet you, Alexis." He stretched out his hand, "I hope you will like me for a brother-in-law. I have heard many, many stories about you, you can believe…."

"Your husband!" Alexander demanded, cutting off Henrik mid-sentence. He turned to his sister Lise, and raised his voice… "Lise? He is your husband?!"

"Well," she returned in defense, "certainly, Alexis, you didn't think I would be alone all my life, did you?" Her words began rolling out quickly, no longer self-conscious, "…after all, you have been out living your life – seeing the world, I imagine. I too have been living, Brother. I have also had experiences of my own. I have changed a lot…" And her voice trailed off. "But you know, I have. You know, Alexis." She said this as if she were charged with an offense. Then, as if realizing that no justification was needed, she recoiled and added in a lighter tone, perfectly calm and at ease, "But why do you look so surprised? Aren't I allowed to grow up and live life too?"

Alexander wasn't too quick to respond. He stood silently glancing about the room.

"How you have changed, Brother!" She looked him over. He, however, didn't pay her any notice. His eyes were following the contours of the room, assessing the situation. Meanwhile, the snow on his shoulders and shins melted in the warmth of the room and the water seeped into the fabric of his coat and trousers. Flickers of firelight danced in his eyes, playing on the bones of his face. His jaw and his chin were rough now. They had been shaved the day before in Krüfsterburg, yet now they were covered in coarse dark whiskers.

Silence settled like dust on cedar walls. Alexander's eyes came to return to meet his sister's gaze. Henrik stood like a cat in a corner, watching, waiting. How she looked different, he thought, looking at her. She had the same soft face, the same mouth with large sanguine lips, the same giant wondrous eyes, yet now she looked tired. Her hair was tousled and no longer golden. Now it was fair brown like wheat and it gathered on her shoulders in tangles as though she had just woken up in the morning from a heavy night of sleep, though now it was night and in the past it had always been her practice to have her hair combed straight in the evening. Yet what had been her practice may now be no longer. She was a woman, now. She was a woman and she was a wife. The wife of a man. His little sister was the wife of a man and it was very difficult for Alexander to come to terms with this for some reason. He looked at her continually, searching in her eyes.

"Where is Father?" he finally asked.

More silence. Silence, stirred only by the intermittent crackles of sap and the hisses of moist wood burning in the fireplace.

"Where is Father, Lise? Has he gone hunting?" His question flitted through the room, seeping up into the rafters. It then drifted down like a falling leaf, sweeping the air with yet more silence. Alexander walked over to the hook by the front door. He began taking off his frockcoat, and as he did so, he asked again, "Has he gone hunting? Tell me, Lise."

His sister made no reply. She made no reply but she walked over to him. She walked to him and reached out, brushing his hand with hers. She then took his coat from the hook where he had hung it, and carried it over to put by the stove where it would dry more quickly.

Over the old woodstove, the coat hung to dry. Alexander ran his fingers through his damp hair to shake some of the water out. Lise came over to him and took his hand and led him to the table of planks. The two then sat together, across from one another, looking at one another. Silence. Lise sat and bit her lower-lip. She sighed and looked on away. Henrik tried to be of use and boiled coffee for everyone. Lise didn't want coffee but Alexander accepted a cup. Did he want sugar? "No, but milk if there is any." Lise took tea for herself instead and brought the coffee and tea and milk for all to drink; and here at the old dinner table, brother and sister sat; and here they began a conversation. It was a conversation that was long and went around many places and spoke of many things. It had begun with a serious question posed by a man, and was then led by a woman into a light place, then it turned back to serious matters. This was the first time that Alexander and his sister spoke to each other as two adults. It was the first he was no longer Alexis to her.

"Alexander," she laughed, "I'm not sure if I can get used to calling you that name!...I'll try anyhow. I like it though. It's more masculine...more grown-up." She liked it that he was more masculine now, more adult. She was impressed by fancy city clothes, his new bizarre mannerisms. He was much different, his gestures were fluid; his accent, nondescript. His face too had changed completely, having lost its youthful softness and rosy pallor, which she considered before cherub-like and fitting only for a boy. Now he was a man, and she liked what he had become.

"I'm not sure if I can get used to you being someone's wife!" Alexander laughed back at her.

"And somebody's mother!" Henrik put in, who all the while had been sitting as an onlooker at the end of the table, pinned to the wall, one hand clasped on his coffee cup; the other, fidgeting with the tallow on the solitary candle burning alight in the center of the table. He had hitherto been watching the conversation in rapt delight, obviously enjoying having the privilege of being a part of this intimate family affair... "And somebody's mother, now doubt!" he laughed, apparently quite proud of himself.

With this admission, Alexander threw a questioning glance first at Henrik, then at Lise. What was it he'd said? Somebody's mother? Lise cast a look of annoyance at her husband. Then she smiled lightly and turned back to Alexander. She pushed her chair back slightly and cinched the fabric on her nightgown. The light from the candle sent a warm glow on her soft and tired feminine face, and sent shadows across her nightgown, illuminating the folds and creases of the fabric. She tilted her head to the side while making a slight and coy smile. Then she brought her hands before her and touched the tips of her fingers together to make a frame; and this she set against her small belly which formed a firm mound beneath the thin cloth of the nightgown. She touched her belly around the naval and looked even more coyly. She looked shyly, almost embarrassed, at her brother. "It is not easy to tell. I haven't much of a stomach yet…but a slight one. But it will grow and then it will go away. And when it goes away, you will be an uncle."

Alexander stared between the frame of his sister's fingers, studying her form. It did not look pronounced. He never would have noticed if they'd said nothing, but now he saw it was slightly swollen.

'A strange life, this one, indeed,' he thought to himself, looking on at his sister who, self-satisfied from the confession, pulled her chair back in towards the table and smiled, taking a light-hearted sip from her teacup, shrugging off whatever tinge of embarrassment she might have had with a single dip of her head to the side and a blow of air from her lips. Henrik smiled too and let out a small strangely sounding chortle. He told Alexander then that they weren't sure if he would ever return. And so the baby's name was to be Alexis if it were a boy. Henrik explained that Lise wanted there to be an Alexis in the house. Henrik said all this in a way that made it appear that Henrik thought such an admittance would earn him brotherly embraces and tender words from his new in-law; but Alexander merely nodded and searched the room with his eyes as though very deep in thought.

After all these serious confessions, Lise lit up brightly, as if only now suddenly realizing that it was her one and only brother whom she was seeing again after all this time, and with a look of sudden immense joy, she stood and ran around the table and embraced him. She embraced him, and he her, and here the two spent a moment together, until she dropped the embrace. She let her hands fall from his neck. She pushed him back to look in his eyes. And here, the joy was over. The playful confessions of marriage and the birth to come, the mutual laughter, over coffee and tea, of childhoods surrendered, and the sentimental, almost teary, recognition of adulthood and experience attained…all as if this were just practice for the real events to come – rehearsal for the real words to be spoken. Lise let her hands drop from her brother's body and withdrew. She went back around to her place on the other side of the table. Here she sat a moment, thumbing at the rim of her cup full of tea gone cold.

"Your sister and I," Henrik put in suddenly in a gay tone, as if trying to ease the mood that had turned from spirited to somber in a flash, "We decided it will be Alexis if it's a boy, and if it's a girl, she will be called Sofie, after my mother."

Alexander gave a start upon hearing this name. "Sofie," he repeated in a voice of disconcert. But then he smiled calmly, lightheartedly; then Henrik continued...

"And you should have a look at the upstairs room. A look at the attic. Do you want to?" Henrik lifted his shoulders and said this with a voice of such intended charm, as though just one mere brotherly gesture from Alexander would set him at complete ease. But Alexander made no such brotherly gesture, and so Henrik lowered himself back down in his chair, a little deflated. He then continued in a less animated tone, "Well, anyway, you should see the attic. We've changed it into a room for the baby. And we're just down here..." And as he turned his eyes down the long corridor to the far end of the hall, his wife, Lise, threw him the most horrid glance imaginable. And here Henrik stopped dead in his words, as he knew what he had done wrong. Barely audible, he cursed himself to himself, and stood shamefaced and looked at his wife who looked angrily at him. And without another utterance, he left the table and walked over to the closet by the front door, took out his coat, put it on, and silently went outside. He went outside to hunt another log from the yard to put on the fire which was by then dying down into a dull and lightless pile of soot and ashen embers.

Once Henrik was gone from the house, Alexander jumped up from the table and focused his eyes on the corridor. Here Lise, seeing what he was about to do, also leapt up and ran around the table to stop her brother from going down that corridor. But it was too late. While her nightgown tore a rip from where it caught on the arm of the chair, Alexander made it across to the holy part of the house. And here, at the far end of the corridor, he turned the copper knob and entered that room which had remained holy for the two's entire lives; and he saw now what bed was standing there. He saw whose clothes were now draped on the post of this bed, whose sheets now sat rumpled, smelling of whose bodies and whose scents; and seeing that all had changed and realizing now what had changed, and knowing now for sure exactly what had changed, his body fell back in a slight and barely visible seizure. A tiny groan escaped from his lips. He looked to his sister. He looked at that face he had known. It was a look of question. A pleading look. And upon that face of hers, that he had known since the day she was born, he could read easily and clearly what the answer was. She looked at him as his forehead flushed. His head felt clammy, cold and waxen, nausea filled his throat and he realized he was about to fall.

Lise stood beside him, poised like a wooden fish draped in a nightgown. He reached out for her. She took him here, and for once it was she, the little sister, who supported the older brother. It was she who led him back down the corridor. And when he sunk in fever in the chair at the table, she held him and remained beside him until he was breathing right again, until his eyes opened again, until the color returned to his face.

Yes, while he had been out experiencing life, Lise had been here in this cabin in the Great Northern Woods also experiencing life. She had had her love and her loss. Her richness and poverty. Her longing and attainment. She had had her own joy and her own misery. And now, she had her own stories to tell. She had her own marks of the passage of life and time to describe. And so, the two sat up into the night for many, many hours and talked. They talked and cried and embraced one another. They embraced and laughed and joked with one another. Their entire lives were retold in all their grim beauty and joyful sorrow; and Henrik, meanwhile, spent a great deal of time out in the yard hunting logs for the fire. Not that the forest was short of logs, nor that his axe was dull, or his arms, weary. He knew all too well now what was happening in the house. Though before, he'd displayed only a foolish naïvety towards the two's relationship and the whole scene involving his wife's brother's homecoming, he now knew his place. He knew his place and he knew their place and he understood how separate he was from their place; and so he spent a great deal of time that night out wandering around in the dark, among the heavy snowdrifts, hunting for logs. When he finally did reenter the house, dawn was creeping up over the edges of the birch and cedar trees, a white pale and cold sky came seeping into the star-laden darkness, and by this time much had changed and many things had altered.

Lise and her brother spent that whole night at the table. Then, just before dawn, her brother, who despite his acceptance of all that is inevitable in this, our procession of life, was considerably stricken with grief, and thus finally crept off to sleep on the makeshift bed his sister had prepared for him between the hearth and the window – the same place where his father had slept while his mother was dying long ago. The same place where his father had been sitting on that day long ago when his son had come to him to tell him he'd be leaving to go in search of the Great City. "I knew it would be like this," his father had said. He had a clear picture of him in his mind, as he sat there whittling a block of wood with a knife, sifting through the shavings on the floor by his mud-caked boots, flinging life and death into the fire where it crackled and burned. And here, where his father had slept on the wooden frame stretched with leather, Alexander lay a long time after, and here he fell asleep, fast asleep and soundly so, in spite of it all.

Lise, his sister, on the other hand, though very tired, waited up all night that night and all through the dawn, watching over her brother; she drank tea after tepid cup of tea and thought. Her hair became more and more tousled. Her skin, more swollen. The skin beneath her eyes darkened further from fatigue, but awake she remained, demonstrating that ability to tolerate extreme amounts of pain peculiar to all women; while her husband remained outside bearing the pain of the cold and his own significant fatigue, the burden of which a man can bear. He did not dare reenter the house during the nighttime, at least not while the fire still glowed through the window panes. Henrik now understood that this night was one where he needed to sacrifice himself – a night he needed to give himself up to wandering in the snow, in the cold, in the wilderness, around the stumps and lumber, in the darkness, beneath the still and changing sky.

Chapter XXI

"The Farewell"

It was after dawn when Henrik reentered the house – an hour when the air outside was thin and brittle and at its coldest, when the windows of the cabin were no longer glowing yellow from fire and lamplight. There, in the blae-blue light of wintertime dawn, Henrik appeared on the porch. He shook the snow from his boots. He entered his home to find his wife still sitting in the same chair, still silently thinking to herself as her brother lay sleeping across the room by the now cold and empty hearth. Lise acknowledged her husband's presence with a blank and listless face. She then returned her gaze to where it had been before, cast across the room at the far window. She stared at the panes of glass steeping in the light of cold dawn. She put the ends of her tousled hair into her mouth with the tips of her thin fingers.

Henrik walked to where his wife was sitting and touched her shoulder with his bare, rough and winter-cracked hand. He then reached down and put this hand beneath her chin and turned her face towards his. He looked at her with heavy eyes. He looked at her strongly, no longer like an outsider, no longer like a complacent guest willing to please, no longer like an unwelcome stranger in this home of brother and sister; instead, now he looked at her like a husband and like a man.

Far off, Alexander was sleeping soundly. Here, at the table, Lise had grown feeble and frail from this long night spent awake, shivering too without a fire. And here in this hollow hour, Henrik's masculine strength returned, and here he took his wife like a man. He took her off down the hall, down the sallow-lit corridor, off into the holy part of the house where the two would come to sleep for many hours, enlaced in each other's arms.

And thus, another short winter's day passed in the Great Northern Woods. When Alexander awoke, it was nearing dusk. Outside, blackish clouds crept over the snowy landscape, over throes of heavy trees, cedars and pines, cracking as they swayed in the dry frozen wind. Being so full of sleep, Alexander looked around himself hardly believing where he was or what had come to pass. He pulled the thin knit blanket that his sister had laid over him tight over his body and shivered. Bumps grew on his skin. A dream taunted his memory. He passed his hand over the length of his body. The down of his hair stood up and bristled. In his dream, he had been sitting with his father beside a spring in the woods – a spring of golden water. With that immense and holy man, he sat and the two spoke. He had been very afraid before, but now seated with his father he had no fear and no sadness, only infinite power and holy joy. Then, when wakefulness flirted with him, and the realization came of the transparency of their meeting, shudders of drowning fear and sorrow flitted through his consciousness. Alexander awoke in the dusky evening. He was numb and lay in a shiver.

Lise, who was already awake, was in the kitchen preparing dinner. Her brother looked up from his narrow cot and rubbed the sleep from his eyes. He saw her pouring some sauce from a large iron pan into three separate bowls. Steam was billowing around her face. Alexander looked at her, and heard himself mumble to himself three words: "Goliva's Holiday Soups." He then felt himself falling back asleep.

Henrik was seated at the table sometime later. When Alexander roused himself finally, he too went there to sit. Henrik had a pan of boiled coffee set aside and it was still very hot. He poured a cup for Alexander, who was sleepily still and mournfully seated at the table; and the latter began spooning brown molasses sugar from a bowl into the thick syrupy coffee. He sipped the coffee slowly.

Henrik asked Alexander how he had slept.

"Strangely," was the reply. Alexander then asked Henrik where his sister was.

"She went for a short walk in the snow. We have dinner ready on the counter." Henrik pointed to the three bowls on a tray by the kitchen sink. Bowls of soup that had grown cold.

'So it hadn't been a dream,' Alexander thought.

"Lise said she'd heat it up when she got back from her walk."

This time with Lise away allowed Alexander and Henrik a chance to talk. Henrik expressed in few but honest words his admiration for Alexander, his devotion to his sister, Lise; and his delight at the fact he will soon be a father. Alexander was quick to see in Henrik, in all his unworldly simplicity, the character of a noble man – a man who was very different from Alexander – perhaps they were even opposites; yet Alexander recognized in Henrik the character of someone bearing masculine greatness. Henrik was a man, he thought, that would reap the joys of a fruitful earth and provide for his family aplenty. This was a man, he thought, that if cursed to suffer drought, would consent to till the barren earth, season after season, if only to reap a mere handful of cracked grain to feed his wife and children. The kind of man who would toil over whatsoever plot he was allotted in this world for those whom he loved, no matter how small and rocky such a plot may be. And if he were given only blighted bulbs to bury in the soil, he would dig deep and bury well and would till and toil and water and pray for generation after generation until by means of the meager food he raised, he was able to see that his children had made children of their own to survive them. From his winter plow, he'd look to the glowing windows in the cabin warm, to imagine his wife there, content, with a breathing babe at her breast. Still, if his life be damned beyond all curse, and poisoned scythe were he given to reap scalding fields afire, this was a man who would find success in flames, and drain the clay cup of worldly failure, bear the sorrows of earthly sin, if only to give a single drop of the honeyed sweat beaded on his knuckles and brow to those he cradled as his kin.

Yes, Henrik was mortal beyond mortally. Of this, Alexander was certain, however, he knew that Henrik would suffer no droughts nor blighted fields. This was a man who would reap food for all aplenty. He would love and be loved. He would live and die. He would cherish his wife, and he would never question his place on this earth. No, Henrik was no wanderer. He was no searcher. He was a man of the earth, not a man of the world, but he was no less a man than Alexander – Alexander realized this. He was thankful for this. He was glad that this man had come to join with his one and only sister, and he, in this short while spent in talking, came to trust him, to respect him and be grateful.

When Lise returned from her walk, all three joined together at the table to eat. Outside, darkness had fallen, but the sky over the snowy earth still retained its ghostly glow. Lise heated up the sauces and soups, boiled some vegetables, and the three were seated at the table of planks. Henrik brought out the bread. There was some diluted brandy left in a small dusty bottle that had been kept away. The three had a small drink and ate with great appetite and they spoke very little. Alexander looked around himself at this home where he was raised. How small everything seemed to be! How immense this house had seemed when he was young, wandering these vast rooms. Now the ceilings were low. It was tiny and strange and unfamiliar and it was clear to Alexander how everything had changed and just how much had changed. Life was running its course swiftly and this day was significant for him as it was solemn. All three in the room understood this and no one tried to lighten the mood with meaningless talk. At one point, Henrik offered to Alexander to make Lise's old room into a place for him to live, or else take the baby's things out of the attic and make that a place for him. He said if necessary, when the baby arrived, they could put its cradle next to the hearth downstairs.

Alexander said no, that this would not be necessary, that he had only returned to see once again his family and visit his old home before setting off back into the world. After this, the subject was dropped and the three resumed their silence and finished eating.

After dinner, they all went to sit by the fire and drink coffee and brandy. Outside, through the window panes framed in frost, the sky radiated with its eternal twilight.

"It's been staying light very late with the snow and all," Lise said casually while the three were settled by the fire. She suggested that Alexander and herself take a walk together later in the yard. He thought that would be a nice idea. She pointed to his coat hanging by the stove and said it was already dry.

"What is that medal in your coat pocket?" she asked him.

Alexander laughed and told her about the war he'd fought in. He told her about Perfory and how he'd given him that medal once the fighting was over. At first Lise thought he was making it all up, but soon she believed him and the whole time she listened with great interest and Henrik did too. When Alexander was finished, Lise asked to hear more and Alexander told more. He recounted many stories, some of which she thought were funny, others horrified or saddened her; and there by the blazing fire, their conversation became light and the mood was happy and they talked and listened for a long while; and when the fire eventually died down, Henrik brought another log from a pile he'd stacked up by the door. Lise made some more coffee and poured the last of the brandy in the men's cups and they all felt happy together and there was much laughter and warmth as the evening progressed into night.

"And you both left just like that?" Lise asked, putting her slender fist in her mouth in anticipation. "And what about her? You never saw her again?"

"Never again," Alexander replied, with a nostalgic toss of his head.

Grief came over Lise's face.

"And truly, Brother, you had no shoes on during all of this?!" She couldn't believe him.

"Not even socks!" he exclaimed a little proud of himself. He told of his empty pockets and the cold hail falling, and described the way his feet froze and bled from the broken glass on the street. "...I'll tell you, Lise, those Great City sidewalks are so filthy, I'm lucky I didn't get an infection. But oh, you two should see that holy city! Tram cars buzzing all around, immense buildings towering overhead, crowds of people everywhere in the streets, crowds like you wouldn't believe!"

"I'd like to see it," Lise said with quiet sincerity. Henrik remained silent while listening.

"But it's too bad you lost her gold bracelet. I would like to have seen that. Was she really very beautiful?"

"Oh, she was beautiful, she was." Alexander said this with no tinge of regret in his voice. He then threw his hand backwards as if he were tossing the past over his shoulder.

"I wish I could see what she looks like. It's too bad you lost those things, Brother."

"Oh, Lise, really I lost nothing. I can honestly say I only gained in all this travel. I lost nothing. As far as objects, the medal means most of all to me...Perfory means most of all and the medal too."

"I wish I could have met this Perfory." Lise perched forward in her chair, "I'm sure I would have fallen in love with him." At this, Henrik flashed his wife a little smile. Henrik was also full of questions. He was most curious to know how it had felt to get shot in the shoulder. Alexander told him he hadn't remembered much because he had gone into shock.

Lise was most ashamed to hear the story of Yeshalem. She also felt sorry that her brother had to work in the basement with those thieves. Whenever he told her about any misfortune he'd suffered, she wondered where she had been at the time and how she had felt. Had she been happy that day, or not? Likewise, Alexander quietly wondered where he was while his sister was being married, while his father was dying. Had he been happy those days?

It was already well into night when the three decided to leave the fireside. The sky was still well lit and with no wind, it was a pleasant night and so Lise and her brother decided to continue on with their plan to take a walk together.

Alexander found his shoes that had been set along with his coat near the stove to dry and put them on while Lise waited by the door. The outside air was brisk. They watched their breath a moment on the porch. Above in the sky, the clouds were parting. The two crossed the yard, traversing the silent snow. Lise asked her brother for his arm and the two walked awhile. Once they passed the fence, she asked him what he thought of Henrik.

"He's a good man," Alexander replied.

"Do you mean it? Sincerely, though Brother, do you mean it?"

"Sincerely I do, Lise. He is a good man. He will be good to you."

The two were quiet a moment.

"This is where we used to walk when we were children." Her voice came out nothing like that of a child. It sounded strange to Alexander.

The two continued on walking.

"Did you find it?" Lise asked all of a sudden.

"What?" her brother replied, "Did I find what?"

"Greatness."

There was a pause.

"I found it," Alexander replied after a moment. "I found it and I am finding it."

"So have I," Lise said afterwards.

The two continued on.

When they were a little farther up ahead, Lise asked her brother if he wanted to see where their father lay.

"He's with mother," she told him, "They are buried in the same place. Henrik helped me. He knew us before, and he was there with us at the end. And he stayed with me after."

Alexander neither turned to her, nor responded. Lise, as though waiting for his eyes or his words, stopped and let go of his arm and took a step back.

"Brother?"

"Yes?"

"Don't you want to go see him?"

"No."

A wisp of silence shook the crackling, brittle, snow-laden branches of the trees. A winter crow flew overhead, drawing the clouds away with its wings. The tip of the moon caught the two sibling's eyes. Alexander held out his arm so Lise would retake it and the two continued walking...

"No," he told her, "I would rather go there alone. The grave is on the way to the road. I will visit it as I'm leaving tomorrow. I will see them as I go."

"And you must leave, Brother?" she turned and looked up at him. But she knew he must leave. She knew he must leave, yet still she stopped and turned to look at him with something like mournful eyes. He stopped and pulled his coat in tight. She asked, "But you must leave?"

Hers was a voice of affection. It was a voice of sorrow, a voice of longing, of disappointment and regret. Yet in these words of hers there was also another tone which she could not conceal. It was a voice that also wished that he would leave, that he would go back out onto the road, back on his voyage, back to his life of passing through the world's numerous cities and countries. She knew he was no longer a boy of the Great Northern Woods. He was a man of the world now and she wanted him to return to this life. Likewise, she was different too – no longer the little girl playing in the forest with her big brother; now she was a woman with a husband and a new family, an unborn child. With them, she now belonged. The past was gone; and so of course in the profundity of all, she hoped that her brother would be leaving.

Had Alexander questioned his sister's feelings on this, no doubt she would have denied any wish for him to leave; yet how could he question her on this, and how would she be able to answer him anyway? She could not and he could not. Theirs for now was not to be spoken, and so the two walked through the yard in silence.

Gorgeous was this night. Alexander looked around himself. Yes, his was a different romance. Look at the wintry woods around him. These were the woods that raised him – the young Apollo, smooth and hairless. These were the woods that flung him out into the world to be old. And while his blood belonged to these woods, while his blood belonged to Lise as well, his flesh belonged to the world – his flesh belonged to the world, and so of course he would be leaving.

Yet if he should go and never return? If he should never see these woods, this place, or her, his sister again?

Well, the world has known sadness. It has known tragedy, and its heroes play this desperate game to take whatever joys are allowed. And in the end, and on the way, we reflect on it and it is this which is called a life. Be it tragedy and despair, it is well worth the privilege of being given a chance to wander our great earth. So we will pay what we will, we will take what we are allowed, share in the bounty, and with grateful eyes, it will be this we call a life.

"And so that was my life . . . and so this will be my life." Alexander muttered this to himself while he stood now alone watching, from the clearing on the hill, the crescent moon as it emerged from the thin wisps of clouds parting over snow-covered tops of winter cedars and pines, swaying in the late-night breeze. "How beautiful it all is." And beautiful it was, late into that night, long after Lise had returned inside to sleep, after she had left her brother to himself, to his thoughts and memories.

Beneath his footsteps, the snow crunched. Far off in the woods, an animal scurried. It was beautiful, this vast forest. In the distance, coyotes bayed. It was beautiful, this private reunion with himself. There was tenderness in everything. Now the sky was clear and the moon reflected off the patches of snow, lighting the path where Alexander finally decided to walk down that night after all, to where his father and mother lay.

There was tenderness at that grave, at that holy mound where he spent a long time that night offering renewed greetings and private adieux. And having toasted a tearful farewell to his past and their lives gone away, he walked solemnly back through the trees to the house in the northern woods feeling that he had given himself to the dead and that he could now again give himself to the living. It was a pretty feeling, this understanding; yet even with this he was solemn. And when he returned inside, in grief he fell asleep.

The morning came crisp and bright with a light through frosted window panes. Outside, Lise had found some early flowers pushing through the snow, and she went to gather them. The sun had finally come that day and the snow was beginning to thaw. Winter would soon end. When Lise returned inside she was smiling. In her woolen sweater, she cradled the yellow flowers she had picked. Henrik was happily building the first fire of the day. Lise told him she saw robins building nests in the trees. Spring was not far off.

Alexander and his sister and her husband, all drank coffee together and the breakfast was good. Lise baked the black bread fresh. By the stove Alexander's clothes were warm and dry. He put his frockcoat on.

"Do pin the medal on, Brother," Lise implored.

"No," he shook his head, a little bashful, "I like to keep it safe in the inside pocket."

"Oh, do put it on, it will look handsome!"

"Alright," he agreed. He could always take it off later. He took the medal out and pinned it on his coat. Lise smiled with delight.

Once the three had left the house and were in the yard, Lise turned to Alexander, "But Brother, where will you go?"

"Why, to the city, of course!" he exclaimed in a playful tone.

She then returned his playful tone... "But do you have any idea *to which* city?"

Certainly Alexander had an idea to which city. He knew exactly where he was headed. "Alright, little Sister. I'll tell you which city. I'll tell you about it the next time we see each other." He said this smiling and cheerful. Great radiance shined from his singular gaze. And it was with this cheerful smile and renewed radiance that she remembered him that morning as he departed again to see the world, just as he had done long before when still a youth. She remembered how then she had cried while she watched him go... just a lad, skipping off with her yellow handkerchief tied to the strap of the sack slung over his back. He still shined with that same radiance, but things were now altogether different. He was a man now and he said farewell like a man. He stood and gave a final wave, dressed handsomely in his dark coat, that medal of gold pinned to his chest, a slight dust of snow on his shoulder from where a tree branch dipped from the weight of a landing bird, dropping powder from its needles. This is how they both remembered him.

And this is how Alexander remembered the two of them: standing at the fence in the thawing snow, saying goodbye; Henrik waving and smiling with his simple and benevolent face, and Lise, his dear sister, that blessed woman – gazing at him with her soft and giant tired eyes, while her hand rested gently on the curve of her swollen belly.

There were no tears in anyone's eyes. There was only gladness.

And so, with a wave of his hand, he bid so long, and walked through the thawing snow, on down the winter path that would lead to the spring-lit road. A new day was beginning, and as he walked, he felt the sun fresh and clean, shining down upon him.

Printed in the United States
208886BV00001B/66/A